THE HYDRA HEAD

THE
HYDRA
HEAD

CARLOS FUENTES

Translated from the Spanish by
MARGARET SAYERS PEDEN

SECKER & WARBURG
LONDON

Originally published in Spanish under the title
La cabeza de la hidra.
Copyright © 1978 by Editorial Joaquín Mortiz, S.A., Mexico

First published in England 1979 by
Martin Secker & Warburg Limited
54 Poland Street, London W1V 3DF

Translation copyright © 1978 by Farrar, Straus and Giroux, Inc.

SBN: 436 16762 X

This book has been published
with financial assistance from
the Arts Council of Great Britain

Printed in Great Britain by
REDWOOD BURN LIMITED
Trowbridge & Esher

To the memory of

(in strict order of disappearance)

Conrad Veidt

Sydney Greenstreet

Peter Lorre

Claude Rains

La Renaudière, Margency, summer of 1977

Une tête coupée en fait renaître mille
Corneille, *Cinna*

PART ONE

HIS OWN HOST

1 AT EXACTLY 8 a.m. Felix Maldonado arrived at the Sanborns on Madero. Years had passed since he had set foot inside the famous House of Tiles. It had gone out of style like all of downtown Mexico City, the historic center Hernán Cortés had ordered built upon the ruins of the Aztec capital after personally drawing up the plans. This was in Felix's mind as he pushed the wood-and-glass revolving door, made a full turn, and emerged again into the street. He felt guilty about arriving late for an appointment. He was known for his punctuality. He was the most punctual official in the entire Mexican bureaucracy. Easy, some said, no competition. Extremely difficult, Felix's wife, Ruth, said, easier to let yourself drift with the current in a country governed by the law of least resistance.

This morning Felix could not withstand the temptation to waste a couple of minutes. He paused on the sidewalk across the street and for a long moment admired the magnificence of the blue- and white-tiled façade of the ancient colonial palace, with its wooden balconies and churrigueresque cresting outlining the flat roof. Again he crossed the street, quickly entered Sanborns, hurried through the sales area, and pushed open the beveled glass door leading to the translucent glass-roofed patio restaurant. One of the tables was occupied by Professor Bernstein.

Felix Maldonado attended a political breakfast every morning. A pretext for exchanging impressions, ordering world affairs, plotting intrigue, conspiring, and organizing cabals. Small early-morning fraternities that serve, above all, as a source of information that would otherwise remain unknown. When Felix spied the professor reading a political journal, he said to himself that no one would ever understand the articles and editorials if he was not a devoted regular at the hundreds of political breakfasts celebrated daily in chains of American-style quick-food restaurants—Sanborns, Wimpys, Dennys, Vips.

He greeted the professor. Bernstein half rose and then let his massive body fall again onto the rickety chair. He offered a soft fat hand to Felix and questioned him with a look, as he stuffed the journal in his jacket pocket. Handing an envelope to Felix, he reminded him that the annual National Prizes in the Arts and Sciences would be awarded at the National Palace tomorrow. The President of the Republic himself, so the invitation read, would honor the recipients. Felix congratulated Professor Bernstein for winning the Economics Prize and thanked him for the invitation.

"Please don't fail to be there, Felix."

"How could I, Professor? I'd die first."

"I'm not asking that much."

"I know. But, besides being your disciple and your friend, I'm a public official. You don't refuse an invitation from the President. What luck to be able to shake his hand."

"Have you met him?" asked Bernstein, staring at the water-clear stone sparkling in the ring on his sausage finger.

"A couple of months ago I attended a work session on oil reserves at the Palace. The President came at the end of the meeting to hear our conclusions."

"Ah, the famous Mexican oil reserves! The great mystery. Why did you leave Petróleos Mexicanos?"

"They transferred me," Felix responded. "They have some idea that an official gets stale if he stays in one post too long."

"But you've spent your whole career with Pemex, you're a specialist, what idiocy to waste your experience. You know a lot about the reserves, don't you?"

Maldonado smiled and remarked how odd it was to find

4

himself in the Sanborns on Madero. Actually, he hoped to change the subject, and he blamed himself for having brought it up, even with someone he respected as much as Bernstein, his old economics professor. Almost no one ever ate here now, he said. Everyone preferred the restaurants in the newer residential areas. The professor looked at him soberly and agreed. He suggested that Felix order, and a girl in a native Indian costume wrote down orange juice, waffles with maple syrup, and American coffee, weak.

"I saw you reading a journal," said Felix, believing that Professor Bernstein wanted to talk politics.

But Bernstein said nothing.

"Just now, as I came in," Felix went on, "I was thinking how you can't understand anything the Mexican press says unless you attend political breakfasts. That's the only way you can understand all the allusions and veiled attacks and unprintable names hinted at in the newspapers."

"Neither do they print important news like the sum total of our oil reserves. It's curious how news about Mexico appears first in foreign newspapers."

"Right." Felix's tone was neutral.

"But that's how the system works. Anyway, it isn't classy any more to come to this Sanborns," the professor replied in the same tone.

"But we come to these breakfasts to be seen by other people, to make it clear that we and our circle know something no one else knows." Felix smiled.

Professor Bernstein was in the habit of sopping up his eggs-and-hot-sauce with a piece of tortilla and then slurping noisily. Sometimes he even spattered his rimless spectacles, two thick, naked lenses that seemed to float before the professor's invisible eyes.

"This isn't a political breakfast," Bernstein said.

"And that's why you invited me here?"

"That's unimportant. What matters is that Sara's returning today."

"Sara Klein?"

"Yes. That's why I asked you to come. She's returning today. I want to ask you a great favor."

"Of course, Professor."

"I don't want you to see her."

"You know we haven't seen each other in twelve years, ever since she went to live in Israel."

"Precisely. I'm afraid you'll have a strong desire to see each other after such a long time."

"Why do you say 'afraid'? You know very well there was never anything between us. It was a platonic affair."

"That's what I'm afraid of. That it will cease to be platonic."

The costumed waitress placed Felix's breakfast before him. He seized the opportunity to look away, so as not to offend Bernstein. At that moment he disliked the professor intensely for interfering in his private affairs. Furthermore, he suspected that Bernstein had favored him with the invitation to the Palace to blackmail him.

"Look, Professor. Sara was my ideal love. You know that better than anyone. But maybe you still don't understand. If Sara had a husband, it would be a different story. But she never married. She's still my ideal, and I'm not about to destroy my own idea of what's beautiful. Don't worry."

"It was a simple warning. Since we'll all be together for dinner tonight, I preferred to speak to you first."

"Thanks. You needn't worry."

The sunlight beaming through the glass roof was intense. Within a few minutes, the dazzling patio of Sanborns would be an oven. Felix said goodbye to the professor and stepped out onto Madero. He checked the time by the clock in the Latin American Tower. It was too early to go to the Ministry. And it had been years since he'd walked down Madero toward the Plaza de la Constitución. Like the nation, he mused, this city had both developed and underdeveloped areas. Frankly, he didn't care for the latter. The old center was a special case. If you kept your eyes above the swarming crowds, you didn't have to focus on all the misery and poverty but could, instead, enjoy the beauty of certain façades and roof lines. The Templo de la Profesa, for example, was very beautiful, as well as the Convento de San Francisco and the Palacio de Iturbide, all of red volcanic stone, with their baroque façades of pale marble. Felix reflected that this was a city designed for gentlemen and slaves, whether Aztec or Spaniard, never for the indecisive muddle of people who'd recently abandoned the peasant's white shirt and pants and the worker's blue denim to dress so badly, imitating middle-class styles but, at best, only half successfully. The Indians, so handsome in the lands of their origin, so slim and spotless and secret, in the city became ugly, filthy, and bloated by carbonated drinks.

Madero is a narrow, boxed-in avenue that was originally called the Street of the Silversmiths. When he reached the huge square of the Zócalo, Felix Maldonado recalled this, as he was blinded by a dark, brilliant, harsh sun as remote and cold as silver. The sun in the Zócalo dazzled him. He couldn't see a thing. He felt the disagreeable sensation of an unexpected and undesired contact; a long tongue pushed up his shirtsleeve and licked his watch. His eyes adjusted rapidly to the glare and he saw that he was surrounded by stray dogs. One was licking him, the others watching. An old woman swaddled in black rags was apologizing, "I'm sorry, señor, they're just playful, they're not really bad, no, they're not."

2 FELIX MALDONADO hailed a one-peso cab and relaxed, the first client in this collective taxi. In front of the Cathedral, a man dressed in overalls was skimming a long aluminum tube above the paving stones. He was crowned by headphones connected to the tube and to a receiving apparatus strung across his chest and secured by suspenders. He was muttering something. The cab driver laughed and said, Now you've seen the Cathedral nut, he's been searching for Moctezuma's treasure for years.

Felix did not reply. He had no desire to converse with a taxi driver. All he wanted was to reach his office in the Ministry of Economic Development, wash his hands, and lock himself in his cubicle. He took out his handkerchief and wiped the hand the dog had licked. The driver rolled along the Avenida 5 de Mayo with his hand stuck out the window, index finger raised, announcing that his taxi cost only one peso, and followed a fixed route from the Zócalo to Chapultepec Park. The previous evening Felix had left his own car with the doorman at the Hilton so he wouldn't have to drive in a Chevrolet for which there was no parking place.

The taxi stopped at every corner to pick up passengers. First, two nuns got in on the corner of Motolinía. He knew they were nuns by the hair severely drawn back into a bun, the absence of makeup, the black dresses, the rosaries and scapulars. Since they were forbidden to go out in the street wearing their habits, they'd found a new uniform. They chose to get in front with the driver. He treated them like old friends, as if he saw them every day. *"Hel-*lo, Sisters, how's it going today?"* The nuns giggled and blushed, covering their mouths with their hands, and one of them tried to catch Felix's eye in the rear-view mirror.

When the taxi stopped at Gante, Felix drew back his legs to make room for a girl dressed in white, a nurse. She carried cellophane-wrapped syringes, vials, and ampules.

8

She asked Felix to slide over. He said no, he would be getting out soon. Where? At the Cuauhtémoc traffic circle across from the Hilton. Well, she was getting out before that, in front of the Hotel Reforma. Come on, she was in a hurry, she had to give an injection to a tourist, a gringo tourist dying of typhoid. Moctezuma's revenge, Felix said. What? Don't be a creep, move over. Felix said certainly not, a gentleman always gave his place to a lady. He got out of the taxi so the nurse could get in. She looked at him suspiciously while behind the peso cab a long line of taxis were tooting their horns.

"Step on it, they're about to climb up my ass," the driver said.

"So who said chivalry's dead?" The nurse smiled and offered an Adams chiclet to Felix, who took it, not to offend her. And he made no effort to press against the girl. He respected the empty space between them. It wasn't empty long. In front of the Palacio de Bellas Artes, a dark, fat woman stopped the taxi. To prove to the nurse that he was gallant with ugly as well as pretty women, Felix attempted to get out, but the fat woman was in too much of a hurry. She was carrying a brimming basket, which she lifted into the taxi. She sprawled face-down across Felix's legs, her head plowing silently into the nurse's lap. The nuns giggled. The fat woman propped her basket on Felix's knees and, groaning, struggled to seat herself. Dozens of peeping yellow chicks erupted from the basket, swarming around Felix's feet and climbing his shoulders. Felix was afraid he was going to crush them.

The fat woman settled into her seat, clutching the empty basket. When she saw that the chicks had gotten out, she flung the basket aside, striking the nuns, grabbed Felix by the neck, and flailing about, tried to collect the chicks. Felix's face was plastered with feathers like adolescent down.

Ahead, a student with a pile of books under his arm was

flagging down the taxi. The driver slowed to pick him up. Felix protested, sneezing through a myriad of feathers, and the nurse seconded him. There wasn't room. The driver said yes, yes of course there was room. Four could ride in the back. "In the front, too," one of the nuns giggled. And when the fat woman shrieked, "God help us, the chicks have escaped," one of the nuns giggled, "Did she say Gold help us, we're about to be raped?" The driver said he had to make his living any way he could and anyone who didn't like it could get out and get a taxi all to himself, two and a half pesos before the meter ever started ticking.

The student approached the halted taxi, running lightly in his tennis shoes in spite of his load of books. He ran with both arms crossed over his chest. Maldonado, hissing in protest, noted this curious detail. A girl with a head of tight curls emerged from behind a statue whose pedestal bore the inscription "Malgré tout"—in spite of everything. She grabbed the student's hand and the two piled into the rear of the taxi. They said excuse me, but inevitably stepped on several chicks. The fat woman shrieked again, struck at the student with her basket, and the girl asked whether this was a taxi or a mobile food-stamp market. Felix dreamily gazed at the receding statue, a marble woman in an abject posture, naked, poised for the outrage of sodomy, "Malgré tout."

Books spilled to the floor, killing more chicks, as the student perched on the nurse's knees. She didn't seem to mind. Felix took his eyes from the statue to glare with scorn and anger at the nurse through the crook of the fat woman's arm, and pulled the student's girlfriend toward him, forcing her onto his knees. The girl slapped him and called to the student: "This pig's trying to feel me up, Emiliano." The student took advantage of the diversion to turn to the nurse, wink, and stroke the back of her knees. "Are we going to have to get out," he said to Felix, "and settle things? You're asking for it, not me."

The student spoke in a nasal voice, his girl urging him on:

"Let him have it, Emiliano"; and Emiliano: "Keep your hands off my baby." Through the open window, a lottery vendor thrust under Felix's nose a handful of black and purple sheets still smelling of fresh ink. "Here's your dream come true, señor. Ending in seven. So you can marry this nice lady." "What lady?" Felix retorted with assumed innocence. "You're looking for trouble and you're going to get it," growled the student. The nuns giggled and asked to get out. The girlfriend noticed that the student was eyeing the nurse with interest and said, "Let's get up in front, Emiliano."

As the nuns were climbing out, the student got out of the left side of the taxi to avoid stumbling over Felix, and the driver said, "Don't go out on that side, you stupid jerk, I'm the one who'll get the fine." The girlfriend with her head like a woolly black sheep pinched Felix's knee on the way. Only Felix noticed in the midst of the confusion that the giggling nuns had stopped beside one of the many statues of heroes along the Paseo de la Reforma. One of them raised her skirts and whirled her leg as if dancing the can-can. The taxi shot away, leaving the student and his girl scuffling in the middle of the street. Then he remembered his books, shouted, "The books," and ran after the taxi, but couldn't catch up.

"They got out without paying," Felix said to the driver, absurdly inhibited at the idea of interfering in something that was none of his business.

"I didn't ask them to get in."

"Are you going to keep the books as payment?" Felix insisted.

"You heard me. I asked them not to get in," the driver said, as if the matter was settled.

"But that isn't true." Felix was scandalized. "You wanted them to get in, this nurse and I were the ones who protested."

"My name's Licha and I work at the Hospital de Jesús,"

said the nurse, tapping the driver's shoulder as she got out in front of the Hotel Reforma.

Felix made a mental note, but just then the fat woman hit him again with her basket and yelled, "It's all your fault, don't try to look so innocent, why are you making that face, all you had to do was move over a little, but no, you wouldn't move over, all you had on your mind was feeling all the women's bottoms as they got in and out, I know your type all right." She also accused Felix of killing all her chicks, but Felix ignored her. There were dead chicks on the floor and on the seats, and a few crushed against the taxi windows. Books were strewn over the floor of the taxi, open and trampled, black shoeprints obliterating black print.

"I know I'm going to get fined," said the driver. "It's just not fair."

"Take my card," said Felix, offering it to the driver.

He got out at Insurgentes and watched the taxi drive away with the fat woman's head and fist sticking out the window, her fist threatening him as the statue of Cuauhtémoc with upraised lance seemed to threaten the conquered city. He reached the door of the Hilton and the doorman greeted him, touching a hand to the visor of his military cap, powder-blue like his uniform. He handed Felix the keys to his Chevrolet, and Felix gave him a fifty-peso bill. The cardboard silhouette of the senior Hilton beckoned from behind glass doors, BE MY GUEST.

3 SEÑORITA MALENA was the only person in the office, and at first she didn't see Felix Maldonado come in. Señorita Malena was a little over forty, but her particular idiosyncrasy was to pretend that she was still a little girl. Not merely young, but truly childlike. She wore bangs and curls, flowered dolls' dresses, white stockings, and patent-leather Mary Janes. It was well known in the Ministry that this was how Malena kept her mother happy. Ever since Malena was a little girl, her mother had said, I hope you always stay a little girl, I pray to God you never grow up.

Her prayer was heard, but none of this prevented Malena from being an efficient secretary. She was absorbed in folding a little lace handkerchief on the desk before her, and Maldonado coughed to let her know he was there without startling her. He didn't succeed. Malena looked up, left her handkerchief, and opened wide doll's eyes.

"Oh," she yelped.

"I'm sorry," Maldonado said. "I know it's early, but I thought we might get started on several matters."

"How nice to see you again," Malena managed to murmur.

"You say that as if I'd been away a long time." Maldonado laughed, walking toward the door to the cubicle on which were spelled out in black letters: Bureau of Cost Analysis, Chief, Licenciado Felix Maldonado.

Malena straightened up nervously, wringing the handkerchief, stretching out an arm as if she wished to intercept him. The Chief of the Bureau of Cost Analysis noticed the movement. It struck him as curious, but he gave it no thought. As he opened the door, he thought that the secretary seemed almost to swoon. He heard her sigh as if bowing before the inevitable.

Maldonado turned on the fluorescent lights in the windowless cubicle, removed his jacket, hung it on a hanger, and sat down in the leather swivel chair behind his desk.

Each of these actions was accompanied by a nervous movement from Malena, as if she hoped to prevent them, but, failing, was forced to blush with shame.

"If you would bring in your pad, please," said Maldonado, staring with increasing curiosity at Malena, "And your pencil, of course."

"I'm sorry," Malena stammered, nervously toying with a corkscrew curl, "but what matters are we going to take up?"

Maldonado was on the verge of snapping, "What business is it of yours?" but he was a courteous man. "The unit program, and the international cost index of raw materials."

Malena's face was illuminated with happiness. "The Under-Secretary has that dossier," she said. Maldonado shrugged his shoulders. "Then bring me the file on paper imports from Canada." Malena sighed with relief. "That dossier is locked in the file. The fact is," the secretary concluded, "you've arrived a little early, Licenciado. It isn't even ten yet. The file clerk hasn't come in and everything's still locked. Why don't you go out and get a cup of coffee, Licenciado? Won't you, please, Licenciado?"

So the sympathetic and childlike Malena was protecting the file clerk, who was late. That explained everything. It was his own fault, Maldonado thought, putting his jacket on again, for being the first one there.

"Please ring my wife, Malena."

Malena stared at him with horror, petrified on the threshold.

"Didn't you hear me?"

"I'm sorry, Licenciado, but can you give me the number?"

This time Felix Maldonado could not contain himself. Red with anger, he said, "Señorita, I know *your* telephone number by heart, how is it possible you don't know mine? For six months, for exactly one-twelfth of a six-year presidential term, you have been calling my wife for me at least two or three times a day. Do you have a sudden case of amnesia?"

Malena burst into tears. She covered her face with her handkerchief and scurried from Maldonado's cubicle. The chief sighed, sat down at the telephone, and dialed the number himself.

"Ruth? I got in early from Monterrey. On the first flight. I had to go directly to a political breakfast. Sorry I couldn't call until now. Are you all right, darling?"

"Fine. When will I see you?"

"I have a lunch at two. Then remember that we're having dinner at the Rossettis'."

"Always lunches."

"I promise I'll go on a diet next week."

"You needn't worry. You'll never get fat. You're too nervous."

"I'll be home to change about eight. Please try to be ready."

"I'm not going to dinner, Felix."

"Why not?"

"Because Sara Klein's going to be there."

"Who told you that?"

"Oh, is it a secret? Angelica Rossetti, early this morning when we went swimming at the club."

"I only found out at breakfast. Anyway, it's been twelve years since I've seen her."

"It's up to you. You can stay home with me, or go see the great love of your life."

"Ruth, Rossetti is the Director General's private secretary, have you forgotten?"

"Goodbye."

He was left with a dead receiver in his hand. He pressed a button on the intercom and heard Malena's voice on the extension.

". . . I think I've seen him before, that is, I seem to remember having seen him, but the honest truth is I don't know who he is, Licenciado. If you'd like to come by and see him, he's asking me for classified dossiers, and acting as if he owned the office, if you could just . . ."

Maldonado hung up the receiver, walked out to the main office, and stared at the secretary. Malena put a hand to her mouth and hung up the telephone. Maldonado approached her desk, planted his fists on the sheathed typewriter, and said in a very low voice: "Who am I, Malena?"

"The chief, sir . . ."

"No, I mean, what is my name?"

"Uh . . . Licenciado . . ."

"Licenciado who?"

"Uh . . . just Licenciado . . . like all the others . . ."

She burst into uncontrollable sobs, invoking the immediate presence of her mommy, and again hid her face in the lace handkerchief with the little yellow chicks embroidered in a circle around the initial M.

4 FOR MORE THAN AN HOUR, a perplexed Felix Maldonado walked about aimlessly. What he most disliked about the Ministry was that it was in such an unattractive part of the city, the section where all the streets were named after doctors. A run-down mass of low buildings dating from the beginnings of the century, and an all-pervading concentration of cooking odors issuing from squalid little lunchrooms. An occasional tall building loomed like an excessively inflated glass tooth in a mouth filled with cavities and badly healed extractions.

He walked as far as Doctor Claudio Bernard, trying to put his thoughts in order. He was unpleasantly distracted by the odors from the shabby eating places opening directly onto the sidewalk. He turned to make his way back to the

Ministry. He bumped into a stand where ears of corn were being steamed over boiling kettles. He pushed his way through crowded streets filled with itinerant vendors selling sliced *jícamas* sprinkled with lime and chili powder and paper cones of scraped ice that like a blotter absorbed redcurrant and chocolate syrups.

His strongest impression was one of a faltering will. He inhaled deeply, but was offended by the smells. He set off down Doctor Lucio and, a block before reaching the Ministry, saw a beggar woman with a tiny baby sitting on the sidewalk. It was too late to turn his back to them. He could feel the woman's black eyes observing him, judging him. These were the dangers of walking through the streets of Mexico City. Beggars and the unemployed, even criminals, everywhere. That's why you had to have a car, to go directly from a well-protected house to the tall office buildings besieged by the armies of the hungry.

He reflected, and told himself that on any other day he would have done one of two things: walk straight ahead, unperturbed, without even glancing at the woman with the outstretched hand and the tiny baby, or turn his back to them and walk back the way he'd come. But this morning all he dared do was cross to the opposite side of the street. Obviously, the most cowardly and least dignified solution. How could it have hurt him to walk past the pitiful pair and give them twenty centavos?

From the opposite sidewalk, he could see that the girl was an Indian, very young, not more than twelve. Barefoot, dark-skinned, filthy, with the tiny baby wrapped in her long shawl.

Is it hers, Felix Maldonado asked himself. Is it her child or her brother?

Is it hers, he repeated, as if someone had asked him the question, and then answered in a low voice: "No, señor, it isn't mine."

The girl continued to stare at him, hand extended. Felix

felt an urgent need to rush back to the office to sort things out. He walked faster, until he reached the Avenida Cuauhtémoc. Unable to resist, he turned once again to look at the pair, the child-mother and the son-brother. Two nuns were bending over the two beggars. He realized that they were nuns by their black skirts and the hair pulled back into a bun. One of them looked up, and Felix thought he recognized one of the sisters who had ridden with him in the taxi that morning. The nun turned away, covered her face with a veil, took her companion's arm, and the two quickly walked away, without looking at him again.

5 FELIX ENTERED the Ministry building and walked to the elevator. If he was lucky, he'd meet some friend going up. And the elevator operator himself would know him, of course. We ask your indulgence. The operator is not on duty. We respectfully request the public to use the self-service elevator to the left. Felix recalled the elevator operator, remembering him in clear detail. A small, ageless man, very dark, with high cheekbones and watery eyes, a sparse moustache, and a gray uniform with copper buttons and the initials MED embroidered on the breast pocket. If he remembered the elevator operator, Felix said to himself as he ascended surrounded by strangers, it was only logical that the elevator operator would remember him.

Ordinarily, Malena cashed his bimonthly paycheck for him at the cashier's office. All he had to do was sign the payroll. But today he decided to go in person. He got off the elevator and walked toward the cashier's window. There was a long line. He stood at the end, deciding not to pull rank. The two girls ahead of him were engaged in animated conversation. The elevator operator, his acquaintance, the dark little man, joined the line directly behind him. Felix smiled at him, but the man was absorbed in contemplation of a coin.

"How are you? What are you looking at?" Felix asked.

"This silver peso," said the elevator operator without looking at Felix. "Can't you see?"

"Yes, of course," Felix said, hoping the man would look at him. "But what about it? Haven't you ever seen a peso coin before?"

"The eagle and the serpent," the man said. "I'm looking at the eagle and the serpent on the coin."

Felix shrugged. "It's the national emblem, man. It's everywhere. What's so unusual about it?"

The elevator operator shook his head, never raising his eyes from the tarnished silver coin. "Nothing unusual. It's just that it's beautiful. An eagle on a cactus, eating a serpent. I like it better than what it's worth."

"What do you mean?"

"I mean, I don't care what it's worth. I like the design."

"Oh. I see. Listen, won't you look at me?"

The operator finally looked up and observed Felix with watery eyes and a stony smile.

"Every day I go up to my office in your elevator," Felix blurted impulsively.

"Lots of people go up. If you only knew."

"But I'm an important official, the chief of . . ." Exasperated, Felix left the sentence unfinished.

"I'm the only one who doesn't go anywhere. Everyone looks at me. I don't look at them," the operator said, again staring at his coin.

To avoid standing there like an idiot, staring at the elevator operator staring at the eagle and the serpent, Felix turned his attention to what the two secretaries were saying. Now they were near the cashier's cage.

"If a girl doesn't have respect for herself, who will?"

"You're absolutely right. Besides, everyone should get the same treatment, you know?"

"If only we could. But you'd have to be blind not to see she's his favorite . . ."

"It's undemocratic. And I told him so. You know?"

"You did? You told him that?"

"You don't believe me? Well, I'm fed up to here, dear, you know? I said, you're giving special treatment to Chayo, you can see it a mile away. That's what I told him, you know? And I said, on the other hand, did you bother to come to our Christmas party last year? No, you didn't, did you? Excuse me, but I call that discrimination."

"You told him that?"

"Well, practically. I sure wanted to tell him. You bet your bottom peso I wanted to, you know?"

"Well, you'll have to forgive me, but I would've said it. Yes. We all have our dignity. I'd've said, just because you don't think we're quite as high up as you, that's no reason to insult us, Licenciado."

"Well, you know how it is, that Chayo thinks she's the queen bee. I guess it's not all her fault, and the truth is, the chief, old Maldonado, 's a pretty good guy . . ."

They signed the payroll, cashed their checks, and walked away counting the bills in their pay envelopes. Felix was torn between following them and cashing his check. The man at the window looked at him impatiently.

"May I help you?"

"Maldonado," said Felix. "Cost Analysis."

"I'm sorry, but I've never seen you before. Do you have any identification?"

"No. Look, my secretary usually comes to take care of this for me."

"I'm sorry, sir. I'll have to have some identification."

"All I have with me is my credit card. Here."

"Is your name American Express? We don't have anyone with that name on the payroll."

"Isn't my signature enough? You can compare it with the ones on the previous checks."

The cashier shook his head severely and Felix left the window, determined to look for his driver's license, his passport, his National Party card, even his birth certificate, if necessary. How could Malena cash a check in his name every two weeks without any problem if he, the one the check was made out to, had to have identification? Angry, he walked toward the elevator. Without success, he looked for the two secretaries who'd been talking about him. Was there another Maldonado in the Ministry? Well, why not? It wasn't an unusual name.

6 ONCE in the self-service elevator, again surrounded by strangers, he told himself that the simplest thing would be to send Malena, as he always did; Malena dear, run down to the cashier's for me, will you? He got off the elevator on his own floor, still annoyed because he had had no identification with him. He walked down the narrow, crowded hallway and paused to look out at the low flat roofs in the surrounding Colonia de los Doctores, each roof with its own water-storage tank.

His life was so predictable, he thought, so orderly, and he always went only to places where he was known. He was given special treatment in the bars and restaurants where all he had to do was sign with his American Express card. Except for some small change for tips, that was all he ever needed. But an idiot cashier had asked for what no one ever required at the Hilton or the Jacarandas Club, an identifying photo.

"Underdeveloped as hell," he muttered as he entered his office, "the idiot still isn't aware of the existence of credit cards. They must pay him with glass beads."

Malena and the two secretaries who'd stood before him in the line had their heads together by the door to his office. They might have been in a football huddle. He coughed, and Malena trembled. They broke apart, guiltily, and the two girls said offhandedly, "We'll see you around, Mallie, ask your mother to let you come see the rodeo on Sunday," and Malena, who could not contain herself, cried: "You bitches! Don't leave me here all alone."

She sobbed, and sat down at her ancient Underwood, protected by its bulk.

"Why don't you wear the typewriter cover for a witch's hat; you're certainly acting the part," Felix said brutally.

Suddenly Malena became calm. She arranged a silken curl, picked up the telephone, dialed a short number, and said, with no trace of tears but with an expression that seemed to Felix one of a vengeful, tattletale child: "He's here now. He's back."

Felix Maldonado entered his private office, turned on the fluorescent lights, and automatically took out his felt-tip pen to sign the stack of daily communiqués and memoranda. Customarily, the efficient Malena had all the papers needing his signature ready a little after one. But today, pen in hand, Felix saw that the folder was not on the desk.

As he reached out to buzz his secretary, a short, blond man entered without knocking. One of those short skinny towheads, thought Felix, who thinks he's hot stuff and because he's light-skinned and good-looking can get away with murder. He's the kind who thinks being short allows him to be aggressive, that being a runt excuses all his excesses and commands everyone's respect. But this one was even more annoying than usual because of the penetrating odor of clove drifting from the artfully arranged handkerchief in his breast pocket. Felix wanted to say all this to this man who'd intruded so impertinently.

"Yes? What can I do for you?"

"Sorry. May I sit down?"

"I thought you already were."

"What did you say?"

"Sure. Make yourself comfortable," Felix said, at last gratified. If he's asking my permission, that means he knows this is my office.

"My name's Ayub. Personnel. Simon. Uh . . . what shall I call *you?*" He coughed.

"Whatever you want," said Felix coldly, thinking, *Ayub,* that's strange, a blond Lebanese. If he'd heard the name without seeing its owner, he would have imagined a thick moustache and an olive complexion.

"What's going on . . . Licenciado . . . uh?" said Ayub, questioning but discreet. "What's going on is that we've found an abnormality in the personnel time cards."

"Whatever you say, Ayub. I'm an official. I don't punch time clocks."

"But the fact is . . . Licenciado . . . the fact is that all morning we've been combing the area for a man who . . . usually . . . works in this office . . . uh, unsuccessfully."

"Express yourself clearly. He works unsuccessfully, or you're looking for him without success?"

"That's what I mean, Licenciado, that's what I mean."

"What?"

"That we can't find him."

"What's his name?"

"Felix Maldonado."

"*I* am Felix Maldonado."

The blond man stared at Felix with desperation. He swallowed several times before speaking. "Well, that's not to your advantage, believe me, Licenciado . . . uh?"

"It's not to my advantage to be myself?" Felix asked, disguising his discomfort with a blow of his fist that cracked the protective glass covering of the desk.

"Don't get me wrong," Ayub said, between coughs. "We're trying to see this from a global point of view."

Felix stared with irritation at the green vein of broken

glass running like a scar across the photograph of his wife, Ruth.

"You'll have to pay for the damage to government property," said Ayub, in an absolutely neutral voice, also looking at the scar on the official's desk.

Felix considered it beneath his dignity to reply.

"The Director General told me to tell you to see him today at six," Ayub said abruptly. He stood up, excused himself, and walked out the door, trailing a wake of clove. "So long. Good luck."

This reminded Felix that he had to be at the Restaurante Arroyo in Tlalpan by lunchtime. With the traffic as it was, it would take him at least an hour. He glanced at his watch: one-thirty. When he went out to the main office, he found that Malena had already left. The typewriter was covered with precision; a single violet exhaled in a crystal bud vase, and a worn teddy bear was ensconced in little Malena's desk chair.

The rest of the Ministry of Economic Development seemed to be functioning like clockwork, smoothly and silently. The normal time to leave for lunch was between two-thirty and three.

7 IT TOOK a little longer than the predicted hour to drive to Tlalpan. It was Friday and many people were leaving for a long weekend in Cuernavaca. Several times he was stalled in the choked traffic, and once he even fell asleep at the wheel, to be awakened by a concert of furious honking.

From the street, he could hear the mariachis in the Arroyo. As he parked, he tried to recall the reason for the luncheon, and shuddered. He, especially he, could not

24

afford the luxury of forgetting anything, or forgetting anyone.

Aggressive, self-congratulatory, gray sideburns and a black moustache; a coarse, ugly, ruddy face. Felix said hello, and retained a single impression: an ugly man with beautiful hands. And a woman beside him, greeting the guests.

"Hello, Felix."

"Hello, Mary."

He freed his hand from Mary's grasp. His confusion was understandable, he rationalized, walking toward the table of hors d'oeuvres. He had not only touched the hand and looked into the eyes of the woman he most liked to touch and look at in the world. More. She had recognized him. She had said hello Felix, with complete naturalness. Of course—he gulped down the small glass of excellent tequila —the man with the ugly face and beautiful hands was her husband. He would never have recognized him without Mary. Who would ever remember the owner of a chain of supermarkets? He needed Mary in order to identify her husband. That was all. He hadn't actually forgotten him. Mary's husband, in spite of his florid appearance and aggressive behavior, was not memorable. That was all, he repeated, as Mary approached and told him that the meal was very informal, everyone was to help himself, everyone was to sit where he pleased and with whom he pleased.

"Besides, the mariachis are an ideal cover for intimate conversation, don't you agree?" Mary asked, half closing eyes as violet as the solitary flower on Malena's desk.

Violet eyes flecked with gold, Felix recalled, helping himself to tortilla chips with guacamole, an extraordinarily beautiful Jewish woman with black hair and a preference for décolletage. She oiled the line between her breasts so the cleavage would be more noticeable.

His eyes followed her as mushroom canapés were being passed and the mariachis bleated in the distance, remote but overpowering. Mary was aware that Felix's eyes never left

25

her. She moved like a panther, black, lustful and pursued, beautiful because she was pursued, and because she knew it. Mary.

Felix glanced at the time. Three-thirty, and still no lunch. Tequila and hors d'oeuvres, nothing more. He was always exasperated by these four- or five-hour Mexican lunches; and the Director General was expecting him at six on the dot. Mary winked at him from across the room as waiters entered carrying clay crocks of *mole*, boiled rice, nut- and spice-stuffed peppers topped with cream and berries, platters of steaming tortillas, and several kinds of chili, brown chili, tiny *piquines*, the fieriest of all, *serranos*, and *jalapeños*.

He served himself a heaping plate and joined Mary; the woman with the violet eyes smiled at him and offered him a beer. They walked together from the table, balancing their plates and glasses of beer, speaking in voices drowned in the racket of the mariachis, threading their way among the guests.

"What's the occasion for the party?" Felix asked.

"My tenth wedding anniversary," laughed Mary.

"So many years?"

"Ten's not so many."

"Exactly as many as it's been since we've seen each other. I'd say a lot."

"But we do see each other from time to time at cocktail parties and weddings and funerals."

"I mean physically together, Mary, as we used to be."

"That's easy to remedy."

"You know that all I want is the physical part, don't you?"

"You mean you never loved me? I know that very well. I never loved you."

"More than that. I never desired you."

"Oh? That's something new."

"I can only touch you when I don't desire you. Touch

26

you and touch you, kiss you and screw you, but without desire. Do you understand?"

"No, but it's enough for me. It excites me. I like the way you touch me. Ten years is a long time. Look. Go to the motel just down the street. Leave your car in front of your room, so I can see where they put you. That way I can run my car behind the building where it can't be seen. Wait for me there."

"I have a very important appointment at six."

"That's all right, I'll disappear after a while. Abie won't even notice. Look at him."

Felix didn't want to look at a man he would never remember, and he pressed Mary's arm.

"And listen, Felix," said Mary, falsely brazen. "Don't expect me to be the same as before; I've had four children."

Felix said nothing. He moved away as Abie announced with grandiloquent gestures and elaborate passes of an imaginary cape that he was going to fight four yearling bulls at the end of the party. Torero! He'd shaved carelessly; there were several nicks on his chin.

When everyone had moved to the bullring beside the restaurant, Felix left and drove to the neighboring motel. He followed Mary's directions and took a room, notable for damp sheets and the smell of disinfectant. He must have slept. He was awakened by throbbing and acid indigestion. For a moment he imagined how it would be to be at the shore, away from the altitude of Mexico City, by the sea, digesting his food normally in an unattainable paradise of simple, short meals served at fixed hours.

Through the motel window he could hear the olés! from the small bullring. He imagined a ruddy-faced Abie, aggressively fighting his bull, his beautiful hands hidden beneath the red cape. Surely the first Jewish torero. Few people knew that many refugees from Hitler's Europe had come to Mexico, where they effortlessly assimilated the customs, even the rituals, of the Mexicans, as if nostalgic for

Spain before their expulsion. He laughed. A Jew in a bull-ring, facing a snorting reddish-brown bull, was the Sephardic revenge against the Catholic Queen Isabella.

He also imagined Mary sitting on one of the narrow tiers of seats, watching the absurd posturing of her husband. He did not desire her. He had to see her before he wanted to touch her. His physical relation with Mary could not tolerate either the time of dream or the space of separation. It could not tolerate desire.

8 THE DOWNPOUR BEGAN as Felix Maldonado, belching painfully, was driving down the Avenida Universidad. It was an early-evening rain typical of the tropics, a phenomenon born of topographical perversion, a cloudburst more appropriate to virgin jungle than to a chilly plateau two thousand meters above sea level.

No temperate climate would ever witness the sheets of water, the dark, steaming rain whipping against the windshield of Felix's Chevrolet. The wipers refused to function. Felix had to get out of the car in the driving rain to set them in motion. Even as he was getting soaked, he laughed a little, thinking of a washed-out Abie, the rain-soaked tables, the interrupted bullfight, and Mary, motionless beneath the rain, staring at mountains as violet as her eyes.

As he parked the automobile in the basement of the Ministry, Felix nervously consulted his Rolex. Ten minutes after six. Ten minutes late, he repeated as he stepped onto the elevator operated by his little friend, who greeted him amiably, as if he recognized him. No, he greeted everyone that way, it was one of his duties as elevator operator. Outside working hours, it was up to others to recognize *him*.

28

Felix got off the elevator and, almost running, still soaked and breathless, reached the Director General's reception room. The secretary was an extravagant bleached blonde with large breasts and small hips. She tried to disguise the red moles on her face by painting them black.

"Good evening, Licenciado."

Felix closed his eyes. With a great effort he recalled, this is Chayo, the conceited secretary her two envious colleagues had been discussing that morning at the cashier's window.

"How's everything, Chayo?"

He awaited her response. There was none. Impossible to tell whether or not she recognized him.

"I have an appointment with the Director General."

Chayo nodded. "Please take a seat, it will be just a moment."

"I get fed up with the Latin vice of never being on time, Chayito," Maldonado commented as he sat down. "It bothers me much more than it does the people who have to wait for me. You understand what I mean?"

Chayo again nodded, and continued typing to the rhythm of her chewing gum, or vice versa. A buzzer sounded and Chayo stood up, wriggling her bust instead of her non-existent hips. "If you'll come with me, please." Maldonado followed her down a long cedar-paneled corridor decorated with photographs of former Presidents of the Republic beginning with Ávila Camacho.

Three times Chayo pressed a red button beside the door; it lighted, and she pushed open the door. Felix entered the dimly lighted office of the Director General. Chayo disappeared, and the door closed.

Felix had difficulty locating the Director General in the vast, deliberately murky penumbra of the windowless office, where an occasional lamp seemed strategically placed to blind the visitor and protect the Director General, whose photophobia was well known.

Finally, Felix was able to make out the reflection of tinted lenses. Pince-nez had been the trademark of the number-one villain of modern Mexican history, Victoriano Huerta, and only the Director General would dare wear them. But he had the excuse of his extreme sensitivity to light.

His host's voice guided him; also an additional gleam in the darkness, a gold wedding band. The pale hand beckoned, "Sit down, Licenciado, I beg you; here, please, facing me at the desk."

Hastily, Felix sought the place indicated by the Director General and, equally hastily, replied, "I hope you'll forgive me. Being late drives me up the wall. I put myself in the place of the person who's waiting, and hate myself as much as I hate anyone who makes me wait. The wait-that-exasperates, you know."

The Director General laughed hollowly, a dry laugh that stopped abruptly at the very crest of the merriment. As usual, he passed without transition from laughter to severity. "We know that you are always punctual, Licenciado Maldonado. You are a man of many virtues. Some say too many virtues."

"Since when is virtue a defect?" Felix asked, speaking only to cover his intense desire to kneel before the Director as before the Pope, and to kiss his ring; for the first time in this entire day, a member of the Ministry staff had spoken his name, Maldonado.

The Director General swiveled his chair slightly. Felix's superior favored a military haircut, and in the light of the desk lamp his round head bristled like a white porcupine. He consulted a blue card before him.

"You also have too many lives, Licenciado. We know you as a distinguished economist with a degree that earned you your title, an efficient and punctual bureaucrat, n'est-ce pas? an individual gifted in his amorous encounters, a man of sudden tempers, isn't that true? a disciplined member of the National Party, a devotee of political breakfasts, a friend of certain influential people, a convert to Judaism, a husband and . . ."

"We have no children," Felix interrupted, fearful of the next assessment his conjugal life might provoke, irritated by the repeated lack of respect for his privacy evidenced throughout the day. "But we hope to have a child soon."

"As soon as you achieve a more stable economic and social position, isn't that right?" smiled the Director General.

"Yes," Felix agreed nervously, "and my wife wouldn't have married me if I hadn't converted to . . ."

"What a varied existence. It reflects your personality well, cold and passionate, adept and excitable."

"Do you pretend to know me so well, sir?"

"Why not?" The Director General wagged his head and then rested his chin on clasped hands. "You give yourself the luxury of being all things, Machiavelli and Don Juan. A bit of Al Jolson, and a bit more of Othello . . ."

"Al Jolson? You're joking." Felix laughed weakly.

"A Jew disguised as a black, a Mexican disguised as a Jew. Where's the difference? You're a well-entertained and entertaining man, Licenciado, a courtier and a politician, at home in the salons of the wealthy and in . . ."

"We all lead several lives." Maldonado interrupted again, now with open irritation. "Don't you?"

"Licenciado," the man with the crew cut spoke glacially. "It is not I who is being judged."

"I *am?*" Felix parried.

"No, you are not being judged. You have already been found guilty."

The Director General saw Felix's face and laughed his high, thin, abruptly suspended laugh. "Don't be irritated. Don't take it so to heart."

"How do you want me to take it?" Felix swallowed the thick, bitter knot in his throat.

"Listen carefully. Pay close attention."

"Only as you merit, sir."

"Good. Let us suppose that a superior official orders a subordinate official to invite, and if necessary compel, a third official, inferior to the second, to commit a crime."

"I'll suppose it if you wish, but I don't know what you're getting at. Why beat around the bush?"

"To avoid a series of difficulties."

"I still don't understand."

"We prefer to obtain the desired results without need for extensive proceedings or troublesome, at times even cruel, interrogations, n'est-ce pas?"

"And if the second official fails to persuade the third, or if he cannot force him?"

"Then the second official will be guilty of not having known how to persuade *or* to force."

"In that case, is the third official exonerated of blame?"

"He is not."

"Then there must necessarily be a culprit?"

"No. There must only be a crime. Understand this clearly. We have nothing personal against you."

"Imagine if you did."

"Don't attempt irony. Understand that we wish to help you."

"To achieve that more solid economic and social position you mentioned a moment ago?"

"Why not? I repeat: understand that we wish to help you. Allow us to . . . forget you."

"Sir, I don't understand a single word of what you're telling me. It's as if you were talking to another person."

"The fact is that you *are* another person. Don't complain, man. You have many personalities. Discard one of them and keep the rest. What harm is there in that?"

"I still don't understand. What makes me uneasy about all this is that you're talking to me as if I were someone else."

"Have you forgotten the very purpose of this interview?

32

Is it possible you don't remember what I've been saying to you?"

"That would be serious?"

"Extremely."

"What do you recommend?"

"Do nothing. Be calm. Situations will present themselves. If you are intelligent, you will recognize them, and will act accordingly."

The Director General stood up, the upper part of his body disappearing into shadow. The lights illuminated only his lean stomach, one hand resting lightly on the buttons of his jacket.

"And remember this very carefully. We are not interested in you. We are interested only in your name. Your name, not you, will be the criminal. Good evening, Licenciado . . ."

"My name is Felix Maldonado," Felix said aggressively.

"Easy, easy." The hollow voice of the Director General grew more distant in the shadow.

Felix paused with one hand on the bronze doorknob and asked, without turning to look at his superior. "I'm already forgetting. What is the crime the third in the hierarchy is invited or forced to commit?"

"That is for the interested party to ascertain," replied the Director General, his voice hollow and distant as if on a recording. And almost immediately: "Don't bother to turn the knob. It's merely an ornament."

He pressed a button and the door clicked open electronically.

He didn't allow me even that freedom. I wasn't allowed even to open the door. I was manipulated like a damn fool, like a puppet on a string. Felix strode from the office, avoiding the eyes of the sumptuous Chayo.

9 HE WAS EXHAUSTED as he drove from the Ministry to his apartment in the Polanco district. He tried to recall the conversation with the Director General. It was essential that he not forget a single detail, that he reconstruct faithfully every word uttered by his superior. It frightened him that he felt drowsy. He pinched his leg as if to force himself to stay awake, to avoid an accident. He would have to have a cup of coffee before leaving for dinner. He pinched himself a second time. With whom had he just spoken? What had he said to him? He quickly rolled down the car window, welcoming the rush of cold, rainswept air that follows a storm.

He honked his horn three times to announce his arrival to Ruth. It was an affectionate custom of long standing. He parked in front of the twelve-story condominium. He took the elevator to the ninth floor. Sometime he should count the number of times per day he ascended and descended in a elevator. Perhaps what he really needed was a gray wool uniform with copper buttons and the initials MED embroidered across the breast. Maybe in the future that was the only way he would be recognized at the office.

As he entered his apartment, he called several times: Ruth, Ruth. Why did he feel the need to announce his arrival from the street, and again on entering, when he knew perfectly well that his wife would be angry with him, that she would be lying on the bed waiting for him, pretending not to be, leafing through a magazine, the television turned on but the volume down, dressed in a silk night-gown and bed jacket as if she were debating whether to go to bed early, still in her makeup, still not in her night creams, indicating that she was available and could be persuaded to go with him to the Rossettis'.

Before he opened the bedroom door, he studied the life-size reproduction of the Velázquez self-portrait hanging in the hall. It was one of their private jokes. When they'd seen the original in the Prado, they'd laughed in that ner-

34

vous way one laughs to break the solemnity of museums, but had not dared say that Felix was the painter's double. "No," Ruth said, "Velázquez is *your* double," and bought the reproduction as they left. He opened the bedroom door. Ruth was watching television. But she hadn't fixed her hair, and was removing her makeup with Kleenex. This disconcerted Felix. Hello, hello Ruth, he said, but she did not reply. Felix walked directly to the bathroom. He called in a loud voice cloaked by running water and the sound of his electric razor: "It's eight o'clock, Ruth, the invitation is for nine. You're not going to be ready."

The face in the mirror recalled the resemblance to Velázquez, the black almond eyes, the high olive-skinned brow, the short curved nose, Arab but also Jewish, a Spanish son of all the peoples who'd passed across the peninsula —Celts, Greeks, Phoenicians, Romans, Hebrews, Muslims, Goths—Felix Maldonado, a Mediterranean face, high prominent cheekbones, full sensual mouth with deep fissures at the corners, thick black wavy hair, wide-set but heavy eyebrows, and again the black eyes that would have been round, round to the point of obliterating the whites, were it not for their vaguely Oriental elongation, black moustache. But Felix's face did not have the smile of Velázquez, the satisfaction of those lips that had just tasted plums and oranges.

"You're not going to be ready," he repeated. "All I have to do is shave, take a quick shower, and change my clothes. It takes you longer. You know I don't like to be late."

Several minutes passed and Ruth still did not answer. Felix turned on the taps and unplugged his electric shaver. Patience and compassion, the rabbi who had married them had exhorted; he remembered the words now, and kept repeating them under the shower. Patience and compassion, as he scrubbed himself vigorously with the towel, sprinkled himself liberally with Royall Lyme, smoothed the Right Guard beneath his arms, hefted the pouch of his

35

testicles, and checked the size of his penis, not looking down at it, because from that vantage it always appeared small, but from the side, in profile before the full-length mirror, as women see it. Sara, Sara Klein.

Consciously naked, he walked into the bedroom, pretending to be drying his ears with the towel, and repeated what he had previously called. "Didn't you hear me, Ruth?"

"Yes, I heard you. How nice that you bathed and perfumed yourself, Felix. It's very unpleasant when you go to dinner still smelling of the day's sweat and office odors and dirty undershorts. Of course, I'm the one who'll have to pick them up."

"You know I don't always have time. I like to be punctual."

"And you know I'm not going. That's why you showered and soaked yourself in cologne."

"Don't talk nonsense, and hurry it up. We'll be late."

Ruth hurled her *Vogue* at him with fury. Felix stepped aside, remembering the knife-sharp pages of the student's books in the taxi killing the chicks.

"Late, late! That's all you ever think about. You know perfectly well that if we arrive on time there won't be a soul at the Rossettis'. He won't be home yet from the office, and she'll just be rolling her hair. Who're you trying to kid? God, how you irritate me. You know that if they invite us for nine they mean for us to arrive at ten-thirty. Only foreigners who don't dig our ways arrive on time and embarrass everyone."

"Who don't 'dig' our ways? Did you pick that up from a Yankee friend, darling?"

"And stop parading around naked, you'd think you wanted to show off that pencil penis," Ruth screamed.

Felix laughed. "Ah, it was much bigger before you forced me to be circumcised. How about that, circumcised at twenty-eight. Just to please you."

He was angry now. His patience had run out, and he dressed hurriedly. It was always like that—first, good humor, then suddenly real anger, not feigned like Ruth's. Just for you, I changed my religion, my diet, my foreskin, and got myself married in a fucking little skullcap.

She watched him. "I was thinking . . ."

"You?"

"You're going to pull off those buttons, Felix."

"Just call me Wimpy."

"Don't try to be funny. Come here, sit beside me for a minute. I'll do your cuff links. You never can manage. I don't know how you'd get along without me. I've been thinking that for months now we've been like enemies, and the only reason we've stayed together is to convince ourselves we should separate."

"You may be right. The kind of life we lead is certainly a good argument for separation."

"You're away so much. What can I believe?"

"It's my work. You ought to respect it."

"I'm sorry, Felix. It's just that I'm afraid."

Ruth put her arms around him, and Felix's heart turned over. He was about to ask her, do you know something, do you understand what's going on. But she spoke first, to dispel the doubt. "Felix, I know what role I've played in your life."

"I love you, Ruth. You must know that."

"Wait. Please. I mean why you chose me over Sara and Mary."

"You sound as if you think they were better than you."

"The truth is, they were. I'm not as intelligent as Sara or as good-looking as Mary. I've spent the day thinking about it. You always put Sara on a pedestal. You went to bed with Mary. But for you either a pure, even intellectual, love or pure sex without love doesn't work. You need a woman like me to solve your practical problems, to handle the details of your career and your social life, and as long as our everyday affairs go smoothly, you happily love and screw the same woman, one woman, me. I'm your untouchable ideal at times, and sometimes your whore, but always the woman who has your breakfast ready and your suits pressed and your bags packed—everything, the dinners for your bosses, everything. Am I right?"

"It's all too complicated. But I've been listening all day to things about myself that seem to refer to someone I don't know."

"No, Felix. It's perfectly simple. I was never your pure ideal, like Sara, or your piece of ass, like Mary. I'm both of them but only half of each. That's the problem, don't you see?"

"Ruth, it's not important that Sara Klein will be at the Rossettis'. I haven't seen her for centuries. What is important is to go there with you, for them to see us together, and happy, Ruth."

"In me you have what Sara Klein and Mary Benjamin each gave you."

"Of course, of course, that's why I preferred you. Don't keep harping on it."

"You love me ideally, like your Sara, and physically, like Mary."

"Do you have any complaints? What's bad about that?"

"Nothing, except that now you're idealizing both of them, both are becoming what Sara Klein once was; you're idolizing them from afar, the equilibrium is about to be broken. My intuition tells me, Felix, if you see Sara tonight you won't be able to resist the temptation. She'll be back on her pedestal. And you'll take my place from me."

"Which place, Ruth, your ideal or your sexual security? Please explain, since you seem to know more about it than I do."

"I don't know. It depends. Did you go to bed with Mary today?"

"Ruth, I haven't seen Mary today."

"She called me herself to ask if I was ill, why I didn't come with you to their anniversary party at the Arroyo."

"What time did she call you?"

"About six this evening."

"But you were angry when I first called you this morning."

"Because of Sara Klein. I'd forgotten about Mary. Mary made me remember them both. But I'm not angry now. I feel as if you'd split me down the middle, Felix. What I wanted to give you in me, united in me, you'd rather have from two women. It's as if you wanted to go back, to be young again."

"That fucking Mary," Felix muttered.

Ruth looked at her husband, and frowned. "Don't do it, Felix. You're still young."

"Do you know you're talking to me the way a Jewish mother talks to her son?"

"Don't make fun of me. Just believe that we can live together and grow old together and die together."

Felix grabbed Ruth by the arms and shook her. "Don't play the Jewish mother with me, I can't stand it. I can't take your wise Jewish mamma warnings. I'm going to the Rossettis' because Mauricio is the Director General's private secretary, and that's that. Sara Klein has nothing to do with it. I think your theories are totally idiotic."

"Please don't go, Felix. Stay here with me. I'm not playing games now, I'm asking you sincerely. Please stay. Don't jeopardize yourself."

10 RUTH'S FACE haunted him all the way from Polanco, along the throughway, and out to San Angel. She'd never before looked at him just that way, her eyes filled with tears and tenderness, slowly shaking her head, her brows knit, warning him, as if this one time she knew the truth but didn't want to offend him by speaking it. As he drove, he wondered whether her words masked the truth, whether she was lying to let him know, without hurting his feelings, that she suspected the gravity of everything that had happened during the day.

Felix had never played off Sara and Mary against Ruth. Ruth realized that the mere fact of her presence gave her the advantage over any aspect of Felix's past, Felix said to himself, accustoming himself to speak of himself in the third person; Ruth is Felix's wife, he thought as he searched for a parking place near the narrow Callejón del Santísimo. Ruth has freckles she tries to cover with makeup, the way Chayo tries to disguise her red moles. When Ruth perspires, the sweat gathers on the tip of her nose. Maldonado's wife is a pretty Jewish girl, charming, active, a Hebraic geisha, Madame Butterfly with the Ten Commandments from Mount Sinai cradled in her arms instead of a son, Madame Cio-Cio-Stein, an empty basket in the bulrushes. Ridiculing her, he worked himself up to detesting her as he entered the Rossettis' white colonial house. It's true, Ruth does keep my shirts ironed, she does put my cuff links in for me.

Standing in the exact center of a white rug, a glass in her hand, Sara Klein seemed to be waiting for him. The light of the open fire formed a halo around her; an enormous painting by Ricardo Martínez served as a backdrop. After twelve years, Sara Klein was suspended within a luminous drop in the center of his world.

He feared to burst the golden bubble. He closed his eyes and reviewed faces from the past.

When he was studying economics at Columbia University, he'd seen all the films at the Museum of Modern Art.

He had escaped at lunchtime, sometimes going without eating in order to see the old films on Fifty-third Street. For Felix Maldonado, the cinema became the counterpoint and nemesis of economics. Economics is an abstract science, sadly and finally innocuous when its true nature is revealed: the science of economics is personal opinion converted into dogma, the only opinion that makes use of numbers to justify itself. Film is a concrete art, happily and ultimately deceptive when it proves itself to be everything *except* art: a simple catalogue of faces and gestures: uniquely individual, never generic.

He concentrated on these memories as if trying to prolong coitus, trying not to come too soon. Not yet. He denied himself the pleasure of looking again at Sara; as yet, he didn't want to go to her. Ruth had implored him, don't go to that party. Like Mary Astor in the final scene of *The Maltese Falcon,* incredulous, prepared to transform the lie of her love into the truth of her life if Humphrey Bogart would save her from the electric chair. Except that poor Ruth hadn't been pleading for her own life but, in some obscure way, for his. And now, and here, Sara before him, as enigmatic as Louise Brooks in *Pandora's Box.* So like her, her hair black as a raven's wing, worn in bangs and a pageboy, icy diamonds in her gaze, fatal availability in her body. But as interpreted by Louise Brooks, Lulu was a clear warning—a warning with no possibility of misunderstanding—of all the misery that lies in store for a man who loves a promiscuous woman. Sara Klein was Felix's ideal, his untouched woman.

He opened his eyes and saw an unchanged Sara. Young Napoleon at the Bridge of Arcole, a picture postcard from the Louvre, Sara Klein, her hair combed like Bonaparte's, the same profile, the same military-style suits and overcoats. Sara Klein, aquiline and dark-skinned—*aguileña y trigueña*—the description was practically a theme song. She was entranced by the Spanish *Ñ*.

41

"Mexico is an *X*," Felix had told Sara when they were both still very young. "España is an *Ñ*. You will never understand the countries if you don't understand the letters that characterize them."

Sara, the young Jew, the only one of them who had not spent her childhood in Mexico, had learned Spanish as a young adult. She had grown up in Europe, unlike Ruth and Mary, who had been born in Mexico and were second-generation Mexican Jews. He wondered whether Mary was looking at him. And he recognized that something incomprehensible had happened. The rhythm, not only of the day, but of his life as well, had been broken the instant he entered the Rossettis' house and saw Sara Klein standing motionless on a white rug.

At that moment, something changed in Felix Maldonado. He thought differently. He recalled forgotten associations, references to films, to history, to the present, everything that had to do with Sara Klein, the quintessential woman, untouched and untouchable, but at the same time the one most deeply wounded by history, the European girl who had known suffering Ruth and Mary could not even imagine. Auschwitz had real meaning for Sara. That was why he'd never been able to touch her. He'd been afraid he would add pain to her pain, that he might hurt her in some way.

"It wasn't what they did to us individually. It was what they did to us as a whole. What happens to one person is important to everyone. Mass extermination ceases to be important, it becomes a question of statistics. They knew that, and that's why they hid the individual suffering and glorified collective suffering. In the end, the most important victim is Anne Frank, because we know her life, her home, her family. They couldn't reduce Anne Frank to a simple number. She is the most terrible witness of the Holocaust, Felix. A young girl speaks for everyone. A pit with fifty corpses has no voice. Forgive me for what I'm going to say. I envy Anne Frank. I was only a number at Auschwitz, one more nameless Jewish child. I survived. My parents died."

The bubble burst as the tall, obese figure of Professor Bernstein approached Sara.

Mauricio and Angelica Rossetti, his hosts, came to speak to Felix, concealing their surprise that their guest hadn't greeted them.

"Will we be seeing you tomorrow at the Palace for Professor Bernstein's prize?" Rossetti asked in his deep-throated voice, but Felix had eyes only for Sara Klein.

The Rossettis introduced him to Sara: "You already know Professor Bernstein. What a shame Ruth isn't feeling well."

They introduced him to Sara Klein, and he wanted to laugh. He wrinkled his nose as if to pronounce "n-yeh," and she remembered, and understood, the joke of their youth, *araña, mañana, reseña, enseña, nuño, niño, ñoño, ñaña, ñandú*, they laughed together, *moño, coño, retoño*.

Felix took Sara's hand and said how fortunate it was that they had the whole evening before them. She hadn't forgotten the terrible Mexican hours? And she replied in her husky voice, "I remember that everything is very late, very exciting, not like the States. What time is it?"

"Barely ten-thirty. We won't eat before twelve. First, everyone has to drink a lot of whiskey to build up pressure. If not, the party's a flop."

"And then?" Sara smiled.

"We have to stay till five in the morning for the party to be considered a success. I've heard about hosts who swallow the key so no one can leave." Felix stepped aside to include Bernstein in the circle. "Isn't that right, Professor?"

"I guess so," said Bernstein, watching the pair attentively, his eyes narrowing behind the thick lenses. "We Mexicans have a temperament for fiestas, music, and color.

On the other hand, we are completely lacking in talent in the two most essential professions in the world today: film and journalism. What you said this morning as we were breakfasting together was right, Felix. You can't understand what a Mexican newspaper says if you don't have access to confidential information."

"Who knows? That's a Jew's point of view, not a Mexican's," Felix said rudely. Why didn't Bernstein go away? Why didn't he leave him alone with Sara? Was he going to spend the whole evening hovering over them?

"You should know," Bernstein replied. "You're married to one Jew and in love with another."

Without a moment's hesitation, Felix Maldonado reached out and yanked off the rimless eyeglasses, the two thick, naked lenses that seemed to float before the professor's invisible eyes.

"I can't believe it," said Felix, examining the lenses. "The tomato sauce from breakfast is still here."

Bernstein's naked, astounded eyes swam in the depths of a personal ocean and then leapt nervously on deck like gasping fish. Contemptuously, Maldonado hurled the eyeglasses into the fire. Sara cried out, and Mauricio Rossetti rushed to the fireplace to rescue the glasses. Several guests, amused and alarmed, gathered around as Mauricio fished the eyeglasses from the fire with the fire tongs, and Sara stared at Felix with her cold diamond eyes and all the contradictions of her complicity. Felix looked at Sara, first to decipher and then to attempt to distinguish among attraction and repulsion, scorn, homage, and an urge to laugh. Pure perversity, Felix said to himself, gazing at Sara, as Mauricio rescued Bernstein's damned eyeglasses from the flames that purified all things—conjunctivitis, secretions, and the morning's tomato sauce.

Felix leaned close to whisper in Sara's ear. "Darling, we must risk a change in our relationship."

"It wouldn't last," Sara replied, hiding her ear beneath

the crow's wing of her hair. "I have already given you something I couldn't give if our relationship changed. Let things be as they've always been. Please."

"Are you trying to tell me that what we had is no different from what you've felt for other men?" Felix, nibbling the tip of Sara's ear, enunciated this badly.

Laughing gravely, Sara moved her head away. That laugh was her hallmark.

"Our relation is unique. Do you expect me to be the same to all people if I'm to be totally different with you? Do you realize what you're asking?"

Mauricio sent a servant to the kitchen to cool Professor Bernstein's eyeglasses, then officiously stepped between Sara and Felix. "I must ask you to leave, Maldonado. Your bad manners know no bounds. You are in my home now, not your own."

"What do you mean?" Felix caricatured surprise. "Don't you always say 'my house is your house'?"

I cannot understand your conduct," Mauricio said coldly. "Perhaps the Director General will be able to explain it in the morning when I report to him what happened here."

Felix laughed in Rossetti's face. "Why, you fucking little gondolier. Are you trying to threaten me?"

"I beg you to reflect on your behavior, and conduct yourself in a proper manner, Licenciado."

"Ass-kisser."

"Who will help me evict this . . . creature?" Rossetti inquired of the amazed and obviously stunned guests.

The professor intervened between Maldonado and Rossetti. How different he looked without his glasses; his surprise evaporated, his normally suspicious and tense face acquired a kind of Yuletide good nature. Bernstein-without-glasses resembled a lovable old woodworker who'd lost his eyesight carving toys for good little boys and girls. The professor told his host that he'd been the one insulted, and begged him to forget the incident. Rossetti insisted. Maldonado had offended all his guests. "This upstart must be taught a lesson, Professor."

"I beg you. For me. Please."

Rossetti yielded with a disdainful shrug of his shoulders. "This is the last time you will set foot in my house, Maldonado."

"I'm aware of that. It's fine with me. Sorry."

The servant returned Bernstein's glasses to him, and with them, the professor's lost face. Bernstein patted Felix's shoulder paternally. From the professor's fat finger, the water-clear stone in his ring sparked pinpoints of light.

"Our host is very Italian, even though four generations of his family have lived in Mexico. The Italians understand nothing of the old or the new, only the eternal. They find the accidents of history inconsequential, even laughable. Rossetti doesn't understand that we Jews are parricides, while all Mexicans are filicides. In Christ we tried to kill the Father, terrified that we might find the Messiah incarnate in a usurper. This makes sense, especially if you consider that each time a Redeemer appears, our destruction hangs in the balance. On the other hand, Mexicans wish only to kill their sons. What tortures you is the idea of offspring. Any form of continuation serves as proof of your degeneration and bastardy. No, Mauricio doesn't know these things. There are many things Mauricio doesn't know. My image is too paternal for you to want to kill me, isn't that right, Sara?"

"You are my lover," Sara spoke in a sterile tone. "What do you want me to say?"

Bernstein looked straight at Felix, neither smiling nor in triumph.

"You would never kill your father, Felix, that's what our poor little Mauricio cannot understand. You would kill only your sons. Am I wrong?"

A devastated Felix glanced toward Sara, but then, to avoid her eyes, studied the painting by Ricardo Martínez over the fireplace. Massive forms, Indians squatting in the

46

middle of a cold and windswept plain with swirling mists nibbling at the outline of human contours.

Finally he spoke. "Then I deserve to get what everyone else is getting."

"Poor Felix," said Sara. "You were never vulgar as a young man."

Bernstein interrupted his protective patting and, still smiling, pressed his face dangerously close to Sara's.

"I warned you not to come," said the fat man with the ring as watery as his eyes.

"Poor Felix," Sara repeated, and touched the hand of the man who loved her. "Now you know that I am like all your women. Poor Felix."

"That's a laugh." Abruptly, Felix burst out laughing. He laughed till he was doubled over, and finally had to support himself by grasping the edge of the mantelpiece decorated with reproductions of tiny sixth-century Jaina figurines. "What a joke! Mary turns out to be the only woman I haven't laid a hand on in at least ten years. A lifetime, right? Mary, Miss Mary Hotpants, will have to be my ideal woman from now on. I give you my word never to go to bed with Mary."

"He's crazy." Sara's composure had vanished. "Bernstein, do something. Remind this imbecile that he never touched me, and he never shall. He's going to go around telling everyone that Mary's the *only* woman he hasn't had in the last ten years."

"I just spent five minutes mentally fornicating with you," Felix told Sara. "Why, Sara? And why Bernstein, of all people?"

"May I tell him, Bernstein?" Sara glanced toward the professor to ask his permission. The professor nodded, but the exchange infuriated Felix, and once again he was on the point of yanking off his former professor's eyeglasses.

"Don't treat me as if I were a fool," Felix said to the two. He would have to get used to them as a couple. How disgusting. How ridiculous. To think that he'd tried to demean his poor Ruth, so loyal, so noble . . .

"Like the newspapers . . ." the professor tried to interject.

"Oh, sure," Felix cut him off. "We've been going to political breakfasts for ten years, Professor. Before that, you were my instructor in the history of economic theories at the university. Sure I know."

"The truth isn't found in the texts of Charles Gide and Charles Rist," Bernstein joked weakly.

"I like to tie up loose ends. I know you've served the cause of those who track down war criminals. I know that. Men who flush the Nazis from their burrows in Paraguay and then place them in glass cages for judgment. And Sara went to live in Israel twelve years ago. *You* go to Israel twice a year. Right? It fits together perfectly. Where's the mystery?"

"The word 'mystery,' my dear Felix, has many synonyms," Bernstein replied with perfect equanimity.

A long, long moment of silence passed. Felix took note of Sara's grimace and Bernstein's silent plea: let's drop it here, let Maldonado believe this, let him believe whatever he wants, what importance does Felix Maldonado have, anyway? Sara tugged at Bernstein's sleeve, but the professor removed her hand affectionately. Angelica Rossetti decided to speed things along, and invited the guests to come in to dinner. She glared with undisguised displeasure at Felix, as she would at a cockroach unworthy of eating the cannelloni set out on the buffet table.

"Won't you come in, Sara?"

Bernstein escorted the mistress of the house into the colonial dining room, and Sara Klein, arms crossed, leaned against the mantelpiece. Maldonado realized it was the first time since he'd entered the room that she'd changed position. An oppressive dankness rose from the living-room floor in spite of the fire. Homage to the cold stone floor, the proximity of the garden attempting to penetrate the house

48

through the French doors, the mud after the rain, the water-logged desert plants, a monstrous dampness.

Sara Klein stroked the hand of her old friend, and Felix felt warmth and life returning to him. He dared not look at her, but he knew once again that he truly loved her, and would always love her, whether she was near or far, pure or sullied. Now he understood. As long as he had known her, he had falsified his feeling about Sara Klein. The truth lay in admitting that he loved her, and that he didn't care who possessed her. It was no longer Felix or no one.

Sara saw what was passing through his eyes. "Felix, do you remember the time we celebrated your twentieth birthday together?"

Felix nodded. Sara stroked his cheeks and cradled in her hands Felix's curl-ringed, dark-skinned, slim, virile, moustached, Moorish face.

Sara had said that all celebrations are sad. She remembered very few that had really been celebrations, and many that could not be held because the dates were there but the people were not any longer.

"You were sad on that birthday. We went dancing. It was fourteen years after the war. You set yourself the task of teaching me everything I'd missed. Films and books. Songs and styles. Dances and automobiles. I'd missed all that as a child in Germany. Then the orchestra began to play Kurt Weill, the theme song from the *Dreigroschenoper*. Louis Armstrong had made it popular again, you remember? And something very strange happened. The twenty years of your life, my childhood in Germany, that song united us magically, as nothing had before."

" 'Mack the Knife,' I remember."

"You were telling me about a song in vogue in 1956, and I remembered that it was one my parents used to hum. They had a version recorded by Lotte Lenya before the war, before the persecution. A poor, scratched record. Everything joined together to make your melancholy authentic. We were infected by sadness that night. You told me something, do you remember?"

"How could I forget, Sara? That one's death begins with his twentieth birthday."

"And I told you it was a very romantic phrase, but completely false for me, because for me death had never begun, and would never end. I told you that for me death had nothing to do with age. Felix, we knew that night why we could never marry. You were a young and melancholy Mexican. I was a sad, ageless German Jew. We suffered much. That is true. It had nothing to do with sex or our countries or our age."

"I know. That's why I love you, and don't want to cause you more sorrow."

Sara kissed Felix Maldonado. She moved away, and her eyes were no longer icy diamonds. Now they were the turbid waters of a shallow, artificial lake, uselessly and violently roiled. She withdrew until only their hands, their fingertips, were touching.

"If you truly wish not to hurt me, stop loving me, Felix."

"That's difficult. You see, I know that you're Bernstein's lover, and still I love you."

The tense face, the dark brilliance of her eyes, were those of Bonaparte at Arcole.

"I'm not asking you to love me."

"But how can I stop, Sara?"

"By helping me."

"I don't understand."

"Yes. You must help me justify what I'm doing."

"What you and Bernstein are doing?"

"Yes. The thing that truly unites us, not sex."

"Don't you go to bed with him either?"

"Yes. Sometimes."

"That's a relief. It would be too much if you were Bernstein's virgin."

"I'm not. Help me justify the fact that yesterday's victims are today's executioners."

Maldonado tried to step closer to the woman who was suddenly changing before his eyes. Sara Klein was shedding the image he remembered and emerging in a new, stark, candid light.

"There's no virtue in revenge," said Felix, "but it's understandable."

"Tell me how to disguise the truth, Felix."

"The truth is clear. The former victims are now the executioners of their former victimizers. I understand that. I accept it. There's the truth. Why do you want to disguise it? But going to bed with Bernstein seems to me a very high price for truth and revenge."

"No, Felix," Sara answered abruptly, as she had when they were students together, Bernstein's disciples arguing over an economics theory they'd read in Gide or Rist. "No, Felix."

Maldonado dropped her hand.

"No, Felix. That's all over. We've found and judged all our executioners. Now we're executing new victims."

"Which is what your executioners wanted," Felix said flatly.

"I believe they did," Sara replied.

"You're an intelligent woman. You know they did."

"How painful, Felix."

"Yes. It means that your executioners have triumphed over you from the grave. It's what they wanted," said Felix, and turned away.

Felix left the Rossettis' house and walked the length of the Callejón del Santísimo, choked with parked automobiles, to where the cobblestones ended and the mud of the streets of San Angel began, the mud of many streets of Mexico City following a rain, as if they were country roads.

From the midnight mists emerged motionless figures

huddled in the mud, like the figures in the painting by Ricardo Martínez. Felix wondered whether those shapes were actually Indians, human beings squatting in the middle of the night, wrapped in their dusk-colored sarapes, rent by the fangs of blue fog.

He didn't know, because he had never seen anything like it before. He would never know, because he did not dare approach those figures of misery, compassion, and horror.

11 PATIENCE AND COMPASSION, patience and compassion, the rabbi who'd married them had exhorted. Felix drove rapidly along the throughway to the Petróleos fountain and there emerged as if from a cement whirlpool in the direction of a National Auditorium rising gigantic against a sleepy sky. He continued along Reforma, fresh, rain-washed, perfumed by humid eucalyptus trees, inventing meaningless sentences, dreams of reason, Sara, Sara Klein. When we were young, we thought that purity would save us from evil. We didn't know that an evil of purity can be fed by the purity of evil. That was the complicity between Felix and Sara.

He stopped in front of the Hilton, and handed the keys of his Chevrolet to the doorman. The doorman knew what to do. Felix entered the lobby, asked for his key, and the desk clerk handed him a card, his own card, Felix Maldonado, Chief, Bureau of Cost Analysis, Ministry of Economic Development. Felix regarded the desk clerk questioningly.

"A woman left it, Señor Maldonado."

"Mary . . . ? Sara . . . ? Ruth . . . ?" first incredulous, then alarmed.

"I beg your pardon? A heavy lady carrying a large basket."

"What did she say?" Felix was relieved.

"She said flat out she wasn't going to make any trouble for you because it was easy to see you were a big wheel, that's what she said."

"She said that? How did she know I have a room here?"

"She asked. She said she saw you get out of a taxi and come in here."

Felix Maldonado nodded, and tucked the card in his pocket.

He walked through the lime-green lobby to the elevator.

A small man sitting on one of the lobby sofas dropped the newspaper he'd been reading. Felix could smell the penetrating odor of clove.

Ever polite, Simon Ayub rose to greet Felix. "Good evening. What a pleasure. Can I buy you a drink?"

"Thank you, no. I'm too tired."

"If you like, I can drive you home," Ayub offered tranquilly.

"No, thank you," Felix replied dryly. "I have some business here in the hotel."

"Of course, Licenciado, I understand." Always the slightly superior tone.

"You don't understand shit." Felix spoke through clenched teeth, but immediately he repented. He was going to end up fighting everyone he saw. "Sorry. Think whatever you want."

"Will we be seeing each other tomorrow morning, Licenciado?" Ayub inquired cautiously.

"Ah, yes. Where?"

"The President is awarding the National Prizes at the Palace. Have you forgotten?"

"Of course I haven't forgotten. Good night."

Felix started to turn away, but Ayub committed the unpardonable sin, he grasped Felix's arm. Felix looked with astonishment and anger at the well-cared-for hand, the manicured fingernails, the topaz rings with incised scimi-

53

tars. The repugnant aroma of clove assailed his nostrils.

"What the fuck?" Felix flushed beet-red.

"Don't go to the ceremony." Ayub's voice dripped honey. His eyelids drooped in a very Arab, very Mexican manner, veiling any intent of threat. "I'm telling you this for your own good."

In Felix's laugh, scorn triumphed over anger. "I swear to God this has really been my day. All I needed was for *you* to tell me what to do, you overdressed little runt."

Felix jerked free of Ayub's delicate hand.

In the elevator, the figure of the senior Hilton invited, BE MY GUEST. Felix Maldonado clutched his room key in a hand that reeked of clove, following his contact with Ayub. There are people who can be their own hosts only, never the guests of others, he responded silently to Mr. Hilton. Only a man fed up with too many hosts can finally purge himself of them all, along with all the resentments, the nostalgias, the ambitions, the cowardly acts, all the ragtags of his life, the baggage of his soul, fuck them all, anyway.

He entered his room. He didn't have to turn on the lights: the fluorescent light above the dressing table illuminated the shambles. He started to call the desk to protest. Again he smelled the odor of clove. The locks of the drawers he had converted into filing cabinets had been forced open and ransacked. Papers were strewn across the carpet.

He fell exhausted upon the king-size bed, called room service, and asked for breakfast to be sent to him precisely at 8:00. He slept without removing his clothes or turning off the light.

12 HE DRANK his orange juice and two cups of coffee, and by 8:30 he was in the elevator in a clean, pressed suit, one of several hanging in the closet of his room. He left orders for the valet service to dry-clean the suit he'd worn to dinner at the Rossettis'; the cuffs were caked with mud.

He waited at the hotel entrance for the doorman to deliver the Chevrolet. The doorman handed him the keys. "You won't be taking a taxi this morning, Licenciado? The traffic's fierce, it always is at this hour."

"No, I'll be needing the car later, thanks." He tipped the doorman.

He progressed slowly down Reforma and the Avenida Juárez, even more slowly down Madero, and turned into Palma to leave his car in a five-story parking garage. From there he walked down Tacuba toward the National Pawn Shop on the Plaza de la Constitución.

There he walked faster. The immense plaza stirring in the early morning, the naked space, the ancient memories of Indian empires and Spanish viceregencies, the treasures lost forever in the depths of a vanished lake, evoked scenes of rebellions and crimes, fiestas, deceit and mourning. In front of the Cathedral, an old woman was throwing dry tortillas to a pack of hungry dogs. At one of the Palace gates, Felix showed his invitation to the soldiers of the guard, olive-colored uniforms and olive-colored skin, and then to an usher, who directed him to the Salón del Perdón, where the ceremony was to be held.

Many people were milling around the great brocade-and-walnut Salón dominated by the historic painting of the rebel Nicolás Bravo pardoning his Spanish prisoners. Felix quickly located the faces that most interested him. The small, blond Simon Ayub, strolling unaccompanied. Felix didn't have to get any closer, the odor of clove spanned the distance like an indecent love letter addressed only to him. Farther away, the taller, nearsighted Bernstein, one of those

55

to be honored. Felix strained to see whether Sara Klein was with him, but was distracted by the sight of the Director General in violet eyeglasses, visibly suffering in the bright daylight, the flashes of the press photographers, and the television lights. Beside the Director General, whispering into his ear, Mauricio Rossetti, looking slightly hung-over and staring straight at Felix. There was a moment of heightened whispering, followed by an impressive silence.

The President of the Republic entered the Salón. He advanced among the guests, greeting them affably, probably making jokes, pressing certain arms, avoiding others, effusively offering his hand to some, coldly to others, recognizing one man, ignoring the next, illuminated in the steady, biting television lights, intermittently divested of shadows by the flashes. Recognizing. Ignoring.

He was approaching Felix.

Felix prepared his smile, his hand, adjusted the knot of his necktie.

If the President of the Republic spoke to him this morning, it would prove once and for all that he was indeed Felix Maldonado. The President of the Republic did not speak to persons who were not who they said they were. That would teach a lesson to the people trying to wrest his identity from him, even if only the identity of his name. Yesterday's nightmare would vanish forever. He was attending the ceremony in which the National Prizes in the Arts and Sciences were being awarded, and every person who doubted his identity, or was asking him to renounce it, was present. Not the President, no. He would speak to him. He would recognize him. He would say, How are you, Maldonado? What's the latest on those costs? Maldonado could reply with a light joke, Costly, Señor Presidente, only up, Señor Presidente. But he wouldn't; he'd limit himself to a slight nod in recognition of the honor bestowed. At your service, Señor Presidente, thank you for recognizing me.

Felix tried to fix in his mind the President's physical

appearance, to recall his face. He couldn't. Impossible. And not just because of the dazzling white glare of reflectors and flashes. The President suffered the same malady as Felix Maldonado. He had no face. He was nothing but a name, a title. He was Presidential pomp and ceremony, an aura of power. He was without a face or a name of his own; he was a protecting, all-dispensing, all-recognizing hand. Maldonado glanced at the cluster of Presidential assistants. Unsuccessfully, he searched for familiar faces dispersed throughout the mob, obliterated in the white darkness surrounding the President. He couldn't see Bernstein, Ayub, Rossetti, or the Director General.

The President was within a few steps of Felix Maldonado.

PART TWO

THE MEXICAN AGENT

13 HE WAS a long time awakening. He reflected fuzzily, as one does in sleep, that he was dead. Then, that this was an eternal sleep—which was the same thing—and only later he reasoned that he was asleep, alive but in a comatose state. Finally, he realized that the time spent struggling to wake was nothing compared to the time he had been asleep.

His vision was limited by the circumference of two white tunnels. To overcome the length of those tunnels, he had to look straight ahead, more or less follow the imaginary north of the tip of his nose. A normal range of vision was denied him. The slightest movement of his eyes to the right or the left met with black walls. But, even looking straight ahead, he could see only a kind of whitish space, undulating uncertainly.

He saw nothing, but even the nothingness was extremely limited, distant, the bifocal vision of shortsightedness that minimizes everything. Voices came to him from a great distance, diminished, as if they had passed through walls of cotton as white as his sight. As he was getting used to both what he could manage to see and hear, neutral voices and white space, they vanished, and Felix Maldonado was alone.

Again, against his will, he sank into a dreamless sleep, not counting sheep, mulling over the mysterious fact that the Spanish language makes no distinction between the act of sleeping and the act of dreaming; he was arguing against a faceless enemy named Felix Maldonado. In exchange for that seeming poverty of expression, Spanish, with its *ser* and *estar,* is the only language with two verbs for *to be: to be,* the permanent state; and *to be,* the temporary condition. Spanish makes that distinction, but none between dreaming and

sleeping, sleep/dream is unique, sleep/dream is everything, sleep/dream is the image of itself.

He awakened with a start. Now he could see nothing at
all, no matter how hard he tried to penetrate the darkness
of the tunnels. Weakly, he rolled his eyes in dry sockets. He
had the terrible sensation that his orbs of sight were scrap-
ing against the bed of nerves and fibers and blood on which
they normally rested, shredding themselves like Parmesan
cheese on a grater.

He was about to sink again into the heavy and imprison-
ing sleep that so avidly pursued him. To escape, he asked
himself, or rather, he asked Felix Maldonado, did he exist
—to be, permanently; or did he exist—to be, temporarily?
He wondered whether what was happening to him and to
Felix Maldonado was something they were activating or
something being inflicted on them. To escape sleep, he took
inventory of his physical being. Was he temporarily motionless? Was he permanently stilled?

He tried to raise his arms. His limbs were leaden. He
called on his nerves and muscles. Patiently, he invoked a
twitch of the fingertips of his right hand, a latent spasm in
the pit of his stomach, a tickling in the sole of one foot, a
contraction of his sphincter, a sensation of flowing sap in his
testicles. He was whole. He was one. And he was lying
down.

Much later, he felt he had the strength to sit up. The
shadow had yielded not an inch. He groped about him in
the darkness. Nothing. He moved his legs until he sensed
they were without support.

His feet sought a footing. When he felt some contact, he
sat for a moment on something he imagined to be a bed.
He resolved to stand up.

His feet were not really a base of support. They were two
stone wheels. He felt the floor moving under him, he was
falling. He reached out with heavy arms and, still on his
feet, but stumbling, fell against a flat surface. He tried to

pull himself erect, clawing at that smooth space, and then growled with strange jubilation. The enormous head of mute cotton that had become Felix Maldonado was pressing against a cold, smooth surface, was returning to him a proof of life, moistness, a breath.

His extended arms girded the contours of the object that was holding him upright and breathing with him, upon him, at the same time he breathed. He feared it was something alive, another being embracing him, holding on to him to keep from falling down dead.

Suddenly the lights went on, and Felix saw the reflection of a mummy swathed in bandages, with no apertures but the holes for eyes, nose, and mouth.

14 Now he was awakened by the clearly defined chink of glass against metal, familiar, unmistakable sounds, liquid being poured from a bottle, a spoon stirring the contents of a glass, rubber-soled shoes, tiny catlike footsteps squeaking on a composition floor.

Then he felt a painful jab on the inside of his forearm, and heard a woman's voice: "Hold still. Please don't move. Don't move your arm. You must have your intravenous solution. You haven't eaten in forty-eight hours."

He moved the other arm, and touched his body. A sheet covered him from the stomach down, a shortsleeved gown above. He touched his head and realized it was still wrapped in bandages.

"I asked you to be still. I can't find the vein. Since you can't make a fist, it's really hard."

Felix Maldonado inhaled deeply, but identified only the aseptic and neutral scent of alcohol-soaked cotton and a lingering scent of chloroform that seemed to cling to the ceiling like a recalcitrant early-morning mist.

Then he smelled the odor of clove.

Desperately, Felix rolled his eyes in their irritated sockets. There was no one in his field of vision.

"Leave us alone, Lichita," said Simon Ayub.

"His condition isn't good at all. Don't let him move his arm."

"We'll worry about him. He's the one who doesn't know how to take care of himself." Felix heard a hollow, cutting laugh that was interrupted abruptly, severed like a thread. Felix moved his bandaged head, and through the tunnels of his vision saw the Director General sitting before him.

"Well, please be careful," said the woman's voice.

Felix tried to place that voice; he'd heard it somewhere, but the effort exhausted him. It wasn't important. He supposed the woman was the nurse who'd been attending him during the forty-eight hours she'd alluded to earlier.

It didn't matter, especially in view of the fact that he knew perfectly well who was in the room: Simon Ayub, outside his range of vision but, by the aroma of clove, certainly present, and the Director General, an unlikely presence in the echoing chamber of this sickroom, a hospital maybe. Tinted lenses could not contend with the glare from white-enameled walls assaulting the eyes of his superior, forcing him once and again to remove the pince-nez between thumb and index finger of his left hand to rub the dry eyes deprived of their protective penumbra.

"Lower the blinds, Ayub," said the Director General, "and draw the curtains."

Felix heard the corresponding movements. The Director General replaced the violet-colored glasses on the bridge of his nose and looked inquisitively at Felix. "For the moment, you cannot speak," he said, when Ayub had darkened the room. "It's better so. That will prevent you from asking unnecessary questions. I recall your disagreeable buffoonery when you came to my office. You thought you were the cock of the walk. Perhaps now you will listen to reason. I repeat that what we are doing is for your own good."

Felix attempted to speak, but the sound emerged as a death rattle. Intimidated, he accepted his passive role. Simon Ayub laughed discreetly. Out of the corner of his eye, Felix thought he could see the Director seize Simon Ayub by the necktie. As he tugged him toward him like a marionette, Felix could clearly see the small Lebanese, his mouth grotesquely agape, brought to his knees before his chief.

"Don't mock our friend," said the Director General in a serene tone inconsistent with the violence of his action. "He's been of service to us, and we're going to prove to him how fond we are of him."

He released Ayub and again stared intently at Felix. "Yes, you've been of service to us, but not in the discreet manner we would have desired. Do you object to my smoking?"

The Director General extracted an English cork-tipped cigarette from an engraved silver case.

"The day you came to my office, I asked to borrow your name. Merely borrow your name. But you felt obliged to intervene personally in a matter that did not concern you. You did only minor harm, and that can be corrected. That's why you're here, to correct the harm. Everything was planned, mmh? so that only your name would be guilty. You should have understood what was happening and accepted the arrangement we were offering you. That would have avoided any complications. I told you that in my office. I don't like annoying details, prolonged negotiations; in sum, red tape. So. I'm going to tell you exactly what happened, n'est-ce pas? No more, no less. The facts. If you attempt to secure more information, you must assume the responsibility, and the risk. I warn you once again, mmh? You are not guilty of anything. But your name is."

65

"You're the guilty one," Simon Ayub interjected angrily. "You should have prevented him from ever showing up at the ceremony at the Palace."

"Ah, but the Licenciado, at heart, is overly sentimental." The Director General smiled. "I agreed with Rossetti that the inevitable contretemps with Bernstein at Rossetti's house would be sufficient to convince our friend to absent himself, n'est-ce pas? out of decency or pride or simple temper, from the ceremony honoring the professor. But no, by heaven! His gratitude and warm memories as one of Bernstein's former students prevailed, instead."

"You're out of your head!" Ayub laughed. "He went out of pure vanity. He wanted to shake hands with the President."

"Doubtless," continued the Director General, overlooking the impertinence, "at this instant our friend is asking himself whether in fact the highest official in our nation recognized him and offered him his hand, n'est-ce pas?"

"What he must be asking is why you always call him 'our friend' instead of addressing him by name." Ayub was being sarcastic.

The Director General exhaled a mouthful of smoke into Felix's face. It drifted in through the holes in the bandages, and Felix coughed painfully.

"Don't treat him so rough," said Ayub in a tone of mock seriousness, smothering his laughter. "Remember what the nurse told us? His condition isn't good at all."

"Well, my friend," the Director General continued. "There wasn't time. The President never reached you. How shall I explain it? There was an accident. An instant before he reached you, there was a shot. The President's security agents shielded him with their bodies, forcing him to his knees. A sight never witnessed before that moment, if you'll allow me to express my amazement, mmh? In the confusion that followed, all eyes were on the President, who rose with dignity, brushing aside his zealous bodyguards, and murmured some obligatory phrase, I die for Mexico, or, They can kill me but they can't kill the fatherland, something of the sort, n'est-ce pas? I imagine every chief of state has some *bon mot* prepared for the fatal moment."

The Director General laughed hollowly, the dry laugh that ended almost as it began. "Can you hear me, my friend? Nod if you do. Does it pain you?"

Felix nodded mechanically, then shook his head, then admitted passively that he was worse than a prisoner; he was a worm they were toying with cruelly, cutting into little pieces, and prodding to see if it still moved.

"He's alive and he hears us," said Ayub, waving his perfumed handkerchief before his nose. "This place stinks of chloroform."

"Such drastic and unnecessary measures!" sighed the Director General. "If only you'd made yourself scarce and allowed us to carry out our plan."

"I warned you, he's stubborn, and proud, and always worrying about his dignity." Simon Ayub sniffed with disdain.

"As if that mattered in cases like this!" The Director General threw up his hands like an Egyptian priest affronted by the presence of a monotheist. He paused dramatically, to emphasize the extent of his outrage, then punctuated his speech with French. *"Passons. Bref,* the pistol was in your hand, my friend, and the only thing no one could explain is why, having the opportunity to assassinate the President of the Republic at such short range, point blank, as they say, your bullet went astray and passed instead through the shoulder of the honorable Professor Bernstein, a member of our National Academy, a professor of the Universidad Nacional, a recipient of the National Prize in Economics ..."

"And a hired agent of the state of Israel." The diminutive Ayub pretended to wipe tears from his eyes.

"Is there no ashtray?" asked the Director General, stubbing out his cigarette on Simon Ayub's lapel.

"My best Cardin!" screamed Ayub.

"I don't know why I put up with such an inept and insolent assistant." The Director General's laugh echoed hollowly.

"You know why," shrieked Ayub. "Because you have me by the balls!"

"Obviously," the Director General continued, unperturbed, "I must have a warm spot in my heart for you. Imbecile. It's my own fault. Why did it ever occur to me to send a cockroach like you to dissuade our friend from attending the ceremony? But I prefer dissuasion to violence."

Felix could see Simon Ayub as he came dangerously close to the Director General, the delicate fist, manicured nails, the rings with the topaz scimitars, raised threateningly. "I'm getting fed up to here," he cried hysterically. "Yesterday this small-time Romeo called me an overdressed runt and now you call me an imbecile. The day will come when I can't take any more. One day I'm going to explode . . ."

"Calm yourself, Simon. Sit down and be quiet. You know you'll do nothing of the kind. You just said why very graphically."

"One day . . ."

"One day you'll wake up and find yourself an orphan, no?" said the Director General affably, and again turned his attention to Felix. "Let's get down to brass tacks, Licenciado. Exactly as I informed you during our very pleasant interview, *you* are not responsible for the attempted assassination of our President. But your name is. And your name, Licenciado, no longer exists."

"Say his name, say it to him." Ayub whined like a whipped dog.

The Director General sighed with relief. "At last. Felix Maldonado."

He laughed, a laugh that broke off at its crest.

"Let me savor the syllables, like a good cognac, better still, a Margaux. Fe-lix Mal-do-na-do. Aaaaaah. Only a name, n'est-ce pàs? The man behind the name no longer exists. Quickly, Simon, remember the nurse's instructions. Don't try to sit up, my friend. You see, if you make those sudden movements, you will pull the needle from your arm. Please look to see if it's all right, Simon."

Gloating, Ayub approached Felix's recumbent body, and Felix, concentrating all his strength, struck blindly at him. Ayub bore the brunt of the blow in his chest, fell to the floor, rose coughing, and lunged toward Felix, who gritted his teeth at the pain of the loosened needle. The Director General stretched out a foot and tripped Ayub, who fell against the metal bed.

He clambered to his feet, groping for the Liberty print handkerchief drooping from his breast pocket. "I don't know which of you I despise more," he said, dabbing at the blood trickling from the corner of his mouth.

"It is of absolutely no importance," said the Director General, "but if it is any comfort to you, that was more painful for our friend than it was for you. *En fin.* Let him replace the needle, Licenciado. We don't want you dying of starvation."

The Lebanese approached Felix's bed with glee. In Ayub's hand, the needle resembled one of the scimitars adorning his topaz rings.

"Furthermore," the Director General continued, "your Calvary is far from over. You must build your strength to prepare for what still awaits you. As we were saying, n'est-ce pas? your presence at the ceremony complicated our plans, but in the end it worked out well. Felix Maldonado, the presumed assassin, attempted to escape night before last from Military Camp Number One, where, given the nature of his crime, he had been incarcerated for greater security. As is the custom in these cases, he was shot while attempting to escape, mmh?"

The Director General removed his purplish eyeglasses and examined his prisoner through half-closed lids.

69

"Three well-placed bullets in the back, and the private and official life of Felix Maldonado was ended. The burial took place yesterday at ten o'clock in the morning, with the discretion demanded by the occasion. One must not overinflame public opinion, n'est-ce pas? Several theories have been advanced concerning the frustrated attempt to assassinate our President. You know how those things are. The myth that a Mexican President never dies in his bed is international in scope. Actually, Obregón was the last President assassinated in this country, and that was in 1928. On the other hand, in a more civilized country like the United States, mmh? Presidents drop like flies, and their families and followers as well. Myths. Myths."

Ayub had reinserted the needle in Felix's vein and the liquid flowed again.

"Hold his arm, Simon. Our patient is very high-strung. What must he be thinking about all this? What a shame he can't tell us. I'll try to calm his fears by telling him that the family and friends of Licenciado Felix Maldonado, in small number, attended the burial in the Jardín Cemetery. The wife of the defunct, his widow, Ruth Maldonado, in the place of honor. Very dignified in her grief, n'est-ce pas? And one or two interesting women, the married Mary Benjamin, for one, and the unmarried Sara Klein, recently arrived from Israel, mmh? I believe she also attended the rendezvous with dust. And my own secretary, Mauricio Rossetti, along with Angelica, his wife. They'd forgiven Maldonado's unfortunate vulgarity at their home. Hebrew rites were observed, naturally."

The Director General laced thin fingers across the front of his jacket and allowed himself the luxury of a satisfied smile, without the accustomed laugh. "There will always be doubts, my friend. Did Felix Maldonado mean to avenge himself on Professor Bernstein because he had outstripped him in winning the favors of Sara Klein? Or was it all part of an attempt on the life of the President? We shall suppose, mmh? just suppose, that the government as well as public opinion favors the second hypothesis. I'm telling you all this, Licenciado, so that you can understand just what was at stake. On one side of the scale, place an internal political crisis of international dimensions and on the other, your wretched life as a second-rate bureaucrat and a third-rate Don Juan. You, a converted Jew, unstable, as proved by your recent actions, are a madman who throws his professor's eyeglasses into the fire, creates scandalous scenes in a fit of jealousy, and without provocation insults everyone in sight. You might easily take your revenge on Bernstein. On the other hand, it's equally plausible that you were using your irrational behavior to cover a cold and calculated assassination attempt. But even then, n'est-ce pas? doubts persist. No one will ever be absolutely sure whether at the last moment your desire for revenge overrode political purpose, or whether in fact a kind of mild schizophrenia overcame Felix Maldonado and he tried to kill *both* Bernstein and the President. Mysteries that will never be cleared up, since the possibilities are varied. The fact is, regardless, that Maldonado's dead and buried."

The Director General smiled, and studied his fingernails. *"Tiens!* That was practically a poem. Perhaps we should write a ballad, mmh? The Song of Long-Gone Felix?"

His smile vanished. Unexpectedly, he stood up and peremptorily ordered Ayub to summon the nurse and to stay with her while she removed the patient's bandages.

"Everything would have worked out as I wished it, beautifully executed, if you hadn't interfered. What a shame," said the Director General. "Goodbye forever, Licenciado."

15 FOR SOME FIFTEEN MINUTES Felix Maldonado knew he was alone in the room with the short Lebanese. What was worse, to lie here impotent, immobilized by his bandages, with no one to look after his needs, or to be attended by a humiliated and vengeful dwarf? One thing he knew, any cruelty of Simon Ayub's was preferable to what the Director General had forced him to endure.

"I'll never let this happen again," Felix Maldonado said to himself. "No one, ever again, is going to make me swallow his words when I can't get back at him."

"Did you see what I had to swallow because of you?" Ayub asked insolently, as if reading Felix's mind. "Well, now we'll see how you can take it, old asshole buddy. Let's see what's beneath those bandages, Licha."

"It's too soon, he'll be scarred," Felix heard the woman's voice say.

"Hurry it up, you bitch." Ayub attempted to imitate the Director General's authority, but his high-pitched voice was unconvincing.

Felix heard the quick, nervous steps of the woman named Licha, and curtains being violently pulled back. The light forbidden by his photophobic superior flooded the room, and the woman cried, "That's mean, Simon, I can't take off his bandages in that glare."

Ayub replied that the chief was the only one bothered by the light. Anyone else could go fuck himself.

"But it might ruin his eyes," the woman protested.

"For what he's going to see, he won't need good eyes."

As she sat beside him on the bed to properly insert the needle Ayub had incorrectly replaced, the woman at last moved into Felix's field of vision. The arm was purple.

If Felix Maldonado had had a kangaroo in his chest, it couldn't have leaped more wildly than his heart the moment he saw and recognized Licha. She was the girl carrying the cellophane-wrapped syringes and ampules who'd entered his taxi several days ago at the corner of Gante. "My name is Licha and I work at the Hospital de Jesús," she'd said as she got out in front of the Hotel Reforma on her way to give a shot to a Yankee tourist suffering from typhoid fever.

Perhaps she was able to read Felix's eyes in the depths of their white tunnels; perhaps she merely noted her patient's accelerated pulse rate. She raised her eyes from her task and looked at Felix, begging him not to give her away, not in front of Ayub, please.

When she finished, Licha squeezed Felix's wrist, and told him he was doing fine.

Ayub ground the topaz rings into the open palm of his left hand, like a boxer training for a match. "I owe you one for that dirty punch, I swear, I owe you one. Come on, Lichita, get those bandages off."

Licha said she wanted to bandage Felix's swollen arm first, but Ayub pushed her aside and began to tear at the gauze strips binding Maldonado's head. Felix tried to ball his hands into fists; he felt he was going to faint from the pain.

"Don't be such a creep," the nurse cried. "Let me do it, you have to unfasten the clips first."

Felix closed his eyes. Along with the pain, he tried to block out Ayub's scent of fresh clove and his acrid perspiration, as well as the sound of his ragged breathing.

"Look what you got yourself into by being such a fuckup," said Ayub, as Licha carefully unwound the bandages. "Everything was all laid out by the chief. If you hadn't been there and stuck your nose in, no one would have noticed a thing after the shot except what was happening to Number One. They'd all have thought the criminal got clean away. They wouldn't have found a trace of a killer *or* a weapon, and by this time every law-enforcement agency in the country would be looking for a fugitive named Maldonado. We had everything ready for you to make a getaway, all we wanted was your name. It was picture-perfect—passport, tickets, a little bread for you and your wife . . . perfect. And then you had to butt in. Who put the pistol in your hand? Try to remember that much, at least. See if you can't make us feel a little sorry for you, you bastard, because now you've got nothing, no bread, no passport, no tickets, no wife, no name, nothing . . ."

Ayub's brusque movement echoed his frenzied words as he seized an oval hospital mirror with a slightly tarnished chrome frame and held it to Felix's face.

His name was Felix Maldonado. The face reflected in the mirror belonged to a different name, not Felix Maldonado. No moustache, curly hair cut close to the scalp, shaved in places, an unnatural slickness at the temples, receding hair at the browline, as if his head were a practice field for transplants and grafts. Some of the facial incisions hadn't healed; in some places the skin was stretched taut, like a false face, held by clamps behind the ears. The swollen eyes looked vaguely Oriental. Invisible stitches paralyzed the mouth.

Felix Maldonado stared with blind fascination at the mask Simon Ayub offered him. He couldn't hold his eyelids open, and he heard Licha say, "You've probably ruined his eyes, you jerk. Come on, will you get out of here?"

"When do you think he'll be able to talk?"

Licha did not reply. Ayub said, "Let us know as soon as he can," and left, slamming the door.

16 "DON'T WORRY, honey, you'll see," said Licha as she dressed his incisions. "As soon as the swelling goes down, you're going to look fine, and little by little you'll get used to your new face. After a while, you'll recognize yourself, easy . . ."

She changed the cotton pads on his eyes and said that later that afternoon they could remove the clamps. It was a good job, she added, they hadn't used one of those butchers, but a first-rate surgeon. "You can't tell by the first days, honey; you'll get used to it and forget you ever looked any different. Some things, like the eyes, you can't change."

Perched on the side of his bed, she held Felix's hand. "You don't mind if I call you honey, do you?"

Felix shook his head, and Licha smiled. He could visualize her, the Playboy Bunny type, small but shapely, everything in the right place, well stacked. She tried to minimize her dark complexion by dying her hair ash blond, but actually achieved the opposite effect; the blond hair made her look darker. She hadn't been to the beauty shop recently, and the center part showed a half inch of dark roots. Her makeup was discreet, as if in nurse's training they'd told her that flashy nurses don't inspire confidence.

She smiled, pleased that Felix hadn't thought she was too forward. But then she moved away from the bed, anxious, unable to think of anything to say after breaking the ice. She puttered about the room, pretending to be absorbed in little details of his treatment but, in truth, searching for the right words to resume the conversation.

Finally, with her back to Felix, she said surely he must be wondering what had happened to him, he must be thinking she was mixed up in it somehow. Well, she wasn't. She didn't know any more about it than what Simon Ayub had told him. Simon had contacted her for this job. She'd asked for a brief leave from the Hospital de Jesús, where she usually worked, and she'd followed Ayub's instructions to a T.

75

"There's something I want you to know right off," she said, turning to look at Felix, as if inflicting a penance upon herself. "I was Simon's girl for a while, but that was a long time ago." She paused, waiting for a sign of some kind from Felix, then realized none was coming.

"Um-hmm. About a year ago," she went on. "He's quite a ladies' man, and he looks like a nice enough guy, all those fancy clothes . . . You get a little carried away. And he's good-looking, and well, short, you know. It's easy to fall for him. It isn't until afterwards you find out what he's really like. He talks so sweet at first, but when he knows you better, dirty isn't the word! Well, anyway, I can't complain. Like they say, it was an experience, and, you know, honey, I'm still a little fond of him, because, well, he gave me some good times." She clicked her tongue and grimaced, half asking forgiveness, and half saying, what the hell! She seemed to feel that after getting that off her chest she could go on to more serious matters.

"When he asked me to help him out, it seemed like a good thing. Climb into a taxi and come take care of a man who'd had facial surgery. That's all Simon told me, and I know as much about it as you do, honey. It looked like an easy way to earn a little quick cash in no time at all. At the hospital where I work, they don't pay too well, if you know what I mean. But it's steady work, and I have insurance, and little by little you work up to pretty good overtime, and seniority. It's not so bad, even if it's a charity hospital and all you see are poor people, really a lot of beat-down people who go there to die because they don't have the time or the money to get well. Well, I guess everybody has time for dying, you might say. It's different here at this clinic. Just a few rooms, all private, with TV and everything. And security! You can't get in without a special pass. They even have guards downstairs. It must cost an arm and a leg, and an eye as well. Sorry. I shouldn't have said that. You feeling okay?"

Felix nodded, helpless, his questions frustrated on the tip of an immobilized tongue.

"That's good. Now don't you worry, honey. I'm going to look after you, I won't leave you for a minute. The fact is, they wouldn't let me leave, anyway. The deal was that I'd sleep in as long as you're sick."

And now Licha went about her tasks happily, as if she'd justified her familiarity by confessing her affair with Simon Ayub, and then by being so professional in explaining their situation. "Honest, honey, I didn't know you weren't in on this deal," she said as she busied herself rearranging a shelf full of bandages, cotton swabs, and rubbing alcohol. "I supposed you'd ordered the surgery yourself, though I did wonder why at the time. A cute fellow like you."

She must have thought it was cowardly to say this without looking him straight in the face. She left her bottles and bandages and turned toward Felix. "No kidding, I liked you the minute I saw you in the taxi. I really went for you, the way you carry yourself, the way you look, everything."

Felix took the opportunity to try to pantomime something with his hands. He held out his arms and Licha took the gesture as an invitation. She approached him with a combination of hesitancy and her version of allure, but stopped, disconcerted, as Felix's hands imitated the motions of leafing through a newspaper. He repeated the pantomime of the reader unsuccessfully searching for a story, rapidly turning invisible pages, running his eyes up and down columns, and tracing imaginary headlines across the top of a page.

"What is it? What do you want? Didn't you hear what I just told you?" said Licha, with another of her contradictory attitudes, curiosity now mixed with resentment. "You're not interested? Hey, are you trying to put me down or something? Oh? You want me to read to you? *You* want to read something? No, that wouldn't be good for you. Why don't I read you something? A magazine?"

Licha giggled and her dark cheekbones flushed with the

high color of her distant Indian forebears, the color of apples and cold early mornings in the sierra.

She went to the window to be sure it was closed, tried unsuccessfully to draw the curtains tighter still, and then sat on the bed beside Felix Maldonado. She slid her hands beneath his hips.

"You're trying to find out something that isn't going to be in the newspapers. Don't worry about your face. I tell you it's going to be okay. And I'm going to take good care of you. Real good care of you. Wouldn't you like to find out whether you're still a man?"

17

LATER THAT AFTERNOON, Licha removed Felix's clamps and stitches. She alternated her professional attention with hugs and kisses, and surges of tenderness, cuddling Felix, afraid of hurting him, patting the sound parts of his body, everything except his face, asking, Wasn't that good? Didn't you think that was super?

She dozed awhile, lying as close to Felix as she dared. When she awakened, she raised her head and gazed at him with the eyes of a hobbled calf, strangely pleading for a love that would set her free. Felix saw in her Bunny's gaze: Love me, or I'll be a slave forever.

"You'll be able to talk soon," she told him. "I skipped your novocaine injection. Can't you move your tongue a little better already? Look, before you can talk, I want you to listen to me a bit. I know you'll say I was taking advantage of you when you couldn't talk, but it's easier for me if you listen and don't say anything just now. Then later, if you say yes . . . great. And if you don't say anything, I'll understand."

She hid her face against Felix's chest, and idly played with one of his nipples. "Did you like me? Honest, wasn't it pretty good?"

Felix stroked Licha's bleached hair.

"Yes?" said the girl. "Are you listening? Look, I thought that now you're a different person, like Simon said . . . and you don't have anyone, and aren't really anyone yourself . . . I thought that maybe you could love me a little . . . and live with me even if just a little while, while you get well . . . and if you like me, maybe . . ." She raised her head and looked at Felix with fear and desire. "I know I'm being pushy, but God, I'd do anything for you. I've never known anyone like you. What makes you tick? Why did you do it that way? Who taught you that?"

Felix moved a furry tongue, seemingly not related to the unhealed lips. "He-clp me-eee."

"What is it you want?" Licha asked eagerly, pressing her nose to Felix's neck. "Anything. Anything at all, sweetie."

In desperation, Felix pushed her from him, seized her shoulders, and shook her. "You know," he said, thick-tongued. "A newspaper." Licha got up, unruffled, almost happy that Felix had treated her so familiarly, a little violently, patted her hair in place, and told him she had strict orders not to take anything into or out of Felix's room. He was in isolation because his was a very special case.

"Look," Licha said, pushing the button at the head of Felix's bed. "It's disconnected. And look here"—mimicking Felix's violence, ripping aside the curtains and throwing open the windows. "This room is on the third floor. It's the only one with bars at the windows. They keep it for special cases, for the nuts . . . oh, I'm sorry, the mentally ill patients."

Licha removed a chiclet from her uniform pocket and stood for a moment, pensive. "I've got it," she said suddenly. "The women come by at six to clean the rooms. They always leave the rubbish bins in the hall. I'm sure they throw the old newspapers in there."

Again she lay down beside Felix, repeating over and over, "It was so good, who taught you that, no hands or anything, without touching me, just looking, honest to God, I never knew a man to come before just from seeing me naked, never. Who taught you? It makes me feel really good. I swear it makes me feel like something special."

"You're very sweet, and a very pretty girl," said Felix, clearly enunciating the syllables, and Licha threw her arms around Felix's neck, curled around him like a snake, and kissed his neck again and again.

About six-thirty she returned with a wrinkled, egg-stained copy of the noon edition of *Últimas Noticias.* Breathlessly, desperately, Felix scanned the headlines. Not a single reference to what he was looking for. Not a word about an attempt on the life of the President of the Republic, or its aftermath, no editorial comment, and nothing, less than nothing, about the fate of the presumed assassin Felix Maldonado. Nothing. Nothing!

He swallowed thickly, and desolately folded the newspaper. He remembered his conversation with Bernstein at Sanborns. The real political facts never appear in the Mexican press. But this was too much, absolutely incredible. No one could have such control of the press that they could prevent the printing of news of an attempt against the Chief of State in the Salón del Perdón in the National Palace of Mexico during an official ceremony before scores of witnesses, photographers, and television cameras.

His head was whirling. He could not believe his burning eyes. He wasn't blind. He wasn't delirious. Several times he checked the date of the newspaper. The ceremony in the Palace was on the tenth of August. The newspaper was dated the twelfth. No mistake, but there wasn't the least reference to the events of scarcely three days ago. There had been only two previous attempts, one against Ortiz

Rubio, and the other against Ávila Camacho, and those had been known, and reported. It wasn't possible. Licha was watching him with alarm. She walked toward the bed.

"Now don't get excited. I told you, it's not good for you. Don't try to get up. Wouldn't it be better if I read something to you? I'll read you the police reports; that's always the best part of the paper."

Felix lay back, exhausted. Licha began to read in a monotonous, halting voice, with a tendency to give an exotic pronunciation to words she didn't recognize, charging at punctuation like a bull at a red cape, and bucking like a young mare before the obstacle of a diphthong. Fastidiously, she read the accounts of a rape, a burglary in the San Rafael district, an armed robbery at the Masaryk Branch of the Banco de Comercio, and then the details of a particularly gruesome crime: this morning, at daylight, at the Suites de Génova, a woman had been found brutally murdered, her throat cut.

The preceding evening the victim had requested the concierge to wake her at 6 a.m. to catch an early flight. Because of the request, the concierge, uneasy that the victim did not respond to his repeated calls, let himself into the room using his master key, and found the naked body on the bed, throat slit from ear to ear. Suicide was ruled out inasmuch as no sharp instrument was found anywhere near the deceased, although the officers in charge of the investigation do not exclude the possibility that the weapon was removed following a suicide by a person or persons of unknown motivation, to suggest a perfidious crime. The coroner fixed the time of death as sometime between midnight and one o'clock yesterday morning. An additional fact that casts doubt on the possibility of suicide is that the deceased had carefully packed all her clothes and personal belongings, clearly indicating her intent to carry out her announced trip. All that was found in the room occupied by the deceased were a half-used tube of toothpaste, a new box of sanitary napkins, and the furnishings belonging to the hotel, a television, a stereo, and a collection of 45 rpm records which, according to the concierge, are also the property of the management. An inspection of the contents of the suitcases has thrown no new light on the circumstances of death. The only personal documents found in the flight bag were a folder of traveler's checks, a round-trip air ticket—Tel Aviv–Mexico City–Tel Aviv, the Tel Aviv–Mexico City portion already used, the return flight for today confirmed via Eastern to New York, and via El Al from the City of Steel to Rome and Tel Aviv. The deceased's passport stated her to be of Israeli nationality; born in Heidelberg, Germany. Name: Sara Klein—although in this regard the Israeli Embassy, in the person of a Second Secretary questioned at an early hour by our reporter, wished to make no comment, and refused to confirm the identity of the victim . . .

Licha read con*cer*gee, Em*bas*sy, *New* Yorr, as Felix thought to himself: Sara wasn't at my funeral. She was already dead. Everybody's been lying to me. But he showed no reaction, and suppressed his emotion as well. He told himself he shouldn't squander his feelings, not now, not for some time to come. He must save his grief for a single instant. When? The time would come. Sara Klein deserved that much. His love for Sara Klein deserved that much. A single, final act should consecrate his emotions at having known her, lost her, and found her again for one night in the home of the Rossettis, before losing her forever.

Neither did he want to conjecture about the reasons for or the circumstances of the death of the Jewish girl he'd taken dancing one night in some nightclub in vogue at the time. Where had they gone? Yes, the Versalles, in the Hotel del Prado. They'd danced in celebration of Felix Maldonado's twentieth birthday. The orchestra had played "Mack the Knife," the ballad that Louis Armstrong's recording had made popular again.

82

He asked Licha to help him escape from the hospital. She said it would be very difficult. She looked at him suspiciously, as if afraid that Felix already wanted to get rid of her. But she put the idea aside, and again said it would be difficult. "Besides, what about me? Ayub will never forgive me, and he scares me to death."

"Don't you think I'm capable of protecting you against that little shrimp?" asked Felix, kissing Licha's cheek.

"Oh, yes," she said, and stroked Felix's hand.

"How can I get out of here, Lichita?"

"There's no way, I swear. I tell you it's a real exclusive place. They have guards at all the doors."

"Where are my clothes?"

"They took them away."

"Are there elevators?"

"Yes. Two. One holds three people, and there's a bigger one for stretchers and wheelchairs."

"Are they self-service?"

"No. They have some pretty tough guys running them."

"Is there a dumbwaiter?"

"Yes. For all three floors. The kitchen's on the ground floor."

"Is there anyone in the kitchen at night?"

"No. After ten, the nurses fix anything that's needed."

"Can you get to the street from the kitchen?"

"No. The only way's through the main entrance. No one comes in or out without being seen. You have to have a pass, and the guards keep a list of every time anyone goes in or out, the staff, the patients, the visitors, messengers, everyone."

"Where are we?"

"On Tonalá, between Durango and Colima."

"What kind of patients do they have here?"

"They're mostly Turks. It's practically reserved for them, since the clinic's run by the Arabs."

"No, I mean, what kind of sick people?"

83

"Lots of maternity cases on the second floor. The first floor's for accident cases; up here, the serious cases, heart, cancer, everything . . ."

"Couldn't you get me out if I was all bandaged up, and say I was someone else?"

"They know me. They know I'm only to take care of you, nobody else."

"Doesn't anyone die? Can't I go out as a corpse?"

Licha laughed heartily. "You have to have a death certificate. You're going way too fast. They'd take one look at your face and give you a pinch that'd revive you in a hurry! You must be kidding."

"Then there's only one way."

"Whatever you say."

"If I can't escape from here like the Count of Monte Cristo, then we'll have to make them believe that the Count of Monte Cristo's no longer here."

"I'm sorry, honey, but I don't follow you."

"Can you steal some trousers and some men's shoes for me?"

"Well, I'll see if I can find anyone asleep. I'll try. What's your plan, sweetie?"

"Since I can't leave the building alone, Lichita, I'll leave accompanied by everyone in the building, patients, nurses, *and* guards."

"I guess I'm dumb, but I don't get what you mean."

"You just do what I tell you. Please."

"You know how I feel about you. And besides, I wouldn't mind shafting that rat Simon a little, especially now that I know what he did to you. Okay. You just tell me what I'm to do. But don't be so sad, honey. I really meant what I told you, honest. If you want to stay with me afterwards, swell. If not, you haven't lost anything."

"Lichita, you're one hell of a woman. I don't think I deserve you, word of honor."

"But you're so sad, honey, anyone could see that."

"Don't worry about it. It's hard for me to leave a woman."

"Any woman, honey?"

"Yes." Felix forced a smile. "Sometimes death takes one away from me. But I carry them all with me all my life, dead or alive, the way a snail carries its shell."

"You're really something!"

18 LICHA PLAYED her part to perfection. From the sidewalk across the street, Felix Maldonado watched the fire destroy the private clinic on Tonalá. He was invisible among the patients, some lying unconscious on the street, some suffering from shock, a few on stretchers or in wheelchairs, a few on foot; women wept, their wailing newborn infants, hastily wrapped in blankets, in nurses' arms; one nurse was shouting, This baby will die out of the incubator; one man was moaning about the cardiac pain in his arm; confused and excited nurses held aloft bottles of serum they'd managed to save during the sudden panic; a woman lying on the ground was crying out, her labor inopportunely precipitated by fear; some patients had been almost asphyxiated by the smoke; and one jaundiced man, seemingly near death but smiling and highly diverted, clung to a scrawny tree, the same tree that supported a silent, heavily bandaged Felix Maldonado indistinguishable in the human maelstrom.

Licha wept hysterically. Befuddled, wringing her handkerchief, she was arguing with one of the clinic guards, pointing first to the left and then to the right. "Well, why don't you go look for him. Don't be so damned stupid, he can't have gone very far in the state he's in, can he?"

"Shut up, you little nitwit. This was a carefully planned

operation," one of the guards said, frothing with rage. "You'll answer for this, I'll see to that . . ."

"I was only in the bathroom for a second. Can't a girl even take a minute to pee? And since he couldn't move . . ."

"Naturally, his accomplices got him out. But how?"

Felix had put on the trousers and shoes, and Licha had led him to the dumbwaiter on the third floor, where he flattened himself into a corner like a sardine, praying that no one would summon it at that hour. Licha had gathered together all the wastepaper, newspapers, and Kleenex she'd found in the wastebaskets and the dispensary, along with dirty sheets, pillowcases, and towels, and piled everything on the mattress in Felix's room. Then she poured alcohol over everything, set fire to it, and ran down the hall, screaming, Fire, fire. She pressed the button to make the dumbwaiter descend to the ground floor, and as smoke curled from Felix's room, patients and nurses erupted into the hall. Then Licha had run down the stairs to the ground floor, rushed to the kitchen, opened the door to the dumbwaiter, and run back toward the main door screaming, "The one in 33's escaped! I went to pee and when I got back he was gone."

"He didn't come out here," one of the guards said.

"He must still be in the building," a second added. "Come on!" He started to run upstairs to look for Felix, but couldn't push his way through the nurses running downstairs, yelling fire. The guard tried to halt them: "You irresponsible bitches. Get back up there with your patients."

"But the elevator's full of smoke," one nurse cried.

The guard at the entrance shouted an obscenity and ran to the elevators. His efforts were hampered by ambulatory patients hurrying toward the exit.

Faceless in his bandages, yelling like all the other patients, Felix emerged from the kitchen and joined the stream of fleeing patients, as the guard at the door ran back to telephone the Fire Department.

The fire trucks were very slow in arriving. The guards and nurses continued to evacuate the patients, and Licha spun out her hysterical scene until the guard got fed up with her, called her a dirty bitch, and said it was her fault they were in the mess they were in. "But you'll pay for your carelessness. You'll never work in another hospital in this city. Stop that screeching and try to do something useful. Help the patients, at least. This is going to ruin us."

For a while, Felix stood among the sick, lost amid the confusion. Then little by little he moved away, mingling with the curious who'd come from neighboring houses to watch.

It will be interesting to see whether they keep this out of the newspapers, Felix murmured dryly, and casually started walking down the quiet, dark Colima toward the Plaza Río de Janeiro. He removed his bandages and threw them in a gray receptacle labeled KEEP YOUR CITY CLEAN.

He cut across the deserted plaza toward the corner of Durango. From afar, he could see the brick building that had been constructed at the beginning of the century, the first apartment house in the city, a red monstrosity with slate-roofed, feudal towers pointed like witches' hats, a four-story castle designed to resist the wintry blasts of the Norman coast.

This architectural anomaly, transplanted onto a tropical plateau, had degenerated until it had reached its present state, a tenement for low-income families. Licha had told him to go here, and had penciled a message in the margin of the *Últimas Noticias* Felix had kept tightly folded in the back pocket of the trousers stolen from a sleeping patient.

He pushed open the rusted iron gate and entered the dark, dank passageway. The second door on the right, Licha had told him, on the first floor. Felix rapped once with his knuckles. Blinding pain ran up his arm.

In agony, he struck at the door with the folded newspaper, but succeeded in making about as much noise as the

87

scratching of a wounded cat. He felt like a wounded cat. A terrible weariness fell over him and settled permanently at the back of his neck. He beat on the door with his open palm, and a voice from the other side replied, "I'm coming, I'm coming, hold on to your shirt."

The door opened and a man in undershirt, suspenders dangling to his knees, trousers flapping, asked, "What can I do for you?"

Felix, the cinema buff of Fifty-third Street, thought of Raimu in *The Baker's Wife*. It was the driver of the one-peso cab who had taken him from the Zócalo to the Hilton. The man stared at Felix with suspicion, and Felix again remembered Raimu, but also remembered that he recognized the driver but the driver couldn't recognize him.

"Licha sent me," Felix said tonelessly, offering the folded newspaper to the driver, who read the message and scratched his bald head.

"That woman of mine is a regular sister of charity," he grumbled. He turned away from Felix, waving him in. "Come on in. What happened to you? Where'd you get so banged up? No, don't tell me. My wife thinks this house is a hospital. The dumb-bunny says she has the gift of healing, and that it hurts her to see anyone in pain. She'd do better to clean up this place first. Excuse the mess."

The room contained a rumpled, unmade bed, an aluminum-leg table, and two oilcloth-covered chairs. Felix looked around the room for a telephone; Licha had assured him there was one. The driver pointed toward an electric hot plate with two burners, and a battered lunchbox. "There's some beans in the frying pan and tortillas in the lunchbox. They're cold, but tasty. There's a little Delaware Punch left there. Help yourself while I look for some clothes for you. Ah, Lichita, baby, if you weren't so sexy . . ."

"Could I have the paper back?" Felix asked.

"Here you are." The driver tossed the paper on the

table, and as he wolfed down the beans and tortillas, Felix reread the notice of Sara Klein's death. Then he turned to the obituary columns, and found what he was looking for.

The taxi driver gave him a clean shirt, socks, and a jacket. He looked curiously at Felix's eyes as he handed him the clothing.

"Hey, what happened to your eyes? No, don't tell me. They look like fried eggs. Here, put on these dark glasses. You look to me like even the moon would make you squint."

Felix put on the clothes and the dark glasses, thinking of the photophobic Director General, and asked if he could use the telephone. "You do have a phone, don't you?"

"Imagine a taxi driver without a telephone." He laughed. "It's cost half my ass to get it and the other half to keep up with the bills. It's my one luxury."

He lifted one of the pillows. There was the telephone, nestled like a jealously incubated black duck. Felix felt like a man about to be forced to leap from a burning ship into the sea. He measured the taxi driver carefully. He was heavy, but not very solid, having gone soft from too many hours behind the wheel, too many carbonated drinks and too many beans. Felix made the leap.

"May I use it?"

"Help yourself."

He dialed a number and got the telephone operator at the Hilton. "Give me the desk, please. Hello. Maldonado speaking, room 906."

He saw the driver stop, like a toy on a string. Then, just as suddenly, he went on toward the table, and picked up the bottle of Delaware Punch Felix hadn't tasted.

"Right. How's it going? Look, I'm in a hurry. I'm at the airport."

As he spoke, he was trying to weigh which was harder, a soft-drink bottle or the telephone receiver. Which was a better weapon to crack a man's head? The driver tipped back the bottle and emptied it.

"After a while I'll be sending someone by the hotel. He'll bring a note with my instructions, written by me. Let him put the things I want in a suitcase. Of course it's a serious matter. Wake the manager. Thanks."

The driver set the empty bottle on the table. He stared at Felix with unassuming irony. Felix hung up.

"Look, who wants to get mixed up with the dead?" the driver asked.

"No. Better leave them in peace."

"You know, if a man was to get paid, that'd be all there was to it, right?"

"You'll get paid double, I promise."

Felix left, thanking the driver.

"It's okay, chief. Just don't ever get married. If only that Lichita wasn't so damn sexy."

19 AT THE HILTON, Felix produced the note he'd written in the clinic on a piece of paper Licha had salvaged from a wastebasket. The night clerk recognized the handwriting. Licenciado Felix Maldonado was an old client. The manager had been advised and would be down in a minute.

The clerk accompanied him to room 906, and Felix packed a light suitcase with several articles of clothing, toilet things, and traveler's checks. He flipped through the checks: each bore the signature of Felix Maldonado in the upper left-hand corner. Then he dialed a number. As he heard my voice, Felix said:

"When shall we two meet again?"

"When the battle's lost and won," I replied.

"I have but little gold of late, brave Timon," Felix said to me.
"Wherefore art thou?" I asked.
"At my lodging," he replied.
"All's well ended if this suit be won," were my last words
before I hung up.

When Felix reached the lobby, the manager was waiting,
every silver hair in place, as impeccable as if it were ten
o'clock in the morning. He told Felix that they had to be
sure, he knew he understood, he was so sorry, his only wish
was to protect Licenciado Maldonado's interests, such a
respected client, but the handwriting, carefully examined,
seemed unsteady, and the paper was of very strange quality.
Could he present additional credentials, he inquired of the
ill-dressed, unshaven, battered man wearing dark glasses
and carrying Felix Maldonado's suitcase in one hand.

"You'll be receiving a telephone call any minute now,"
said Felix.

The manager was obviously perturbed when he heard
Felix's voice, but at that moment was advised that he had
an urgent telephone call. Ostentatiously, he shot his sleeves,
revealing, as was his intention, ruby cuff links. He listened
to my instructions attentively.

"But of course, sir. Absolutely. Anything you say, sir,"
the manager said to me, and hung up.

Felix walked the short distance separating the Hilton
from the Gayosso Mortuary on Calle Sullivan. The suitcase
was very light, and he ignored the pain in his arm. Strength
of soul, not the strength of a bruised body, was what was
required to walk the distance to the mortuary. The sheaf of
bills the manager had given him sat warm and comforting
in his trousers pocket.

He stood before the main door of a three-story mauso-
leum of gray stone and black marble that was a way station
in the stone geography of this city in which even the parks,
like the one stretching between Melchor Ocampo and
Ramón Guzmán, seemed made of cement. He climbed the

stairway of volcanic stone and read the directory: SARA
KLEIN, SECOND FLOOR. A gray-uniformed man with the
face of a small, friendly monkey sat dozing in the concierge's office.

The body of a woman lay in the non-denominational
chapel. From the next room came the drone of Ave Marías
and the pervasive odor of funeral wreaths. The chapel contained no floral offerings from friends, business associates,
or family. Only a Menorah with lighted candles. Felix approached the open coffin. A still-damp sheet covered Sara's
face and body. Someone had fulfilled the ritual of washing
the body. Who? Felix asked himself as he set down his
suitcase beside the gray lead casket.

Only Sara Klein's feet were visible. Felix knew what he
had to do. He touched Sara's naked toes, pressed them, and
knew that for the first and only time he possessed the body
that life and death, sisters in their complicity, had forbidden
him.

Still clasping Sara's foot, he asked her forgiveness. It was
ritual, but even though ritual is intended more to resolve
one's own personal feelings than to identify the attitudes of
others, it meant much more than that to Felix. The clinging
sheet was a palimpsest upon which Felix could read every
configuration of the woman who had been Sara Klein. He
studied the features hidden beneath the white mask. He had
never known her body naked. He obeyed an irresistible
impulse and removed the sheet.

The face was the face he had known, except that a thick
bandage separated it from the body. He recalled that in the
clinic he had promised himself to reserve all his emotion in
order to experience it in a single instant. This was the
moment, the moment he discovered for the first time the
mystery of a beloved body. But hers was no different from
other bodies. He had looked many times at naked, sleeping
women; few things excited him so much as gazing for prolonged periods at a naked and defenseless woman possessed

by sleep. Sleep divests a woman of something more than the clothing that is a part of conscious amorous conventions. For Felix, sleep stripped a woman of the habits of her battle against man, the feigned reticence, the modesty, the coy— or brazen—invitation, the negation or the affirmation of her body. An unconscious, sleeping woman became his merely by the contemplation, even as abandoned in sleep she was lost to him and his competitor became sleep itself. If, before, sleep had been the rival of his passion, now his rival was death. Felix started to draw the sheet over Sara's body. He paused. There was something, after all, an object that set sleep apart from death, the thick bandage separating Sara's head from her trunk, a necklace of necessity bloody. His Lulu had been murdered by Jack the Ripper.

He studied that face. It did not mirror either sleep or the death that resided there. He saw something more. He was compelled to repeat the words that forced him to enter into the ritual that was no longer a spectacle to be observed but an act in which he must participate. He had realized at the home of the Rossettis that he would love Sara forever, whether she was near or far, pure or sullied. Now he must add: living or dead.

"Living or dead," he murmured, and saw what it was in Sara's face that distinguished it from the mortal sleep of other women, living or dead. The motionless face of Sara Klein was the face of memory, a consuming memory unable even in death to find repose in forgetfulness.

Felix had come here to concentrate and to consecrate his love. He had come prepared to offer that love to the woman he had loved so deeply. Instead, it was she who offered him something, the light of a face washed clean of makeup, eyes forever closed, the mystery of a face that in life would have accepted death had it promised forgetfulness, but which in death seemed forever fixed in the rictus of painful memory.

Desolate, he covered Sara's body. Stop remembering now, he entreated, forget your persecuted and orphaned

93

childhood, your adult remorse, Sara. He heard steps. The candles in the Jewish candelabrum were burning low. Undoubtedly, the person responsible for attending Sara Klein's body was coming to replace the candles. He turned, expecting a mortuary attendant. Instead, approaching him he saw a Mexican Bunny Licha, tense and somewhat hesitant. Even in his fury, he noted that she had taken the time to change into a black miniskirt and dark, low-cut blouse. She had exchanged her white rubber-soled shoes for abominations of black patent leather with monstrous platforms and clicking heels. A fake-patent-leather handbag was swinging from her arm.

"What are you doing here?" Felix asked in the hushed voice death imposes.

"I was hoping I'd find you here."

"How did you know? How dare you?" Felix was devastated by the rupture of the unique moment and he detested Licha for profaning it. In addition, he was physically exhausted by the unconcluded transferral of Sara Klein's memory to his own, a transferral interruptus that like unconsummated coitus wearies beyond words the bodies so sadly unfulfilled.

"I'm sorry, honey. I already told you I'm a big coward."

"What are you talking about?" Felix asked impatiently, tearing his eyes from Sara Klein's naked feet.

"I just couldn't tell you before about poor Memo. I didn't have the nerve."

"Who the fuck is poor Memo?"

"My husband, honey, the driver, where I sent you. Better if he finds out for himself, I told myself. If he loves me, he'll forgive me, and if he doesn't, well, I already told you, what the hell . . . ? I can tell you're really mad at me."

For an arrogant instant, Felix almost smiled. "You think *that's* the reason . . ."

Licha struck the pose of a peevish little girl, pointing her toes together and grinding one heel on the marble floor.

"Now don't say anything. Listen to me. Memo's a good man, he's been more like a father to me than a husband. You don't know, honey. On the street where I lived, nobody comes out a nurse. The only way you get out of there is as a hooker or a servant. Memito protected me and made me feel secure. He gave me the money to go to school, and if I don't come home for several nights in a row, he says it's because I'm taking care of patients. He never asks for any explanations. He's satisfied knowing we're married in the eyes of the law. That's enough for him. And I know I owe him everything. You understand?"

"Fine, it doesn't matter to me," Felix said.

Licha tripped toward him on the tips of her toes. "Really? Then it's on?"

Lovingly, she clasped her hands behind Felix's neck. He pushed her from him and held her at arm's length to look in her eyes. A look wasn't enough. You had to phrase questions precisely for this girl, and pry the answers out of her with a shoehorn.

"What are you trying to say?"

"Sweetheart. I've never been with a man like you. You're the only man I'd ever leave Memo for, in spite of everything I owe him."

Felix had known painful memory in Sara's forever-closed eyes. In Licha's wide eyes, he saw smiling menace. He couldn't laugh at her, or even be angry with her. He turned from her to Sara's coffin. In some mysterious manner, these two women who could not possibly have had less in common in life were in this house of death finding some common ground, sharing, to some degree, this and other sorrows. Suddenly he saw each of them in a new light, as bearers of secrets, terrible sibyls.

"Who brought this woman here?" Felix decided to confront this new vision of Lichita. "Who put the notice in the newspaper about the death, the mortuary, and the cremation?"

95

"What if I told you it was the people at the Israeli Embassy, would you believe me?" Licha smiled.

"You're asking me not to believe you."

Licha winked a shoe-button eye. "Right you are. One thing you're not, and that's stupid."

"The newspaper said that the Israeli Embassy claimed no knowledge of her. Who, then? Bernstein was wounded. Is he dead, too?" Felix asked of himself as much as Licha. "If they didn't do it, then who?"

The nurse's sly silence seemed eternal in the sputtering of the dying candles. Felix hesitated to precipitate what he most dreaded, Licha's idiotic ideas, the conditions this woman he'd never wanted to see again wanted to impose on him.

"Sweetheart, I tell you there's only one man in this world who could make me betray my Memo, who's been so good to me."

"Simon Ayub, I suppose?" Felix asked brutally.

Licha clung to his lapels. "You, darling, you, only you, only you, like the song says. I'll give to you what you give to me, true love, darling, true love."

"No," said Maldonado, seizing the tail of an intuition that streaked like a comet through his mind. "I was asking you whether Simon Ayub had handled the arrangements."

A vague wave of his hand included the coffin, the naked feet, and the fading Menorah, but ended beneath Licha's blouse, caressing her breast, and his eyes signaled yes, everything was fine, anything she wanted.

"You think it was him?" Licha pulled away, wiggling triumphantly, but Felix sensed that for the first time she was surprised. She extracted a stick of gum from her shiny handbag and carefully unwrapped it. Felix grabbed her by the arm and squeezed hard.

"Ayyy! Don't hurt me."

"You know," said Felix, in the voice of violent familiarity that in fact pleased Licha—he remembered she had no defenses against that line of attack. "You know," he repeated, "all women are alike, you have to put up with them."

"Not me, honey. I'll make you love me," the nurse squealed.

"You just put up with them," said Felix, without releasing Licha's arm. "Any woman, a special woman, it's all the same. No escaping it. Even after you try to get rid of them, you have to put up with them."

He picked up his suitcase and hurried from the mortuary chamber. Licha, the stick of gum folded in her mouth, unchewed, stood paralyzed for an instant, stunned by Felix's changes of mood. Then she ran after him. She caught up with him at the stairway. She tugged at his sleeve to stop him, then ran ahead of him and stood in his way.

"Let me by, Licha."

"All right, you win, don't be mean to me any more," she said, with a toss of her head. "Simon handled everything. You're right. He brought her here. He said you'd follow her anywhere because she had you on a string . . ."

Felix slapped her, interrupting the surly, hysterical gush of words. She stumbled against the marble wall, and sudden tears left a smear of moistness there that reminded Felix of the sheet covering Sara's body.

"Who does Ayub work for?" Felix continued down the stairs. His grief was temporarily allayed by his outrage at Licha's presence. He had been deprived of the moment he'd hoped to consecrate to Sara Klein by a vulgar, stupid woman who was trying to worm her way into his life because she thought he had no life, no name—nothing—of his own.

"I don't know, sweetheart, honest."

"Where did he get the authority to claim the body? Who delivered the body to him? Why do you say he wanted to draw me here if he had me in his hands at the clinic? Why did we go to all the trouble to rig that elaborate charade of the fire? Why did I have to escape in the first place?"

"I don't know, I swear on my mother's grave." Licha's voice was shrill. "He said all he wanted was to lay into you till you sat up and begged, that's what he said . . ."

"He could have done that in the hospital."

"Here, let's have a little respect," called the monkey-faced concierge as they reached the vestibule. "We respect the dead here."

Felix stopped, surprised to see the memorable face he'd already forgotten; he turned to gaze at the stone stairway that separated him from the body of Sara Klein. Her face had defined memory, and death. Only then did he realize that he had looked at her from a face that didn't belong to him, the face of a man taking Felix Maldonado's place. If Sara had awakened, she wouldn't have recognized him.

It was early morning. As they emerged into the street, Felix smelled the renewed and familiar burnt-tortilla odor of Mexico City.

Once again, Licha threw her arms around him. "That's why I came, sweetie, I swear it, to warn you. Hurry, we can go together. I know where we can hide, where they can't find you. Honest, I don't know anything more."

Felix hailed a taxi, opened the door, tossed his suitcase inside, and got in without looking back at the nurse.

"Let's go together," she whimpered. "I want you to be my man, don't you understand, I'll do anything for you . . ." Licha removed a stiletto-heeled shoe and hurled it after the taxi fast disappearing down the deserted street.

The watchman with the face of an ancient ape had followed them, and asked Licha if she wouldn't like to go up and sit awhile with the woman on the second floor. She had no mourners, and that was bad for their image. They would pay her by the hour; they budgeted in a little to hire someone off the street now and then.

"Oh, go off to the zoo and hire your shitass mother, cheetah," Licha said, glaring with hatred. She recovered her shoe, slipped it on, and clicked off toward Insurgentes.

98

20 FELIX CALCULATED, successfully, that at the Suites de Génova they would assign him the room they'd had the greatest difficulty renting. At first, the man at the desk observed with ill-disguised displeasure Felix's barely healed face and the dark glasses attempting to disguise it, and his initial reaction was to say he was very sorry but they were completely booked. A second clerk whispered something in his ear.

"Well, we do have one suite available," the first clerk allowed, a thin, dark-skinned young man with oily eyes and hair.

Felix longed to ask him, Where the hell did you come from, you low-class bastard, that you think you can look at me like that? Buckingham Palace, or Skid Row? He wanted to ask them how many people during the last two days had requested any suite but the one vacated by the woman who'd had her throat slit, with all that publicity in the papers . . .

"Name, please? Please fill out this card."

The clerks exchanged congratulatory looks, as if saying to each other, What about this clown! as Felix wrote the name Diego Velázquez. Born: Poza Rica, Veracruz, 18 December 1938. Current Address: 91 Poniente, Puebla, Puebla. I had told him it would be best always to include some element of truth in his lies. He hesitated before signing the name of the artist he no longer resembled, and observed the thin clerk remove the key to 301 from its pigeonhole; it clinked against its twin, and then the clerk escorted Felix to the third floor, where he surrendered the key to him. The bellboy deposited the suitcase on the folding luggage rack. Felix tipped him twenty dollars. The clerk saw the size of the tip, and they bowed and scraped their way from the room.

Once alone, Felix looked around him. If anything had been left in the room to mark Sara's presence, the police would surely have removed it. He had no evidence that she had died here except his own imagination and will. That was enough. He had returned to the site of Sara's death to conclude the homage interrupted by Licha. But thinking of the nurse made him remember Simon Ayub, and the thought that the diminutive, perfumed Lebanese had seen and touched Sara's naked body irked Felix; an awful nausea followed the irritation.

He put all thought aside and yielded to weariness. He took a long bath and then stood before the washbasin and studied his face. The swelling had subsided considerably and the incisions were healing well. He touched the skin of his cheek and jawbones and it felt less tender. Only his eyelids were still purple and puffy, obscuring the ineradicable pinpoint identity of the eyes. He realized that the old resemblance to the Velázquez self-portrait that had been his and Ruth's private joke was returning with the beginnings of his moustache. He soaped five days' growth of beard and carefully shaved, a difficult, often painful task. He spared the burgeoning moustache.

He ordered breakfast, but in spite of his hunger, he was unable to eat, and he fell asleep on the wide bed. He lacked the strength to dream, not even of the affront of Ayub's hands pawing Sara's body. It was dusk when he awakened, the time the fashionable Zona Rosa comes alive with young Lotharios roving the streets, the horns of convertibles blasting the Marseillaise. He got out of bed to close the window, and drank a cup of cold coffee. He stared indifferently at the furnishings typical of such hotels, modern, low-slung furniture, Mexican fabrics of solid and audacious colors—lots of orange, lots of indigo blue—drapes of rough native cloth. Listlessly, he flicked on the television; nothing but stupid soap operas, unctuous voices resounding in vacuous décors.

He switched off the television and turned to the stereo, a small set much the worse for wear that played only 45's. In the bookcase he found a few records in worn jackets, and flipped through them without interest. Sinatra, "Strangers in the Night"; Nat "King" Cole, "Our Love Is Here to Stay"; Gilbert Bécaud, "Et Maintenant"; Peggy Lee, several mariachi groups, Armando Manzanero, and Satchmo, the great Louis Armstrong, the ballad of "Mack the Knife," the song of his twentieth birthday and the Versalles nightclub and Sara in his arms, the bitter and witty ballad of a criminal of Victorian London who asked: Is it worse to found a bank or rob one, "Mack the Knife," the song of youth and Sara Klein and Felix Maldonado's love for each other, a song jolted out of the Berlin of the thirties, bridging the horror of those crimes and contemporary ones, the persecution of the child and the murder of the woman, a succession of murderers, Mack the Knife, Himmler the Butcher, Jack the Ripper. This was the only new album. Felix was sure Sara had bought it to play in the room. Meaning for him to hear it, too. He removed the record from its still shiny envelope, pristine in contrast to the worn, ripped, dull jackets of the other records. It bore the sticker of the shop where Sara had bought it, Dalis, Calle de Amberes, Mexico City, D.F. He switched on the stereo and placed the huge mouth of the disk over the beige plastic spindle. The record dropped noiselessly and began to spin; the needle was inserted without pain. Felix awaited Satchmo's trumpet. Instead, he heard the voice of Sara Klein.

21 "FELIX. I must be brief. I have only five minutes on each side. I loved you when I was young. We thought we would spend our lives together. But I was afraid. You overidealized me. You couldn't share my sorrow. Bernstein could. He took advantage of our mutual suffering. He convinced me that it was my duty to go to Israel and involve myself in building a homeland for my people. He said it was the only way to respond to the Holocaust. Death and destruction we would counter with life and creation. He was right. I've never known such happy, clear-eyed people as the men and women and children who were turning a desert into a prosperous and free land with new roads and schools and cities. I was offered a professorship at the university, but I wanted a humbler job where I would know the very roots of our experience. I became an elementary-school teacher. Sometimes I thought of you, but even as I did, I put the thought aside. I couldn't allow affection to stand in the way of duty. Only now I realize that as I stopped thinking about you I also stopped thinking about anything else. I buried myself in my work, and I forgot you. The price was forgetting—rather, ceasing to see, which is the same thing—anything that didn't have a direct bearing on my work.

"Bernstein came over for two months every year. He never mentioned you. I never asked. Everything was clear-cut and defined. My life in Mexico was behind me. Israel was the present. The Arabs threatened us on every side. They were our enemies, they wanted to crush us, just as the Nazis had. All my conversations with Bernstein turned on this, the Arab menace, our survival. Our hope was our conviction. We had to survive this time, or we would disappear from the face of the earth forever. I say 'we' because we are talking about an entire culture. Valéry said that civilizations are mortal. That isn't true. Power passes, not civilizations. My work as a schoolteacher kept my hopes alive. Even if power changed hands, our civilization would be saved, because I was teaching children to know and love it: both the Israeli and the Palestinian children in my class. I tried to teach them that we should live in peace in our new state, respecting one another's particular cultures to form one common culture.

"Of course, I knew of the existence of the detention camps. But I found a justification for them. We didn't kill our prisoners from the Six Days' War, we detained them, and then exchanged them. And the Palestinian prisoners were terrorists, guilty of the murder of innocent persons. And there I closed my file. I had known too much of what happened to us in Europe to be submissive. It was a simple matter of self-defense. Sanity and morality reigned, Felix. What a marvelous way to expiate the guilt of the Holocaust! We were purging ourselves of the sins of others through our own efforts. We had found a place where we could be masters, and not slaves. But more important for me was believing that we'd found a place where we could be masters *without* slaves.

"The change in me came very slowly, almost imperceptibly. Bernstein was very clumsy in attempting to insinuate his affection. He knew what I believed in. I had left you to follow him. But I had followed him to fulfill a duty he himself had pointed out to me. It was no easy job for him to take your place, to offer himself in your place, to dilute my sense of duty by adding to it a love different from the one I'd sacrificed, your love, Felix. Then he tried to confuse my sense of duty with his desire. He began to boast about what he'd been and all he'd done, from his youthful participation in the secret Jewish army during the British Mandate to his participation in the Irgun; and following that, his fund-raising work outside Israel. It was Bernstein who made me think about the fact that Israel had used violence to establish itself in Palestine. I could accept that necessity, but I was shocked by the boastful tone of his arguments and the pathetic intent behind them; he hoped to possess me by causing me to confuse duty with the heroic personality he was creating for himself. The worst of this ambiguous situation was that it kept us from seeing the obvious counterargument. Neither of us expressed the point of view that perhaps the Palestinians, hoping to reclaim a homeland, had as much right to terror as the Israelis, and that our revolutionary and terrorist organizations—the Haganah, the Irgun, and the Stern Gang—necessarily evoked their historic counterparts, the PLO, the Fedayeen, the Black September group.

"Bernstein's sexual desires stood between that terrible truth and my awareness. I was living in a vacuum, and one vacuum contained another: your absence. Then came the Yom Kippur War, and my world and its reasons for being shattered into little pieces. Not abruptly; with me, everything happens gradually. One night Bernstein was particularly aggressive sexually; I was cold and distant, and at first he was embarrassed, but then he redoubled his political arguments. He ranted like a madman about the territories occupied in '73 and how we must never abandon them, not one inch. He spoke of Gush Emunim, and of the town he'd helped build and finance to ensure that we would be irrevocably established in the occupied territories and would erase the last trace of Arab culture. I realized he thought about these lands as he would like to think about me, his occupied territory, and that to him Gush Emunim was tantamount to his virility. Finally I dared speak up to him and say it wasn't territory we needed, because we already had something more than territory, we had the example of our labor and our dignity, and that was all the self-defense and all the propaganda we needed. But all Bernstein could talk about was security; the territories were indispensable to our security. I recalled Hitler's first speeches. First the Rhineland, then Austria, then the Sudetenland and the Polish Corridor. Finally, the world. A world, Europe or the Middle East, vital space, the security of frontiers, the superior destiny of one people. Surely you can understand this, you, a Mexican?

"I decided to request a transfer from Tel Aviv to one of the schools in the occupied territories. My request was granted because they believed I would be an efficient advocate of our values.

"Now I must skip over names of people and places in order to avoid reprisals. In the tiny school where I went to teach, I met a young Palestinian, a teacher like myself, younger than I. He lived alone with his mother, a woman a little over forty. I'll call him Jamil. That he was teaching Arabic to Palestinian children was proof of the good intentions of the occupation, proof that extremists like Bernstein hadn't succeeded in imposing their points of view. But soon I learned that for Jamil the school was trench warfare. I found him one day using the outlawed texts formerly taught in Arab schools, texts filled with hatred of Israel. I told him he was fomenting hatred. He said that wasn't true. He'd copied the old texts by hand, yes, but out of a sense of history; he wanted to preserve all the things our authorities had eliminated as they eliminated hatred of Israel: Palestinian identity, and Palestinian culture, the existence of people who like us demanded a homeland. I read the texts Jamil had copied. It was true. Like me, Jamil was working to keep both cultures alive. Until then, I had reserved that virtue for myself, and not granted it to others.

"Jamil was sure I would inform against him, but he told me not to worry. We belonged to different camps, and probably he would do the same were our positions reversed. At that instant, I realized that our peoples had been fighting each other so long, we could no longer recognize one another as individuals. I did not inform against him. Jamil continued to teach from his hand-copied notebooks. We became friends. One evening we walked to a hilltop. There Jamil asked, 'How many can stand here as we stand and look upon this land and say, This is my country?' That night, we went to bed together. With Jamil, all the frontiers of my life disappeared. I ceased to be a persecuted little German-Jewish girl who'd been exiled for a while in Mexico and later integrated into the state of Israel. Along with Jamil, I became a citizen of the land we stood upon, with all its contradictions, its battles and dreams, its prodigious harvests, and its bitter fruit. I saw Palestine for what it was, a land that must belong to everyone, never to a few, or to none . . ."

The record ended, and automatically Felix turned it over and placed the needle on the second side.

22 "ONE DAY, Jamil disappeared. Weeks passed, and neither his mother nor I had any word of him; I understood that woman who clung to her simple, feudal, traditional life. Was it true, I asked myself, that her values represented backwardness, and ours, progress? I traveled to Jerusalem and exhausted all official channels. I don't know whether I've been under suspicion since then; I simply stated that the young man was my colleague and I was worried about his disappearance. No one knew anything. Jamil had vanished. I contacted a Jewish Communist lawyer I'll call Beata. She was the only person who dared get to the bottom of the matter. What anguishing contradictions, Felix, please try to understand. I am repelled by Communism, but in this case, only a Communist had the courage to expose herself for me and for Jamil in the name of justice. An injustice had been committed against my lover, but in Israel I could count on the means to challenge it through legal channels. Would that have been possible in an Arab country?

"I left everything in Beata's hands and returned to the

village where I taught. Now Jamil's mother had disappeared. She returned a few days later, beyond tears. I thought Jamil was dead. His mother's dry eyes expressed greater grief than any tears. She said no. She didn't want to say more than that. Hours later, Beata informed me that Jamil was a prisoner, accused of being a terrorist. He was imprisoned in a place called Moscobiya in Jerusalem, an ancient inn frequented in olden days by Orthodox Russian pilgrims, and now converted into a military prison. The questions I asked Jamil's mother remained unanswered; I saw only that the woman no longer knew how to cry. She trembled constantly and fell ill with fever. I brought a doctor; she didn't want to see him; I insisted. She fought like a tiger to keep him from examining her. Later the doctor told me; a large object, probably a pole, had been forced into her vagina; it was destroyed.

"Two days later, Beata asked me to come to Jerusalem. She took me to a military hospital where Jamil was a patient. His face was that of an old man. I remembered the happy eyes of Israel. Now I saw the sad eyes of Palestine. Those eyes looked at me and did not know me. I wept, and Beata told me Jamil had been sentenced to two years in prison. She showed me a copy of the confession signed in my lover's hand; he declared himself guilty of acts of terrorism. Beata said she had exhausted all her sources to prove that the confession had been obtained by torture. I went back to our village. After a year, Jamil was freed. He arrived in a Red Cross bus. For the first few days, he didn't speak. Then, little by little, he told me what had happened.

"He'd been taken prisoner as he returned from school, and blindfolded. He lost all sense of direction. Several hours later, the car stopped near heavy traffic, a city, or a highway. He was led to a place where he was asked to confess. He refused. He was brutally beaten. His captors pulled hair from his head and forced him to eat it. Then they placed a hood with two air holes over his head and transported him to a different place. There they made him kneel in a dog kennel. He could hear the barking, but dogs never attacked him. The following day they returned and again asked for his confession. When he refused, they locked him for several days in a tiny cell in which he could neither stand nor lie down. Occasionally he was released and forced to bend over while pressure was exerted on his testicles from behind. Again he was returned to the cement chamber. Later he was released and his hood was removed. His mother was before him. He determined not to recognize her, not to compromise her. But she burst out weeping and told him not to worry, she was the guilty one, she had aided the terrorists, not he, she had confessed. Then Jamil said no, *he* was the only guilty party. They beat him in front of his mother, and he was taken to the hospital. When I visited him there, he had decided not to recognize or remember the people he loved. He spent one year of his sentence in the jail at Sarafand. Beata succeeded in getting his sentence reduced, but a guard told him they were letting him go so that he could return to his village and serve as an example to other rebels. Beata said that this was a standard practice in the occupied territories; to make an example of one person and his family so that his experience would demoralize the others.

"Jamil asked me to leave. He feared for my safety. I accepted his need to be alone with his mother. Before anything else, he had to reestablish his relationship with her. I understood that here was something unfathomable to me, and that it had to do with the Palestinian world of honor. From those depths, Jamil would subsequently learn to remember me. I went to Jerusalem and awaited Bernstein's annual visit. I didn't tell him what I knew. Understand me, please. I became Bernstein's lover to learn more, that's true, to tear down the wall of his pathetic vanity and hear his naked voice. I hinted at the problem of torture. He told me quietly that torture was necessary in a life-and-death struggle like ours. Did I know anything about prisons in Syria or Iraq? I asked him whether we, the victims of Nazism, were capable of repeating the horrors perpetrated by our executioners. He answered that the weakness of the Israeli state could not be compared to the strength of Germany. He didn't give me the opportunity to reply that neither was the weakness of the Palestinians comparable to the strength of the Israelis. He was too busy explaining to me in detail how costly it would be to prevent the investigation of such accusations; he knew it well because that, precisely, was one of his jobs outside Israel.

"But I'm lying, Felix. I went to bed with Bernstein to fulfill the cycle of my own penance, to purge in my own body the perverted reason for our revenge against Nazism; our suffering, imposed now on beings weaker than we. We sought a place where we might be masters, not slaves. But one is master of himself only when he has no slaves. We did not know how to be masters without new slaves, so we ended by being executioners in order not to be victims. We found victims to escape being victims. With Bernstein, I sank into eternal suffering. What unites Jews and Palestinians is sorrow, not violence. Each of us looks at the other and sees only his own suffering in the eyes of the enemy. To reject the other's suffering, inevitably a mirror image of our own, our only recourse is violence. I am not lying, Felix. I went to bed with Bernstein so you would hate him as much as I do. Jamil and I are allies of a civilization that will never die; Bernstein is merely an agent of transitory power. And because power knows itself to be temporary, it is always cruel. Bernstein knows that this is the revenge against civilization anticipated by power. He has forced me to add new names to the geography of terror. Say Dachau, Treblinka, and Bergen-Belsen only if you add Moscobiya, Ramallah, and Sarafand. You can question the history of our entire century, but never the universality of its terror. No one escapes the stigma, not the French in Algeria, not the North Americans in Vietnam, not the Mexicans at Tlatelolco, not the Chileans at Dawson, not the Soviets in their immense Gulag. No one. So why would we Jews be any different? The passport of modern history accepts only one visa, that of terror. It doesn't matter. I am returning to my true homeland to fight, along with Jamil, against the injustices one people impose upon another. This is why I went to Israel twelve years ago. Only in this way can I be faithful to the death of my parents in Auschwitz.

"I didn't want to leave without saying goodbye to you. I will mail this record to you from the airport."

23 THE RECORD continued spinning after Sara Klein's last words. When the needle reached the end of the groove, it retracted abruptly, screeching across the record like a knife across a metal pot. Felix rescued Sara's message and replaced it in the shiny jacket from which Satchmo's blackberry eyes twinkled merrily.

For a long moment he held the record in his hands, poised delicately as if it were a crown without a head to rest on. Then he put it in his suitcase. He mustn't leave a single trace; the less evidence, the better. He walked to the telephone—dial o for an outside line, 1 if you need the assistance of the operator—practicing the phrases he would use. One of them he applied to himself: "My memory has some rights," and he recalled with a painful start that Sara Klein had been cremated that morning. It had been his obligation, professional perhaps, but certainly personal, to be there. But he couldn't help it, he'd been too exhausted, and had slept through it in the room on Génova Street. He wanted to forget; he renounced his right to memory; and besides, no one could be held to an accounting now but Felix Maldonado.

When he heard that the phone had been picked up and that I was waiting silent on the line, he said: *"When shall we two meet again?"*

"When the battle's lost and won," I replied. *"Good news?"*

"Good news!" Felix said in a broken voice.

"Ha, ha!" I laughed. *"Where?"*

"In Genoa," murmured Felix. *"I pray you, which is the way to Master Jew's?"*

"He hath a third in Mexico, and other ventures he hath."

"Why doth the Jew pause?" asked Felix, looking toward the suitcase containing Sara Klein's message.

"Hurt with the same weapons, healed by the same means," I responded.

Felix paused, and I asked: *"What has been done with the dead body?"*

"Compounded it with dust, whereto 'tis kin." There was violence in Felix's words, but immediately he relaxed and asked in the neutral tone we'd agreed upon, *"What news? I have some rights of memory."*

"Go merrily to London," I counseled him. *"Within hours they will be at your aid."*

Felix stared at his reflection in the opaque windows overlooking the bustle of Génova Street. *"Lord, I am much changed."*

"A sailor's wife had chestnuts in her lap. To Aleppo gone, master o' the Tiger," I said, and hung up.

For a moment Felix listened to the dead buzz in the receiver, and then he, too, hung up. He heard a ring, but didn't know whether it was the telephone or the doorbell. He picked up the receiver and heard repeated the distant flight of the bumblebee. As he hung up for a second time, he again heard the sound of muted and insistent ringing. He went to the door and, lowering his eyes, saw Simon

Ayub standing there with a newspaper-wrapped package under his arm and a hotel key in his hand.

"Cool it, man," Ayub said quickly. "I come in peace. The proof: I have the key to your room in my hand, but I rang the bell."

"I see your mentor is teaching you a few manners."

"Tell them to be more careful at the desk. Anyone can get in here. You ask for the key and they give it to you."

"It's a hotel for clandestine lovers and shitty tourists, didn't you know?"

"At any rate, they should be more strict. This isn't even any fun."

Ayub tried to look over Felix's shoulder, sniffing at the air he was tainting with his accent of clove. "May I come in?"

Felix stepped aside, and Simon Ayub entered with the blond-conquistador swagger that had so annoyed Felix ever since the Lebanese had first come to his office in the Ministry of Economic Development.

"For once, I'll save you any unnecessary questions," said Ayub, rocking back on the Cuban heels that increased his stature. He avoided looking at Felix. "Three to one, you would come here, and nine out of ten, you'd be in this apartment. Correct?"

"Correct," said Felix. "But those weren't my questions."

"Oh, is that right?" said Ayub indifferently, scrutinizing the four walls of the apartment.

"Why didn't anything about the attempt on the President's life appear in the newspapers? What really happened? Who died in my name, and with my name? Why was it necessary to kill anyone? Why didn't they capture me and kill me? Why did we have to go through the charade of my escaping from the hospital if that's what you wanted? Who do you and your chief work for?"

"This is a nice place," smiled Ayub, ignoring Felix's questions. "The things that go on here!"

"Now," said Felix, approaching Ayub like a cat. "Who killed Sara Klein?"

"No one comes here but tourists, or lovers." Ayub continued to smile, allowing himself the excesses permitted those who are small, light-skinned, and good-looking.

"What are you doing here?"

"This isn't the first time I've been here." Ayub was unbearably cocksure. Felix grabbed his lapel.

Ayub patted Felix's hand. "Are we feeling better now, friend? Do you want to go back and let Lichita take care of you?"

"Remember, I knocked you down with one hand, dwarf," said Felix, still grasping Ayub's lapel.

"I'm not forgetting anything." Ayub's eyes suddenly clouded with rancor. "But I prefer to bring that up on another occasion. Not now."

Smoothly, Ayub removed Felix's hand, as his self-congratulatory smile returned. "That's two lapels ruined; the Director General got one with his cigarette the other day, and now you, twisting and pulling. If things go on like this, I won't be earning enough to pay my tailor's bills."

"Who's your tailor? Lockheed?" Felix stared at Ayub's bright Braniff-colored suit.

"Classy, mmh?" Ayub smiled, stroking a lapel. "But what a way to greet a friend. Especially a friend who's bringing you a present."

He offered Felix the newspaper-wrapped package, which Felix accepted with marked reluctance. "Okay, I've had enough of this clowning around. What do you want, Ayub? If you're thinking of beating me up, you'll have a hard time of it unless you've brought a gang of gorillas with you. I'll kick the shit out of you."

"Aren't you going to open my present?" Ayub smiled as if secretly he thought there was no greater gift than his presence. "It isn't a bomb, I give you my word." He laughed almost hysterically.

"What is it, then?"

"Open it with care, friend. It's Sara Klein's ashes. Don't want to let them fly away."

Felix checked his impulse to punch Ayub, because the eyes of the little man who smelled of clove and dressed like a DC-7 had lost any trace of mockery or aggression or complacency. His cocky attitude refuted it, but his eyes shone with a tenderness that reflected a kind of pain, a kind of shame.

"You accepted the responsibility for Sara Klein's body?" asked Felix, the package in his hands.

"The Embassy claimed to have no knowledge of her."

"She was a citizen of the state of Israel."

"They said she had no relatives there and that she'd lived in Mexico longer than in Israel."

"But you aren't a relative."

"All I had to do to get them to release her body to me was say that I was her friend and would take care of the details. It was easy to see she was a hot potato in the Israelis' hands. They snapped at the chance."

"Bernstein was her lover. It should have been up to him."

"The good professor is, how shall I say it . . . incapacitated."

"Did Bernstein kill Sara Klein?"

"What do you think?"

They stared at each other in a pointless duel; each fought with the same, mutually invalidating, weapons: disbelief and certainty.

"Just remember," said Ayub, "that the professor has more important aims in this life than chasing after a woman, even if she is a good piece." He took three steps back, upturned palms extended. "Just keep your cool, my friend. Things are as they are. Careful, don't drop the package. If you break the urn, we'll both have to sweep up."

"You dirty bastard son-of-a-bitch," said Felix, clutching

the package. "You saw her naked, you touched her with your filthy little manicured pig's hands."

Ayub stood silent for a second, rejecting the insult, studying his hand with its topaz rings and carved scimitars.

"Sara Klein was the lover of my cousin, a schoolteacher in the occupied territories," Ayub said simply, his usual braggadocio stripped away. "I don't know whether she told you that story. Maybe she didn't have time. I know you loved her, too. That's why I brought you her ashes."

He turned his back to Felix and walked to the door, again the strutting conquistador. As he opened the door, he turned to look at Felix. "Take care, my friend. When we meet again, there'll be blood in our eyes, I promise you that. Don't think I've forgotten that low punch you landed. I want to even the score, I give you my word. Now more than ever."

He left, closing the door after him.

24 AT EIGHT O'CLOCK that evening, Felix entered a café on the Calle Londres. Leather banquettes and a bar of polished wood were intended to suggest an English pub, but the image was distorted by the strong fluorescent lights, and the beveled mirrors repeated only sparks of a dead star.

Felix walked to the copper-rimmed bar and asked for a beer. He looked around the room and was grateful, after all, for the horrid glare that permitted him to see the patrons. That may have been why the lights had been installed, so the bar wouldn't become a haunt for hot lovers.

It didn't take long to spot them. The boy in bell-bottom blue-jeans and a blue-and-white-striped jersey with a big anchor across the chest. The girl with hair like a curly black lamb he recognized immediately. The question was whether they would recognize him. He walked over to them with a glass of beer in his hand. The girl was carefully shelling chestnuts in her miniskirted lap; discarded hulls clung to her laddered stockings. She was feeding the nutmeats to the boy.

"August isn't the season for chestnuts," said Felix.

"My sailor friend brought them to me from a long way away," the girl said, not looking up, absorbed in shelling the nuts.

"May I?" asked Felix, as he sat down.

"Scoot over, Emiliano," said the girl. "These seats aren't very wide."

"*Your* seat's too wide, baby," the boy replied, mouth filled with chestnuts. "I don't know why they say those English women are so jolly, they must be thin in the butt."

"You should know," said Felix. "A girl in every port."

"No," purred the girl, caressing her companion's neck. "He's not much, but he's all mine."

"We fit fine," said Felix. "Better than in the taxi. Did you get your books back, Emiliano?"

"No, man. You know the truth of it? I'm a professional student. Right, Rosita?"

The curly-headed girl smiled, and nodded. "Want a chestnut?"

"What I want is to know where you got them."

"I told you, Emiliano brought them to me."

"Where did they come from?" Felix insisted.

"From far away." Emiliano raised his eyebrows. "What *I* need to know is what boat they came on, and who was at the helm."

"They came on a ship called the *Tiger,* and Timon was the captain's name."

"Umm," Emiliano mumbled. "The captain told me to tell you to keep your cool, and that the chestnuts came from a place called Aleppo."

"Haven't the three of us traveled together before?"

"That's right, man," said Emiliano.

"Who was aboard our ship?" Felix asked.

"Umm, it was jammed. A driver, two nuns, a nurse, Rosita here, and me, a fat woman with a basketful of chickens, and a man who looked like a government type. End of report."

Rosita shook the chestnut hulls from her lap, and the three studied one another. Then, avoiding their eyes, Felix asked, "Who killed Sara Klein?"

"The fuzz haven't picked up the trail," Emiliano replied, scarcely lowering his voice.

"The crime took place between midnight and one in the morning. At that hour, it's easy to check who came in and went out of a place like the Suites de Génova."

"Tell him, Emiliano, can't you see he loved her?" said Rosita, eyes brimming.

"Rosita, take care of your chestnuts and listen, but keep your mouth shut."

"Whatever you say, gorgeous," Rosita grinned, and simpered to Felix, "He's my man. We're crazy about each other. That's why I can understand how you feel. The woman they killed led you down the dark alley of grief, didn't she?"

Emiliano pinched Rosita's exposed thigh.

"Owww!"

"And pick the shells out of your stockings; it'll be like getting in bed with a cactus. There's always something caught in your bloody stockings."

"Then why do you ask me to leave them on when we go to bed?" mooed Rosita.

Felix was insistent. "What did you start to tell me?"

"The doorman swears no one suspicious went in or came out, only registered guests."

"Can you trust him?"

"He's been a doorman all his life. He's not too bright, but he's worked there nine years and no complaints."

"Years at his job, and old, he can be bought. Look into it."

"Right. He told me no one asked for Señorita Klein and no one sent her any messages or packages. Nothing."

"What was going on outside?"

"What's always going on in the Zona Rosa? Some kids in a convertible, pretty stoned, stopped in front of the hotel with some mariachis. A serenade, they said, for some lady tourist who didn't want to leave Mexico without being serenaded. The cops moved them right along. And a nun who asked the doorman if he'd donate something to some charity. That's the only thing out of the ordinary, a nun out alone at midnight. He didn't give her anything, and she left."

"How did he know she was a nun?"

"You know, the hair pulled back in a bun, zero makeup, all in black down to her ankles, a rosary in her hands. The usual bit."

"Were the serenaders and the nun there at the same time?"

"Umm, that I don't know."

"Find out, and report to the captain."

"Okay, Batman."

"Are you sure that Bernstein didn't enter the hotel sometime, or wasn't registered in advance?"

"The maestro? No way. He's been in the hospital with a gunshot wound in the shoulder. That night he was in the English Hospital, and never budged from there."

"Where is he now?"

"That we do know. In Coatzacoalcos, Hotel Tropicana."

"Why did he go there?"

"What I was just saying, to recover from the shot."

"Why didn't it come out?"

"What, man?"

"Anything about Bernstein's wound."

"Why would anything come out, and where?"

"In the newspapers. He was shot at the Palace."

"No, no. It was an accident, in his home. No reason for it to be in the newspapers. He said he shot himself accidentally, cleaning a pistol. That's what the hospital admission record shows, too."

"And not at the Palace the morning they awarded the National Prizes? Wasn't there an attempt on the President's life?"

Emiliano and Rosita stared at each other, and the boy reached for Felix's beer and drained it at a gulp. He stared at Felix, baffled. "Sorry, man. Hit me with that again. What attempt?"

"I thought someone tried to kill the President in the Palace," Felix explained patiently, "and that Bernstein was shot by mistake . . ."

"Jeez, are you stoned or something?" said Rosita.

"Shut up," said Emiliano. "No, not true. What made you think that?"

"Because I thought I'd fired the shot." A cold chill settled in the nape of Felix's neck.

"We didn't hear anything about that," said Emiliano, a flicker of fear in his eyes. "And nothing was in the papers, and the captain didn't know about it."

Felix clasped the boy's hand, and squeezed it.

"What did happen in the Palace, I was there . . ."

"Cool, brother, keep your cool, those're the instructions . . . You were there and you don't remember what happened?"

"No. Tell the captain what I've told you. It's important for him to know. Tell him that one side knows and tells things the other side doesn't know, and vice versa."

"Everyone in this whole affair's been lying. Cap knows that."

"All right," Felix said, more calmly. "Tell him to find out two things for me. I can't make it if I don't find out."

"Don't get excited. That's what we're here for."

"First. Who was jailed under my name in Military Camp Number One on August 10 and shot that same night while trying to escape? Second. Who's buried in my name in the Jardín Cemetery? Oh, and the license number of the serenaders' convertible."

"Okay. The cap says don't leave any tracks, and keep it cool, and he says most of all that he understands but you shouldn't let your personal feelings get in the way. That's what he said."

"And you remind him he gave me carte blanche to do whatever I think best."

"I'll tell him, man, fancy words and all."

"Tell him not to mistake anything I do for any motives of personal revenge."

Emiliano smiled, satisfied. "Cap says all roads lead to Rome. You get cultivated, being around him."

"See you later."

"Alligator."

"Take care," said Rosita, making sheep's eyes. "Maybe you'll invite us for another taxi ride. I liked sitting on your lap."

"I liked fooling around with the nurse," countered Emiliano.

"How can you be so mean, Emiliano?" whined Rosita.

"I wasn't being mean, fatass, just reminding you that two can dance that tango."

"Whew, aren't we rough tonight?" laughed Rosita, and hummed the first bars of the bolero "Perfidia."

They didn't even turn to look at Felix, and as he left the imitation pub, they were still arguing and making barbed jokes, as anonymous as any run-of-the-mill sweethearts. Felix told himself that brave Timon had gathered about him some very strange aides.

He stopped at the Red Cross Clinic on the Avenida Chapultepec to have them take a look at his face. They told him it was healing fine—"Who cut you up like that?"—and that all he needed was some ointment; rub it in and continue the treatment for several days.

He bought the ointment at a pharmacy and returned to the room on Génova. It was almost eleven and the young and oily desk clerks had gone off duty. The doorman opened the door, a somnambulist-faced, ancient Indian in a navy-blue suit shiny from wear.

The windows of the room were opened wide, and the bed was turned down, with a wrapped little chocolate on the pillow. He opened his suitcase. The package containing the ashes was still there, but the record with Satchmo on the jacket had disappeared.

25 FELIX LANDED at the airport of Coatzacoalcos at four in the afternoon. From the air, he had seen the expanse of the Petróleos Mexicanos refineries in Minatitlán, the stormy Gulf in the background, the industrial citadel inland, a modern fortress of towers and tubing and cupolas glinting like tinfoil toys beneath a storm-sated sun, the busy port with its railroad tracks extending onto the docks, and long, black, sleek-decked tankers.

As he descended from the plane, he breathed the hot humid air laden with the scent of laurel and vanilla. He removed his jacket and hailed a broken-down taxi. Swift glimpses of coconut-palm forests, zebu cattle grazing on brick-colored plains, and the Gulf of Mexico whipping up its early-evening thundershower yielded to a view of a port city with low, ugly buildings, their windows blasted out by hurricanes, and dirty neon signs, unlighted at this hour, a whole consumer society installed in the tropics, supermarkets, television-sale and -repair shops, and in the foreground the everlasting Mexican world of tacos, pigs, flies, and naked children in mute contemplation.

The taxi came to a stop before an open market. To Felix, everything was red, the long bloody sides of beef hanging from giant hooks, bunches of flame-colored bananas, red-leather sling chairs stinking of recently sacrificed cattle, and machetes of blackened metal, bathed in blood and thirsty for blood. The driver carried his suitcase to the entrance of a three-story rococo palace dating from the beginning of the century; the top floor had been destroyed by fire and converted spontaneously into a cooing dovecote.

"Hit by lightning," the driver said.

High above, buzzards wheeled in great circles.

The neon letters that spelled out Hotel Tropicana protruded like a wounded finger from the façade of sculptured stucco, angels with voluminous buttocks and cornucopias of fruit painted white but turning black from lichen and the incessant labors of the air, sea, and smoke from refinery and port. Felix registered under the name of Diego Silva, and a *cambujo*—half black, half Indian—servant dressed in a white shirt and shiny black trousers led him through a patio roofed in stained glass that filtered the hot sunlight. Many panes had been broken and not repaired; great blocks of sun were trying to assume precise positions on the chessboard of the black-and-white marble floor.

At his room, the bellboy unlocked the padlock on the door and turned on the wooden ceiling fan that hovered over the room like one more vulture. Felix gave the *cambujo* ten pesos and he smiled his way from the room, revealing gold teeth. A notice hung above the mosquito-netted brass bed:

SU RECÁMARA VENCE A LA 1 P.M.
YOUR ROOM WINS AT ONE P.M.
VOTRE CHAMBRE EST VAINCU A 13 HRS.

Felix telephoned to ask for the number of Dr. Bernstein's room. Room number 9, he was told, but the professor was out and wasn't expected back before sundown. Felix hung up the phone, removed his shoes, and lay back on the creaking bed. Little by little he began to feel drowsy, lulled by the sweet novelty with which the tropics receives its visitors before unsheathing the claws of its petrified desperation. But for the moment he was happy to be free of the burden of Mexico City, increasingly ugly, strangled in Mussolinian gigantism, locked into inhumane options: marble or dust, aseptic confinement or gangrenous incontinence. He hummed several popular songs, and it occurred to him as he drowsed that all the great cities of the world have their special love songs, Rome, Madrid, Berlin, New York, San Francisco, Buenos Aires, Rio, Paris. But no love song for Mexico City, he thought, and fell asleep.

He awakened in darkness with a start; his nightmare ended where sleep had begun; mute pain, a howl of rage, that was the song of his city, and no one could sing it. He sat up in terror; he didn't know where he was, in his bedroom with Ruth, in the hospital with Licha, or in the Suites de Génova with Sara's ashes. In his delirium he touched the pillow in the lustful night and imagined beside him the naked body of Mary Benjamin, her hardened nipples, her moist mound of Venus, the smell of an unsatisfied and sensual woman; he had forgotten her, and only a nightmare had brought her back, the lovers' rendezvous in the motel beside the Arroyo Restaurant was never consummated; the bitch had called Ruth.

He rose bathed in sweat and felt his way toward the bathroom. He took a cool shower and dressed quickly in clothing inappropriate to the heat, socks, shoes, city trousers, and shirt. He studied the face in the mirror attentively. The moustache was growing rapidly, the hair more slowly. The eyelids were less puffy, the incisions visible but healed.

He called the switchboard and was told the professor had returned. He took the newspaper-wrapped package from his suitcase and walked from his room down a corridor lined with large porcelain glass-incrusted flowerpots to room number 9.

He rapped on the door. It swung open and Bernstein's nearsighted eyes, swimming in the depths of the thick rimless eyeglasses, regarded him without surprise. One arm was in a sling. With the other he invited him to enter. "Come in, Felix. I've been expecting you. Welcome to Marienbad-in-the-Tropics."

26 INVOLUNTARILY, Felix put a hand to his face. Bernstein's watery gaze became unfathomable. His former student shook his head as if to free it of a spider's web. He entered the professor's room, on his guard against a trap. Doubtless the pockets of Bernstein's weightless but bulky mustard-colored jacket held more than parlor tricks.

"Come in, Felix. You seem surprised."

"You recognize me?" murmured Maldonado.

Bernstein's smile was one of amazed irony. "Why wouldn't I recognize you? I've known you for twenty years, five at the university, our breakfasts, there's never been a time I stopped seeing you—or wanted to. Would you like a drink? It doesn't go to your head in this heat. But come in and sit down, my dear Felix. What a pleasure and what a surprise."

"Didn't you just say you'd been expecting me?" asked Felix, taking a seat in a squeaking leather chair.

"I'm always expecting you and always surprised by you." Bernstein laughed, walking to a table replete with bottles, glasses, and some ice cubes swimming in a soup plate.

He poured a shot of J&B into a glass and added ice and soda from a siphon. "As long as I've known you, I've always said that boy is extremely intelligent and will go far if he doesn't get carried away by his excessive imagination, if he will only be more discreet and stop meddling in affairs that don't concern him . . ."

"This is something that concerns us both," said Felix, offering the package to the professor.

Bernstein laughed, shaking like a bowl of custard. Sweating in the tropic heat, he resembled an enormous mass of melting vanilla ice cream.

"So, you haven't forgiven an old man his ridiculous love for a younger woman. I expected more of your generosity," he said, carrying Felix's whiskey toward him.

"Take it," Felix insisted, still proffering the package.

Again Bernstein laughed. "I have something for you, and you have something for me. What a curious coincidence, as Ionesco and Alice would say."

Bernstein held the glass of scotch in his slightly trembling good hand, its ring finger adorned by the huge stone so clear it seemed of glass.

Felix said flatly, ignoring the professor's buffoonery: "These are Sara's ashes."

It seemed impossible that Bernstein's vanilla-ice-cream face could pale. But it did. His trembling increased, spilling whiskey on his jacket. Then he dropped the glass and it shattered on the black-and-white marble floor.

"Forgive me," said Bernstein, suddenly red, brushing at the whiskey trickling down the bulk of his jacket. Felix wondered if the magician's tricks in the pockets would be ruined from the sudden dowsing.

"They were given to me by the only person who took responsibility for Sara. He thought I had a right to them because I loved her," Felix said without emotion. "But I never possessed her. I prefer to give them to someone who's been her lover. Perhaps you'll accept this obligation at least?"

With his good hand, Bernstein snatched the package from Felix and clasped it piteously to his breast. He grunted like a wounded animal and threw it on the bed. He stumbled, and almost fell beside the package. Felix checked an impulse to rush to his aid, but the professor regained control of his gelatinous mass and half fell into a rattan chair.

For some seconds, the only sound was the humming of the ceiling fan.

"Do you believe I killed her?" Bernstein's voice caught in his throat.

"I don't believe anything. I was told that you were in the hospital when Sara was murdered."

"That's true. I never saw her again after the dinner at the Rossettis'. I had a fit of jealousy. I *warned* you not to see her again." The professor spoke with his gaze riveted on the tips of his perforated tropical shoes.

"Would her death have been avoided if I hadn't attended the dinner?"

Bernstein looked up suddenly and stared at Felix with the eyes of an ailing basilisk. "Did you see her before she died?"

"No. But she spoke to me."

Bernstein rested his weight on the arms of the chair that surrounded him like a throne. "When?"

"Four days after her death."

"Don't play games with me, Felix," said Bernstein, modulating his infinite repertory of tones. "We both loved her. But she loved you more."

"I never touched her."

"You're a man who should never touch what doesn't concern you. There is suffering that has nothing to do with you. Be thankful for that."

"I'm still waiting for the whiskey you offered me."

Bernstein struggled laboriously to his feet, and Felix

added: "There is something that does concern me. What happened at the Palace the morning of the prizes?"

"What! Hasn't anyone told you? But it's the joke of the breakfast circuit. Where have you been the last week?"

"In a hospital with my face bandaged."

"You see? Bad company," said Bernstein, measuring the whiskey with squinting, myopic eyes. "Just as the President reached you, you fainted. You blacked out," he added, and dropped one, two, three cubes of ice into the glass. "No big deal. A little scene. An incident. You were carried unconscious through the crowd. The President didn't flick an eyelash; he continued greeting people. The ceremony went ahead normally."

Bernstein suppressed a trembling, roguish smile. "There was no dearth of jokes. A minor official of the MED fainted just at the sight of the President. What emotion! There's been nothing like it since Moctezuma."

"You say you wounded yourself cleaning a pistol?"

Bernstein solemnly offered Felix the glass. "Someone shot me that evening when I was alone at my home. A bad shot."

"Maybe he didn't mean to kill you."

"Perhaps."

"Perhaps? It wouldn't be easy to miss someone your size."

Bernstein did not reply. He prepared his own drink and raised it as if to propose a toast. "May the devil," he said, "cut off all noses that find themselves in others' business."

He turned away from Felix, a sweat-stain continent on his back. "In your room at the Hilton, you had a dossier on all my activities."

"Was it you who rifled my files?"

"What difference does it make?" replied Bernstein, his back still to Felix. "I know you know everything about me. But many people have that information. It's no secret. You can parrot it till doomsday and nothing will happen."

127

"Recite like a good pupil?" Felix smiled. "But it is important. Leopoldo Bernstein, born 13 November 1915 in Krakow with all the handicaps: Polish, Jew, the son of militant socialist workers; emigrated to Russia with his parents following the October Revolution; given a fellowship by the Soviet government to study economics in Prague, and charged with establishing relations with Czech universities and officials in the Beneš government on the eve of the war; fails in carrying out his charge; instead of seducing, allows himself to be seduced by Zionist circles in Prague; following Munich, and before the imminent conflict, takes refuge in Mexico; author of a pamphlet against the Ribbentrop-Molotov pact; his parents disappear and die in Stalinist camps; the Soviet Union declares him a deserter; a professor in the School of Economics at the University of Mexico, requests leave and travels for the first time to Israel; fights in the Haganah, the secret Jewish army, but finds it too temperate and joins the terrorist Irgun; participates in multiple acts of murder and reprisal bombings of civilian sites; returns to Mexico and obtains his citizenship in '52; from that time, he is responsible for raising funds in the Jewish communities of Latin America, and following the war of '73, he helps found Gush Emunim, with the aim of preventing the return of the occupied territories . . ."

"Publish it in the newspapers if you want," interrupted Bernstein, again installed in his rattan throne.

"Shall I also publish the fact that out of jealousy you ordered a Palestinian teacher jailed and tortured, ordered his mother to be tortured, her sexual parts destroyed, ordered the teacher, stripped of his will, sent back to Sara, all out of revenge?"

"I don't know how Sara spoke to you following her death, but I see she did," said Bernstein, with celluloid eyes.

"Who killed Sara?"

"I don't know. But as you seem to know, she, too, moved in bad company."

"The Israeli Embassy refused responsibility for her body."

"She'd gone over to the enemy. That was no reason to kill her, but, simply stated, we were no longer responsible for her."

"But the other side had even less motive to kill her."

"Can you be sure? The internal conflicts of the Palestinians are no tennis game. If you ingratiate yourself with one group, you immediately alienate another."

"You should know. The Jewish terrorists of the forties also had their disagreements."

Bernstein shrugged. "Sara was very prone to leaving messages. And you to swallowing them."

"Isn't what I've said true?" Felix asked tranquilly.

"In context, yes. Outside it, no. The boy was a terrorist."

"As you were in the Irgun. And with the same motives."

Bernstein laboriously crossed fat legs. "Do you remember your classes in law? Palestine, ever since it was taken from us, has been a no-man's-land, *res nullius,* through which all armies and all peoples have passed. Everyone has claimed it, Romans, Crusaders, Muslims, European imperialists, but only we have the original right to it. We have waited two thousand years. Ours is the real claim to Palestine. Our patience."

"At the price of the sorrow of the people who've been living there for centuries, with the right or without it? You suffer from the sickness of a lost Paradise."

Bernstein again shrugged his shoulders impatiently. "Do you want to return the island of Manhattan to the Algonquins? Shall we throw ourselves into what the French call an eternal Café du Commerce debate?"

"Why not? I listened to Sara's reasons. I can listen to yours."

"I fear I may bore you, my dear Felix. A Jew is as ancient as his religion, a Mexican as young as his history. That's why you constantly renew your history, each time imitating a

129

new model that quickly becomes obsolete. Then you repeat the whole process, losing everything. In the end, you do maintain the illusion of perpetual youth . . . *We* have persisted for two thousand years. Our only error has been always to wait for the enemy that hated us to leave us in peace, peace in Berlin and Warsaw and Kiev. For the first time, we have decided to win our peace, instead of waiting for it to be conceded to us. Is it only in suffering that people who, like you, have nothing to lose respect us?"

"You might choose less fragile enemies."

"Who? The Arabs, a thousand times better armed and more powerful than we?"

"You might have demanded a fatherland in the very places where you suffered, instead of imposing one upon other peoples."

"Ah, Sara taught you well. Bah! No one loves the Palestinians, the Arabs least of all. They're the albatross around their necks. They use them as an arm of propaganda and negotiation, but in their own countries they impound them in concentration camps. So much for the farce of Arab socialism." Bernstein narrowed his eyes and leaned forward over his gross belly. "You must understand, Felix. The only intimate ties the Palestinians have are to us Jews. To no one else. They must live with us or be the pariahs of the Arab world. With us, they have what they have never had: work, good salaries, schools, tractors, refrigerators, television, radios. I hate to think what it would be with the Arabs . . ."

"The Yankees would give us the same if we became less independent."

"And why don't you?" snorted Bernstein, amused. "It's what Marx recommended. Anyway, you're not independent, you simply lack the advantages of total integration with the North American world. Compare California to Coahuila. The whole American Southwest would still be a flea-bitten wasteland in the hands of Mexico."

"Sara said in her message that she believed in civilizations that endure, not in transitory powers."

"And for believing the same as she, we were persecuted and murdered for centuries. A civilization without power is already archaeology, whether it knows it or not." He removed his eyeglasses to emphasize his lack of defenses. "A destiny that one suffers deserves compassion, but a destiny one controls is detestable. We will not be detained by this paradox. We worked hard. Nothing was ever *given* to us. Have you ever asked yourself why, with fewer arms and fewer men, we always defeated the Arabs? I'll tell you why. When Dayan founded the 101st Commando, he established one ironclad rule: no wounded soldier would ever be abandoned on the field of battle and left to the mercy of the enemy. All our soldiers know that. Behind them stands a hard-working, democratic, and informed society that will never abandon them. Our weapon is called solidarity, and it is serious, not second-hand rhetoric as it is in Mexico. Do you understand?"

"I fear a society that feels itself absolved of all guilt, Professor."

"Apparently, our only guilt is that of controlling our destiny. And when destiny is controlled, you're right, it is called power. For the first time, we have it. We have assumed its responsibilities. And its inevitable pitfalls. Would you go so far as to claim that Hitler was right? After all, his final solution would have avoided today's conflicts. Think about it: only total extermination in Nazi ovens would have prevented the creation of Israel. Men create conflicts. But conflicts also create men. During the Mandate, the British had concentration camps for Jews and Arabs in Tel Aviv and Gaza. What right did they have to judge the Germans at Nuremberg for identical crimes?" He replaced his spectacles, his eyes focused, the fish ceased to swim. "Throughout history, there have been only executioners and victims. It's a banal observation. It is less banal to stop being victims,

131

even at the cost of becoming executioners. The other option is to be eternal victims. There is no power without responsibility, including responsibility for crimes. I prefer that to the consolation of being a victim, even to the applause of posterity and the compassion of good souls."

Bernstein rose from his chair and walked to the window and opened it. The sounds of Coatzacoalcos were accompanied by a dizzying rush of elemental odors, fruit, sugarcane, excrement, mixed with the artificial odors from the refinery.

"Look." Bernstein leaned from the window and waved his good hand toward the market. "They're slaughtering cattle. An esthete might say it recalls a painting by Soutine. On the other hand, through the eyes of an animal lover or a vegetarian . . ."

He closed the window and wiped the sweat from his forehead with his jacket sleeve. Felix sat motionless, empty glass in hand.

"Professor," he said, finally. "Your power depends on others. Arms and money. You recruit both. That's all right. But every day they will be more difficult to obtain. You know it. Jewish families in Mexico, in Argentina, in the United States, everywhere, are becoming more Mexican, more Argentinian, more North American, they're drifting away from Israel, and in a few years no one will give you anything. Why don't you give a little before it's too late and you find yourself alone once again? Alone and hated and persecuted."

Bernstein wagged his head and a strange resignation appeared in his eyes. "Sara accused me of being a hawk. You know, the third floor of this hotel was destroyed by lightning. Doves took over the ruins. And as no one ever repairs anything here . . . Vultures fly high overhead, especially here, around the market slaughterhouse. Every day, they kill a vulture or two trying to feed on the dead flesh of the cattle. Dead meat is what the buzzards like, they don't bother the doves. It's true. Someday we'll be forced to abandon the occupied territories. Oil weighs more heavily than reason. But we shall have left behind cities and citizens, schools and a democratic political system. When the Arabs return, there will be peace only if they respect our new pilgrims, those who remain there. That will be your famous meeting of civilizations. That will be the acid test of peace. If not, everything will begin all over again."

Again Bernstein approached the window. He peered in vain through the sheer curtains. A sudden tropical downpour had been unleashed.

Bernstein whirled to face Felix. "What are you thinking?"

"I'm remembering the conviction with which you used to expound economic theories at the university. From your lips, every theory was convincing, from Quesnay to Keynes. It was why we loved your classes. It was why we followed and respected you. You never pretended to be objective, but your subjective passions had the effect of being entirely objective. Professor, you didn't come here to recover from a wound inflicted by a mysterious bullet. Much less to convince me of the rights and motives of Israel. Enough talk. I'm going to ask you to hand over what I came here to get . . ."

It wasn't caramels in the bulging pockets of Bernstein's wrinkled, sweat-stained jacket. Felix leaped from his chair and grasped the professor's fat neck; he twisted the injured arm, pulling it from the protective sling, and Bernstein howled with pain, his free arm upraised, a tiny Yves-Grant .32 clutched in his hand. He let the pistol fall on the chessboard floor. Felix released his grip on Bernstein and picked up the automatic. He leveled it at the professor's trembling belly.

His aim never wavering, he emptied Bernstein's suitcase, tossing aside all its contents. He ordered Bernstein to precede him to the bathroom, where he opened the leather kit

133

of personal toilet articles; he squeezed out the toothpaste, he tore open capsules of medicine, he removed the straight-edge razor and ripped out the lining of the kit bag. With Bernstein before him, he returned to the bedroom and slit open the lining of the suitcase. He searched the closet and, for good measure, shredded the blue-striped seersucker hanging there. He repeated the process with pillows and mattress. He tore down the mosquito netting to examine its yellowed canopy. Throughout, Bernstein, seated on his precarious rattan throne, watched, unmoving, the grimace of pain yielding to an insulting smile.

"Take off your clothes," Felix ordered.

He searched the clothing. Naked, Bernstein resembled a gluttonous child who'd turned into the mountains of cotton candy he'd consumed.

"Open your mouth. Remove your bridge."

Only one orifice remained. Felix knelt. He pressed the barrel of the pistol against Bernstein's kidney and inserted a finger up his rectum. He felt only the convulsions of the old man's uncontrollable laughter.

"Nothing there, Felix. You're too late."

Pistol in hand, Maldonado rose to his feet and cleaned his finger across Bernstein's lips. Even the professor's gesture of revulsion could not check his amused chortles. "Nothing, Felix. You find yourself with empty, if slightly filthy, hands."

Felix's eyes were clouded with sweat, but the pistol never wavered. There could be no better target than the massive bulk of his former mentor. "Tell me just one thing, Professor, so I don't go away empty-handed. After all, I brought you that . . ." He waved the pistol toward the newspaper-wrapped package.

Bernstein made a slight nervous movement. The Yves-Grant again pointed at Bernstein's navel.

Felix asked, "How did you recognize me?"

Now Bernstein's laughter was gargantuan. He bellowed

like a Santa Claus on holiday, naked in the tropics, far removed from his icy workshop. "Such imagination. I told you! Ever since you were in college . . ."

"Answer me. I don't need an excuse to shoot."

"I don't have the background, my dear Felix. I don't understand why you think I shouldn't recognize you."

"This, and this, and this," said Felix, with the rage of futility and fatigue. One by one, the pistol barrel pointed out the scars on his face. "And this, and this. I have a new face, can't you see?"

Bernstein's laughter was explosive. When it subsided, he settled his naked bulk in the only chair capable of sustaining him. "They made you believe that?"

"I can see myself in the mirror."

"A touch here, a slight modification there?" Bernstein smiled. "Your hair cut short, a new moustache?" He crossed fat hands across his belly, but did not achieve the desired resemblance to a benign Buddha.

"Yes," replied Felix, willing to be convinced. He felt that only by abandoning all strength could he recover his capacity for it. And there was something more, the dark little seed of an idea beginning to sprout in his guts, working its way toward his chest.

"The only surgery performed on you was that of suggestion." Bernstein smiled, but immediately erased the smile. "It's enough to know that a man is being sought. After that, everyone sees him differently. Even the man himself. I know what I'm talking about. Have a drink. It's too late. Relax."

Bernstein indicated the table cluttered with bottles, glasses, and ice, repeating the earlier wave of his hand through the open window toward the teeming market. The ring with the clear stone was no longer on the professor's finger.

The seed exploded in Felix's intestines, branched through his chest, and blossomed like a sunburst in his head.

As he ran from Bernstein's room, still carrying the pistol, he could hear the professor's steely cry, strong at first, then dissipated by street noises, then once again erupting from the open window: "It's too late! Be careful! Watch out!"

27 THE CAMBUJO from the Hotel Tropicana was standing beneath Bernstein's window, facing the market. He was ready, fists clenched, legs planted sturdily, and smiling; Felix could read the caution signal flashing from his gold teeth.

He stuck the pistol in a pocket and limbered his leg muscles. He meant to take a running jump with both feet on the servant's belly, but the *cambujo* broke into a run toward the market, swinging the beef carcasses aside, turning over crates, scattering straw in his wake. Blood from the sides of beef stained Felix's shoulders, and huge clusters of bananas struck him in the face; the machetes glittered more by night than by day. Felix grabbed one at random as he ran by. Better that no shots be heard that night in Coatzacoalcos.

The *cambujo* continued his flight through the market, zigzagging back and forth and sowing obstacles in Felix's path. A mix of Olmec Indian and black, he was short in stature but fast, and Felix was unable to overtake him. They emerged at the far end of the market onto the railroad tracks, and Felix saw the mestizo bounding along the rails like a rabbit, following the tracks toward the port outlined in the distance by scattered yellow lights. Felix followed his dark hare, who had an obvious advantage; he'd played there as a child.

Maldonado tripped over a spike and fell, but he never lost sight of his prey; the *cambujo* seemed not to want to be lost from view; as Felix fell for the second time, he stopped and waited for Felix to get to his feet before he went on running.

The rainstorm had ended with the same abruptness with which it had begun, magnifying to an even greater degree the pungent odors of the tropical port. A moist lacquerlike film shone on the long expanse of dock, the moribund rails, the asphalt, and the distant hulks of oil tankers. The *cambujo* ran along the length of the dock like a swift Veracruz Zatopek, with Felix some twenty meters behind him, harboring the burning conviction that this was not a normal chase; the *cambujo* was a false hare, and he a false turtle.

The pursued slowed his pace and the distance between them narrowed dangerously; Felix clasped his machete more tightly in his hand; at any moment the *cambujo* might turn with a pistol in his hand, his pursuer now within sure range. He stopped beside a black rain-washed tanker sweating gray drops of water and oil; Felix dropped the machete and threw himself upon the dark little man.

The tanker whistled one long blast. Felix and the *cambujo* fell to the ground and rolled along the dock, the mestizo offering no resistance. Felix straddled the heaving chest of his oddly passive adversary and planted his knees on the outspread arms. The prisoner twisted his wrists, teasing Felix with balled fists. For an instant they stared in panting silence, Greek masks. Felix's face was the grimace of pain, the mulatto's the mask of comedy, black, sweating, gold teeth shining. Felix felt beneath his weight that the wiry little man had yielded completely, with the exception of those clenched fists.

Felix seized one fist and tried to pry it open. Worse than the iron gauntlet of a medieval warrior, it was the claw of a beast with its own secret reasons for not ceding. The tanker sounded a second blast, more guttural than the first. The *cambujo* opened the hand, grinning like the little laughing heads of La Venta artifacts. There was nothing in the pink-palmed hand crisscrossed with lines promising eternal life and good fortune for the *cambujo.*

His captive turned round eyes toward the ship as Felix struggled to open his other fist. The ship's gangplank began to rise from the dock toward the portside rail of the tanker. Felix reached for the abandoned machete and held the edge to the *cambujo's* throat.

"Open that fist or I'll cut off your head, and *then* your hand."

The fist opened. Bernstein's ring lay there. But not the stone as transparent as glass. Felix leaped to his feet, grabbed the neck of the *cambujo's* shirt, jerked him to his feet, and roughly ran his hands over his body, felt the shirt, the trousers. He released him, as the ship cast off its lines.

Freed, the *cambujo* trotted back toward Coatzacoalcos, but Felix had no further interest in him. A cameo of light on the dark tanker had captured his attention, a circle of light on the poop deck, doubly bright, illuminated by brightness as strong as if from a reflector and by a face as brilliant as the moon, framed in the oval of a porthole, an unforgettable and unmistakable face, with bangs and crow's-wing hair emphasizing the luminous whiteness of the skin, the icy diamonds in the gaze, the aquiline profile, as the woman turned her head.

The gangplank was halfway between the dock and the port rail. Felix thrust the ring into his trousers pocket and, still clutching the machete, ran desperately along the ship and lunged for the gangplank, managing only to brush the ends of the thick ropes dangling from the treads.

A freckled gringo, about forty, with a face marked by thin lips and a flattened nose, shouted from the rail: "Hey, are you nuts?"

"Let me on. Let me on!" shouted Felix.

The gringo laughed. "You drunk or somethin'?"

"The woman. I must see the woman you have on board."

"Shove off, buddy, dames don't travel on tankers."

138

"Goddammit, I just saw her . . ."

"Okay, greaser, go back to your tequila."

"Fuck you, gringo."

The man laughed and his freckles danced. "Meet me in Galveston and I'll kick the shit out of you. So long, greaser." He secured the gangplank and thrust an obscene finger toward Felix.

Felix threw himself against the side of the tanker still bumping against the dock, and, swinging his machete, an unlikely Quijote, attempted to pierce the body of the slowly moving giant. As the ship eased away from the dock, the cutting edge of the machete scratched fresh paint, leaving a long shining scar along the hull.

The tanker churned the dark waters of the Gulf of Mexico. The night of rotted mangoes and sweet nicotiana evaporated like the puddles following the shower. Felix read the name on the tanker's stern, *S.S. Emmita, Panama,* and saw the flag of four fields and two stars floating limply in the heavy air.

The face of Sara Klein, a paper moon suspended in a circle of light, had disappeared.

PART THREE

OPERATION GUADALUPE

28 FELIX BOUGHT a white fiber hat at the Coatzacoalcos airport and took the first Mexicana flight. In Mexico City he caught a Pan-American Airlines flight to Houston. He had a visa for multiple entries into the United States, and the immigration officials saw no discrepancy between the photograph on the passport and the moustached face of the man wearing a white hat and black sunglasses. Bernstein was right; these men weren't looking for him.

In Houston he rented a Ford Pinto at the airport Hertz desk and got on the highway to Galveston. He had a day to kill; the Port Authority at Coatzacoalcos had told him that the *Emmita* made no ports before Galveston; she was carrying a cargo of natural gas from Mexico to Texas, and in Texas she was taking on refined products destined for the East Coast of the United States. It was her normal trading route, and she called in at Coatzacoalcos every two weeks except in the winter, when the northers held her up a little. Her captain was named H. L. Harding, but he hadn't made this run because of illness. And no one had seen a woman go aboard.

The August heat on the barren plain between Houston and Galveston is unrelieved by hills or woods or aromas— except that of gasoline. Felix was grateful for the long, straight highway that allowed him to drive without major distractions and see before him, instead of the dirty Texas sun, the opaque moon of the face he'd glimpsed in the porthole of the *Emmita,* a face he'd always compared to Louise Brooks's in *Pandora's Box;* the more he thought about it, the more the cinema buff in him substituted a second, the stark white face of Machiko Kyo in *Ugetsu*

143

Monagatari, the flesh consciously artificial in its mortuary whiteness, the false eyebrows tracing an arc of conjecture over the real, shaved-off brows; the phantom gaze merging into the vigilant sleep of Japanese eyes, the painted mouth a rosebud of blood.

Felix was dizzied by the contrast between the daylight scene of the reverberating Texas plain and the nocturnal vision of Japan, a misty moon following a rain, a night of ancient spirits and sorceresses who take possession of the bodies of virgins in order to effect a festering revenge, visions echoed in the night he'd spent in Coatzacoalcos, the bloody beef carcasses, the vultures, and dovecotes installed in the ruins of a fire, the silvery cupolas of the refinery, Bernstein's room, the rococo hotel, the *cambujo . . .* and the white profile of Sara Klein glimpsed against the darkness of the *S.S. Emmita.*

The vision was so confused and so powerful that he felt ill and had to stop the car; he crossed his arms over the steering wheel and rested his head; he closed his eyes and repeated wordlessly that from the beginning of this adventure he'd sworn to be wholly accessible, ready to respond to any situation, to be led by any suggestion, to be open to all alternatives, and—and this was the most difficult of all— to keep his mind razor-sharp, assessing the deliberate or the chance accidents others created for him, to be aware of them, but never to prevent or avoid them.

"For a few weeks, you'll be living in a kind of voluntary hypnosis," I'd told him as I explained what he might encounter. "If not, our operation may fail."

"I don't like the word hypnosis," Felix had said, smiling his Moorish smile, so like that of Velázquez. "I'd rather call it fascination. I'll allow myself to be fascinated by everything that happens to me. Maybe that's the fulcrum between the exercise of will you're asking of me, and fate."

"No parking on the expressway." Someone was tapping Felix on the shoulder.

"I'm sorry, I didn't feel well," said Felix, raising his head from the wheel to see the beefy arm of a State Policeman.

"You a dago or a spick? You people shouldn't be allowed to drive. I don't know what this country's coming to. Ain't no real Americans left. All right, get going," said the patrolman with the broad, red Irish face.

Felix drove on. A half hour later he was in Galveston, and drove directly to the offices of the Port Authority. He asked for the date and the hour of the arrival of the *S.S. Emmita*, en route from Coatzacoalcos under the Panamanian flag.

The shortsleeved clerk told him, first, to close the door or the air conditioning wouldn't do any good, and second, that the *Emmita* wasn't going to arrive anywhere, for the simple reason that she'd been undergoing repairs in dry dock. Why didn't he speak with Captain Harding who was supervising the work.

There is no more insolent sun than one struggling through a veil of clouds, and the thermometer was hovering around 98 degrees when Felix located a bare-chested old man standing beside the disabled hull of the *S.S. Emmita, Panama.* A frayed cap with a worn leather visor protected him against the burning sun. Felix asked if he was Harding. The man nodded yes.

"Do you speak Spanish?"

Again the old man nodded. "I've been in and out of the ports along the Gulf and the Caribbean for thirty years."

"And you never get sick?"

"I'm too old to get the clap and too tough for anything else," Harding replied good-humoredly.

"I saw the *Emmita* weigh anchor last night in Coatzacoalcos, Captain."

"The sun's pretty strong," Harding replied kindly.

"It's the truth."

"Dammit, my tanker isn't the *Flying Dutchman*. Look at 'er, no wings."

"Well, I have wings. I flew here today from Coatzacoalcos. Your tanker left the dock at midnight and should reach Galveston tomorrow afternoon about four."

"Who spun you that fairy tale?"

"The Port Authority, and a freckled sailor who promised to kick the shit out of me here."

"You're sick, mister. You better get in out of the sun. Come along with me and we'll have a beer."

"When will your ship be repaired?"

"We sail day after tomorrow."

"For Coatzacoalcos?"

The old man nodded, scratching the white horsehair mattress on his chest.

"They said you weren't aboard because you were sick."

"The bastards said that?"

"If what I'm telling you is true, can I count on your help?"

The old man's eyes flickered like tiny stars in a sky of wrinkles. "If some bastard's knocking around the Gulf using the name of my ship, you wait and see, I'll be the one who'll knock the shit out of the whole kit and caboodle, damn pirates! Maybe they fooled the Mexican authorities and they're headed for another port."

"I don't think Freckles was lying. He said Galveston all right. He saw my machete and thought I was a drunken Indian."

Felix accepted Captain Harding's hospitality and spent the rest of the afternoon asleep on the sofa in his little gray wooden house by the slick, oily waters of the Gulf. Harding left him, and returned about ten that night. He'd hurried the repairs along, and had brought beer, sandwiches, and a list of all the tankers due to dock the next morning in the port of Galveston. They read it together, but the names told them nothing. Harding said they were all names of legitimate ships, but if those buccaneering pigs were changing names in every port, there was no way they could find out.

"Do you have any way of recognizing her if you see 'er, fella?"

Felix shook his head. "Only if I see the man with the freckles. Or the woman on board."

"Never had a woman on my tanker."

"That's what they tell me. There was one on this one."

"It's hard to tell one tanker from another. We don't get rigged up for a carnival like the cruise ships and all those fag outriggers on the Caribbean. All a tanker has to do is change her name." Again he read the list aloud: the *Graham*, the *Evelyn*, the *Corfu*, the *Culebra Cut*, the *Alice* . . .

Felix slapped the captain's strong, age-spotted hand. "The *Alice!*" He laughed.

"Yessir, and the *Royal* and the *Darien* . . . You always so tickled at the names of ships?" Harding, slightly annoyed, interrupted his reading.

"Bernstein's lapse." Felix laughed, striking his knees with his fists. " 'What a curious coincidence, as Ionesco and Alice would say.' Really. Curiouser and curiouser . . ."

"What the hell's the matter with you?" said Harding, again afraid that Felix was either crazy or sunstruck.

"What time does the *Alice* dock tomorrow, Captain?"

29 AT FOUR O'CLOCK on the afternoon of the following day, the S.S. *Alice* docked beneath low-hanging clouds in Galveston. The Stars and Stripes drooped above a bow proclaiming Mobile as the tanker's port of origin. Harding had situated Felix in the best place to see without being seen. The freckled sailor was freeing the chain to drop the gangplank, calling to the stevedores on the dock.

Leaning against the steel side of a warehouse and hidden behind a latticework of similar columns, Felix watched a tall, elegant man in white walk the length of the dock toward the gangplank: Mauricio Rossetti, the Director General's private secretary. He stopped and waited for the completion of the docking maneuvers.

Aided by the freckled sailor, the false Sara Klein descended. She saw Rossetti and ran happily toward him. She started to kiss him, but he discreetly declined, took her arm firmly, and led her toward the exit gate. The woman was closer now and Felix could see that the imitation, if an imitation had indeed been intended, was crude, and appropriate only for deceiving fools like him hopelessly in love with women unattainable either in life or in death. But there was no mistaking the intent: the Louise Brooks haircut, the powder-whitened Machiko Kyo face, the slate-blue tailored suit.

Angelica Rossetti had studied Sara closely during the dinner party the previous week in the San Angel home filled with paintings by Ricardo Martínez. But everything about her was false; the only truth was the clear stone ring sparkling on her finger, an inter-stellar combat of luminous pinpoints in the dusk. The mounting was new. Felix rubbed the stoneless ring in his pocket.

He followed the couple from a distance. As he passed the tanker, his fingertips brushed the flagrant scar inflicted by his machete. Felix, never taking his eyes off the Rossettis, raised his arm, and Harding, who had been awaiting the signal, rushed the ship with three port policemen. The freckled sailor watching from the rail dropped his rope and disappeared into the ship. Harding and the police went aboard. Our stubby friend Freckles won't have an ounce of shit left in his body, Felix thought.

Angelica's only luggage was the dressing case she was carrying. She and her husband got into a Cadillac limousine driven by a chauffeur sweating beneath his gray cap. Felix climbed into the Pinto and followed them as they headed directly for the expressway to Houston.

The Rossettis' limousine came to a stop before the white elegance of the Warwick Hotel. Felix drove to the nearby parking lot. Suitcase in hand, he entered the refrigerated comfort of the hotel. The Rossettis were registering. Felix waited until a clerk had led them through the lobby and along a row of exclusive boutiques. That meant they'd been given one of the rooms on the large crescent ringing the swimming pool. The sweating chauffeur delivered the Rossettis' suitcases to the doorman; they still bore the Mexico–Houston luggage tags. As Felix reached the desk, the clerk was instructing the bellboy to carry Señor Rossetti's suitcases to room number 6. Felix told the clerk that he enjoyed an early swim, and requested a room by the pool.

"It's nice at night, too," the Chicano clerk told him in Spanish. "The swimming pool's open till twelve midnight. And we have facilities for parties in the cabanas."

"How about 8, is it free?" Felix was betting that rooms facing the pool all had even numbers.

The Chicano said yes, the room was available. The bellboy carried Felix's suitcase to his room and opened the heavy drapes for the guest to admire his private terrace and view of the swimming pool. He left, after explaining how to regulate the thermostat.

Felix undressed, but even though his body felt as sticky as a sucked caramel, he didn't dare shower. He stood near the communicating door between his and the Rossettis' rooms, hoping to overhear something; nothing but the clinking of glasses, muffled footsteps, drawers opening and closing, and once, the strident voice of Angelica, no, not now, not after the way you greeted me, and Rossetti's inaudible reply.

Then the door of the adjoining room opened and closed. Felix half opened his door and peered down the hall in time to see the tall and elegant figure of Mauricio Rossetti. Felix was paralyzed with indecision. If Rossetti had the stone with him, it wouldn't be impossible for Felix to recover it, only more difficult. He hurried to the bed and pulled on his swim trunks, preparing to follow Rossetti; after all, he knew where Angelica was, but the private secretary was leaving the hotel. As he leaned over, he saw a reflection in the sliding door to the terrace.

On the neighboring terrace, two hands grasped the light blue railing, unaware of the game of reflections facilitated by the sudden darkness. On the finger of one of those hands shone the ring with the clear stone.

He waited. Maybe Angelica would take a nap, and he would only have to vault the low parapet separating the two terraces. Again the Rossettis' door opened and closed. Felix watched a white-robed, barefoot Angelica walk toward the pool; after making sure no lights were on in his room, he stepped onto the terrace. Angelica Rossetti was wearing a bikini beneath her robe; she dived into the water. Felix hurriedly donned the white robe hanging in his own bathroom, placed the room key in the pocket, and ran toward the pool.

Angelica emerged from the water and climbed onto the diving board. Again she dived. Felix tossed aside the robe and plunged into the opposite end of the pool.

The water was overly warm, the pool illuminated with submerged lights. In spite of the chlorine, Felix kept his eyes open; he saw Angelica, eyes closed, cleansed forever of the mask of Sara Klein, moving toward him in the water with regular strokes of arms and feet.

Felix rolled slightly and seized Angelica by the neck; she uttered the strangled cry of a wounded shark; the water shattered like crystal around them, a Laocoön-like figure shot toward the surface, though in this case each must have believed the other the serpent.

Felix could only imagine the terror in Angelica's eyes. He clamped his hand over her mouth and again thrust her beneath the surface, her body yielded, and he was reminded of a woman who for a moment resists an overture for the sake of appearances, then suddenly surrenders. He grappled for Angelica's hand and tore the ring from her finger. In other circumstances, this strong-minded, athletic woman, who went swimming every day with Ruth at the Chapultepec Sports Club, would have defended herself better; she now seemed incapable of offering resistance, and Felix's arms again embraced her, this time to lift her from the pool.

The contact with the almost inanimate body excited him; some women are at their most beautiful at rest, and Angelica, normally aggressive and very much the lady, now resembled a goddess rescued from the sea, proud, solitary and sensual, as Felix left her almost lifeless beside the pool.

He dressed hurriedly, left the hotel, and drove off in the Pinto. Once on the superhighway to Galveston, at moments when the lights from a passing car allowed it, he held the stone round as a marble, clear as the waters of the swimming pool, and sparking a thousand lights of its own, between his thumb and index finger to study it, seeking its secret, its flaw. He was driving ninety miles an hour, and had no time to stop.

When he reached Captain Harding's gray cottage, he tested the stone in the mounting of Bernstein's ring; it fit perfectly, and he replaced it in its original setting. Even as he did so, he laughed at himself; how many mountings had it enjoyed, this indecipherable object, whose secret, he was sure, would turn out to be as obvious as Poe's purloined letter.

Harding was waiting for him. He recounted without dramatics how the captain of the *Alice* and the freckled sailor had been arrested and charged with conspiracy, illegal exercise of authority, fraud, and misrepresentation; they'd thrown the book at them, he said. No lack of charges. And Harding added that he'd even managed to punch Freckles in the mouth when he admitted it was he who, suspended on a painter's rig somewhere between Coatzacoalcos and Galveston, had changed the white letters on the stern of the ship. The *Emmita* would sail in the morning at six and within forty-eight hours be in Coatzacoalcos. Could he do anything for Felix?

"Would this ring fit your finger, Captain?"

Harding observed the stone with some reservation and tried it on his finger. "Fits all right, but the boys'll have a good laugh. I'll look like a Lolla Palooza sporting a rock like this."

"Like who?"

"Guess you didn't read the funny papers? Forget it. Before your time. Don't worry. To think they insulted me that way, my ship, my name, my reputation, everything. They retire sick old men, you know. My friend, I love the *Emmita* like a woman. She's everything I have in the world. It's like those bastards buggered her. Who do I give the ring to?"

"Do you know *The Tempest?*"

"I've known 'em all." The old man laughed.

"A boy and girl will be waiting for you at the dock at Coatzacoalcos. They will ask you if you've come on behalf of Prospero, and you'll tell them yes. They'll ask you where Prospero is, and you'll say in his cell. Give them the ring."

"Prospero," repeated Harding. "In his cell."

"The sea has its sadness, doesn't it, Harding?"

"Like a mother who outlives her children," the old man replied.

30 HE HAD NO DIFFICULTY identifying the sounds in the Rossettis' room. When he returned from Galveston, he left his door ajar and called me in Mexico City to relay the quotes from *The Tempest*. Before hanging up, he added with the blend of defiance and humor so typical of my friend Felix Maldonado: *"Your sister's drown'd, Laertes."*

"Too much of water hast thou, poor Ophelia," I replied, first because I wasn't willing to be outdone by Felix, but also because it was my way of letting him know that, as with him, my personal emotions occasionally became entangled with my professional obligations, and that, like me, Felix must learn to keep the two separate. *"And therefore I forbid my tears."*

Felix held the receiver to the open door so I could hear the movement of doctors and nurses and resuscitation equipment; apparently, he even expected the odors of antiseptic and medication to flow through the telephone lines from Houston to Mexico City. It was I who hung up.

Felix slept peacefully; he had sufficient evidence that Angelica was the dominant one and that Rossetti wouldn't make a move until his wife had recovered. A drowning person either dies instantly or is instantly saved. Death by water admits no twilight zone; it is black, immediate night, or day as luminous as the one Felix discovered when he opened the drapes. A wind from the north was sweeping the heavy gray clouds toward the sea, washing clean the urban profile of Houston. I, on the other hand, dreamed uneasily of my dead sister, Angelica, floating in a river like a sylvan siren adorned with fantastic garlands.

About three in the afternoon, the Rossettis left their room, Angelica leaning heavily on her husband's arm, and entered the Cadillac waiting at the hotel entrance. Felix again followed in the Pinto. The limousine stopped before a building soaring toward the sky like an arrow of copper-colored crystal. The couple got out, and Felix double-parked, so as not to lose sight of them, and hurried into the building, just as the Rossettis were getting into the elevator.

He watched to see where the elevator stopped and then consulted the building directory to match the stops with the names of the offices on those floors. His job was facilitated by the fact that the Rossettis had taken the express elevator that served only the floors above the fifteenth. But he couldn't complain of lack of variety: investment brokers, import–export companies, architectural firms, the private offices of lawyers and insurance underwriters, businesses serving the shipping and port industries, petroleum technologists, and public-relations firms.

The elevator had stopped on the top floor, the thirtieth, and Felix considered that the Rossettis' mission might be important enough to have taken them to the penthouse executive suites. But that was the simplest deduction, and surely those two had thought of that. Felix read the names of the offices on the twenty-ninth floor. Again, lawyers' names in lengthy lists strung together by chains of hierarchical snakes, & & &; Berkeley Building Associates; Connally Interests; Wonderland Enterprises, Inc.

"Is there a communicating stairway between the thirtieth and twenty-ninth floors?" he asked the Chicano doorman.

"Right. There's an inside stairway that serves the whole building. With fire-retardant paint and everything. This is a safe building with all the latest. It's only been open about six months."

"Thanks."

"For nothin', *paisá.*"

Felix took the elevator to the twenty-ninth floor and walked to an opaque glass door with the painted sign WON-DERLAND ENTERPRISES, INC. He was struck by the old-fashioned glass door in such modern surroundings; all the other offices discreetly announced their functions with tiny copper plates on doors of fine wood. He entered an ultra-air-conditioned reception room furnished with light leather couches and dwarf palms in terra-cotta pots. Presiding over all this from behind a half-moon desk was a blonde with the face of a newborn kitten, a kitten precariously teetering on the brink of forty. She was reading a copy of *Viva,* and she looked Felix over as if he were the centerfold in living color.

More than her question, her look invited him. "Hello, handsome. What's on your mind?"

Felix looked in vain for a mirror, to confirm the receptionist's compliment. "I have something to sell."

"I like things free," said the secretary, grinning like the Cheshire cat, and Felix took as a good sign the blonde's unconscious literary allusions.

"I'd like to see your boss."

The feline blonde pouted. "Oh. You're really on business, are you? Whom shall I say is calling?"

"The White Knight." Felix smiled.

The secretary stared at him suspiciously and automatically slid one hand beneath the desk; her magazine fell open to a nude man sitting in a swing. "Bossman busy right now. Take a seat," the blonde said coldly, hastily closing her magazine.

"Tell him I'd like to join the tea party," said Felix, approaching the receptionist's desk.

"You get away from me, you dirty Mex, I know your kind, all glitter and no gold. You ain't foolin' this little girl."

With his best James Cagney grimace, and wishing he had a grapefruit in his hand, Felix Cinema-buff flat-handed the dish face of the jittery blonde, now more humiliated than Mae Clarke; he pressed the button she was trying to conceal beneath a freckled hand that revealed both her age and her intention, and the leather-covered door swung open. The secretary shrieked an obscenity, and Felix entered an office even colder than the reception room.

"Good afternoon, Señor Maldonado. We were expecting

you. Please close the door," said a man with a head too large for his medium stature, a leonine head with a lock of gray hair falling over a high brow. Fine, arched, playful eyebrows lent an air of irony to icy gray eyes, brilliant behind the thickest eyelids Felix had ever seen outside the cage of a hippopotamus. The body was strikingly slim for a man of some sixty years, and the blue pin-striped suit was expensive and elegant.

"Please forgive Dolly," he added courteously. "She's stupid, but lovable."

"Everyone seems to be expecting me," said Felix, looking toward Rossetti, still in white, perched on the arm of Angelica's light leather chair. She was disguised in black sunglasses, her hair hidden beneath a silk kerchief.

"How did you . . . ?" said Angelica in alarm, her voice harsh from having swallowed so much chlorine.

"We were very careful, Trevor," Rossetti said, hoping to divest himself of any blame.

"Now you know my name, thanks to our friend's indiscretion." The man with the thin lips and the curved nose of a Roman senator spoke with edgy affability. Yes, that's what he reminds me of, Felix thought. Agrippa Septimus & Severus fortuitously dressed by Hart, Schaffner & Marx.

"I thought you were the Mad Hatter," said Felix in English, in response to Trevor's unidentifiable, too-perfect Spanish, as neutral as the speech of a Colombian oligarch.

Trevor laughed and said in an impeccable, British public-school accent, "That would make him the Dormouse and his spouse a slightly drowned Alice. Drowned in a teacup, of course. And you, my friend, would have to assume the role of the March Hare."

His smile was replaced by a tight, unpleasant grimace that transformed his face into a mask of tragedy. "March Hares are easily captured," he continued in Spanish. "The poor things are trapped between two fatal dates, the Ides of March and April first, the day of fools and dupes."

156

"As long as we stay in Wonderland, I don't give a *sombrilla* what the dates are."

Trevor laughed again, thrusting his hands into the pockets of his pin-striped suit. "I adore your Mexican sayings. It's true, of course. An umbrella is of very little value in a tropical country, unless one fears sunstroke. On the other hand, in countries where it rains constantly . . ."

"You certainly should know; the English even sign their peace treaties with umbrellas."

"And then win the war and save civilization," replied Trevor, his eyes invisible behind thickened eyelids. "But let's not mix our metaphors. Welcome to Wonderland. I congratulate you. Where were you trained?"

"In Disneyland."

"Very good. I like your sense of humor. Very like ours. Which undoubtedly explains why we chose such similar codes: we, Lewis Carroll, and you, William Shakespeare. On the other hand"—he stared scornfully at the Rossettis —"can you imagine these two trying to communicate via D'Annunzio? Out of the question."

"We have Dante," Rossetti countered weakly.

"Oh, be quiet," said Trevor, the threat underlined by the immobility of his hands in his jacket pockets. "You and your wife have done nothing right. You overplayed everything, as if you'd wandered into an opera by Donizetti. You completely missed the point that the only way to proceed secretly is to proceed openly."

He reserved particular scorn for Angelica. "Disguising yourself as Sara Klein so no one would know you'd left Mexico, and hoping everyone would be racking their brains looking for a dead woman. Bah! Balderdash!" Trevor's Spanish was curiously archaic, as if he'd learned Spanish watching comedies of manners in Madrid.

"Maldonado was in Coatzacoalcos, and getting close to the ring. He's a wild man, Trevor; you should have seen him in my house the other evening, the way he treated

Bernstein. He was mad about Sara, I only wanted to stir him up a little," said Angelica, with strident and artificial energy.

Trevor withdrew his hand from his pocket and slapped Angelica squarely across the mouth; her jaw dropped open as if she were again drowning, and Rossetti jumped to his feet with all the indignation of a Latin caballero.

"Imbeciles," said Trevor, through tight lips. "I should have chosen more efficient traitors. My own fault. The lady allows the ring to be taken from her while she's imitating Esther Williams. The gentleman doesn't dare strike me because he's hoping to collect three ways, and the money means more to him than his honor."

Rossetti, pale and trembling, resumed his position beside Angelica. He tried to put his arm around his wife, but she shrugged him off.

Trevor turned to Felix as if inviting him to a cricket match. "My friend, that ring holds absolutely no value for you. I give you my word of honor."

"I place about as much stock in the word of an English gentleman as in that of a Latin caballero," Felix commented with the counterpart of English phlegm—Indian fatalism.

"We can avoid many disagreeable scenes if you return it to me immediately."

"You surely don't believe I brought it with me."

"No. But you know where it is. I trust your intelligence. Try to get it back for me."

"How much will my life be worth if I do?"

"Ask our little pair here. They know that I pay better than anyone."

"The stakes may go up," Rossetti managed to say with painful bravado.

Trevor looked at him with amazement and scorn. "Do you think you can collect four times? Greedy little bastard!"

Felix observed the Director General's private secretary with interest. "That's right, Rossetti. You can collect from the Director General because you convinced him you were informing on Bernstein's activities; you collect from Bernstein because he believes you were his accomplice, and for revealing the Director General's plans to him; you collect from Trevor here by informing against your other two benefactors. And if you really want to sing, I'll pay you more than the other three together. Or are you planning to return to Mexico, inform on us all, and get out of this with both your honor and your bankroll intact?"

"You bastard, why did you have to get in our way?" Angelica's question was rhetorical.

"How much is the famous ring worth?" Felix asked her, his voice equally neutral.

Regaining control of himself, it was the private secretary who answered Felix, ingratiatingly, as if he'd discovered hitherto unseen virtues in this obscure chief from the Bureau of Cost Analysis. "I don't know. I only know that Bernstein had arranged everything in Coatzacoalcos so that Angelica could take it to the United States."

"And instead of delivering it to Bernstein's accomplice, you double-crossed him and brought it to Trevor."

"It's true," Trevor interjected before the Rossettis could respond, "that my friends the Rossettis, how shall I say it? diverted the course of normal events to bring the ring to me. Alas, you intercepted it. Whatever the case, Bernstein's consignee must be biting his nails somewhere on this vast continent, awaiting our Angelica's arrival on another ghost tanker we'll call, shall we—not to deviate from our previous allusions—the *Red Queen*. You know, the one who demanded the head of the Knave of Hearts for stealing her tarts. I must ask that you take us to the missing ring, Señor Maldonado."

"I repeat, I do not have it."

"I'm aware of that. Where is it?"

"Traveling, slowly but surely, like Alice's Mock Turtle."

"Where, Maldonado?" said Trevor, his voice steely.

"Paradoxically, to the very place that Bernstein intended," said Felix, not flickering an eyelash.

"I told you, Trevor." Angelica's voice was guttural, and hysterical. "He's a convert to Judaism; it's not for nothing I'm one of Ruth's good friends. He was bound to align himself with the Jews. He's Bernstein's former student, he knows Mann, and he's sent him the ring. He already knows Bernstein didn't kill Sara . . ."

Trevor feigned resignation before Angelica's unrestrained babble.

Rossetti attempted to soothe his wife. "Don't say more than you mean to. Please be more discreet, darling. We have to go back to Mexico . . ."

"With Bernstein's money, and Trevor's, we have enough to live somewhere other than that land of trained fleas," retorted the ungovernable Angelica.

"I promised you that we'd go wherever you wanted, darling." Rossetti was kindlier by the minute, though more than half his kindness was reserved for himself.

"I'm sick and tired of watching you crawl up one bureaucratic step every six years! What will you be in twelve years? Bill collector? Milk inspector? What?"

"Angelica, we should at least spend a few months . . ."

"Don't you ever get tired of living off my money . . . you pimp!"

"I said a few months, until everything gets back to normal. That's only prudent, Angelica, we'll have plenty of money . . ."

"But Trevor slapped me. Who's going to repay that, you ball-less wonder," shrieked Angelica, tearing off the black sunglasses to reveal her chlorine-streaked eyes.

"I will, if only you'll shut up," said Felix, and buried his right fist in Rossetti's stomach at the same instant the private secretary took a knife from his pocket and pressed it to release the switchblade.

Rossetti's gaze glittered with every imaginable threat, as,

moaning and doubled over with pain, he fell on the sofa. Felix picked up the knife and pressed down the blade between a nail file and a corkscrew.

"Perfect." Trevor smiled. "Neapolitan technology. Clean nails for the body beautiful, along with a sure way to open bottles in airplanes without fear of being poisoned. Right up Rossetti's alley. What do you think, Maldonado? Was he going to slit Angelica's throat or demand that I hand over the promised money?"

"He was going to pin back my wings like a butterfly's," Felix replied coldly.

"Oh, yes?" Trevor lifted arched eyebrows. "May I inquire why?"

"First, because I was witness to his wife humiliating him."

"As well as I."

"You're not Latin. It's a matter of clans."

"And second?"

"Because I'm the only person who might betray him. All the rest—you, Bernstein, the Director, Angelica—have good reason to keep his secrets."

"You're sure of that? Well, it doesn't matter. We must be grateful to our friends for this edifying conjugal scene."

"You're a bachelor?" Felix smiled.

"Witness my good health." Trevor returned the smile.

"He's a fag," spat Angelica.

"Politics has no sex, my dear, and because you believed the contrary, you have allowed yourselves to become embroiled in futile passions. Let's get to the point, Maldonado. If you're lying to me, you're wasting your time. The ring is useless to your side. First of all, to use it requires something beyond Neapolitan or Aztec technology. Examine it to your heart's content, the ring will tell you nothing. If you shatter it, you automatically destroy the information it contains. And, finally, you already possess the information."

"Then it won't matter if the stone is destroyed," said Felix, wondering why Trevor was telling him all this.

The Englishman provided the answer. "You're not interested in knowing what we want to know about you? Don't be so elementary, my dear Maldonado."

"The ring will be delivered to Mann," said Felix, clutching at the straw of Angelica's gaffe.

"Blast and damn!" exclaimed Trevor, with another of his Wodehouse comedy expressions. "To *whom?*"

"To Mann, Bernstein's accomplice," Felix repeated.

Trevor's laugh was forced. *"Man,* not Mann. But you speak English."

"Don't let him fool you, Felix. Bernstein told us we were to take the ring to Mann in New York," cried Angelica, totally disoriented in her allegiances, divided in her excitement between menace and alarm, pity and scorn for her husband, the misdirected attempt to blackmail Trevor and her confused belief that by punching Rossetti Felix had somehow avenged her for Trevor's slap. Felix had a vision of Angelica in a mental hospital. They'd be afraid to admit her.

"All right," said Trevor before Angelica could speak again, and, moving diagonally like a Bishop in a chess game, countered, "The lady wants to be paid and be on her way, is that it?"

"Exactly!" cried Angelica.

All four stared at one another in silence. Trevor pressed a button and Dolly appeared.

"Dolly, the lady is leaving. I hope her husband will follow her. They are very tiresome."

"I'll make you a present of him," said Angelica, motioning toward the groaning figure of Rossetti. "I'll take the money."

"But you didn't do your job, Angelica," Trevor chided. "I don't have the ring."

"What about the risks we ran? I was nearly drowned.

You promised us the money, no matter what. You promised, Trevor. You said the risks involved merited it."

"Yes, Angelica, you are correct."

Trevor opened a drawer, removed a fat envelope, and handed it to Rossetti's wife. "Count it carefully. I don't want any complaints later."

Angelica greedily thumbed through the green bills, her lips moving silently. "Very well, Trevor. Business is business."

"And your husband?"

"Get him a job in a pizzeria," said Angelica, and, following Dolly, exited with her usual arrogance.

 "WELL." Trevor inhaled deeply. "Now we can talk in earnest."

"What about him?" Felix nodded toward Rossetti.

"Have you ever asked yourself, Maldonado, who the one guilty party in all this might be?" Trevor sighed.

"Guilt seems to be the one thing in this affair that's evenly divided," Felix replied without humor.

"No, you don't understand what I mean. Gather together all the guilt, yours and mine, the Director General's and his boy Ayub's, Bernstein's, plus that of the lady who just left us. That adds to a lot of guilt, don't you agree?"

Rossetti was shaking now, and starting to rise to his feet. "No, Trevor, no . . ."

"The wise thing, the clean thing, would be to pile all the guilt on one head, to make one person responsible. I'm looking at that person right now. Do you see him, too?"

"It's all the same to me," said Felix. "But there is one thing I don't want you to make Rossetti responsible for."

Trevor took Rossetti gently by the shoulder and forced him back on the sofa. "Ah, yes. And what is that?"

"Angelica, Angelica," Rossetti was mumbling grotesquely, his face hidden in his hands.

"The death of Sara Klein," said Felix. "I'll take care of that."

"Agreed. Now listen to me. Look out those windows. Houston isn't a beautiful city. It's something better, a powerful city. See that blue glass skyscraper? It's the headquarters of the world's most advanced petroleum technology. It belongs to the Arabs, and it cost them five hundred million dollars. See the Gulf Bank sign? Eighty percent of their transactions consist of managing petroleum dollars for their Arab clients. Did you see the names of all the legal firms in this building? All working for Arab money. I invite you to take a stroll through any company in this building. Every one is dedicated to a single proposition, participation in the development programs of Arab countries; they're gambling two hundred billion dollars. Stop blubbering, Rossetti. What I'm saying should be of interest to you."

"Angelica . . ."

"You'll be joining her soon. Be patient. First, you'll have to justify my having given her the money. Half of all the commercial transactions between the American private sector and the Arab world are realized in Houston: four billion dollars annually. From here flow pipelines, liquid-gas plants, petrochemical technology, agricultural know-how, even university professors, to the Arab world. One single firm of Texas architects has signed contracts for six billion dollars of exports annually from the United States to the Arab countries."

Trevor clasped his hands behind an impeccably tailored back and contemplated the face of Houston beneath the newly cloudy, dirty, hot sky, as if he were observing a field of cement mushrooms nurtured by black rain. "This building, right here where we are standing, is the property of the

164

Saudis. Do I bore you with my statistics?" He turned and directed his tight smile toward Felix.

"If you're trying to impress me with your audacity, I admit you're succeeding," said Felix.

"Audacity?" Trevor inquired sarcastically.

"You're the one who said it," Maldonado replied. "The real secrets are those that are open secrets. Houston is an ideal site for an Arab secret agent."

Both Trevor and Rossetti laughed, and regarded Felix like a pair of wolves regarding a lamb.

"Tell him the truth, Rossetti," ordered Trevor, more than ever the Roman senator.

"Bernstein told me to deliver the ring to Trevor," said Rossetti, more sure of himself now. "Mann doesn't exist. It was a code name."

"Madame Rossetti earned her 'bundle' in good faith." Trevor smiled. "The ring, therefore, is not on the way to the mythic Mr. Mann in New York."

"The things you learn." Felix's voice was drowsy but his internal clock began to tick more rapidly. "I didn't realize that Wonderland had its capital in Jerusalem."

"I lend my professional services," Trevor said in a velvet voice.

"To the highest bidder?"

Trevor extended his arms in an expansive gesture rare to him, as if embracing the office, the building, the entire city of Houston. "There's no mystery. On this occasion, and in this place, I represent Arab interests."

"But Bernstein sent *you* the ring."

"Don't recriminate against your former professor. He knows me as an Israeli agent, and made me the ring's recipient in all good faith. He doesn't know that I practice the virtue of simultaneity of allegiances. Can you distinguish between Tweedledum and Tweedledee?"

"I know that if you crush one, the other will fall like Humpty Dumpty."

"Except that all the king's horses and all the king's men would have to put me back together again. I'm too valuable to both parties. Don't try to crack the egg, Maldonado, or you're the one who'll end up as an omelette. Remember that if it were my wish you would never leave this room alive," said Trevor, pacing like a cat on the thick office rug.

"You can't kill me," said Felix.

"Poppycock! Are you immortal, my dear Hare?"

"No. I'm dead and buried. Visit the Jardín Cemetery in Mexico City someday and see for yourself."

"Do you realize that you're proposing to me the ideal way to kill you without leaving a trace? Who'd be looking for a 'dead' man who's already dead?"

"But if I die, no one will find Bernstein's ring."

"You think not?" said the Englishman, his face more innocent than that of a Dickens heroine. "All I have to do is retrace, link by link, the chain of events you so imprudently ruptured. The actors in the plot are perfectly interchangeable. Particularly the dead ones."

Felix couldn't control his pounding blood, the invisible enemy betraying the impassivity of his face. He was grateful for the scars that helped sustain the rigidity of his mask. Felix had had no physical contact with Trevor, but now the Englishman was affectionately patting his hand, and Felix flinched at the dry, sweatless touch.

"Come now, don't be afraid. Consider the game I'm proposing. Let us call it, in honor of the Holy Patroness of your nation, Operation Guadalupe. A good Arabic name, Guadalupe. It means river of wolves."

Even without intending it, Trevor's features assumed a lupine expression. "But let us not dwell on philology; let us consider, instead, probable scenarios. Perhaps brutal scenarios. Combine the elements in any way you desire, my dear Maldonado. The perfectly calculated pretext of the Yom Kippur War and its equally calculated effect: the rapid acceleration of oil prices; Europe and Japan brought to their knees, once and for all stripped of any pretense of independence; Congress's granting funds for the construction of the Alaska pipeline because of the oil panic, and the multiplication by millions of the earnings of the Five Sisters. Listen, and marvel: in 1974 alone, Exxon's profits rose 23.6 percent, as compared to 1.76 percent in the ten previous years; those of Standard Oil rose 30.92 percent, compared to 0.55 percent during the preceding decade."

He relinquished Felix's hand and turned toward the window. "Look outside, and see the evidence of petrodollars. Let's say we play Israel against the Arabs and the Arabs against Israel. Houston is the Arab capital of the United States, and New York the Jewish capital; the petrodollars flow in here and out there. Does *anyone* know for whom he's working? But let's confine ourselves to our game. All scenarios are possible. Even—or especially—one for a new war. Depending on the circumstances, we can close the New York valve and suffocate Israel, or close the Houston valve and freeze Arab funds. Follow the moves in our game, please. Imagine an isolated Israel plunged headlong into a war of desperation. Imagine the Arabs refusing to sell oil to the West. Choose your script, Maldonado; who would intervene first, the Soviets or the Americans?"

"You're speaking of a confrontation as if it were a good thing."

"It is a good thing. The present state of coexistence was born of the confrontation in Cuba. Conditions resulting from being on the brink of war provide the necessary shock that prolongs an armed peace for fifteen or twenty more years. A generation. The real danger is that the peace is weakened in the absence of the periodical crises that revitalize it. Then we enter the realm of chance, stupor, and accident. A well-prepared crisis is manageable, as Kissinger demonstrated at the beginning of the October War. On the other hand, an accident brought about by the simple material pressure of accumulated arms that are fast becoming obsolete is something that cannot be controlled."

"You're a perverted humanist, Trevor. And your imaginary scenarios appear every day in newspaper editorials."

"But also in the councils of the nuclear powers. What is essential is that we take all eventualities into account. None must be excluded. Including, my dear friend, the nearby presence of Mexican oil. That's more than a scenario, it appears to be the only solution at hand."

"And is Mexico not to be consulted?"

"There are collaborationists in your country, just as there were in Czechoslovakia. Some are already in power. It would not be difficult to install a junta of Quislings in the National Palace, especially during a time of international emergency, and in a country without open political processes. Mexican political cabals are like amoebas: they fuse, divide, subdivide, and fuse again in the obscurity of the Palace, without the slightest awareness on the part of the public."

"From time to time, we Mexicans awake."

"Pancho Villa couldn't have resisted a rain of napalm."

"But Juárez could, as Ho Chi Minh did."

"Save your patriotic exhortations, Maldonado. Mexico can't sit forever on the most formidable oil reserves in the hemisphere, a veritable lake of black gold stretching from the Gulf of California to the Caribbean Sea. We simply want to be sure that Mexico profits from it. For the good, preferably. All this can be done without disturbing President Cárdenas's sacred nationalization. Oil can be denationalized, by Jove! without changing appearances."

"It won't please Our Lady of Guadalupe that you're using her name for this musical comedy." Felix was only half joking.

"Don't be difficult, Maldonado. What's at stake here is much bigger than your poor corrupt country drowning in poverty, unemployment, inflation, and ineptitude. Look outside again, I beg you. This once belonged to you. You did nothing with it. Look what it's become without you."

"That's the second time I've heard that song. It's beginning to bore me."

"Listen to me carefully, and repeat everything to your chiefs. The contingency plans of the Western world require precise information about the extent, the nature, and the location of the Mexican oil reserves. It is vital that we anticipate every possibility."

"And that's the information Bernstein was sending from Coatzacoalcos?"

Perhaps Trevor would have answered, perhaps not. In any case, he was denied the opportunity. Dolly burst into the office, her kitten face transformed, as if she were being chased by a pack of vicious bulldogs. "Oh, God, Mr. Mann, a terrible thing, Mr. Mann, a horrible accident. Look out the window . . ."

Felix couldn't see the look exchanged between Trevor/Mann and Rossetti. Dolly opened the window and the conditioned air flowed out, along with the momentarily frozen words of the double agent; the three men and the weeping woman leaned out into the sticky Houston air, and Dolly pointed with a poorly manicured finger.

In the street, a swarm of human flies was gathering around a body sprawled like a broken puppet. Several police cars were parked nearby, sirens howling, and an ambulance was threading through the traffic on the corner of San Jacinto.

Trevor/Mann slammed the window shut and told Dolly in a nasal Midwest accent: "Call the cops, stupid. I'm holding the dago for the premeditated murder of his wife."

Mauricio Rossetti's mouth dropped open, but no sound emerged. Trevor/Mann had an automatic in his hand and was pointing it straight at Rossetti's heart, but it was an unnecessary gesture. Rossetti had crumpled on the sofa, and was weeping like a child. Trevor/Mann ignored him,

169

but held on to the pistol. It was ugly in his scaly hand.

"Console yourself, Rossetti. The Mexican authorities will ask for your extradition, and it will be granted. There is no death penalty in Mexico, and the law is understandingly benign when a husband kills his own wife. And you won't talk, Rossetti, because you'd rather be considered a murderer than a traitor. Think this over while you're luxuriating in the Lecumberri prison. And consider, too, that you're well rid of a terrible harpy."

Trevor waved the pistol in Felix Maldonado's direction. "You may leave, Señor Maldonado. Bear me no rancor. After all, you've won this round. You have the ring. I repeat: it is of no value to you. Go quietly, and ruminate on how Rossetti gathered facts little by little, partially from the offices of the Director General, partially from Minatitlán and other centers of the Pemex operation, and delivered the raw information to Bernstein. It was your professor who put everything in order and turned it into coherent cybernetic data. Don't worry; Rossetti prefers the responsibility of a crime resulting from conjugal problems to one caused by political indiscretions. On the other hand, our unfortunate Angelica, now united with her homonyms, will not be enjoying her customary privilege of unbridled chatter."

"And what about me, aren't you afraid I'll talk?" said Felix, with sinking spirits.

Trevor/Mann laughed, and again assumed a British accent. "By gad, sir, don't push your luck too far. Talk is precisely what I *want* you to do. Tell everything. Transmit our warnings to whoever it is who employs you. Allow me to demonstrate my good faith. Do you want to know who killed Sara Klein?"

Felix could only nod, humiliated before the assurance of the man with the features of a Roman senator, the stubborn lock of hair, and the anachronistic interjections. Merely by mentioning her name, Trevor/Mann was verbally pawing

Sara, the way Simon Ayub had physically pawed her in the mortuary.

"Look to the nun." A veil like ashes masked his gray eyes.

"And another thing, Señor Maldonado. Don't try to return here with bad intentions. Within a few hours, Wonderland Enterprises will have disappeared. There will be no trace either of this office or of Dolly or of myself, your servant, as you Mexicans say with such curious courtesy. Good afternoon, Señor Maldonado. Or, to quote your favorite author, remember when you think of the Rossettis that ambition should be made of sterner stuff, and when you think of me, remember that we are all honorable men. Pip, pip!"

He bowed slightly toward Felix Maldonado.

32 AGAIN he was driving toward Galveston, pursued now by a black angel of presentiment but also driven by the desire to put the greatest possible distance between him and Angelica's horrible death. He had been assured in the offices of the Port Authority that the *Emmita* would dock punctually in Coatzacoalcos at five o'clock on the morning of August 19. Captain Harding's schedule went like clockwork. Felix drove by the little gray house beside the exhausted, oily waters of the Gulf. The door was unlocked. He went in, and smelled tobacco and beer gone flat and scraps of ham sandwich in the garbage. He resisted his longing to spend the night there, far from Houston and Trevor/Mann and the Rossettis, one very dead, one a walking corpse. He was afraid his absence from the Hotel Warwick might cause suspicion, so a little after midnight he returned to Houston.

For the same reasons, he decided to stay at the hotel through Wednesday. He bought a return ticket to Mexico City for Thursday afternoon. By then, the *Emmita* would have reached Coatzacoalcos and Rosita and Emiliano would have received the ring from Harding's hands. Felix engaged a cabana by the swimming pool, sunned, swam, and had a club sandwich and coffee for lunch. He went in swimming several times, hoping to cleanse his memory of Angelica, but he kept his eyes open underwater, afraid he would find her broken body at the bottom of the pool.

Everything seemed normal in the hotel, and the Rossettis' room was quietly emptied of their belongings and occupied by another couple. Felix could hear them from the balcony; they spoke English and were talking about their children in Salt Lake City. It was as if Mauricio and Angelica had never been in Houston. Felix faded into the protective coloring of the hotel and took advantage of the dead hours to try to order his thoughts, an undertaking that led nowhere.

Thursday afternoon, he left behind him the burning plains and humid skies of Texas. Soon the sterile earth of northern Mexico dissolved into dry, dark peaks, and these yielded before the truncated volcanoes of the center of the Republic, indistinguishable in form from the ancient pyramids that perhaps lay beneath their petrified lava. At six o'clock in the evening, the Air France jet hurled itself down into the circle of mountains half hidden in the lethargic haze of the Mexican capital.

Felix took a taxi to the Suites de Génova, where they asked whether he wanted the same room. Thanks to his memorable tips, they fawned over him as they led him to the apartment where Sara Klein had been murdered. The thin and oily employee ventured the comment that Felix looked very well after his trip. As he removed the white sombrero he'd bought in the airport at Coatzacoalcos, Felix confirmed in the bathroom mirror that his hair was beginning to grow back thick and curly and his eyelids had lost their puffiness; only the scars from the incisions were still noticeable. Somehow his moustache was obliterating the memory of the operation and returning to him the face that, if not exactly his own, more and more resembled the face of his private joke with Ruth, the Velázquez self-portrait.

Thinking of Ruth, he almost telephoned her. He'd forgotten her all the time he'd been away; he'd had to put her out of his mind; if not, that most intimate and commonplace of all relationships might have diverted him from the mission I'd commended to him. He was also restrained by the fact that to his wife he was a dead man. Ruth had attended the burial in the Jardín Cemetery organized by the Director General and Simon Ayub. The widow Maldonado had not had much time to accustom herself to her new role. As Felix had felt he must reserve a sacred moment with Sara's body, he felt now he must reserve a special moment for his reunion with Ruth. A disembodied voice over the telephone would be too much for such a domestic woman, a woman who solved all his practical problems, who prepared his breakfasts and pressed his suits.

His feeling for Sara, living or dead, was a different matter, something akin to the sublimation of adventure itself. She was the most fervent, but also the most secretly guarded, motivation for his actions. My instructions had been clear. No personal emotion was to stand in our way. There is no intelligence mission that does not inevitably evoke one's emotions and weave an invisible but inescapable web between the objective world we set out to control and the subjective world that, whether we wish it or not, controls us. Had Felix realized during this strange week that, no matter how wide-ranging, events never move us far from the place where we are our own hosts, and that no external enemy is greater than the one residing within us?

Later Felix told me that as he was dialing my number after his return from Houston he remembered the joking way he'd announced Angelica's death before it had occurred: *"Your sister's drown'd, Laertes."* I'd set aside my personal feelings, although at that point Angelica's role in this intrigue was ambiguous. He felt he didn't need to say anything more when he telephoned me from the Suites de Génova, didn't have to find a quote from Shakespeare to tell me that, instead of drowning, Ophelia had died a broken doll upon the steamy pavement of a Texas city.

"When shall we two meet again?"

"When the battle's lost and won."

"But tell us, do you hear whether we have had any loss at sea or no?"

"Ships are but boards, sailors but men: there be land-rats and water-rats, land-thieves, and water-thieves."

"What tell'st thou me of robbing?"

"The boy gives warning. He is a saucy boy. Go to, go to. He is in Venice."

I hung up. I had noted with uneasiness an impatience and reticence in Felix's voice. I had the feeling he was hiding something from me, and I feared that. Our organization was very new, it was testing its wings, and no one, not even I, could pride himself on having the tough skin of our Soviet, European, or North American counterparts. That accursed subjectivity was, irrationally, seeping through the cold sieve of the means which should have been identical to the ends. The Golden Rule of espionage *is* that the means justify the ends. I couldn't imagine a single individual on the long list of those we emulated, from Fouché to Ashenden, perturbed by any personal emotion; they would brush sentiment aside like a mosquito. But it was also true that no Mexican spy would ever come in from the cold; the suggestion, climatologically speaking, was ludicrous, and I imagined my poor friend Felix Maldonado looking for a refrigerator to crawl into in Galveston or Coatzacoalcos.

I lighted my pipe and, not in the least at random, opened my Oxford edition of the complete works of Shakespeare to the graveyard scene in *Hamlet*. As I began to read again, I told myself that was the only thing I could do, to begin again where I had left off when Felix telephoned. Laertes is telling the Priest to lay Ophelia in the earth so that from her fair and unpolluted flesh violets might spring. The Priest refuses to say the Requiem for a suicide; the soul of Ophelia will not depart in peace. Laertes rebukes him; Ophelia, he says, shall be a ministering angel when he lies howling. This fearful curse is followed by the equally terrible action of Laertes. He asks the earth, that of the grave, and also that of the world, to hold off a while till he has once more caught his sister in his arms. He leaps into the grave beside the body of Ophelia. Hamlet, in spite of his emotion, watches this scene with strange passivity, the usual passivity of this actor who is the always distanced observer of his own tragedy. The whole of the Renaissance is contained in this scene. Man, in his world, has discovered an excessive energy that he hurls like a challenge into the face of the heavens; at the same time, he has discovered his insignificance within the gigantic cosmos, and knows he is smaller even than Providence had augured. Only an impassive irony like Hamlet's can reestablish the equilibrium; others judge him mad.

I watched the curling smoke ascend toward my library ceiling. In spite of her name, I could not imagine Angelica dispensing the favors of heaven to man. But, in this story, which of the women whose threads were always broken before they reached my hands deserved divine favors? Of Sara and Mary and Ruth, all Jewish, which would look into the face of God? If Angelica were not Ophelia, which would be our Ariadne? If I were an inglorious Laertes, would my friend Maldonado know to be a Hamlet with method in his madness, or would he lose himself within the labyrinth of modern Minotaurs?

It was one of those moments—and there were many more than I imagined then—in which Felix and I were on a telepathic wavelength. Sara was present, dead or living, mysterious in the persistence of her reality, strangely close in her absence; so, too, Ruth, whom we must not frighten by telephoning, even if she suffered a while longer; when the time came, we would explain things calmly, to the degree that explanation was possible. And Mary, why hadn't we been thinking of her?

I feared I was falling into the greatest of detective-novel commonplaces, *cherchez la femme.* I closed my book, and my eyes. There was so little time. I thought about my sister, Angelica.

33 ON THE OTHER HAND, Felix did not check his second impulse; he dialed Mary Benjamin's number, and a servant answered. "The señora may be busy, may I say who's calling?"

Mary was the one woman who could take it: "Felix Maldonado."

She was listening on the extension; a light click had betrayed her presence on the line, and immediately he heard Mary's irritated voice. "Whoever you are, I don't appreciate your sick jokes."

"Don't hang up," said Felix, with an affectionate inflection Mary should recognize. "It's me."

"I told you . . ." Mary's voice was still irritated, but slightly tinged with doubt and fear.

Felix laughed. "You sound a little shaky; this is the first time I ever heard that from you."

"There's always a first time." Mary was struggling to compose herself. "Felix was very big on black humor, wasn't he?"

"Prove it."

"Don't be stupid, I don't have a televiewer on my phone yet."

"Génova Suites. Room 301. Eleven-thirty tonight. Be there. The last time, you stood me up." Felix hung up.

Italian restaurants abound in the Zona Rosa. The Osteria and Alfredo's, facing one another across the arcade between Londres, Hamburgo, and Génova, sounded too Roman, and the Focolare on Hamburgo, too generic, so Felix walked toward La Góndola on the corner of Génova and Estrasburgo. He says he was thinking of me. For the first time, he had deliberately betrayed my instructions. He needed a woman, too much adrenaline had been pumping through his body the last few days; he hadn't had a woman since Licha. It meant coming out in the open, but after ten years without touching her, he wanted to go to bed with Mary Benjamin. Mary Benjamin was exactly what he needed, a hot, passionate bitch, and if he'd consulted me, I would have racked my brain to come up with a quote from Bill Shakesprick to tell him to get himself a call girl in one of the hotels in the Zona Rosa. But Felix had other things in mind.

There weren't many people in La Góndola that night, but it was filled with penetrating odors of tomato and garlic and basil. Emiliano and Rosita sat facing each other, hands clasped, elbows on the red-and-white-checked tablecloth. Felix sat down beside the "saucy" boy who was bringing him a warning, facing the girl with a head like a woolly black lamb. The young couple's faces betrayed their uneasiness, they could dispense with the preliminaries.

"Did Harding give you the ring?"

They shook their heads.

"What happened?" asked Felix impatiently. Mary was boiling in his blood, a soft, warm Mary was clasped between his thighs. "Did you forget the code from *The Tempest?*"

"We didn't get a chance," said Emiliano, dropping Rosita's hand. "The old man was dead."

"They killed him, Emiliano, tell him," said Rosita, playing with some toothpicks, not daring to look at Felix.

"When?" Felix asked, paralyzed within a triangle of stupor, impatience, and disbelief.

"After the tanker docked, this morning," said Emiliano, helping Rosita in the construction of a toothpick castle.

"How?"

"A machete, in the neck."

"Where was he?"

"In his cabin, probably getting ready to go ashore."

"And the ring?" Felix asked carefully; he could hear his voice rising.

"It wasn't there."

"How can you be so damn sure, my beardless friend? Did they let you search the old man? Did they let you in the cabin?"

"Hey, Feliciano," Rosita interrupted. "We're on the same side, what the hell's with you?"

Felix ducked his head to acknowledge the rebuke, and Emiliano continued. "We thought the scene was coming down pretty heavy, so we got in touch with the chief. Within a half hour, the cops were swarming all over the *Emmita,* searching everything. Not a whiff of the ring, man."

"Tell him, Emiliano, tell him about the girl."

"The mate thought the cops were looking for something else. He told them Harding kept an old silver locket hanging over his hammock, with a faded snapshot of a girl in it, signed Emmita. He couldn't believe they'd waste the old guy for such a nothing thing, though sometimes at sea they tell tales of feuds that last to the grave."

"The locket wasn't worth a penny to anyone except him," Rosita said excitedly, covering her mouth with the napkin. "It was gone, nothing but a faded circle where it used to hang."

"The fuzz pulled in the thief almost before he could turn

around. They found him a little after six, drunk out of his mind, in one of those all-night bars on the docks. He was carrying a big roll and the locket was around his neck."

"The snapshot was gone, the bum'd thrown it away," moaned Rosita. "He was trying to con some girl into going to bed with him, telling her she'd be his new sweetheart and he'd put her picture in the locket."

"They put him in jail, but when they searched him, he was clean. He said he'd found the locket on the dock, and that he'd never been on the *Emmita*. The hiring agent, though, said they'd been shorthanded and he'd signed on the *cambujo* part-time as a stevedore."

"The *cambujo?*" Felix interrupted.

Emiliano nodded. "Yeah, he usually worked in the Hotel Tropicana. He does a little bit of everything, though, even butchers beef sometimes in the market. They call him El Machete."

He looked at Felix with pride, like a student who's passed his exams with honors. "Old Bernstein packed up lock, stock, and barrel, and checked out of the hotel a half hour after the *Emmita* docked."

"The sea had its sadness," murmured Felix. He removed one toothpick and the whole rickety structure collapsed on the tablecloth.

"What?" said Rosita.

Felix shook his head. "Have you been watching Bernstein?"

"He's back home. His servant girl has orders to say he's very busy preparing his courses for the fall and he can't receive any visitors. We found out he's leaving for Israel tomorrow morning. An economy-class round-trip ticket, good for twenty-one days."

"Did the Coatzacoalcos police interrogate the *cambujo* about his connection with Bernstein?"

"The chief said it was hopeless. The prof had paid him off. Besides, El Machete knows he's well covered, and Mexican justice being what it is, he'll be out of the tank before you know it."

"Well, Bernstein has the ring, that's the one thing we can be sure of," said Felix.

"He wasn't wearing it." Rosita laughed.

Felix remembered the man who'd called himself Trevor, and Mann, and God knows how many other aliases. The only way to proceed secretly is to proceed openly.

"The chief has men watching him night and day," said Emiliano.

"Since when?" Felix inquired skeptically.

"Since before he left for Coatzacoalcos."

"Then the chief's up on everything, my brief adventure in the Tropicana, my fight with the *cambujo* on the dock, and the connection between El Machete and Bernstein."

"Don't be a masochist, man," said Emiliano, looking at Felix's face. "The situation's very fluid, and we've all got to work together. The prof hasn't made a move we don't know about, he hasn't sent any letters or packages, and he hasn't communicated with anybody. He even stopped paying his telephone bill a couple of months ago, so they'd cut off his service."

"We had to go to his house and talk to his servants; we said we were students of his," Rosita added.

"He's really putting it on that he's living like a hermit and has nothing to do with anything. He must be scared."

Emiliano was interrupted by the waiter, who placed a plate of lasagna under his nose, and a plate of spaghetti bolognese in front of Rosita.

"He even went to the Basilica to light a candle in thanksgiving for getting well so fast." Rosita laughed. "And him a Jew and all."

"He went to the Guadalupe shrine?"

Felix glared at the waiter, who was asking for his order. He'd looked the same way at Bernstein during the eyeglasses incident. The waiter, as if he'd lost his last friend, scurried away to whisper with the cashier.

"Right. When he got back from Coatzacoalcos, he went straight there from the airport," said Emiliano. "He got a candle and lighted it to Our Lady of Guadalupe."

"Does the chief know this?"

"In spades, and he's busting his brain. Always with the culture, you know; he says in Mexico even the atheists believe in Guadalupe, but not the Jews. You know what he meant?"

"I think so."

Felix pushed away from the table and regarded their faces in the strange light of the Góndola Restaurant's Venetian stained glass. "Keep an eye on Bernstein's departure tomorrow. If the ring leaves Mexico, it will go with him."

"Son-of-a-bitch, man, that's a big operation and the chief's going to have a fit if you aren't there. We're greenhorns."

"Like you said, my boy, it's a question of teamwork. No one's indispensable."

"Is that what I tell the chief?"

"No. Tell him I'm following a different trail. At any rate, with the ring or without it, meet me at ten."

"On my word, man, Rosita and I aren't hungry for glory, we don't want to take anything from you, you know? We'd never take the ring to the chief without seeing you first."

"Ten o'clock."

"Where?"

"The Café Kineret. I'll treat you to a kosher breakfast."

As he left, he wasn't thinking about Bernstein but about the old man who'd told him he loved the *Emmita* like a woman: "She's everything I have in the world."

34 THE DOORMAN at the Suites de Génova came on duty at 11 p.m. Felix greeted the somnambulist-faced, ancient Indian wearing a navy-blue suit shiny from wear, as he opened the door. He never smiled; and his expression remained unchanged when Felix handed him a hundred-peso note and told him he was expecting a lady at eleven-fifteen. The doorman nodded and tucked the money in his pocket.

"Do you remember me?" asked Felix, attempting to penetrate the drowsy gaze.

Again the doorman nodded.

Felix pursued the point, handing him a second hundred-peso note. "Do you have a good memory?"

"They say I do," said the doorman, his voice both guttural and melodious.

"When was I here?"

"You left about six days ago, and just came back."

"Do you always remember people who come back?"

"The ones who come often, yes. The others, only if they're nice people." He didn't hold out his hand, but it seemed as if he had.

Felix handed him the third hundred-peso bill. "Do you remember the nun, the night of the murder?"

The doorman studied Felix through veiled eyes and realized there would be no more bills. "Yes, I remember. Sisters never come begging for charity that time of night."

"I want you to tell me later whether the woman who's coming in a few minutes looks like the nun."

"Sure. Whatever you say, chief."

He never smiled; but the leathery wrinkles around his eyes twitched slightly. He gave no other indication that he hoped there would be more tips later.

Felix had just showered, shaved, and sprinkled himself liberally with Royall Lyme when he heard the tapping at the door. It was a little after eleven-thirty.

He opened the door. In the film library of Felix's memory,

he had always equated Mary Benjamin with Joan Bennett, after she'd changed the color of her hair to distinguish herself from her sister, the adorable blond Constance, as well as to compete with the sensational, exotic Hedy Lamarr. Now he would have to add another impression to the layers of masks; like Angelica on the docks by the Gulf of Mexico, Mary had combed her hair like Sara Klein, the bangs and crow's-wing hair of Louise Brooks playing Wedekind's Lulu in G. W. Pabst's cinematic version. For an instant, he felt that a silver screen separated him from Mary; he was the spectator, she was the projected image, the threshold was the dividing line between the inadequate dreams of the movies and the pitiful reality of the public who dreamed them.

But the violet eyes were Mary's, also the deep décolletage and the oil between her breasts to emphasize the cleavage. Especially it was Mary because she moved like a black panther, lustful and pursued, beautiful because she was pursued, and because she knew it. The panther entered the apartment, asking, "You're the one who says he's Felix Maldonado? You'll have to prove it to me; I knew Felix Maldonado and I attended his burial at the Jardín Cemetery on Wednesday the eleventh of August, more than a week ago. Besides, this room is registered to a Diego Velázquez. Is that you?"

She looked around the room, adding that they were all the same, what lack of imagination. Hadn't Sara Klein died in an apartment like this?

"This *is* the room where Sara was murdered," said Felix, speaking for the first time since Mary's arrival.

She stopped, obviously disturbed, as she recognized Felix's voice. A motion of her hand accompanied the forward swing of the crow's-wing hair from neck to cheek, barely revealing a flushed earlobe. Felix realized that, in keeping with Professor Bernstein's theory, well proved by now, Mary didn't recognize him because she was looking for him.

183

"What are you doing here?" she asked, feigning cool-
ness. "This is a hotel for tourists and lovers."

"And I'm a dead man," Maldonado replied tonelessly.

"I'd hoped you were a lover." Mary laughed.

"Do you usually come when a stranger calls on the telephone?"

"Don't be an idiot, and offer me a drink."

She walked to the small bar set into one of the walls,
opened it, and took out a glass. From that distance, she
stared at Felix curiously, waiting for him to pour her drink.

"A vodka tonic," she said as he approached her.

"I see you do know the place," said Felix, when he'd
located the bottles.

He opened a bottle of quinine water. Mary picked up the
vodka and measured a shot into her glass; Felix added tonic
until stopped by Mary's finger, a snake imbued with a life
of its own.

"Yes, I've been here. On the rocks, please. The refrigerator's under the bar."

Felix knelt to open the refrigerator. Pulsating odors from
her sex assaulted him, without passing through customs.
When he turned his head, he was looking directly at her
crotch.

"Yes, you've been here before," Felix repeated, still
kneeling, squeezing the ice tray to loosen some ice cubes.

"Mmmh. And many places like it. The motel beside the
Arroyo Restaurant, for example. You're the one who stood
me up."

"I told you. I had an important appointment."

"I'm the most important appointment, always. But then,
you're a crummy little bureaucrat who has to go wherever
his chief orders. I prefer men who are their own bosses."

"Like your husband."

"You've got it."

"But he doesn't satisfy you, and the horns are on your
pitiful Abie, not on the yearlings he pretends he's fighting."

184

"I take my pleasure where I want and when I want. Can you hurry up with the ice? I'm thirsty." A tapping toe underscored her impatience.

"You must think you're Tarzan's mate, Mary."

She thrust the glass under Felix's nose, demanding ice; her smile could have substituted for it. "I'm my own Technicolor dream, baby, wide-screen and stereophonic sound, and if you don't believe . . ."

The sentence was interrupted. Felix thrust his hand up her skirt, stretched the waistband of her tiny bikini, and dropped in two ice cubes that instantly began to melt on her burning pussy.

Mary screamed, and Felix rose and took her in his arms. "I'm like you," he said into her ear. "I take my pleasure with the woman I want when I want. And, I told you, I want you only when I can have you quickly, nothing must come between my wanting you and your body, Mary."

With Mary's body, Felix exhausted all the cat-and-mouse games of the past week, all the pretense, all the chance moves and predetermined events. He'd been prepared to be led and deceived and misled, but at the same time he'd been forced to maintain an impossible rational reserve, to ensure that the chance of his actions coincided with the will of others only when his will triumphed. Even at that, it was not his own, his will belonged to an embryonic organization, to Angelica's brother, his chief, the captain, Timon of Athens in code, the second knight in the joust, the man who didn't always acknowledge Felix's importance, who put his faith in beardless youths, who used quotes from Shakespeare so transparent they were obscure, or vice versa. Felix's mind whirled, he was thinking at random, thinking of anything he could to keep from coming too soon, hold back, make her come first, with his scarred face buried between the moist thighs of the suddenly docile woman, the new hair on Felix's head blended with Mary's soft, foamy curls; he made love to her slowly and brutally, with all the soft force his hungry man's body could summon, thinking, thinking not to come, to give her pleasure twice, knowing that the woman is loved only when the man knows she has pleasure less often than the man, but always more intensely than the man.

His face was pressed between her legs. Mary came, and on Mary's body Felix avenged with fury the death of Sara Klein, in Mary's body, the operation in the Arab clinic and his humiliating impotence before Ayub and the Director General, for Mary's body he re-created the struggle with the *cambujo* on the dock at Coatzacoalcos, and with Mary's body he liberated himself of the desire he had felt for Sara's dead body and Angelica's unconscious body beside the swimming pool, in Mary's body he buried his grief for Harding and Harding's love for a vanished girl named Emmita; he assaulted her physically as he had wanted to assault Trevor, he kissed her as he had wanted to crush a grapefruit in Dolly's face, he thrust his finger up her ass to cleanse himself forever of his revulsion for Bernstein, he licked her breasts to erase forever the taste of Lichita, and they came together as he came for the first time and she for the second, and she said, Felix, Felix, Felix, and he said, Sara, Mary, Ruth, Mary, Sara.

"No, stay in a minute, don't get up, please; please don't rush to the bathroom like every other Mexican man," Mary begged.

"When were you here before? Who were you with?"

Mary smiled docilely. "You'll laugh. I was here with my husband."

"You don't have beds big enough in your house?"

"We hadn't gone to bed together for a long time. He suggested we meet here secretly, like two lovers. He said it would be exciting, the way it used to be."

"Did it help?"

"Not a bit. Abie disgusts me. It's worse than physical revulsion. What I can't take is boredom, and not being jealous. That's worse than his disgusting face, always nicked

and cut because he insists on shaving with an ancient razor
that belonged to his grandfather."

"He isn't jealous of you."

"No, I'm not jealous of him. He's jealous, yes. He makes
terrible scenes, but even that bores me. To excite me with
jealousy, you have to have a little imagination. He doesn't
even have that. I should have married you, Felix. Ruth is
too mousy for you. You'd have got ahead with me, I promise you that. Besides, you had every right. You were my
first man."

"Have you told Abie that?"

"It's one of my weapons. I torment him with it, and he
goes up the wall. He's a moron, really, rich, but a moron. But
he knows I'll never leave him, because of our four children.
And he's loaded, and since he never does anything about it,
I've got used to sleeping around wherever I want. What
drives him mad, though, is for me to say anything about you.
You're a dreary bureaucrat who doesn't even have a condominium in Acapulco. I dare him to give me something
besides piles of money, but he doesn't know how to do it. It
nearly gives him a stroke."

"I'm happy I can be of some use to you, Mary."

"Well, it's just my way of turning forty without losing my
mind. What the hell. I like the way you screw. I enjoyed the
roll in the hay. Technicolor and wide-screen."

"We can roll it again. Doesn't cost a thing."

"No. The price is too high, and tonight we both paid."

It was she who left the bed and walked toward the bathroom. "The other day at my anniversary party you told me
you like touching me but never desired me. Tonight I think
you did. And I didn't like it, because that means the show
wasn't free the way it used to be. I'd rather you screwed me
without wanting me, not like tonight, because you did want
something and I was just the way to get it."

Felix sat on the edge of the bed. "I paid for it, too. Desire
doesn't come cheap."

"Or bitterness either, Felix. I only came here to insult your other women. You said their names as you came. And you don't even realize you hurt me. That's the only reason I came here. To humiliate that miserable little Ruth and to tell your marvelous Sara that she's dead while I'm fucking with you." She closed the bathroom door.

It was almost two when Felix walked her to the entrance of the Suites de Génova. The concierge opened the door for them. Mary said her car was in a parking lot on Liverpool and she'd rather walk alone, she didn't want to be seen with Felix at that hour. Felix replied that young drunks in convertibles often wandered around the Zona Rosa, and sometimes they had mariachi bands to serenade American women at the hotels, but Mary made no comment.

They embraced, indifferent to the ancient Indian wrapped in his gray sarape, shivering in the cold, who held the glass door for them.

"Ten years is a long time, Felix," Mary said affectionately. "What a shame we'll have to wait another ten, until we get all the poison out of our systems. By that time, we'll be over the hill."

"Do you know anything about my death?" Felix asked with a twisted smile, his hands on Mary's shoulders, turning her so the concierge could see her clearly.

"You saw that I didn't ask you anything."

"You recognized me."

"Did I? No, Señor Velázquez. That's what I enjoyed about our adventure. I don't know whether I went to bed with an impostor or a ghost. The other possibilities don't interest me. Ciao."

She walked down the street like a black pantheress, lustful and pursued.

"Is she the nun?" Felix asked the concierge.

"No, the sister had a different face."

"But you've seen this woman before?"

"Oh, yes."

"When?"

"She spent the night here about a week ago."

"Alone?"

"No."

"Who was she with?"

"A man with sideburns and a moustache and a face like a ripe tomato."

"Do you remember the date?"

"Of course, señor. It was the same night the lady was killed in 301. How could I forget?"

35 IT WAS EXACTLY ten o'clock. As Rosita entered the Café Kineret, Felix, with an expression of excessive religious zeal, was biting into a bagel with cream cheese and lox.

He had no time to speculate about the absence of Emiliano or about the girl's extraordinary attire. Rosita didn't seem to realize—or perhaps intentionally ignored—that her perennial miniskirts and laddered stockings gave her a slightly dated look, but styles always arrive late in Mexico City. By the time they're accepted in Lomas de Chapultepec and bubbling on the back burner prior to being accepted in the Colonia Guerrero, light-years have passed and Ungaro is showing his new Siberian or Manchurian line. Today, however, the girl with the head like a woolly black lamb was dressed in the coarse, long, flowing habits of a Carmelite penitent, with a scapular flowing over breasts hidden for the first time.

She had washed her face and was carrying a black veil and a white breviary and rosary. She didn't give Felix time to speak. "Hit it, Feliciano. The taxi's waiting."

He left a hundred-peso bill on the table and followed

Rosita to the corner of Génova and Hamburgo. As they entered the taxi, Felix peered into the rear-view mirror to see if he recognized the driver. It was not Memo, of recent happy memory.

"The maestro didn't take the plane," said Rosita as the taxi pulled away.

"Where is he?"

"Don't worry. Emiliano's been following him ever since he left his house."

"When did he leave?"

"Very late. He'd never have made his plane."

"Where are we going?"

"Ask the driver. Where would you go, Felix?" Rosita's smile was gloomy.

"To the Shrine of Guadalupe," Felix directed the driver.

"But, yes, señor," the driver replied. "The sister already told me, the Sanctuary of Our Dark Lady. I can't go any faster."

Rosita didn't preen herself in her triumph. She pretended to read her breviary, as Felix caught a glimpse of the image of Our Lady of Guadalupe, enclosed in a glass oval, swinging back and forth over the taxi driver's head. He burst out laughing.

"You know something, Rosie? The first time I met you two, I said to myself the chief's picked himself some strange assistants."

"Right-o, Feliciano," said Rosita. She kept her eyes glued to the pages of her breviary and thrust her rosary under his nose. "See how well-strung the beads are? No loose ends."

They pushed their way through the throngs that came daily from all parts of Mexico to the place that, along with the National Palace (and perhaps even more than that seat of more or less transitory political power), is the fixed center of a country fascinated with its own navel, perhaps because its very name means "navel of the moon," a nation anguished by the fear that its center, and the pinnacles of that center, the Virgin and the President, might be displaced and, angered like the Plumed Serpent, might flee, leaving us bereft of the protection only that Mother and that Father can provide.

They walked among the slowly advancing penitents, many of them on their knees, their arms spread wide in a cross. Little boys hoping to earn a few centavos kept ahead of them, placing newspapers and magazines under their knees to protect them from the rough pavement. Some wore crowns of thorns and cactus leaves upon their breasts; many were simply there for the sights, and because you had to visit the Virgin, whether or not she'd answered your prayer made back there in Alcámbaro, Acaponeta, or Zacatecas. Sweethearts were drinking Pepsis, and families were having their pictures taken before canvases painted with the image of the Virgin and the humble Indian to whom she'd appeared. Native dancers attired in plumed headdresses and sandals with Goodrich-tire soles were playing Indian flutes; hawkers were selling holy cards, medals, rosaries, books of devotions, votive candles. Rosita purchased a yellowish, short-wicked votive light, and Felix preceded her into the flying saucer anchored in the center of the plaza, the new glass-and-cement basilica that had supplanted the small, slowly sinking, red volcanic-stone church with baroque towers that stood to one side like a poor relation.

Emiliano saw them enter. He jerked his head toward the altar with the image of Our Lady of Guadalupe miraculously imprinted on the coarse fiber cape of a credulous Aztec gardener whose faith was rekindled at the sight of a handful of roses blooming in mid-December; and suddenly the millions of pagans subjected by the Spanish Conquest were converted to Christianity, hungering more for a mother than for gods: *Madre pura, Madre purísima,* Purest of Mothers, intoned by the thousands, the humble, as faithful as the first believer in the Dark Virgin, Juan Diego, the secret model of all Mexicans. Be submissive, or pretend to be, and the Virgin will shelter you beneath her mantle; you will never know hunger or cold, nor will you be a son of Cortés's whore Malinche, but a son of the immaculate Guadalupe.

Bernstein was kneeling before the altar. He lighted a candle and, still on his knees, approached a retable covered with hand-painted ex-votos, prayers granted, thank you for saving me when the Flecha Roja bus went into the barranca in Mazatepec, thank you for returning the power of speech to my little sister mute from birth, thank you for the big one in the lottery; covered, too, with offerings to the Virgin, religious medals, Hearts of Jesus in silver and in tin, rings and bracelets and necklaces. As Bernstein reached out to pluck the ring hanging from a hook among the other offerings, Felix seized his soft, flabby arm.

"I didn't recognize you without your skullcap and Talmud," said Felix.

Bernstein's fingers curled as his fingertips brushed against the ring with the stone clear as water. "Welcome to our sacred Beaubourg, Felix," the professor replied with forced good humor. "Release me, please. We are not alone here."

"I see that. There must be three thousand people here."

"And one of them is named Ayub. Release me, Felix. You're a Jew like me. Don't betray us to our enemies."

"My enemy is Harding's murderer."

"It was the *cambujo*. I told him I didn't want any blood. Stupid idiot."

"The captain was a good man, Professor."

"That's beside the point, Felix. Something more important is at stake."

"Nothing is more important than a man's life."

"Ah, at last you've found your father. You've been searching for him for years, as long as I've known you. First it was I, that's why you became a Jew; then Cárdenas, that's why you defend nationalized oil; then whoever happens to be President, that's why you became a government official . . ."

"And *you* found a mother in the Guadalupe, right?"

"Release me . . ."

Bernstein's vanilla-ice-cream face was melting down the drain of a false smile. A Carmelite penitent with a black veil over her head and a lighted candle in her hands was approaching the Retable of the Miracles on her knees, crooning and repeatedly crossing herself. She paused just long enough to take the ring, and still murmuring, "Oh, María, madre mía, oh my comfort and my joy," Rosita buried the ring in the candle wax—"oh, protect me, give me shelter, and conduct me to the Lord's celestial court"—rose to her feet, and moved away from the altar, head lowered, the candle in her hand.

Bernstein struggled desperately to escape from Felix's grasp. Felix released him with a shove, and ricocheting like a punctured balloon, Bernstein staggered wildly toward the multitudes approaching the altar from the opposite direction. He crashed against a crystal casket containing a recumbent Christ: the wax face and hands were bathed in blood, the body covered by a gold and velvet mantle.

The stunned amazement of the faithful turned into silent menace. Bernstein was sprawled on the glass coffin shattered by his fall; a streak across the glass seemed an additional wound on the sacred body. A wall of black, bovine, impenetrable eyes glared with hatred into the drowned eyes of Bernstein, as clear as the stone of the ring that was irrevocably disappearing with the Carmelite nun; shawl-draped women, white-shirted men, and children in jeans jostled each other, surging forward to gaze at the benevolent image of the Virgin—but, instead, finding in their path this mountainous, befuddled foreigner who had profaned the altar, the very death, of the Virgin's son.

Felix observed the instantaneous transformation of the

193

masks of faith and devotion and submissive good will into something resembling the collective face of violence, horror, and solitude. Several hands seized his shoulders and arms. He smelled the perfume of clove, the warm and aromatic breath of Simon Ayub, who whispered into his ear, "I told you, you bastard, I owe you one for the dirty punch."

A group of Knights of Columbus clad in tailcoats, their plumbed tricorns tucked beneath their arms, intoned in authoritative voices, "We are Christians, we are Mexicans, we will wage war against Lucifer."

36 "YOU'RE a real big man now, you fucking midget." Felix managed to spit out the words before Ayub silenced him with another blow to his already bleeding mouth. Felix was tied to a chair, facing a hooded light that burned into eyes held open by toothpicks broken in half and inserted between the upper and lower eyelids. Two thugs stinking of beer and onions relieved Ayub; they repeatedly beat Felix in the stomach and kicked him in the shins, until the chair tipped over, and then they kicked him in the kidneys and face as he lay on the cold cement of a room stripped bare of any furnishings but the chair, and the hooded light and the men.

The gorillas tired quickly and went back to their beer and sandwiches. Felix could see nothing because he saw too much through propped-open eyelids; his sight was hazy, his mouth was filled with blood, his ears buzzed and he scarcely heard Ayub's half-whining, half-defiant refrain. Stripped of self-pity and cursing, Ayub's words were reduced to the fact that he'd been born in Mexico and felt himself to be Mexican, but not his parents. They had had to go back to Lebanon; they wanted to die in the land of their birth. And they'd taken Simon's little sister with them. The girl had become a militant Phalangist and fallen into the hands of the Lebanese Palestinians. The old people had gone to look for her and all three had ended up in a Muslim village, where they were being held prisoner.

"The Director General said it in the hospital; he has me by the balls. 'You do what we tell you,' he says, 'or we'll send you the heads of your pappa and your mamma and your sweet little sister.' Old fools, they should have gone alone, they never should have taken my sister. But how could they leave her here at fourteen? That's a bad age. You're a Mexican like me. I just wanted to be a Mexican and live a quiet life. Why do you have to go around sticking your nose in things that aren't any of your business? Everyone tells you the same thing, the Palestinians *and* the Jews. 'This is our land, it belongs to us!' They're going to end up killing each other. There won't be anything left but desert when they stop the bombing, and putting people in concentration camps, and smuggling arms that end up in the hands of their enemies. Don't you know that, you shitass! Both sides blindly machine-gun old people and children and dogs and you and poor bastards like me and . . . what the fuck . . ."

As if from far away, Felix heard the Director General's voice, accompanied by the slamming of a metal door, and then by hollow footsteps on a cement floor. "That's enough, Simon. It's useless. He doesn't have the ring."

"But he knows where it is," panted Ayub.

"And so do I. It's useless, I say. Pay off your gorillas and turn off that light. Your friends offend me as much as the glare."

"I wanted to make him talk."

"You wanted to get even. Untie him. Don't be afraid. In that condition, he's not able to strike you."

The Director General was mistaken. Grumbling, the

hired thugs left, carrying their sandwiches. As Ayub untied the ropes binding Felix's legs to the overturned chair, Maldonado kicked him in the testicles. Ayub screamed and doubled over with pain.

"Don't touch him," the Director General ordered, moving like a cat in the shadow. Dexterously, he untied Felix's hands, and carefully removed the toothpicks from his eyelids.

"Help me," he ordered Ayub, ignoring his whimpering. "Help me seat our friend correctly."

"Our friend!" Ayub scoffed, still bent over, offering only one hand to help his chief. It was the hand with the rings; Felix would always remember the metallic taste of the scimitars.

"Oh, yes," said the Director General, softly. "You've been invaluable to us, and you can still be so, n'est-ce pas? It's your vocation, what can we do! A case of love at second sight, *pas vrai?*" He laughed, a laugh interrupted at the peak of its merriment.

He stared somberly at Ayub through his purplish pince-nez. "You may leave us now, Simon."

"But . . ."

"Go . . . Your . . . 'buddies' are waiting for you. Tell them to share their sandwiches with you."

"But . . ."

"But nothing. Go . . ."

Felix felt as if his eyes had been torn from their sockets, and he tried to hold them in place with hands that had become nursemaids to his ruined sight. He could almost believe the hands weren't his. He was distracted by Ayub's swift, receding footsteps and the clanging of the opening and closing of the metal door.

He kept his hands over his eyes. Why try to see if there was nothing *to* see? Only the photophobic Director General could see in that darkness, but Felix was grateful. In that one moment, they were alike.

"Poor devil," the hollow voice commented. "His parents and his sister died last week in a miserable Lebanese village. That's the fate of hostages. The Phalangists and their Israeli allies had killed ten Palestinian hostages in the south of Lebanon. So it became the turn of a similar number of Maronite hostages held by the Fedayeen."

The skull-like face loomed close, as if to ascertain the gravity of Felix's beating. "Such a shame," he went on. "I've lost my hold over Ayub. He doesn't know that yet. But in this all-too-small world someone will soon tell him. It would be better, n'est-ce pas? if that disagreeable pair took care of him once and for all. Exit Simon Ayub. And such a shame for you, too, Licenciado Velázquez. Ayub steadfastly believed that you are the man named Felix Maldonado. No one else believes it."

The Director General stood for a long moment with his arms crossed, awaiting a comment from Felix. Finally, he shook his white porcupine head. "Dear me! It is definitely true. Every time we meet, you are unable to utter a word. I recall our poor departed friend Maldonado one afternoon in my office, the strutting cock. So talkative, yes? Just the opposite of you, the very essence of taciturnity. Dear me. But you mustn't worry. I am a patient man. Here, take my handkerchief. Wipe the blood from your mouth. We'll simply entertain each other for a few moments until your speech returns. When it does, try to avoid the obvious, n'est-ce pas? Our people have been following you ever since, with all the flourish of a Dumas hero, you fled the clinic on Tonalá. I regret that you resorted to such melodrama. A fire! I expected a bit more finesse. But what could we do? We were at the mercy of your caprice. What was important, n'est-ce pas? was that you escaped believing you were truly escaping, never suspecting we fervently desired your success."

"Why?" said Felix, through blood and saliva.

"Hallelujah! In the beginning was the Word!" the Direc-

tor General exclaimed with delight. " 'Why?' Memorable
first words from Licenciado Diego Velázquez, the new
Chief of the Department of Cost Analysis of the Ministry of
Economic Development." The Director General licked his
knife-thin lips as he pronounced the name and the accompa-
nying titles.

" 'Why?' asks the brand-new official. Because someone
was spoiling our plans and we didn't know who. Because
someone unexpectedly transferred Felix Maldonado from
Petróleos Mexicanos to Economic Development. Because,
it turns out, this modest official, who cannot afford to have
children until his salary and position are advanced, allows
himself the luxury of a permanent room in one of the most
expensive hotels in the city. Because all this awakens my
legitimate doubts, and because, following a summary investigation, the information contained in the late Maldonado's
files in the Hilton turns out to be false, placed there pur-
posely to make us suspect everything but learn nothing.
But, as in any war, two can play at the war of nerves. Our
opponents lose their agent Felix Maldonado, but as we are
not niggardly, we counter with the gift of Diego Velázquez,
who baptizes himself to save us the headache, n'est-ce pas?
and who one fine night escapes from a clinic because we
want him to escape."

"Why?"

"Your curiosity is becoming monotonous, Licenciado.
Because we needed an innocent carrier pigeon to lead us
to a hidden nest. From that nest, a not-at-all-innocent vulture whom we both know intends to swoop down and
thwart our plans. Ah, you smile roguishly, Licenciado. You
say to yourself that your friend the Shakespearean buzzard
has won the game and has the ring in his hands. It is for
good reason you call him Timon of Athens. What is it the
immortal Bard says in scene i, Act I of his drama about
power and money—rather, about the power of money?"

The Director General, his arms still crossed, threw back

his head, as if his reverie could illuminate the darkness behind his pince-nez. "See how all conditions, how all minds tender down their services to Lord Timon: his large fortune dues and properties to his love and tendance all sorts of hearts. Do I quote badly, Licenciado? Sorry. My training was not Anglo-Saxon like yours and your patron's, but French, and as a result, I prefer the Alexandrine to blank verse."

"You've confused your birds," said Felix, spitting and licking his lips, testing his tongue against his teeth and lips. "Shakespeare compares Timon to the flight of the eagle, bold and forth on."

"Do not be overly eloquent." The Director General laughed. "I merely wish to indicate that if Timon is powerful and pays well, we are more powerful and pay better. I admit freely, yes, that your patron has the ring. But its loss is secondary. This little drama, you see, has two acts. First act: Felix Maldonado inadvertently foils our mission. Second act: Diego Velázquez, equally inadvertently, leads us to the den of an espionage ring that, in spite of all our efforts, we have been unable to locate or connect with any official branch of the Mexican government. With the result that all sins, yours and mine, will be pardoned in the end, because, thanks to you, we obtained something better than the ring: the thread that leads us to Timon of Athens."

"You have good telephone taps, but nothing more," said Felix, his face resigned and impassive. "Anyone can record a telephone conversation and play with proper names."

"Do you want proof of my good faith, friend Velázquez?"

"Goddammit, stop calling me that!"

"Ah, that's a proper name I don't dare play with. It is too serious a matter. You will see that, my friend. But let me repeat. Ask for proof of my good faith, and I shall gladly give it to you."

"Who is buried in my name?"

"Felix Maldonado."

"How did he die?"

"I've already told you that, in the clinic. Why insist on replaying the first act? Consider the second. It is considerably more interesting, I assure you. Be more daring, my friend."

"Why did he die?"

"I also told you that. He tried to assassinate the President."

"Not a word came out about it in the newspapers."

"Our press is the most easily controlled in the world."

"Don't be a fool. Too many people were there."

"Be careful what you say. Your mouth is ugly enough. We can make it even less pretty, n'est-ce pas?"

"What really happened that morning in the Palace?"

"Nothing. Just as the President approached, Felix Maldonado fell into a faint. Everyone found it funny except the President."

"What was your plan?"

"The one I outlined to Maldonado in my office, mmh? To borrow his name. Only his name. We need a crime, and a crime needs a man's name. You, with your stupid swooning, were the obstacle. So there was no crime, even though there was a criminal."

"What you mean is that you intended to kill the President and hang the death on me."

"You will forgive me, n'est-ce pas? if I fail to answer such an irrelevant question?"

"You asked for difficult questions. I'm asking them."

"Very well, but you won't refuse me the elegance of an ellipsis, mmh? I showed the President the .44 Maldonado was carrying in his pocket. It's an effective weapon, easy to conceal."

"Which appeared like magic; Rossetti slipped it in Maldonado's pocket after he had fainted and been carried from the room." Felix hoped his logic was both unexpected and on the mark, but the effect was spoiled by the quaver in his voice as he referred to himself in the third person.

His apprehension did not escape the Director General's attention. "If you say so. Something had to be rescued from the disaster, n'est-ce pas? We remarked to the President that Felix Maldonado was a converted Jew, and that converts feel a compulsion to demonstrate their zeal in order to be clasped to the bosom of the new family. I cited the reverse instance, recalling the conduct of the Spanish Jew Torquemada after his conversion to Catholicism."

"What did you gain with that gambit?"

"You ask me that seriously?"

"Yes, because I doubt very much that the President would have swallowed that kind of crap."

"It was not our primary intent. But Maldonado had wrecked Plan A."

"To assassinate the President."

"*Passons.* We immediately applied Plan B, which was to sow a simple suspicion in the President's mind. Had Israel actually paid an agent to eliminate the President of Mexico?"

"Why would they? Generally, a tourist boycott by the North American Jews is sufficient when they want to tighten the screws."

"You're at liberty to imagine all probable scenarios."

"But, in all of them, Felix Maldonado appeared to be the ideal sacrificial lamb."

"I repeat; only the name, not the man. But, *en fin.* You know as well as I that in Mexico there are no checks and balances to absolute Presidential power. To exercise that power without regrettable excess requires great equanimity. But how does the poor man know what actually is happening? He lives in isolation, his only information that furnished by the sycophants who surround him. Presidents who listen to the people are very rare. The general rule is that, little by little, the court isolates the President, and gradually and inexorably, n'est-ce pas? the President becomes accustomed to hearing only what he wants to hear. From there, it's only a step to totally capricious rule."

The Director General sighed, as if he were delivering a lecture to an exceedingly slow student. "The first rule in a political system as baroque as that of Mexico is this: Why do things the easy way if they can be made complicated? Thence, the second rule: Why do things well if they can be done badly? And third, the perfect corollary: Why win if we can lose?"

Deliberately, he removed the pince-nez and, with them, the resemblance to Victoriano Huerta. However, the effect was opposite to what had happened with Bernstein; without his glasses, the Director General's gaze did not diminish; if anything, the greenish slits of his eyes gained in intensity.

"The North Americans follow Thoreau's counsel: simplify, simplify; as well as its corollary that nothing succeeds like success. For good or evil, their political system is transparent, a mode accepted by men as disparate as the stupid, well-meaning Eisenhower and the perverse, satanic Dulles. But he who seeks to imitate Machiavelli finds himself drowning in Watergate, n'est-ce pas? In contrast, no Mexican politician is disposed to believe that simple things *are* simple; he suspects something fishy. We Mexicans are, understandably, defensive. Mexico, to continue our ichthyological metaphor, is a fish that has too often taken the bait. One must suspect everything and everybody, and that means that everything and everybody is complicated, *hélas!*"

"Was it the President's orders that I be jailed, shot while trying to 'escape,' and buried?"

"That wasn't necessary. A cabinet member who was present at the ceremony requested an investigation of Felix Maldonado. That caused an Under-Secretary to run to the hot line and order the Chief of the Secret Police to detain

Maldonado. We, oh so happily, handed over an unconscious man to their agents, and they, with a small assist from us, interpreted the President's intentions in their own manner. In view of the enormity of the crime, they tossed the hot potato to the authorities at the Military Camp, saying those were orders direct from the 'Orifice' of the President —if you'll forgive the pun. Of course, *I* was the, shall we say, source, n'est-ce pas? That night I went to Military Camp Number One and spoke to the officer of the guard, a mere commandant, and told him—I have sufficient credentials— I had come on behalf of the President of the Republic to speak with the prisoner. We went to the cell where Maldonado was resting.''

He interrupted his account to emphasize the verb. "I choose my words carefully when I say *resting*. The poor man was dead, wrapped in a coarse blanket scarcely worthy of a recruit. Imagine the confusion of a minor officer who finds he has the corpse of a presumed Presidential assassin on his hands. I suggested that in such instances one must make a virtue of necessity, and that he might distinguish himself if he shot the corpse in the back and said he had been trying to escape. Naturally, he interpreted my suggestion as an order from above. *En passant,* the fact that the prisoner had been shot while attempting to escape relieved me of any responsibility in Maldonado's death; that was transferred directly to the officer of the guard and, thus, to the entire National Army, ah, well . . . The death was a public secret, but everything was clarified and accepted in the higher spheres: a discreet burial the following day, after advising the next of kin of a sudden heart attack, et cetera, et cetera. Finis, Felix Maldonado. Malicious tongues will always say he was struck dead by the emotion of seeing the President at such close range. And that is the felicitous journey that takes us from a simple suspicion voiced in the President's presence and picked up by one of his cabinet, to the brutal decision of a minor army officer—before we are elevated to the plane of appropriate grief at the ceremony at the Jardín Cemetery, mmh?"

"What is the name of the poor devil all this happened to?"

"Felix Maldonado. Felix he wasn't, if you remember your Latin. He was a miserable mediocrity. A mediocre economist, a mediocre bureaucrat, a mediocre Don Juan. Yes, a miserable fellow."

The Director General stared at Felix with judicious ferocity. "Velázquez, place on one side of the scales that miserable, insignificant Maldonado, and on the other an internal crisis with international repercussions. You will see we have no reason to weep over such a man." He replaced his tinted pince-nez. "On the other hand, we must concern ourselves with Licenciado Diego Velázquez. Felix Maldonado did not accept our offer and you have seen what happened to him. A whole world awaits Diego Velázquez: a position with a considerable increase in salary, juicy commissions, trips abroad with generous per diems, everything he could desire."

Felix felt as if his facial muscles were tied in knots. "But I have a wife, remember?"

He could only guess that the Director General's invisible eyes were intrigued. "But of course. And now you can have all the little ones God chooses to send, n'est-ce pas?"

"Right. A litter of fucking little sons of bitches, all named Maldonado!"

The Director General didn't resort to striking Felix. Rather, he leaned close to him; his deeply furrowed, greenish skin, taut over salient bones, was the image of death, if not death itself. The breath expelled from the flaring nostrils and fleshless lips thin as stone knives issued from a cavernous tomb that spoke a threat worse than any beating.

"Listen carefully. The only certainty in this adventure is that you will never know whether you are the true Felix Maldonado or the one who took his place by our orders.

You still deny you are the man buried in the Jardín Cemetery? Reflect upon the moment you awakened in the clinic, and ask yourself whether you can be sure you knew who you were. There will always be a before and an after in your life, separated by a chasm you will never be able to span, do you understand that? From this time forward, what you can recall of your past may only be what we, out of the goodness of our hearts, wish to teach you. Can you be sure of the truth?"

"Ruth . . . ." Felix murmured, hypnotized by the deathly voice and eyes and movements of this man as elusive as an oiled serpent.

"I promise you," continued the Director General, ignoring Felix's mumbled allusion to his wife, "that every time you think of Felix Maldonado's past you will be remembering something I taught you while you were unconscious in the hospital. And as you are living Diego Velázquez's life, you will remember of him only what I tell you. Every choice will lead to its impossible antithesis. If you were the man you were yesterday, can you be sure where your today begins? If you are the man you are today, can you know where your yesterday ended? There's no way out for you, do what you do, go where you go. Felix Maldonado was a nobody who frustrated my perfect plan. Diego Velázquez will bear the curse of that guilt."

From the intensity of the words, Felix knew there must be sweat on the Director General's brow, but like his breath, his brow was mortally cold. The official composed himself, and stood straight, no longer crouching over Felix. "Our poor Maldonado is the ideal man, not because of his debatable virtues, but because he doesn't exist. He will remain dead so that we may continue to profit from his services. His chief agrees."

He gestured disdainfully, inviting Felix to stand. "Follow me, Licenciado. I am going to take you for a ride in my automobile."

Felix got to his feet. He felt dizzy and weak. For an instant, he supported himself by holding on to the back of the chair. The Director General turned away and with deliberation lighted a cigarette, his hand shielding his eyes from the unbearable brilliance of the flame. Felix dropped to his knees, plugged in the light Simon and his cohorts had used to torture him, and the sudden glare—congealed in the room like the breath of the man lighting his cigarette before the lidless eye of the reflector—blinded the Director General. He screamed with anguish and clapped his hands over his eyes. The lighter fell to the cement floor, followed by the cigarette, dropped from his unfeeling fingers and dripping a tiny trail of lava down the Director General's chest.

"Right behind you," said Felix, crushing out the cigarette with his heel.

The Director General suppressed the trailing notes of his cry of agony. He stooped down and groped for his lighter, found it, and again rose, his dignity completely recovered.

"Be my guest," he said to Felix Maldonado.

37 THE METAL DOOR closed behind them and they walked along a glass-and-iron gallery ventilated by draughts of cold night air smelling of the recent rain.

They descended iron stairs to a garage where an ancient long, low, black Citroën was parked. The Director General opened the door and gestured Felix to enter.

Felix climbed into the luxurious imitation coffin. His host followed and slammed the door. He settled back with a sigh, and took the black mouthpiece hanging from a metal hook.

He gave orders in Arabic, and the funeral carriage drove off. The interior of the Citroën was upholstered in black velour; the windows were covered with black curtains, and two sliding panels of black-painted metal separated the unseen chauffeur from the passengers.

Felix smiled secretly, imagining the conversations that could take place between his host and him in this place and under these circumstances. But the Director General was too occupied to talk, absorbed with the drops that would alleviate the pain of the sudden glare. He replaced the bottle in a case fitted into the back of the divider facing them, and with closed eyes leaned back against the cushioned seat.

He spoke with extreme courtesy, as if nothing had happened during the preceding hour. One might think the two men were on their way to a banquet, or returning from a funeral. In tones of modulated affability, the Director General recalled his life as a student at the Sorbonne. There, he said, he'd formed indestructible bonds of friendship with the elite of the Arab world. Doors had been opened to a sensibility that made the Western world seem crude and impoverished. Without the Arabs, he added, the Western world would not be enjoying its own culture; the Greek and Latin heritages had been destroyed or ignored by the barbarians, preserved only by Islam and disseminated from Toledo throughout medieval Europe. The sons of wealthy Palestinians studied in France; through them, he came to understand that their Diaspora, because it was current and tangible, was worse than that of the Jews begun two thousand years before. The Palestinians were the contemporary victims of colonialism in the Promised Land, and were living a destiny Jews could only recall, a destiny that never would have gone beyond a vague Zionist nostalgia had not Hitler once again martyred them. But, while the Jews were rich bankers, prosperous businessmen, and honored intellectuals in pre-Nazi Germany, the Palestinians were already victims, fugitives exiled from the land they, and only they, had truly inhabited.

"The Middle East is an impassioned geography," the Director General murmured. "One need only go there to share its passions—including violence. But the violence of the modern Occident is different from all others because it is programmed, not spontaneous. Western colonialism introduced that violence into the Middle East; the Zionist project prolonged it. Palestinian violence is a passion. And passion is consumed in the instant; it is not a project but a living thing, inseparable from religion and all it implies. In contrast, Zionism is a program that must separate itself from religion in order to be compatible with the secular project of the West whose violence it shares. Consider, friend Velázquez. Palestine was a land already inhabited. But, for the Jews of Europe, anything that was not Europe was, as it had been for European colonialism, land to be occupied. That is to say, colonized, mmh? The Jews forced the Arab world to pay the price of the Nazi ovens. The result was fatal: the Palestinians became the Jews of the Middle East, the persecuted of the Holy Land. But Israel's penance is in its guilt. Little by little the Israelis are becoming Easternized and, like the Arabs, entrenched in a struggle that has become religious as well as secular, passionate and instantaneous. The Easternization of Israel makes a new war inevitable, perhaps many successive wars, since Oriental politics can only conceive of negotiation as a result of, never as an impediment to, war."

Felix didn't wish to reply. He was reaching the end of an adventure in which he couldn't be sure whether he'd been following some plan—either his own or another's—or whether he'd been the blind instrument of chance, completely divorced from will.

The Director General tapped Felix's knee. "Bernstein must have given you his arguments. I shall not persist in mine. You, like poor Simon, must believe you're a Mexican, and what does all this have to do with you? You carry out your assignment, and that's that, n'est-ce pas? But your friends are right. Mexican oil is becoming a more and more important card to be played in the case of continuing war in the eastern Mediterranean. Hence all our efforts, n'est-ce pas? One cannot isolate oneself, Licenciado. History and its passions sift through the universal chinks of violence. Did you study Max Weber? The decisive means of politics is violence. And as each of us, personally, possesses a more or less controlled measure of violence, the encounter is fatal; history becomes the justification for our hidden violence. You may think I quote Weber only because he expresses my own view. But think about it. At this moment you are exhausted, all you want is to bring this to an end. I understand. But I urge you, ask yourself, don't you have a reserve of personal violence completely separate from the political violence surrounding you? Don't you intend to use it to find out the only thing you want to know?"

Felix and the Director General took each other's measure in silence; Maldonado knew that his own gaze was empty, opaque, uncommunicative; in contrast, the two lenses of the Director General's pince-nez glittered like black stars in the black bosom of the ancient Citroën.

"Well." The Director General smiled. "I believe we are almost there. Forgive my chatter. The fact is, I had only one thing to say. Cruelty is always preferable to scorn."

He drew back one of the window coverings and Felix saw that they were approaching the stone bridge of Chimalistac. The Director General again laughed, and said the Spanish had learned from the Arabs that architecture should never be in conflict with the climate, the landscape, or the soul. Such a shame, he added, that modern Mexicans had forgotten that lesson.

"All Mexico City should look like Coyoacán, in the same way that all Paris, in a certain sense, is like the Place Vendôme, n'est-ce pas? One must multiply the beautiful, not isolate it, or destroy it, as unfortunately we do."

The auto stopped, and the Director General's voice again became hollow and dry. "Rest. Relax. When you feel well, return to our office. We will be waiting for you. The same office. Malenita is waiting eagerly. Poor thing. She's like a child, she needs someone who will be a father to her. She will cash your checks punctually, and you won't have to go out of your way or stand in lines. And every month, come by to see my secretary Chayito. Special perquisites aren't processed through the Ministry's public accounting office."

He opened the door and waved his hand. "Please get out, Licenciado Velázquez."

"There's one thing you haven't explained. Why did you tell me in the clinic that Sara Klein had attended my funeral?"

For an instant, the Director General's eyes were as vacant as sand. Then he sighed. "Recall my words. I said that Sara Klein, too, had attended the rendezvous with dust. In this carnival of lies, Licenciado, allow a small metaphorical truth, mmh?"

A wedding ring glittered on the finger of this man with an unimaginable private life. It occurred to Felix that the eight wives of Bluebeard, including Claudette Colbert, had no reason to envy the wife of the Director General.

"Get out, Licenciado Velázquez. I'm going on. And tell our friend Timon of Athens to reflect upon the words of Corneille, with the necessary geographical adjustments. 'Rome, to my ruin, is a monstrous Hydra head; it will, when severed, grow a thousand in its stead.' You see, I, too, know my classics."

Felix got out without offering his hand. But, once outside the car, he turned and thrust both hands inside, the palms with their signs of life, fortune, and love almost touching the Director General's tinted lenses. He said with rage: "See. You've forgotten one thing. My hands. I have my fingerprints. I can prove who I am."

For once, the Director General did not laugh. "No. We thought of that. We decided not to slice off the tips of your fingers this time, Licenciado. One must always have an ace up his sleeve. And cruelty must be gradual. But I'm sure you won't want to expose yourself a second time to our surgery, n'est-ce pas?"

He closed the door and the Citroën pulled away. Felix was standing before the door to my house in Coyoacán.

PART FOUR

WAR WITH THE HYDRA

38 I HAVE WRITTEN the most accurate report possible of everything Felix Maldonado told me during the week he spent recuperating in my home. I have imposed a certain order, for he told his story the way memory works, in disjointed fragments. Felix's memory, as he had already told me over the telephone, had certain rights. And mine as well.

I have transcribed with complete fidelity his feelings of the moment, his descriptions of people and places, events and conversations, as well as the occasional reflections evoked by these events. Some—perhaps too many—peripheral comments are exclusively mine.

I realize as Rosita types my notes that I have accumulated over two hundred pages. The girl with the head like a woolly lamb is an excellent typist, though she doesn't enjoy her secretarial tasks; she feels they are beneath her dignity as a budding Mata Hari. Her Emiliano is much more docile, eager to learn. He is reading with intense interest the pages Rosita transcribes.

The case we, and the triple agent Trevor/Mann, call Operation Guadalupe richly deserves his curiosity. It was the first operation of our embryonic intelligence organization. The lessons we learned from this pilot experience will be of the greatest usefulness in the future.

I came to know Felix Maldonado well some fifteen years ago when we were both postgraduate students at Columbia University in New York. Although we were of the same generation, we hadn't been friends while we were enrolled in the School of Economics at the University of Mexico. Our poorly labeled "maximum house of study" favors neither study nor friendship. The absence of discipline and any entrance standards prevents the former; an indiscriminate mass of two hundred thousand students makes the latter difficult, at best.

Besides, social differences separate the wealthy students from the poor. I came to the university in my own car; Felix, on the bus. Wealthy students like me didn't want to fraternize with poor students like Felix, nor they with us. It created too many problems, we all knew that. They were embarrassed to invite us to their homes; we were uncomfortable at their uneasiness in ours. We spent our weekends in our houses in Acapulco; they, if they were lucky, might get as far as the public bathing beach at Agua Hedionda in Puebla. We had our dances at the Jockey Club; theirs were held in the Clair de Lune Ballroom.

There was also the problem of girls. We didn't want our sisters and cousins to fall in love with them; and they, even if their parents were of a different mind, didn't want theirs swept off their feet by our money.

Felix's case was somewhat different. Everyone knew of his loyalty to the professor who taught economic theory, Leopoldo Bernstein, and of his love for one of our classmates, a Jewish girl named Sara Klein. And this was an additional barrier. Toward the end of the fifties, Jewish families in Mexico still hadn't been accepted in "good" society; the parents spoke with thick German or Slavic accents, it was suspected that their daughters were too emancipated, and, above all, the families weren't Catholic.

Distance spontaneously breached all these barriers. The privileges I enjoyed at home impressed no one in New York; on the other hand, Felix accepted them naturally, but he saw no reason why two young Mexicans living in the United States should perpetuate social divisions; it made more sense to become friends, to share jokes and memories and language.

Felix was overwhelmed by the film series at the Museum of Modern Art, and became infatuated with the art and history of the medium. Several times he invited me to go with him in his explorations of Griffith and Stroheim and Buñuel. I never told him I'd seen them all in Mexico at the Instituto Francés on Nazas, where twice a week we sat in religious silence before the fluid undulations of Swanson and the iron control of *Potemkin,* and then listened as a svelte young Spanish poet with prematurely gray hair gave some three hundred of us lucid lectures on cinematic culture.

As for me, I discovered the theater, and Felix's passion for the movies was equaled only by mine for Shakespeare. I devoted an entire summer to the Ontario Shakespeare Festival and what was called the straw-hat circuit in summer theaters along the New England coast. I invited Felix to go with me, and overcame his reluctance by suggesting that he be my guest at the theater, and I his at the movies.

So we sealed our friendship, and when in September we began our second year at Columbia, we decided to share a room; we rented a small apartment at the Century Apartments on the outmoded west side of Central Park. Felix set one condition: that I limit my monthly allowance to the amount of the fellowship he received from the government. I agreed, and we moved into our furnished apartment, one room, plus bath and kitchenette. We shared the Castro Convertible that was by day a sofa and by night a bed. We worked out an arrangement to entertain girls only in the late afternoon and to hang a sign on the door when we didn't want to be disturbed. We stole a public-works sign on Sixty-eighth Street that read MEN AT WORK, and used it as a signal.

We talked a lot about Mexico, sitting before the view that was our only luxury: the Hudson at dusk from our window on the twentieth floor. Felix's father had been one of the few Mexicans employed by the foreign oil companies. He'd worked as a bookkeeper in Poza Rica for the El Aguila Company, a subsidiary of Royal Dutch.

"My father went to the superintendent's office twice a

month. But he never saw his face. Each time my father entered, this Englishman was sitting with his back to him. That was the custom; you received Mexican employees with your back turned, to make them feel they were inferior, like the Hindu employees of the British Raj. My father told me this years later, when his humiliation had been transformed into pride. In 1938, Lázaro Cárdenas expropriated the English, Dutch, and North American oil companies. My father told me that at first they hadn't known what to do. The companies had taken with them their technicians, their engineers, even the plans of the refineries and wells. They'd said, drink your oil and see how you like the taste! The capitalist countries declared a boycott against Mexico. My father says they'd had to improvise to keep going. But it had been worth it. No more White Guards, the company's private army, stealing land and cutting off the ears of rural schoolteachers. And most important of all, people looked one another in the face."

This is all a well-known fact of modern Mexican history. But to Felix it was a personal and moving experience. He insisted heatedly, as I laughed, that he'd been conceived on the eighteenth of March, 1938, the day of the nationalization, and born exactly nine months later. But if he'd been born nine years earlier, he'd have had none of the advantages he'd enjoyed, the schools Cárdenas created in the oil fields, the medical services that hadn't existed earlier, social security, and pensions. His parents hadn't dared have children before; but Felix went to school in Poza Rica, and his father was promoted and became Chief Accountant in the main offices of Petróleos Mexicanos in Mexico City. Felix was able to pursue his studies and go to the university. His father retired on a pension, but active men die when they stop working. Felix venerated his father and Cárdenas; they were almost one in his imagination, as if their shared humiliation and dignity and destinies, inherited by Felix, were inextricably linked.

He told this story with great warmth and feeling, more than I can recapture here. I didn't offer a similar confession. My life had always been easy, and I was embarrassed to admit that my family, too, owed everything to President Cárdenas. My father's small pharmaceutical factory expanded and diversified following the expropriation, until it became a powerful petrochemical empire. And, along the way, my father cornered a number of concessions; our gasoline stations were strategically located all along the Pan-American Highway between Laredo and Valles, and thanks to all this, I attended not only the university but also the dances at the Jockey Club.

In a way, I envied Felix the vividness of his experiences and emotions; but at the same time I realized they'd marked my friend with a certain eccentricity. I don't mean our religious differences. Where religion is concerned, I'm the one who might be considered an eccentric in a society where everyone claims to be Catholic but only women and children go to church. Felix was the product of socialist schools. I wasn't a Catholic simply because of tradition, but by conviction, and my conviction was based on the very reasons because of which Felix rejected the notion of God: that the Creator could not have created evil.

"But evil is necessary only because there *is* a God," I argued during one of our discussions. "Imagine all evil accumulated on God's shoulders and then you can comprehend His existence; only then will you feel, will you *know*, that God never forgets us. If He is able to bear human evil, it is because we matter to Him."

When news reached Felix of his mother's death, he rejected my company and hung out the warning sign on our apartment door. I came home as late as possible, but the sign was still there, so I spent the night in a hotel. By the following morning I was worried, and I ignored the sign and went in.

Felix was in bed with a very pretty girl. "Let me introduce Mary. She's Jewish and she's Mexican. Last night she lost her virginity."

The girl with the violet eyes didn't seem perturbed. I felt uncomfortable and, I confess, jealous. As long as Felix respected our arrangement and I didn't see the girls that passed through our bed, it didn't matter to me. But Mary's physical presence disturbed me. I rationalized that it was the fault of my good—or bad—training. I would have taken a plane to Mexico City for my mother's funeral. But secretly I also realized that I regarded Felix as somehow mine, the brother who'd lived the hard life that hadn't touched me, the platonic lover who lay beside me every night in the convertible sofa-bed recounting extraordinary films that had never been filmed, or rather, ideal films pieced together from bits he particularly loved, a face, a gesture, a situation, a place immortalized by the camera.

"Who'll pay for the stained sheets and mattress?" I asked grossly, and left them.

I walked to St. Patrick's; Felix wasn't going to pray for his mother.

During the last two months of the life we shared in New York, neither of us again hung the sign on the door.

We returned to Mexico together and promised to see each other often; we exchanged telephone numbers, and went our separate ways. All our good intentions to continue our friendship failed. Felix found a job with Petróleos Mexicanos; his family connections and his Master's from Columbia paved the way. I went back to my old social circle and gradually took over my father's affairs. I heard that Felix was spending a lot of time with the Jewish colony. Sara Klein had gone to live in Israel, but Felix was going around with Mary. Then she married a rich Jewish businessman and Felix married another Jewish girl, named Ruth.

My business affairs prospered, and when my father died, I expanded them even further, but the rewards seemed empty. Because of my two years at Columbia, my friendship with Felix, my love for English literature, I deplored the world of bourgeois Mexicans, ignorant and proud of it, wasteful, voracious in their appetites for accumulating money without any greater purpose, totally lacking in the least measure of social compassion or civic conscience. I held a similar opinion of the government officials I came in contact with; the majority were struggling to amass enough money in a few years to be able to move into bourgeois circles and live and act and think like them.

These two aspects of my life came together in my sister Angelica's marriage; she had all the vices of our class, and the man she married, Mauricio Rossetti, an impoverished aristocrat making a career in government service, had all the defects of his. I imagined how it might have been if Felix had rescued my sister from the idiotic life into which she was pouring her half of our inheritance, only to humiliate her husband. At the same time, she was goading him to profit from government corruption and free himself from her humiliation. I'm not sure, but deep inside I may have resented the fact that Felix hadn't come along, fallen in love with Angelica, and saved her . . .

I cultivated the few exceptions I found, the few lawyers, economists, officials, and scientists who were intelligent, honorable, and, above all, concerned about the future of a country that was needlessly condemned to poverty, corruption, and nonsense. I bought a large old house in Coyoacán. I filled it with my books, the paintings I'd begun to acquire, the music that meant more and more to me as I became resigned to bachelorhood. Almost out of inertia, my business thrived, and I came to be considered a nationalistic entrepreneur.

But always, just beneath the surface, lay those conversations held in a small apartment with a view overlooking the Hudson, when a young student of economics told me what had happened on the day he was conceived.

That day, Mexicans had looked one another in the face.

Following the political and economic crisis of October 1973, my constant recollections of Felix became a real need to see him again. The Yom Kippur War and the Arab oil embargo coincided with the discovery, at a depth of some 4,500 meters beneath the soil of Tabasco and Chiapas, of a large quadrant containing a potential two billion barrels of oil.

It wasn't difficult for the owner of a large petrochemical empire to perceive the warning signals, to measure the greed aroused by the discovery of such enormous oil deposits, as well as the role those reserves might play in an international crisis. I became aware of some things that on the surface seemed quite innocent: the comings and goings of our former professor Bernstein, who claimed to be raising funds for Israel, the contacts he established, the questions he asked; the relation of the Director General of the Ministry of Economic Development with the diplomats and hierarchs of Arab countries. My sister Angelica's indiscretions were incalculable, but I didn't really need them to experience the full pressure exerted upon my own empire to associate with transnational companies and become a part of enterprises that would in the end divest us of our control over our own resources.

I imagined the day when we Mexicans might cease to look one another in the face.

39 I GOT IN TOUCH WITH Felix and made an appointment to see him one evening at my house in Coyoacán. We compared appearances, after thirteen years of not seeing each other. He was unchanged, Moorish, virile, the image of the Velázquez self-portrait, and tall for a Mexican. I, on the other hand, had changed considerably. Relatively short, with a head too large for my small, slim body, I had begun to go bald, and that only emphasized my stature, I attempted to compensate with a thick black moustache.

Without going into great detail, I sketched out what I had in mind. I didn't want Felix to form too many preconceptions. I knew that Felix was motivated solely by personal emotions, not abstract political arguments. Oil was his father's life, not an ideology. He reminded me that he wasn't orthodox but he'd converted to the Jewish faith to please his wife. He asked me whether I'd ever married, he'd completely lost track of me. No, I was a thirty-eight-year-old bachelor. Maybe someday.

We set up a simple code, quotations from Shakespeare. I rented a room in the Hilton to serve as a kind of honeycomb to attract bees of all breeds, and there we carefully planted false documents that had every appearance of authenticity.

Felix objected. "You've given me very little to go on. I may make mistakes."

"It's better this way. No one but you can carry out this mission. When something surprises you, you always react with imagination. When you're not surprised, you act routinely. I know you."

"Then I consider myself free to do whatever I think best."

"Agreed. Our premise is that we have neither information nor plans to forestall the ambitions of those who are a threat to us. We will act alone, our only principals those who deserve our confidence; our only resources, my own personal fortune."

223

Felix looked at me oddly; at times, memory disdains its true name and becomes clouded with emotions that are nothing more than vague recollections. "It's good to see you again."

"Yes, Felix. Very good."

"We were good friends, real friends, weren't we?"

"More than that. At Columbia, they called us Castor and Pollux."

I used the moment to attempt an intimate, personal overture. I placed my arm around his shoulders, hoping some tremor would betray his emotion.

"I'm prejudiced," he said to me. "I'm married. To a Jewish girl. I have many connections in that area."

I removed my arm. "I know that. I also know that the English superintendent at Poza Rica turned his back on your father."

"That can never happen again."

I gazed at him gravely, sadly, intentionally mixing personal and professional relations. "You're mistaken."

"But you know I'd do anything to keep it from happening again, don't you?"

I answered his question indirectly. The sentimental blackmail I was subjecting him to had to be implicit. "Listen to this."

I ran my fingers over the keys of the recorder I always carry in an inside jacket pocket; I pressed one key and my voice emerged. Felix didn't seem to be any more amazed than if I'd been a nightclub ventriloquist, until the moment another voice with a heavy North American accent responded to mine: ". . . in Tabasco and Chiapas. The United States requires six million barrels per day of imported oil for internal consumption. Alaska and Venezuela assure us of only two-thirds of this supply. Mexico will have to send us the missing third."

"Whether or not we want to?"

"Well, it would be better if you did, wouldn't it?"

"Do you think a new war will break out?"

"Not between the great powers, no, because the nuclear arsenal threatens us with either the terror of extinction or a new balance of terror. But the small countries will be the arenas of limited wars using conventional arms."

"And also limited skirmishes using equally conventional economic weapons."

"I was referring to the weapons we used in Vietnam; they're all tied to your profession, you know that; limited and conventional wars mean a boom for the petrochemical industry, you know that, too, napalm, phosphorus, defoliation chemicals . . ."

"And I was referring to even more conventional weapons, blackmail, threats, pressure . . ."

"That's the way it is. Mexico is highly vulnerable because she's dependent on the three valves we can close at our whim: imports, financing, and the sale of replacement parts."

"We'll drink our oil, then, and see how it tastes . . ."

"Ugh. Better to adapt to the future, my friend. Dow Chemical is eager to associate itself with you. That means guaranteed expansion and earnings for your empire, I promise that. In the eighties, Mexico can count on a reserve of 100,000 million barrels, the largest in the Western Hemisphere, second only to Saudi Arabia in the world. You can't sit on it forever like the proverbial Indian sleeping on a mountain of gold . . ."

I stopped the tape. It amused me to wag my index finger under Felix's nose, like the gringo when he visited me in my offices.

"We're on the razor's edge," I said to Felix. "We may wake up some fine day to find all our oil installations occupied by the United States military."

"They'd have to occupy the entire country, not just the wells and refineries," Felix replied, pensively. He looked as if he'd just heard a ghostly dialogue between his father and the English superintendent of Poza Rica.

"You're right."

"I understand why you came to me, you know my sentimental weakness, my father's story," he said without a trace of cynicism. "But you? Why are you doing all this? You should be a conservative."

"I am, Felix. Call me a nationalistic conservative, if you want. I'd like to conserve *that,* keep the oil ours, and prevent outsiders from playing games with us."

"Will I be in contact with anyone besides you?"

"No. Only me. I'll send help when necessary. Money. Friends."

"There are others involved?"

"Only the bare minimum. They think like us. We're few, but we're not alone."

"What shall I call you?"

"Timon. Timon of Athens."

"Why not? We saw that play in the open-air theater in Connecticut. A man of enormous wealth who also buys affection. Isn't that what Shakespeare says, something like that?"

"You'll have to reread the plays so we can communicate."

"You know something? I wouldn't have recognized you on the street."

"I know, Felix. But don't forget my voice. All our communications will be by telephone. We won't see each other until the end. Trust no one."

"But I have my prejudices. Bernstein was my teacher."

"Do you know what the Irgun Zvai Leumi was?"

"No."

"An organization of Jewish terrorists as bent on terrorism as any of the PLO."

"You mean they were fighting for a homeland against the occupying British. Listen, I saw how the British went about things in Poza Rica."

226

"That isn't true. You hadn't been born."

"My father saw it. That's the same thing."

"The Palestinians are also fighting for a homeland. The Irgun didn't limit itself to acts of terrorism against the British; they also exterminated any Arab they found in their path."

"It all seems very abstract."

"I'll give you a concrete example. On the ninth of April of 1948, our Professor Bernstein took part in the slaughter of all the inhabitants of the Palestinian village of Deir Yassim. Two hundred dead, most of them women, children, and old men. This happened three years after the death of Hitler."

The information had no effect on Felix. It lacked the personal element; he would have to know that Bernstein had achieved what he had never tried to achieve, and never had achieved, become Sara's lover. He would have to know Sara's death, the torture of the man called Jamil, Harding's murder, before he understood my parting words, after we'd agreed on the broad outlines of Operation Guadalupe and he was for the first time on his way to the room in the Hilton. "You will learn that no one has a monopoly on violence in this business."

He would have to know the extermination of Simon Ayub's family by Palestinians in Lebanon, and the death of my sister Angelica at the hands of Trevor/Mann and his ally Dolly.

40 I HAVE WRITTEN Felix's version of these events. Now I will give my own interpretation, the broad perspective that Felix lived but only partially understood. My task was made more difficult because Felix—though he never said so, but since he supposed I hadn't left my library at any time during the preceding ten days—thought that, as a participant, he knew more than I. And, once again, he seemed to be the one called upon to play the difficult role, while everything was made easy for me.

More than once during that week in my house, I was afraid that when Felix looked into the mirror and saw his unfamiliar, savaged face his reaction would be anger and self-pity. Knives and fists had played with his very identity, as if it had been modeling clay. I was also afraid that he, recognizing the physical manipulation, would see something even more insulting, moral manipulation. Emiliano and Rosita had told me of Felix's wounded pride when he learned he wasn't my only confidant. And, finally, I feared that his underlying resentment might explode or, obscured by the very real affection that unites us, be turned into grief.

Felix Maldonado's grief takes strange directions, I'd learned following his mother's death. That night he'd deflowered Mary in our bed. And the night he discovered that Sara was Bernstein's lover, he'd physically assaulted the professor in Angelica and Mauricio's home. Grief, followed by the exhaustion of grief, always diverted Felix from his duty, as when he'd made love to Mary, or visited Sara in the mortuary.

I was mulling over these things one evening when we were comfortably settled in my library having a drink, listening to Rubinstein, Szeryng, and Fournier play Schubert's glorious E-flat trio. Only then did I attempt to draw some conclusions from our experience. Ours, I say; for Felix, it was his alone.

"It has nothing to do with the music," I had said, "but

as I listen, it occurs to me that everything you told me sounds melodramatic, you know? But at the same time I feel there's an additional element, possibly something tragic, because neither side is exclusively right; both sides are right and both sides are wrong. Do you know what I mean?"

Felix stared at me a few minutes without speaking, a glass of cognac in his hand. Then, as if to dispute what I'd said, he hurled the glass against the painting of the martyred San Sebastian above the fireplace. The glass shattered and liquid trickled down the painting into the fire, as the flames danced.

"Son-of-a-bitch! I've been here seven days," he said, "I've told you everything I know, and you're still sitting there with your goddamned placidity, listening to your Schubert, quoting your Shakespeare, with your glass of cognac getting as empty as your words." Repeatedly, he thumped his chest with his thumb. "I ran the risk. I stuck out my neck. I have a right to know."

"Where do you want me to begin?" I replied tranquilly.

Felix smiled, and went to pick up the pieces of broken glass from the hearth. "I'm sorry."

I shrugged. "For God's sake, Felix, between you and me . . ."

"Very well. Begin with the part you like best, those grand generalizations, get that out of your system. I understand that both sides wanted information about the Mexican oil reserves, and I'm sure the ring was connected with that. But the performance in the Palace, what was that all about? What did each side have to win?"

"If you'll allow me, I'll try to be systematic. As soon as the record's finished."

With the last chords of the allegro moderato, I folded my hands and lowered my head. I didn't want to look Felix in the eye. "Both sides wanted the information. That's central. That's where everything begins. Why did they want it? For obvious reasons. They didn't know—and thanks to us they

229

still don't—the extent, the precise location, or the quality of our new fields. In case of a new conflict in the Middle East, several things might happen."

"Trevor outlined the hypotheses in Houston," Felix said impatiently. "I know the bottom line: in every case, Mexican oil could be the unexpected ace in the hole. What else?"

"Their specific motivations."

I got up and walked toward Felix. I leaned down. I knew I couldn't expect any intimacy from him; perhaps I thought I might instead provoke the discomfort—the incipient fear —that can result from unemotional physical proximity. "The Arabs wanted the information in order to put pressure on Mexico; our coming into OPEC would strengthen that organization but weaken Mexico. We can support OPEC, but shouldn't join it. We've owned our oil since 1938; the Arabs, no. We don't share earnings with any foreign country; the Arabs do. We're capable of managing for ourselves all the stages of oil production from exploration to exportation; the Arabs, no. To join OPEC would be to let ourselves in for battles we've already fought and won. And, incidentally, we'd lose the benefits of the United States Trade Bill. The Arabs know all this; the gringos as well. Result: the even greater weakness of Mexico. For its part, Israel wants to ensure that Mexico doesn't commit its oil but continues a policy of massive exportation in competition with OPEC, directly or indirectly assuring supplies to the Jewish state. Hence the Israelis' and the North Americans' need to know exactly what reserves the Western world could depend on in case of a new conflict. For it if comes to war, never doubt it, Washington will turn all the screws to make Mexican oil the answer to Arab oil."

"You haven't answered my question about what happened in the Palace."

"Just this. The Director General decided to speed things up. He's an old fox; his intelligence is equaled only by his boldness, and one feeds the other. He's the most dangerous of them all. He realized there was a serious possibility of a more or less disguised surrender of Mexican oil to the United States and Israel. This would be fatal to the Arabs. The Director General decided to risk everything on one throw of the dice. Once he learned about you, you became the ideal candidate for his plan. He suspected that you were working for an unidentified intelligence agency. Furthermore, you were a converted Jew. He decided to kill two birds with one stone. Or rather, three. Because what he was planning was the assassination of the President."

I placed my hand in my pocket and caressed the hidden .44, cold and black, as innocent as a bird in its nest.

In his agitation, Felix ignored the movement. "What *was* his plan?"

"He stationed his people in the Salón del Perdón. As the President approached you, a marksman was to shoot him. In the general confusion, Rossetti would place the pistol in your hand. Like this."

I whipped out the .44 and placed it in Felix's surprised hand; he took it automatically.

"A simple reaction. You would have accepted the gun the way you did just now. You might have dropped it immediately, but in any case you'd have been incriminated."

Felix offered me the gun. I waved it away. "Keep it. You may want to use it later."

Again, I saw flare in my friend's eyes the fear of being blindly manipulated. I countered that threat by frowning, as if planning what I was going to say—though I knew that perfectly well. "The plan was daring," I added hastily, "but had it succeeded, the whole country would have been saying what the Director General wanted them to say: Israel had ordered the assassination of the President of Mexico. He calculated that the inevitable reaction would be Mexico's alignment with the Arab world. In any case, the political crisis would insure that the government would be crippled, and in those muddied waters the Director General counted on being a better fisherman than his rival Bernstein."

"But the plan failed; it failed for the simple reason that I fainted. Why?"

"Because I made sure you *would* faint."

"You?"

I glanced at the pistol in Felix's hand. This wasn't yet the moment I feared. He wouldn't use it, because his astonishment was still greater than his anger.

"Felix, the pharmaceutical house I inherited from my father is thriving. The manager of the Hilton told me the exact hour you'd ordered breakfast for. I was in the hotel."

"You?" He laughed, not scornfully, because amazement still ruled his other emotions. "You who never leave your house . . . ?"

"I'd been in the hotel since the previous evening. I myself placed the precise dosage of propanolol in your coffee. Would you like to know the exact formula? Isopropylamine-1 (naphthyloxy-(1')-3 propanol-(2)). Yes. It's an anti-adrenaline compound. Ingested with food in a quantity of no fewer than fifty milligrams—the amount I placed in your coffee—it works along with the digestion. I knew the hour of the ceremony. The drug would take effect as you were digesting your breakfast, at the moment you were about to speak with the President."

"That's impossible, it would require split-second timing."

"The mechanism exists: the drug is activated two hours following ingestion as the flow of adrenaline encounters the blocking drug. They served your breakfast at 8 a.m. The ceremony took place at ten. You may have confused the signs of hypotension—sweat and general nervousness—with the emotion of the moment. What we know is that as the three factors come together—digestive juices, the drug, and adrenaline—the effect is instantaneous: the blood

232

rushes from the brain to the stomach, and the subject faints. That's what happened to you. And that's how Plan A was spoiled."

"So he activated Plan B."

"Exactly. The real assassin didn't have time to fire."

"Who was he?"

"It doesn't matter. One of many killers on the Arab payroll. The Director General's instructions were absolute: all or nothing. All it took was a slight accident, an unforeseen event, to thwart Plan A. You were that accident. While the Director General was explaining to the President what had happened, his people put you safely out of the way in the clinic on Tonalá. Rossetti was in charge of that; you worked in the same branch of government as he. You'd just fainted, he would take you home."

"But if Plan A hadn't failed, I wouldn't have been taken to the clinic but to the Military Camp, and from there to the cemetery."

"No, the Director General was perfectly honest with you. All he wanted was your name, to fire up official hostility against Israel. He wanted you alive so you, the new you, could escape from the clinic and lead him to me."

"But I still don't understand. Ayub warned me at the Hilton not to attend the ceremony. When I woke up in the clinic, the Director General was berating me for having showed up at the awards ceremony. He said all he'd wanted was my name and that my presence had spoiled his plans; he accused me of meddling and told me that if I hadn't been there, as Ayub had warned me, everything would have worked out the way he wanted."

"They know you too well. They knew you'd do exactly the opposite of what you were told, because you're proud and you're stubborn. The fact was that your presence was indispensable for their plan."

"So why did they keep saying that in the clinic, after it was all over?"

"If you believed them, you'd be diverted from the truth. The Director General doesn't want people going around saying he tried to kill the President. Not even as a theory."

"Is it more than a theory? Is there any proof?"

I nodded nonchalantly. "Mauricio Rossetti is free. He's been extradited. In this case, Mexican justice was expedited. He says Angelica's death was an accident. Trevor's charges didn't stick. Rossetti has been reinstated in his position as the Director General's private secretary. He owes everything to his chief and he knows why: he's the only one who knew about Plan A. The Director General procured his freedom in exchange for his silence, and he's not worried about blackmail. Rossetti would lose something more than freedom if he talked: his life."

"But don't forget, Ayub told me not to go. You say by his chief's orders. But Ayub despises the Director General; he'd have been pleased to have Plan A fail. It would have been his revenge against a man who imprisoned his family in Lebanon and then ordered them killed."

"The Director General ran that risk. But his boldness, I repeat, is always balanced by intelligence. If Ayub hadn't convinced you, the Director General wouldn't have given a damn for Ayub's life, or his family's."

"He didn't give a damn."

"Try to convince a man condemned to die tomorrow that it would be better to die today. That happens only in the folk ballad 'La Valentina.' "

"I suppose I should be grateful. That sinister old bastard has been pretty decent with me, comparatively speaking."

"That's true. If Plan A hadn't failed, he would have given you what he promised in the clinic: passports, tickets, and money for you and Ruth."

The pistol was pointed at my heart, but I knew that Felix's anger wasn't directed toward me any longer.

"Goddammit, then who was shot in the Military Camp and buried the next day in my name?"

234

"Buried, but also exhumed."

I was distracted by the San Sebastian above the fireplace, a good example of sixteenth-century colonial painting. Felix's face may have resembled Velázquez, but his body was that of the martyr—with words as arrows. Deliberately, I returned to my chair and again buried my face in my hands.

"You know, I did a little work myself, Felix. Everyone in this country uses his influence, that's the law of the land. So I was given permission to exhume the body buried in your name."

Felix grabbed me by the shoulders. "Who is it?"

I unclasped my hands and stared into his eyes. "A young Palestinian. A schoolteacher in one of the occupied territories. He fell in love with Sara Klein. He was tortured. The Director General's agents located him and told him Sara was in Mexico with Bernstein, the man responsible for torturing him and his mother. They told him that Sara was Bernstein's lover. The boy went mad. An impassioned Palestinian is passion itself, Felix. The Director General got false papers for him, smuggled him into Jordan, and from there the boy flew to Mexico. Maybe he wanted to kill Sara, or Bernstein, or both, I don't know. He didn't have the chance. They killed him first and placed him in a cell at the Military Camp, saying it was you, unconscious. You know the rest of the story."

Felix released me. "Jamil."

"That's what Sara called him on the recording. His name was Isam Al-Dibi. He looked quite a bit like you. He would have been the ideal murderer of Sara Klein. But the Director General didn't see that far ahead. You can't have everything. He had enough on his mind following you to get the ring. He didn't get it. That's what's important."

"But he did find out about you and the organization, everything that . . ."

"I wanted him to find out. I wanted it because it's impor-

235

tant for both sides to know of our existence. The rule of political discourse is duplicity. That of diplomatic discourse, multiplicity. Espionage is the combination of the two, both double and multiple."

Felix dropped into the chair beside mine, as if to interrupt a conversation about events that were more exhausting to listen to than to have lived. In a daze, he stared about the room, studying the antique mirrors, the coffers with iron corners and iron keyholes, the rich marquetry, the molding, the ironwork and inlay, the hand-turned table legs and chairs of this mansion I'd bought from the heirs of an old millionaire named Artemio Cruz.

Finally he spoke, his voice as hollow as that of the man he unconsciously imitated. "Then the Director General murdered Jamil."

"Isam Al-Dibi, yes."

"But he was a Palestinian, a man who suffered . . ."

"I told you that no one has a monopoly on violence. Or injustice. Much less, morality."

He stared at me absently: "How do you know all this, the Director General's plans, Jamil's death . . . ?"

I hesitated. I was afraid of my answer. But for every subjective reason, even the most objective reasons, I was compelled to tell Felix Maldonado the truth. "Angelica told me. You know how she was. Much too nervous. She couldn't bear feeling guilty. Even less, thinking she'd failed. She told me for one reason: her scorn for Rossetti. She talked a lot. You know how she was."

"*Why* did you want both sides to know about you? I don't think they're frightened. They know we're a small group, pygmies alongside them."

"Exactly. They will think we're less significant than we really are, or will be. They will continue to underestimate us."

"In spite of the fact that you ended up with the ring?"

"Yes. They're convinced it's of no value to us. First,

because we know the secrets it contains. Second, because they don't think we're capable of deciphering its contents. So they'll go through the same routine, and we'll win a second time."

Felix didn't seem convinced. "That's what Trevor said in Houston. I can imagine what was in the ring. But how did you decipher the information, if you did decipher it? There're a lot of things you haven't told me."

I laughed. "Felix, you have to have everything explained to you. You don't figure out anything for yourself, because you're too wrapped up in yourself. When you get over that, you'll be a really good agent."

"Who said I want to be one?" He was laughing at *me.*

I ignored his impertinence. Felix deserved a little self-congratulation, and that would allow me to slip into a neutral topic. He still held the pistol, but it was a toy in his hand.

"It's a devilishly ingenious technique," I explained, and invited him to go with me to the chapel.

4⃝1 I WALKED to a bookshelf and pressed the brittle spine of my folio edition of *Timon of Athens;* the shelf swung upon its hinges, revealing a passageway to the ancient chapel of this colonial mansion. Felix followed, still carrying the pistol. I closed the concealed door behind us and turned on the lights in the tiny whitewashed oratory whose only furnishing was a metal stand.

The floor was paved with red volcanic rock; the wooden altar was painted white, with strips of gold molding. Above the reliquary and the tabernacle hung a painting of Our Lady of Guadalupe.

I opened the tabernacle and removed the water-clear stone from Bernstein's ring. Holding it between thumb and index finger, I showed it to Felix. "Inside this stone are two hundred images reduced to the size of pinpoints. Each one is printed on extremely thin film of high contrast and high photosensitive resolution. But these are not simply photographs that record the differing light intensities reflecting from the object, they're holograms that retain information about all phases of the light waves emanating from the object photographed. In contrast to normal film, if the hologram is cut or blemished, it retains the image of the whole in each portion of the film. This is because the light recorded is not located in one area of the film but is disseminated throughout the space between the object and the hologram."

I placed Bernstein's stone on the revolving top of the metal stand and turned off the lights. I returned to the altar and asked Felix to stand beside me. From the reliquary I removed an electronic control sensitive to the touch of my fingers. I warned Felix not to look toward the light projected from behind us toward precise pinpoints in the ring as it rotated in response to my controls. "What's beautiful about this is that since the prints are made by laser beams, they can be re-created only by light projected from another laser. Look."

I pressed the control and a ray of light as thin as a razor's edge beamed from the left eye of Our Lady of Guadalupe to penetrate the surface of the ring. I pressed the control for rotation.

What we saw on the whitewashed wall was the virtual re-creation, in color and three dimension, of expanses of land photographed from the air. Each image bore the name of the region where it was located, followed immediately—with hallucinatory reality, seemingly so close one could reach out and touch them—by images of the limestone rock corresponding to the region: living reproductions of the electric, magnetic, gravitational, and seismological records of the subsurface; refractory readings of high-velocity beds; pressures and temperatures; holograms of the stereographic projections of the beds and the mathematical calculation of the quantity of fluid each contained: a splendid and frightening portrait of subterranean Mexico, the technological descent of the laser into the mythological hell of Mictlan, an ebullient photograph of the arteries, intestines, and nerve system of a quadrant of land explored meter by meter, as if plumbed by the hundred horrifying eyes of Argus.

Cactus, Reforma, La Venta, Pajaritos, Cotaxtla, Minatitlán, Poza Rica, Atún, Naranjos along the shelf of the Gulf, from Rosarito in Baja California to the plains between Monterrey and Matamoros in the north, from Salamanca in the center of Mexico to Salina Cruz on the Pacific; the complete network of oil, natural gas, propane, and other petrochemical pipelines, platforms for undersea drilling, all the plants for absorbents, lubricants, and cryogenics, the batteries of separators, refineries, and operating fields.

Not a single place, not a single fact, not a single estimate, not a single certainty, not a single control valve in the Mexican petroleum complex had escaped the fluid stone gaze of Bernstein's ring; whoever possessed it and deciphered it had all the necessary information for utilizing, interrupting, or—depending on the circumstances—appropriating the functioning of this machinery, the fertile Hydra head the Director General had referred to, which now was being projected on the wall like the shadows of reality in Plato's cave.

Again I touched the control. The light in the Virgin's eye was extinguished and the stand ceased to rotate. I turned on the lights. I removed the clear stone from the stand and replaced it in the tabernacle.

We returned to the library in silence. I pressed the spine of *Timon of Athens* and the bookshelf returned to its customary position.

239

42 "ANYTHING ELSE you want to know?" I asked, arching my eyebrows as I offered Felix a cognac.

He refused; his hand was toying with the pistol. But he answered my question with another: "Who killed Sara Klein?"

He gazed into my gray eyes as coldly as I gazed at him. "Ah, but that's the only thing I don't know."

"Then I'll have to find out. Do you know who the nun is?"

I sighed deeply, shook my head, and quickly sipped my cognac.

"I told Emiliano and Rosita to ask you to get the license number of the convertible the kids were driving when they serenaded that night . . ."

I took a piece of paper from my pocket and handed it to him.

"Who does the car belong to?" he persisted.

I thrust my hands into the pockets of my pin-striped suit. "I don't know. The plates are registered to a one-peso cab."

"What's the driver's name?"

"A Guillermo López."

"My friend Memo," Felix murmured, and for the first time he stared at me suspiciously.

Feigning indifference, I walked to the fireplace, picked up the fire tongs, and poked at the dying fire. I allowed Felix an opportunity to look at my back, the cut of my finely striped suit.

"Anything else, Felix?" I asked, my back still to him.

"Ruth," said Felix, like a sleepwalker. "I ought to see Ruth. How am I going to explain?"

"You must see her. You won't have any problems. I promise. She'll be happy to know you're alive. Believe me. And after you've seen Ruth, what do you plan to do?"

"The Director General said to call myself Velázquez. He told me I have an office, a secretary, and a salary," said

Felix, with a forced laugh that was far from humorous.

"Accept his offer. It suits us."

"It suits us?"

"Of course. Felix Maldonado is dead and buried. Diego Velázquez is the ideal replacement. No one is looking for him. No one recognizes him. He has no past. He has no outstanding debts."

I heard Felix's footsteps behind me, muffled by the thick Oriental rug. Then his heels clicked on the stone hearth. He seized my shoulders and forced me to look into his eyes. His gaze was dead; it was also deadly. "You're repeating what the Director General told me . . ."

The fire tongs crashed to the warmed stone.

"He was right. Let me go, Felix."

He released his grasp, but remained menacingly close.

"You're more valuable to us than ever," I said through tight lips. "It's to everyone's best interest that you forget Felix Maldonado and take on a new identity. The perfect spy has no personal life, no wife, no children, no house, no past."

I spoke phlegmatically. Again Felix responded with the Mexican counterpart, Indian fatalism. "I don't understand you. It doesn't matter about me. But I don't understand your game. They'll gather all the information again and everything will begin all over."

"For you, it began in a taxi, remember? That was the moment of no return, Felix, that unknowing step from reality to nightmare, the moment when everything that seems real and secure in your life slips away and becomes uncertain, unsure, and phantasmagoric. Do you believe you can simply return to your former life, assume an irretrievable reality, be an obscure bureaucrat and Don Juan and husband named Felix Maldonado?"

I took Felix's hand, though it was a risk; he would feel my dry, lizardlike skin. "I need you, Felix. And you're right. The game will begin again. It's like two cowardly and imperfect knights jousting in a dark labyrinth. The next time, however, they'll find that their adversary is stronger and, what's more, different. And so on and so on. That's why I wanted them to recognize me this time; they won't the next. And you will need me, because I'm the only person in the world who will still call you Felix Maldonado."

"Ruth . . . ?"

"No, no, don't answer. You will offend me deeply if you underestimate me. Don't make the mistake our enemies made. Don't underestimate me, or my ability to disguise myself. You know, baldness can be an advantage. I simply put on a gray wig with an unruly lock of hair, I shave off my moustache, thicken my eyelids with makeup, add a few wrinkles, make my nose a little more acquiline, speak with any one of the many English accents I learned watching Shakespeare with you . . . Although at times I prefer to quote Lewis Carroll. Welcome to Wonderland."

"Trevor."

"And you, my friend, would have to take on the role of the March Hare . . ."

"But Angelica was your sister . . ."

Poor Ophelia. No, hold my hand, Felix, even though my skin repels you. Add a neutral Colombian accent, interjections from the 1890's, poppycock, pip-pip, balderdash . . . Are you following me, Felix?"

"But you were acting for the Arabs in Houston . . ."

"They know me as Trevor, an English homosexual expelled from the Foreign Office as a security risk. The Israelis and the CIA know me as Mann, a mercenary agent whose cover is a traveling job with Dow Chemical. You know me as Timon of Athens, your former classmate and owner of a petrochemical empire in Mexico. I serve them all so I can use them all, and so they will fear me. I'm not sitting in my library waiting for your telephone calls, Felix, while you risk your neck. I received your call in

Mexico City telling me about poor Ophelia—that's the only time you really surprised me—and three hours later I was in Houston looking like a Roman senator and giving a passable imitation of Claude Rains; tomorrow, after a four-hour flight, I'll be in Washington presenting myself to the CIA in Langley as the questionable Mr. Mann, with a slight German accent and another passable imitation, this time of Conrad Veidt . . ."

I released Felix's hand only because I'd run out of breath and couldn't talk, only because I couldn't touch him if I wasn't talking, only because I wanted him to have his hands free to do whatever he pleased. I was giving him that freedom. Finally I had demonstrated that I, too, took risks, that he wasn't the only one living dangerously. I'd finally canceled that debt from our youth.

"But Angelica was your sister," Felix repeated, his voice, his eyes, his body, unbelieving, the hand with the pistol hanging limply.

Now I could look at him calmly. "Felix, what do you plan to do when you leave my house?"

"I don't know. I don't know what to say. Go to Ruth."

"Yes. And then?"

"I told you. I have to find out who killed Sara."

"Why? Sara Klein died twice, once as a girl in Germany and then as a woman in Palestine. Her murder in Mexico was a mere formality."

"You didn't love her."

"Would you compromise our whole operation to rush off on an idiotic chase that has nothing to do with our project? Would you jeopardize everything we've achieved just to satisfy your injured vanity, to avenge the death of an Israeli whore who never went to bed with you but cuckolded your platonic love for her with an old Jewish professor and a young Palestinian terrorist?"

Felix pointed the gun directly at my heart. *"You* didn't love her, you son-of-a-bitch."

"Shoot, Felix. Give one more turn of the screw to the legend. This time Pollux kills Castor. Only one has the right to be immortal, remember? Not both."

"You didn't love her, you son-of-a-bitch."

I approached him and took his hand, this time the hand with the gun. I took it from him; our faces were almost touching. "Ah, passion again rears its fearful Hydra head. Cut off one, and a thousand will grow in its place, isn't that right? Call it jealousy, dissatisfaction, envy, scorn, fear, repulsion, vanity, terror; probe into the secret motives of any of us who participated in this comedy of errors, Felix, and give to his passion whatever name you will. You will always be wrong, because behind every label there is some unnamable, obscure political or personal reality—makes no difference which—that justly or unjustly—makes no difference which—compels us to disguise as action what is actually passion or hunger or suffering or desire or a love nourished out of hatred or a hatred nourished out of love. You think you're being subjective? You're nurturing objectivity. You think you're being objective? You're nurturing subjectivity. Just as the words in a novel always end by saying the opposite of what they mean."

"But Angelica was your sister . . ."

"And Mary your lover, and Ruth your wife, and Sara, I don't know, something bigger than you, something you'll never be able to understand or give a name to. Go. Come back someday and tell me everything. Maybe then I'll tell you how Angelica died, and why."

"I know how. Dolly pushed her out the window."

"But you don't know why. All the better. Don't try to explain it. Not that; not anything."

"Did she know you were Trevor?"

"Of course. When we were children, we used to dress up and pretend to be other people. It was a continuation of our games."

"But she didn't know this game would be fatal."

"No. She thought Rossetti was the one who'd be killed, that we'd get rid of him once and for all. Poor child. Rossetti is harmless, he's useful because he can be controlled. Not Angelica, she was too impulsive, and she talked too much. It's your destiny to be used blindly. Don't complain. Truly bad fortune tends to be monotonous. Passion, without imagination, as you live it, is more entertaining."

"Imagination, without memory, as *you* live it, is to be pitied. I feel sorry for you."

"I'm a Catholic, Felix. I know that when one lacks passion he can be saved by grace. One day when we were young I told you that in my opinion sin and judgment are equally sterile. I prefer to eliminate punishment. The obligation of love is much better than any condemnation. Rossetti didn't deserve love."

"Is that how you loved Angelica?"

"I owe you no explanation. Understand. I have no quarrel with you. I love you, too."

Everything I'd dreaded I saw in Felix's eyes.

"Of course. I understand. There was one thing that powerful Timon couldn't buy. A heart. *'Tis deepest winter in Lord Timon's purse."*

I hoped that wit would disguise my hurt, and I continued the game. *"You're a dog."*

"Thy mother's of my generation," Felix replied. It was the first time someone had called me a son-of-a-bitch by quoting Shakespeare.

My stupefaction was short-lived. I hurled myself on Felix, insulted, angry, wounded by what he was insinuating, robbed of my perfectly phrased, measured, premeditated justifications. He wrested the pistol from my hand, but it didn't matter. I'd been stripped naked by this man, my brother, my enemy, whom finally I held in an embrace of hatred, a struggle in which the bodies that had never touched in the sofa-bed in New York were now locked together in rage—my impotent rage, invalidated by the

245

sweating, straining, passionate proximity of Felix, his hand
jamming the pistol into my armpit, his arm braced against
the pressure of my torso, his leg thrust against my testicles,
the impassioned rejection of a body that didn't desire mine.
He scorned my passions, having discovered the most secret
of them all, transforming me into a living but lifeless shell,
for Felix defended himself against the aggression of my love
coldly, the way someone defends himself against a mosquito. Even though my love meant nothing to him, he loved
me as he always had, his true friend. His memory had no
grief. I wanted him to love me, but I wanted him to fear me
more.

I dropped my arms. I'd been defeated, but I saw in his
eyes that he didn't claim the victory. For him, it was a draw.
I sat down to get my breath back. Felix, too, was panting,
standing beside the fireplace, the .44 in his hand. San Sebastian was dying his eternal death, his gaze vacant, arrows
piercing his body and filling the sky.

"Go, Felix. You'll forget. You'll recover."

He smiled, an unwelcome smile. "No. I'm Mexican. I'll
forget, but I won't recover."

I didn't want to see him any longer. "Understand what
I did, Felix, so I can understand what you're going to do."

"Thirteen years is a long time." His voice was lifeless.
"We don't know each other any more."

He was leaving, perhaps forever. No, in spite of everything, I was sure that someday he'd return to tell me what
he'd done after he left my house. "Felix." I raised my voice.
"I understand you, and I know what you've lost because of
me. Tell me, please. Did you gain anything?"

"Yes. I found a father in the dry docks at Galveston."

I thought he was going to laugh, but if he did, I
didn't hear it. I wouldn't have liked it. He was gone.
Again I savored the cognac on my tongue, and licked
my moustache. Felix was still a long way from being a
good agent. In his own words, he'd told me that Trevor

246

didn't have a moustache. Several times he'd described the tight lips clean as knife blades. No moustache grows in four days.

I sighed. I should be compassionate. Felix Maldonado had been living a nightmare. My breath caught in my throat. After thirteen years, we no longer knew each other. But that wasn't the worst; one thing hurt me even more. I remembered what Bernstein had told Felix. Felix really didn't see me, because he wasn't looking for me. He didn't have the least idea how I looked at forty; he remembered only how I'd looked at twenty. That's what remained in his mind. I didn't exist in the present.

I spent the remainder of the evening leafing through my edition of Shakespeare. I reread the plays of murder at the castle of Dunsinane and of the murder of the Prince of Elsinore. Without interrupting my reading, my thoughts kept pace, weaving in and out among the sentences, sometimes obliterated by the words, sometimes drowning them out. Yes, Felix Maldonado was a bad agent. The James Bond of underdevelopment. But I had to build my organization with whatever Mexico had to offer: Felix, Emiliano, Rosita. Ashenden and Richard Hannay had behind them the heritage of Shakespeare, my poor agents had Cantinflas in *The Unknown Policeman*.

I tried to justify my cruel deceptions of the night. As I deceived Felix, I'd been discovered by him. I told myself that had I not offset the frailty of my human resources and done what I'd done—establish a principle of hierarchy founded on fear—my undertaking would have failed. The base for any action in the future could only be the fear I inspired in my friends and my enemies.

I closed the Oxford edition with bitterness. I could derive only one lesson from this first adventure of the Mexican secret service. Terror is universal, justice is not. Every intelligence organization, however it might strive toward the goal of justice, is perverted by its means—

terror—and finally it becomes the servant of oppression, not the instrument of justice it set out to be. A tiny cell of fascistic structure, espionage, which is intended to protect society, finally becomes a cancer that infects the society in which it takes root. All its heroes are reactionaries, from Ulysses to James Bond. Which explains the exhaustion of its heroism, as ravaged as the plastic features of Howard Hunt.

But as I turned off the lights in my library I was confident that, in spite of everything, Felix Maldonado, my unconscious hero, saddened and exhausted, would return to tell me what he'd done after he had left the refuge of my home.

I thought about him as I climbed the stairs to my bedroom. Oh, if only one day I might compare my probable scenario with Felix's real version. Where would we coincide? Where would we differ? Which of the two endings would be the true one: the one I was preparing to invent, or the one he was preparing to live?

These thoughts went whirling through my mind as I removed the false moustache before my mirrored dressing table. The gum arabic pulled at the real moustache growing beneath the false one.

I placed the luxuriant black moustache neatly in a box of carefully arranged hairpieces: beards, moustaches, eyebrows, and sideburns of various colors, denoting various ages. In the mirrored dressing table and cabinets, I was surrounded by wigs, by new suits and old suits, polished shoes and scuffed shoes, shirts and undergarments and jackets with labels attributing their origins to shops as distinct as Lanvin in Paris, Gath & Chávez in Santiago, Harrods in Buenos Aires, Austin Reed in London, Hart, Schaffner & Marx in Houston, a branch of Marks & Spencer's in Riyadh, the Arrow shirt shop in Tel Aviv, and El Borceguí shoestore in Mexico City.

I stood before the mirror prepared to declaim Macbeth's

famous soliloquy in Act V, scene v, but I felt ridiculous. The sound and the fury had ceased, along with my hour on the stage, even though as I crawled into my loveless bed the night truly seemed a walking shadow.

43

INEVITABLY, he will return to the Suites de Génova and will ask for the same room, the room where Sara Klein died, where he made love to Mary Benjamin. The beds of Felix Maldonado are always occupied by some woman, living or dead. They know him at the hotel; he gives good tips; he's an eccentric; they're not surprised that he's returning with no luggage after a week's absence. I myself had telephoned them: Licenciado Velázquez had been called away unexpectedly and hasn't had time to pack his things, would they please keep his suitcase for him?

"Your usual room, Señor Velázquez?"

It is raining outside my house in Coyoacán. In August, the storms of the high plateau beat against the mountain peaks, spill down the slopes of the ancient snow-topped volcanoes, and in the late afternoon or early evening, like clockwork, unleash their yield, before giving way to the hurricanes along the Gulf, which rage until the onset of autumn—on the Feast Day of St. Francis, when, as they say, the saint's cord-belt lashes them into quietude. Then a luminous and uninterrupted peace consecrates our winters. But soon the crystal of cold sun becomes clouded with the dust of prolonged drought, and the winds of spring raise suffocating dust storms, veritable screams of agony from the dry, cracked tongue of the earth.

Soaked with rain after waiting for a taxi to come along Calzada de la Taxqueña, Felix arrived at the hotel without

249

luggage. The Indian concierge wrapped in a gray sarape recognized him—why wouldn't he?—and waked the night clerk, who'd fallen asleep watching a movie on the kitchen television.

"Your usual room, Señor Velázquez?"

"If it's available," Felix said to the thin, sleepy, hollow-eyed young attendant.

"For you, señor, it's always available."

"I thought by now everyone would have forgotten about the murder."

"Sir? The President of Petroquímica Industrial del Golfo personally called and asked that the room be kept at your disposal."

"He's very considerate."

"Oh, of course. He's one of our most distinguished clients. He sends all his foreign guests to us."

"I know him. He's very careful about details, a real puppet master."

"Sir? Shall we bring up your suitcase, Señor Velázquez?"

"I don't need it. Send it tomorrow."

"As you wish, sir. Here's your key."

He slept uneasily. They brought his suitcase at ten, and after he shaved and ate breakfast, he walked to the Plaza Río de Janeiro. It was recess time in the neighborhood schools and he had to make his way through hordes of happy, yelling children. Red and yellow and blue balloons shone against the glistening leaves of the palm trees. Felix walked to the entrance of the red brick building with the slate towers and pushed open the gate into the dark passageway.

He knew that Memo was working. Lichita might have gone back to work in the Hospital de Jesús, or she might still be on vacation, enjoying the benefits of her service to Ayub and the Director General. He hoped no one was home; he could search at his pleasure, and Memo wouldn't be able to lie to him.

But no. Licha opened the door. Her makeup was streaked and she seemed half asleep. The lace-edged silk robe covering her small, firm breasts clamored for a trip to the dry-cleaners. She seemed stunned, not knowing whether to shut the door or leave it half open and talk with Felix.

Before she could decide, he stepped into the room. Licha threw her arms around him. "Sweetie pie, you're a sight for sore eyes, I thought you'd forgotten me, oh, I'm sorry, I'm a mess, why don't you come back in an hour? let me slick up a little, you go away and come back in a while, hmm?"

She kept her arms around him, trying to push him out into the hall, but Felix planted himself firmly in the doorway. Then she tried to turn him so he couldn't see the bed.

"Did you miss me, honey? I missed you a little, well, that's not true, I missed you more than I can tell. Kiss me, sweetie."

"Where's Memo?"

"Working, where do you think?"

Felix glanced toward the bed and then toward the man's clothes draped carelessly over a chair. "Tell him to get up. I want to talk to him."

"But, sweetie, I just told you, he's working . . ."

"Then who is that in your bed?"

"Shhh, honey, it's a girlfriend. She had a terrible case last night, a dying man, and it was too late for her to get home from the hospital, her house is way out in Azcapotzalco. I told her she could spend the night here, honey. Why don't you come back in a while, mmh?"

"Tell your girlfriend she needs plastic surgery."

"Ha, ha!" Lichita forced a laugh. "Are you going to throw that in my face? I wasn't the one who sliced you up; I took care of you, handsome, and if I hadn't, you wouldn't have come out looking so good."

"It isn't her face, it's her body. Your friend's all out of shape. Things don't seem to be in the right place."

251

Felix ripped the sheet from the bed; a naked boy stared at him in horror. His erection wasn't sanforized. Immediately, his expression changed to anger, and he turned toward Licha.

"Look, stupid. Can't you get your schedule worked out? You said your old man went to work at six this morning and that we wouldn't be interrupted before one." He covered himself with the sheet.

Licha tapped her foot and crossed her arms. "Get going, Sergio. This is serious. See me some other day."

"Hell, no. Let this guy leave. Or stand in line. Makes no difference to me." Sergio settled back with a crooked little smile, his hands clasped behind his head.

"Never mind," said Felix. "Where's your husband's record book?"

"I don't know what you mean." Licha's foot was still tapping.

"The law requires him to keep a record of his fares. If he doesn't, they take away his license plates. A cab hauls passengers, you know, not oranges to market."

"Uh-hmm," sighed Sergio. "If he hasn't had them lifted, he'll lend them to you. Memo's a real sport with his friends. If you pay him enough. He'll lend you anything. Even his wife."

Lichita whirled, to stare at him with fury. "You shut your mouth." Then immediately she stroked Felix's lapels and gazed at him tenderly. Licha could change expression the way you change stations on a radio. "I've been so lonesome, honey."

"I can see that."

"No, I mean it. Did you hear about Simon?"

"They killed him."

"Ooooh, baby!" Sergio laughed from the bed.

The nurse nodded repeatedly, tears in her eyes, her head resting on Felix's shoulder. "I *told* him. That man with the funny eyeglasses doesn't fool around. I told him. He

252

shouldn't have gone to the Hilton that night to tell you not to go to the Palace. He double-crossed old Four-eyes; *he* wanted to be sure you were there at the ceremony with the big shot. I told Simon to go easy, Four-eyes always collects his debts . . ."

"You think that's why Ayub was killed?"

"Sweetheart, you didn't even ask me, but I'm telling you the truth, I want to tell you everything, so you'll love me just a little . . ."

"I already know what happened," said Felix, listening to Licha but looking at Sergio; another blue-eyed blond, short and fair. Obviously, this was the type Licha favored, but this boy wasn't a poor dupe like Ayub. Felix looked more carefully at the gold-buttoned blue blazer tossed over the chair, the gray-flannel trousers, the shirt with the Pierre Cardin label, the black Gucci loafers.

"He didn't have anyone in Mexico, I was his only friend," Licha whimpered.

"I know that, too. How did he die?"

"They left him here for me to find. As full of holes as a sieve. They propped him against the door, so when Memo opened it, he fell into his arms."

"Why here, Licha?"

"I told you, he didn't have anyone else, old Spooky knew that . . ."

"And you think the Director General's shut all the mouths that might talk. Don't kid yourself."

Suddenly all Licha's defenses crumpled; she stopped sniveling, her foot stopped tapping, her jaws began to move as if she were chewing gum, but the gum was her face, dirty, gray gum.

Felix put his hands around her throat. "I want his record book."

"I swear . . ."

He pushed her away and began to rummage through the drawers. He looked in the drawer of the linoleum-covered table, and all the drawers in a kitchen improvised from a hot plate on a battered table, two saucepans, a frying pan, a mortar, empty beer and Nescafé containers, and chipped clay utensils decorated with flowers and ducks.

Licha didn't move a muscle. But Sergio threw off the sheet and jumped out of bed, reaching for his clothes. "You're right, Lichis. I'd better be going."

Felix pushed him back onto the bed and bent over the telephone Memo kept hidden like a treasure in the pillows. Beneath the telephone was a hardcover notebook with marbleized binding.

Licha laughed. "Oh, is that the notebook you meant? I'm so dumb! That's where Memo jots down the addresses of his customers when they call. Is that called a record book? Excuse my lack of ignorance, as they say."

She was talking to Felix, but looking at Sergio. "What are you looking for, sweetie?"

Without speaking, Felix riffled through the notebook. Simultaneously, Licha pressed Felix's hand and shook her head at Sergio. "What's the big mystery, sweetheart? Memo just does the normal things. He works his two shifts, usually from six to three and six till twelve, except when a customer hires him by the hour or wants him to take him out of town, you know, a little pleasure trip . . ."

He showed Licha the paper I'd given him. "Is this Memo's license number?"

"Ye-es . . ." Licha sounded hesitant. She looked at Sergio. "I think so, that kind of thing never sticks in my mind."

"The night of August 10, Memo lent his plates to someone. It isn't entered here. Who did he give them to? Your little Goya *Majo Nude* here already admitted that Memo was in the habit of lending his plates if you paid him enough."

The three of them stared at one another, glances caroming like billiard balls. It was Sergio's shot; he laughed a short, nervous laugh. "That was a joke, man. Old Memo rents out everything, his license plates, his old lady's ass, all of us know that . . ."

"What 'all of us'?" Felix asked.

Sergio narrowed his eyes and scratched a nipple. "Look, are you from the cops, or what? All fuzz are bastards, but you're the champ. I came here to get a piece, not to answer your fucking questions."

"Fine," said Felix, and walked to the door with the notebook under his arm. At the threshold he paused to say to Licha, "Too bad, beautiful. You'll wake up some morning and find that cute little Bunny body's been skewered, but not the way you like it, and not by the persons you like."

Felix turned and left the room. Licha ran after him into the dark, dank hallway. She caught him by the sleeve and again threw her arms around him. From the bed, Sergio watched with amusement.

"Sweetheart, I know what you're after, wait, please."

"You're reading my mind."

"Wait. You want to know who killed that girl in the Gayosso Mortuary, don't you?"

"I told you, you're a regular fortuneteller."

"Sweetie, I'm going to get him out of here, stay here with me, love me a little and I'll help you find who killed her. I promise. How about it, come back in, put down the notebook, and we'll make love, the way only you know how."

"Your baby's waiting, Lichita."

"Don't judge me, sweetie. Everyone has to scratch a little. The centavos don't go very far . . . Come on. Give me the book. I swear it doesn't have anything to do with what you're looking for."

"Then why do you want it?"

"I'm thinking of my poor old Memo, he's such a good man. He'll be ruined without his list of customers. Why be hard on him? What did he ever do to you? Come on, sweetheart, you don't have to . . ."

Felix pushed her away. Her streaked face stretched into a grimace as she bared ratlike eyeteeth. She leaped at Felix, scratching and clawing; she didn't care that her bathrobe fell open, revealing small, firm breasts, or that curses spewed from her twisted lips. "You bastard, what do you know about us? What the fuck do you know about anyone who has to work their ass off to keep from starving, you shiteater."

Felix could hear the whistles of the balloon vendors in the plaza. Licha collapsed in his arms like a deflated balloon. Playfully, he tweaked her red nose. "There, there, Licha. After I get this business over with, I'll come back and see you."

"Honest, sweetheart? You swear it, honey? I'm so crazy about you."

"What is it you want to know, Lichita?"

"You're the one asking all the questions, not me."

"Because you think you'll find out how much I know by what questions I ask."

"Why do you want poor Memo's notebook? You yourself said there's nothing in it . . ."

"Two heads are better than one, Lichita. Maybe I won't understand what's in this notebook, but the Director General will."

"You're not going to show it to *him?*"

"Of course. Those dark glasses will spot in a second why you're so interested in recovering a notebook that doesn't have any entry for the tenth of August."

"I swear it doesn't have anything to do with Simon, or with old Spooky."

"You're that afraid of him?"

"You should have seen Simon, like a Swiss cheese . . ."

"Make up your mind, Lichita. Either all this is tied together, you, Memo, Simon, the Director General, the girl's death . . ."

Licha could only shudder. "No, honey, oh, honey, no, I swear on my mother's . . ."

256

"Or it's two separate things. Make up your mind."

"Oh, yes, honey, it's the way you say. I went to the hospital as a nurse, as Simon's friend, I didn't know what it was all about. It doesn't have anything to do with Memo's taxi, I swear by my mother, it's like you say, two different things."

"Stop trembling, Lichita. If you're telling the truth, you don't have anything to be afraid of. But the police might believe differently. They might think it's all part of the same affair, you know? That you and Memo know something about an attempt against the President's life, understand? And the Director General doesn't fool around, you know that, don't you? He knows how to shut people up forever."

"Sheee-it!" Sergio exclaimed, leaping from the bed and scrambling for his undershorts. "I just came here for a good lay. What the fuck's going on?"

"Think about this, Licha," Felix went on, as Sergio flew into his clothes. "The girl who was murdered was the lover of the Director General's mortal enemy. He's going to figure everything out and then come around to ask for an accounting."

"Not that, honey. Oh no, sweetheart, do anything you want, but don't sic Four-eyes on us . . ."

"Listen, you dumb bitch, what is all this?" Sergio tripped as he tried to put his legs into his trousers. "What kind of mess are you getting me into?"

"All I want is the truth," said Felix, ignoring Sergio.

"But, sweetie, I owe everything to Memo. I told you that already. Don't make me tell on him. I told you, we have to scratch for a living."

"Sometimes the pay is death."

"I'm scared of the old man with the glasses, honey, I'm scared of him!"

"I believe you."

Sergio was knotting his necktie. Licha looked at him, and hung her head, defeated. "Tell him, Sergio."

"I don't know anything about anything, you bitch." Sergio was buttoning his blazer.

Felix examined the small, elegant young man with interest. *"You're* the one who used Memo's plates on August 10?"

Sergio tipped his ridiculous blond head to one side, small even for his small body. "Look, man, you're getting all worked up over an innocent prank. Look how you've upset poor Licha. Okay, be seeing you, Licha."

Felix grabbed his arm.

"Careful, ape-man," said Sergio. "I don't like being pawed."

"Tell him, Sergio," Lichita repeated dejectedly. She had collapsed on a plastic chair. "Tell him, or even though we're not guilty of anything—I swear it—we'll both end up full of holes."

Sergio stroked the sleeve where Felix had seized him. "An innocent prank," he said, and smiled. "That's all it was. A few of us asked Memo for his plates so we could have a little fun that night. We were chasing some blondes, gringas, who were staying at the Suites de Génova. We'd promised to serenade them, you know how they are. They expect to find romance in Mexico and didn't want to leave without a serenade. What's so bad about that?"

"Nothing," said Felix. "But you wouldn't have had to change the plates for that."

"Oh, man. You don't understand. Like everyone else, my old man keeps me on a short rein. The way things are, he says, don't get in any trouble, don't call any attention to yourself, or we'll be kidnapped by the Communists. So what could we do? Just a little fun without letting the old man know, you understand now?"

Sergio lighted a cigarette, dropped the match on the floor, and stared cockily at Felix. He thought he was looking good before Licha, and his vanity was stronger than his fear. "My old man has a lot of influence," he said smugly, with more than a hint of a threat.

"I wouldn't think so, if he can't handle a little racket with some mariachis in front of a hotel in the Zona Rosa. What's influence for? To scold you if you eat a piece of candy before dinnertime?"

Again, Sergio's eyes narrowed. "I said it once before. I never saw a cop that wasn't a bastard, but you top them all. If you don't want to understand . . ."

"You put on a good show. No, I'm not from the police. I'm a member of the Communist conspiracy. Tell your old man to watch out."

Sergio's lips curled in contempt. "Someday we'll pick up where we left off, Lichita. Ciao."

He left, whistling "Blue Moon," and Licha closed her sleep-heavy, love-heavy, fear-heavy eyes. "Stay a while, honey," she murmured.

She opened her eyes. Felix walked toward the door with the notebook in his hand.

"You know the truth now. Leave me the notebook, sweetheart."

"But I'm getting more and more interested in Memo's customers," Felix said. "So long, Lichita. When this is all over, I'll take you to Acapulco."

"Honest, honey? I'm not asking for anything fancy. I'd rather see you steady, once a week, that's enough."

"Can you work me into your schedule?"

"You bastard, I told you the truth. On my soul."

He left her with the sign of the cross on her lips.

44 ON DURANGO, he saw a mustard-colored Mustang pulling away from the curb. He jotted down its license number in Memo's notebook, just below the date August 10.

He returned to the Suites de Génova and asked room service to send up roast beef, salad, and coffee. He studied the notebook carefully. Then he picked up the telephone and asked for the central police station of the Federal District. He reported the theft of a mustard-colored Mustang and gave its license number.

"This is the owner speaking, Licenciado Diego Velázquez, Chief of Cost Analysis at the Ministry of Economic Development. Let's not lose any time on this."

He received obsequious assurances. He looked at his watch. It was three o'clock and the morning sun had disappeared behind heavy, slow-moving clouds. He had time and he needed to rest. He slept until five, with the tranquillity that had been missing the previous evening. He was sure now. Now he knew.

He checked the .44 and placed it in an inside jacket pocket. He walked the block from Génova to Niza and bought a raincoat at Gentry's. The downpour began as he left the men's shop; traffic was snarled and people sought refuge beneath awnings and canopies. He put on the coat, a good Burberry trenchcoat, too new to reflect satisfactorily the image in his subconscious. He smiled as he walked through the rain toward the Paseo de la Reforma. If he hoped outwardly to resemble Humphrey Bogart, inwardly he felt ridiculously like Woody Allen. He remembered Sara Klein in the mortuary, and his smile faded.

At the corner of Hamburgo, he stopped to wait. He had five minutes. He preferred to be exactly on time. He was the most punctual official in the entire Mexican bureaucracy, even though his appointment wasn't with a more or less friendly Under-Secretary but with a more or less savage criminal.

At a quarter to six, the taxi stopped before the Cronopios Boutique on Niza and honked insistently. Young Sergio emerged, laughing and waving goodbye to the employees. He opened the rear door of the taxi and got in. Felix followed closely behind him. He pulled out the .44 and pressed it against the ribs of the small and elegant youth. Memo looked around with alarm.

"Don't worry," Felix said to the driver. "I have bullets for both of you. It depends on which of you wants to die first. Now, let's take our young gentleman to the place you take him every Monday, Wednesday, and Friday at this hour. One false move and Lichita will be a widow."

Greasy sweat broke out on Memo's furrowed brow. He didn't say a word. The taxi crawled at a snail's pace through the congested traffic on Niza toward the Avenida Chapultepec. Felix kept an eye on Memo's neck, but pressed the .44 to Sergio's ribs.

"How's your papa?" he asked the boy.

"Screwing your mother," said Sergio. His pupils were dilated, and he licked his lips.

"No," smiled Felix. "He'd have to be very influential to do that. And millionaires' sons like you don't work as clerks in swank boutiques. They just manage to dress like sons of millionaires. It isn't the same thing."

"Don't go to the usual place, Memo, this guy's full of bullshit. I know him . . ."

Felix smashed the butt of the pistol against Sergio's mouth. The boy screamed and sank down in his seat, wiping blood from his lips with the back of his hand. The taxi turned right on Chapultepec and accelerated slightly.

"The only reason I didn't destroy that big mouth is because I want you to use it to talk."

"Then I'm as good as dead, shitass," spit Sergio.

"You think your chief will protect you? What does he do for you, besides lend you a Mustang to cover his tracks when you act as his messenger boy?"

"I have protection." Sergio smiled crookedly.

"I knew a little pretty-boy like you. He thought he had protection. He ended up full of holes, stacked like a side of beef at a taxi driver's door."

"I just follow orders," muttered Memo. "I go where they tell me."

They moved slowly along the colonial aqueduct that parallels the avenue.

"I know that," said Felix. "I'm grateful that you were so diligent in keeping a record of your calls. Isn't it interesting? Three times a week at a quarter to six you pick up a certain Sergio de la Vega, a supposedly wealthy young man who serenades lady tourists."

"Don't be so thickheaded. I explained that. It was a prank."

"Two pranks. A nun comes to ask for a contribution to her charity and a bunch of boys with mariachis comes to serenade. These two pranks serve to create a distraction in the street while the third prank is taking place inside the hotel."

"I don't know what you're talking about, friend."

"I'm talking about your chief's prank. The murder of Sara Klein."

"The name doesn't mean a thing to me."

"Maybe a bullet in the kidney will mean something."

"You scare me. I'll piss like a sieve."

Felix pressed the muzzle of the .44 against the driver's neck. "Your friend's close-mouthed, Memo."

"I don't know anything, chief." Raimu's double trembled. "They pay me to pick them up and bring them back."

"Memo, the rich can buy protection, but a poor bastard like you would get life as accomplice to a murder."

"Don't tell him anything," said Sergio. "The head man's more powerful than this bastard. He doesn't know anything. He's bluffing. Ignore him. Don't go the usual route, I tell you."

"I know the route," Felix said tranquilly. "Memo put down the address. I know where we're going. And I know who we'll see."

"It won't do you any good. The chief's a super big shot."

"Like your father?"

"Screw your fucking mother."

"I'll say it again, little boy. We'll see whether you believe he's a big shot after the judge sentences you."

"Don't make me laugh. For what? For serenading? For using someone else's plates? Where've you been, dummy?"

"No. For driving a stolen car."

"The chief registered it in my name."

"It's parked in front of your house. By now, the police have located it and are waiting for you."

For the first time, Sergio was sweating like Memo.

"What are you worried about, Sergito? You can prove your big man gave you the car. No sweat. What will they find inside the car? Is that what's worrying you? Is that why your chief put the car in your name, so you'd have to take the rap? Is that the protection you were bragging about?"

At the corner of Melchor Ocampo, the taxi turned onto the main highway around the city, following the sign toward Querétaro. Sergio tried to open the door of the taxi. His head snapped back as Felix grabbed him around the neck; he choked, gagged, and fell heavily to the floor. Felix pulled him up by the collar like a rag doll. Between coughs, in a hoarse, pained voice, Sergio gasped, "She didn't have time, I know she didn't have time."

"We'll see whether she's waiting at Cuatro Caminos," Memo said nervously.

"Don't stop for her," Sergio croaked.

Again, Felix pressed the muzzle of the pistol to Memo's neck. In his fit of coughing, Sergio resembled a tubercular cupid.

No one spoke again until they reached the Cuatro Caminos bullring. A rebozo-wrapped fat woman with a basket over her arm was standing on one corner, waving her free hand at the taxi. She seemed the mother of Indian gods, a stone Coatlicue, imperturbable beneath the rain.

"Don't stop!"

Memo stopped the taxi. The fat woman opened the front door and peered in. When she saw Felix, she paused, but her impassive expression didn't change. Not even when she saw the gun pointed straight at her broad, dark face.

"Get in, señora."

The fat woman sat down beside Memo. She smelled of damp clothing and re-fried beans.

"What do you have in the basket?" asked Felix. "More chicks? Give it to me."

The fat woman turned to hand some keys to Sergio. "Here. I couldn't get to the trunk. The law were all around the car."

Felix took the keys to the Mustang. "The basket."

The fat woman raised the basket to show him the contents; it was filled with lettuce. She hurled it in Felix's face. The woman leaped out with unexpected agility. Sergio tried to follow her, but was stopped by the gun in his ribs.

Memo drove on. Felix and Sergio struggled for an instant, but the boy soon gave up. Behind them, Felix could see the motionless figure of the ancient Aztec goddess fading into rain as gray as the earth she stood on, enveloped in a mist that seemed to emanate from her body.

Felix picked up the basket. Under the lettuce, he found the waterproof packets whose contents weren't what they seemed, not flour, not sugar.

45 THE TAXI DRIVER slowed before the Ciudad Satélite Supermarket. Through sheets of rain, the slim, triangular columns designed by Goeritz resembled the coral sails of a sunken galleon. Felix ordered Memo to stop where he parked every Monday, Wednesday, and Friday. He drove past the main entrance of the huge empty establishment, surrounded at this hour by empty parking places, turned, and parked by the delivery entrance, away from the highway.

"Get out," Felix ordered Sergio, then followed him, pressing the pistol to his back. He left the basket on the rear seat.

Memo stuck his head out the window. Rain plastered his thinning hair. He stared at Felix with the gaze of an ancient priest, humble but dissolute.

"What about me, chief? That night, you promised me you'd pay me double, remember?"

"I'm paying you triple," Felix replied. "Take off, Memo."

"And the stuff?" Memo jerked his tonsured head toward the back seat.

"That's the first prize. Do whatever you want with it. Hand it over to the narcotics bureau and collect a reward. Or sell it through some other channel and take Licha to Acapulco. You both need a vacation. That's your second prize. And the third is that you're getting out of this alive and happy."

Without a word, Memo drove away.

Sergio looked at Felix with curiosity. "Then you really aren't a cop . . ."

"You'll soon see who I am. Open that door."

"Only the head man can open it, from inside. It's an electronic gadget. I have to call over the intercom."

"All right. Listen, Sergio, remember that your chief isn't going to protect you. He's leaving you on the hook with the Mustang and the snow."

Sergio's dilated pupils danced. "What's happened, big talker? Now it's two against one, right?"

Sergio pressed a button, three short and one long. Over the intercom a voice said, "Come in."

The rolling steel door began to rise electronically.

Sergio hesitated an instant, then shouted, "No, chief, don't open it, they've got us!"

Felix rolled beneath the security door and fired three shots. He wasted two bullets; at the first shot, the small blond youth twisted his lips for the last time and fell face forward onto the wet pavement. The third bullet hit the silently closing steel door.

Felix got to his feet in the darkness of the storeroom and started toward the door that communicated with the sales area of the supermarket, guided by the glow of fluorescent lights beyond it.

Before he reached it, the lights were extinguished. Silently, he entered the vast, dark, reverberating cavern. His first thought was that this hangar ought to smell of food, but there was only an overpowering stench of antiseptic. The silence was deafening. Every step, every movement, was amplified in the echoing emptiness. Felix heard his own footsteps and then a distant cough.

He groped his way along high shelves; he touched tin cans and jars and then he shouted, "The game's up, do you hear me?"

The echo resounded in liquid ripples, like waves on a pond after a pebble strikes the water.

"The police have the Mustang. The fat woman gave me the delivery. Sergio is dead outside. The game's up, you hear?"

The answer was an uncannily accurate bullet that burst a bottle next to Felix's head. He heard breaking glass and then smelled whiskey. He crouched down and, still bent over, crept forward, his face almost touching his knees. He moved like a cat, but he told himself this was a battle be-

266

tween bats, a battle in which all the odds were against him. His enemy knew the terrain, he owned this supermarket. Felix collided with an obstacle, tumbling a pyramid of tin cans; the crash of metal was drowned out by a burst of bullets directed at the precise site of the mishap. Felix threw himself to the floor behind a protecting row of shelves.

"Keep talking," a voice said. "You'll never leave here alive."

Felix tried to locate the point from which the voice was originating. It came from a higher level, and he remembered that sometimes the offices in a supermarket are on a second level, from which employees can observe the customers. He removed his shoes. Scattering everything in his path, he ran behind a row of shelves between himself and the trajectory of the bullets—right to left, from a higher to a lower point, and always straight ahead. His rival's advantage was also his limitation. He was hunting from a besieged tower.

"You laid your plans carefully. You registered under an assumed name. You could always say that you were meeting a lover. Actually, it didn't matter if someone saw you. You had the best alibi in the world. You were with your wife. You went together to the Suites de Génova. No one asks questions in a place like that. Tourists and lovers make up the clientele."

Again he was silent, as he ran to a different location. The buckle of his raincoat struck against a shopping cart; he fell to his knees as shots rang above his head. He crawled to the end of the row of carts and took off his raincoat; he draped it over the handle of the cart and gave it a push with his foot. A rain of bullets followed the cart as it careened down an aisle; it struck a display and the barrage was repeated. Felix flattened himself against a sheltering shelf.

"Your wife had challenged you. Why didn't you go to a hotel like lovers, to make it more exciting? But she wanted to add spice to the broth. She said it wasn't enough simply to go to a hotel. Even then, you didn't turn her on. You were furious. She admitted that only when you were jealous were you slightly more attractive. But since you were constantly jealous, even that device was wearing thin. You proposed a new challenge. You asked her to find some way to make you more jealous than ever the night you planned to be at the hotel. She laughed and accepted the challenge. She told you that the night you went to the hotel she would sleep with me before she came to you. She even gave you the number of the room of our assignation, 301. She asked you to reserve a room on the same floor, as close as possible to 301. With luck, you might be able to hear our moans of pleasure."

"You know Mary," the voice said. "Keep imagining."

"Sure, Abie," Felix replied, moving silently along the rows of shelves, being careful to avoid brushing the crinkly cellophane bags with his shoulder. "Mary chose that room for our supposed date because she knew Sara Klein was staying there. You found that out, too, and fell into your wife's trap. She wanted you to know it, so you'd think the challenge was real, so you'd have doubts. Was I taking advantage of my friendship with Sara to use her room for a rendezvous with your wife? Why not?"

Again he ran to a new location, nearer the steps to the upper level. Abie taunted, "Do you know who told Mary that Sara was staying at the Suites?"

Felix again sought protection against some shelves, and said, "It doesn't matter. I'm married to a Jew. I know the tribal customs. It's a tight little community. Everyone knows everything about everyone."

"I know," snorted Abie. *"Do* I know."

"But you didn't know who you were going to kill, your wife or me, or both of us. Your mind was running along two rails, one calculating, the other emotional. Yours and Mary's challenges were like a game of ping-pong. She challenged you, saying that she would sleep with me right under your nose. You returned the challenge with a question: What time did she plan to deceive you? Laughing at you, she set an exact time. Exactly twelve o'clock midnight, the witching hour for Cinderella, something like that, it's her style, right?"

The roar from the upper level was that of a wounded bull. For the first time, Felix fired in the direction of Abie's voice; it was time to let him know that he was armed.

"You prepared your diversions for precisely twelve-thirty. Sergio and his friends with their mariachis would stop before the hotel and sing the serenade. The nun would come by to ask for charity. The police interrupted the serenade and ordered Sergio to keep moving. But you had achieved what you desired. The concierge would remember the two unusual happenings, and the police would pursue two false trails. You were protected. Memo's plates were on the Mustang. Apparently, the police didn't take down the number. A serenade's a normal event; just a prank that interrupts traffic. Sergio slipped the policeman the usual bribe, and didn't even get a ticket. No trace of the Mustang. And you were sure of your people. Memo thought it was a joke, and since no one bothered him, he forgot about it. Sergio was your slave, your drug runner, an addict himself. He never asked questions, he did as he was told. Perfect. Your allies were in the dark, and only you knew what you planned to do."

"And the nun?" The voice laughed. "Do you know who the nun is?"

"No, but you're going to tell me, Abie."

"I might, yes, since you won't be leaving here alive."

Crouched low, Felix moved still closer to the steps. His stockinged foot struck a step. He looked for the nearest cover. His hands touched the icy window of a freezer. He leaned against the cold surface. He was safe from Abie Benjamin's bullets, the staircase ascended alongside the freezer.

"A little before midnight, Mary left the room in her bathrobe. Again, she was both insulting and seducing you. She said she was coming to see me and that she'd be back in half an hour to make love to you as never before. She permitted herself the luxury of a final defiance; she threw the key to room 301 on the bed."

"You're very close. Be careful. How did Mary get the key to Sara's room?"

"I don't know, but I can imagine. In that hotel, the rules are easily bent. Guests visit each other constantly, and receive unexpected visitors at all hours of the day and night. The concierge is used to that. But the most obvious answer is the true one. Mary went down to the desk and took the extra key to Sara's room from its pigeonhole. The concierge was outside, with his back to the lobby. The clerk was sleeping, or watching television in the kitchen."

"Oh, yes, you know her, you bastard. She was a virgin until she met you. You had her before anyone. Before I did. A nobody like you."

"It didn't matter to her. A woman's virginity matters only to the men in her life."

"You've been my nightmare, Maldonado. You've destroyed my happiness. She was always holding you up to me, you, her first man, the only man, the one who really excited her, not me, she wouldn't come near me, you, a goddamned *nobody . . .*"

"I was to be the victim that night."

"Yes. I was going to rid myself of the ten years you've been there in my bed, between my wife and me . . ."

"But when you opened the door to 301, the room was dark. You approached the bed. All the rooms are identical. You groped in the darkness. You touched a woman's body. You heard the music of the mariachis in the street. You didn't care that I wasn't there. She was there. Mary. One way or other, you would avenge yourself for the humiliations of your marriage, and I'd appear to be the guilty one.

270

You'd kill two birds with one stone, Abie. You pulled your straight-edge razor from your pocket, you put your hand over the woman's mouth, and you slit her throat."

"Yes."

"Trembling, you returned to your room and found Mary lying on the bed, laughing with delight. She began telling you how once again, as usual, she'd tricked you; she'd followed you down the hall and watched you from the public bathroom; she'd seen you enter Sara's room, and . . ."

"Yes!"

"Her smile congealed when she saw the razor you still held idiotically in your hand. Fool, she said, nothing but mistakes!"

"Yes."

"You made two mistakes, Abie. You didn't kill me. And you didn't kill Mary. You killed Sara Klein. You killed the wrong person, you son-of-a-bitch!"

Suddenly all the lights in the market flashed on. Felix closed his eyes in pain and surprise.

"I'm coming after you, Maldonado. It's time for a showdown."

He heard Abie's footsteps slowly descending the few steps from the balcony to the ground floor.

"This time I'll make no mistake, Maldonado. You wove your own noose. Tomorrow they'll find your body and Sergio's together in a dump. The Mustang's in his name. There's nothing to tie me to him or to you. Did you grieve over Sara Klein's death? Then it wasn't for nothing. I knew it would hurt you, and you know what? I felt no remorse. It was the same as killing you. Now I'm going to kill you a second time, Maldonado, before I kill you forever. The third time's the charm, they say. And never again will you say anything or hear anything or fuck another man's wife. You know who told Mary Sara was staying at the Suites de Génova?"

Pressed against the freezer, Felix saw the tip of Abie's shoe appear, only a few feet away.

"Ruth," said Abie.

Felix felt the unremembering, unhating tension of a leopard. The instant Abie moved into his line of vision, Felix leaped on him, but prevented his falling by throwing a hammerlock around his neck. Abie's back pressed against Felix's chest; each grasped a weapon in his right hand. Felix pulled the trigger and the gray-haired, black-moustached man screamed and the pistol fell from his fingers. Felix dropped his own .44, opened the door to the freezer, and pushed Abie inside.

The man with the coarse, ugly, ruddy face fell to the icy floor in the midst of hanging sides of beef and extended his beautiful, imploring hands toward Felix.

Felix slammed the freezer door. He knew that those doors had no opening on the inside—as if the slaughtered steers might slip from their hooks and escape their icy tomb. No one would arrive before six o'clock the next morning. Nine hours at a temperature of fifty degrees below zero is a long time.

He looked at Abie, locked inside the freezer, the floridity and aggression gone forever. In his eyes, the cold of terror anticipated the cold of death. He pushed aside the sides of beef, rose, slipped, and fell forward against the frost-framed glass door.

With his bleeding hand, he scratched six letters in the frost of the door. Felix read them in reverse, red on white, as with a grimace of terror Abie placed his hand over his mouth, closed his eyes, and remained kneeling, like a penitent in Antarctica. He had managed to scratch *nun eht*.

46 THE BURBERRY SCARECROW had more life than Abie Benjamin. Felix Maldonado retrieved his trenchcoat from the shopping cart and put it on. He went upstairs, where he found Abie's control panel on the desk. First he punched the key marked SECURITY DOOR, STOREROOM. He depressed it for an instant only, enough to allow him to leave as he'd entered, on his belly; he didn't want to arouse suspicion by leaving the rolling door wide open.

Next he turned off the fluorescent lights. The antiseptic cathedral sank into an almost sacred darkness; only the frost in the freezer glistened dimly, like tiny votive candles.

He squeezed beneath the steel door and then returned once more, dragging Sergio de la Vega's rain-soaked body. He didn't want Abie Benjamin's vacation in the snow to be interrupted because of this Cardin-shrouded corpse. He propped the body against some cartons of Ajax and derisively bade him farewell. "Tend the store for Abie."

For the last time, he wriggled through the opening between the rolling door and the concrete floor. In the rain, he walked to the Mexico City–Querétaro highway and, without much hope, stood waiting for a taxi or a bus. Clusters of men wearing sarapes and sombreros trotted along the highway, numb with cold. A city of thirteen million, Felix thought, and not even the most elementary means of public transportation. The horse and the wheel had come late to Mexico, after centuries of foot travel. Now a man without a car was a pariah, a peasant condemned to repeating the journeys of his ancestors. As he watched them jogging stolidly by, he recalled the figures he'd seen the night of his last meeting with Sara Klein, the figures resembling the paintings of Ricardo Martínez. He'd been unable to describe them, because he hadn't dared approach those creatures of misery, compassion, and horror.

The unremitting rain washed from his trenchcoat the

273

emblems of honor won in the joust against Abie Benjamin: dust, mud, and grease. It wasn't much of an accomplishment, but for the first time since he'd accepted this mission in the name of his father's humiliation, Felix felt free. Finally he had done one thing on his own, without orders from me, without finding himself in circumstances where he was forced to follow my wishes, believing he was acting on his own. He had avenged Sara Klein. And he had not compromised the humble, Memo and Licha and the fat woman.

Automobiles and trucks ignored him as they roared by on the road. Alone beneath the rain, his own host, he conceded that Abie was right, Felix Maldonado was a nobody, the kind of man who achieves certain outward signs of prosperity, without being rich. But that is the secret of modern societies: to make the greatest number believe they have something when they have nothing— because the few have everything. He looked across the highway at Abie Benjamin's market, a modern-day cathedral. Again he thought of Sara Klein, of her enormous faith in the egalitarian society of Israel and the efforts of its people, in the democracy of that land where a Communist lawyer could defend a poor man like Jamil. Sara herself had compared all this to the inequality, the injustice, the tyranny of Arab countries.

Now that he was alone in the rain, facing the red and yellow and blue columns of the Ciudad Satélite, he remembered my warning: no one has a monopoly on violence in this business, much less truth or morality. All systems, whatever their ideology, generate their own injustice; perhaps evil is the price of life, but you cannot stop living because you fear evil, and for Felix on that night, at that hour, in that place, that awareness was truth. He bestowed that truth upon those who demanded life above every other thing, even if the price were evil: upon the boy Jamil, who'd loved Sara more than Felix had; upon the Palestinians, who, because they had no life, countered with evil the lives that denied theirs.

A long, low, black Citroën stopped before Felix. A black door opened and a pale hand beckoned. Automatically, Felix got in. The Director General glanced at him, smiling ironically. He gave an order in Arabic over the intercom, and the coffin-on-wheels drove away.

"I've been looking for you, Licenciado Velázquez, mmh? But you're soaking wet. I'll take you to your hotel; have a warm bath and a good rubdown and a glass of cognac. You'll get pneumonia. That would be ironic, after surviving so many dangers."

The dry laugh was a spider's thread cut suddenly by invisible scissors.

"Why were you looking for me?" said Felix, again defeated, thinking how much he preferred his freedom beneath the rain to the warm comfort of the Director General's automobile.

The Director General laughed, stopped laughing, and spoke with grave deliberation. "You were very unwise to say the Mustang was yours. The police found twenty kilos of M & C, morphine and cocaine, in the trunk. They immediately contacted me, since you'd identified yourself as an official in my Ministry. But it worked out well. The matter's settled; they attribute the contraband to a certain Sergio de la Vega; the car was registered to him." He gazed at Felix with an intensity ill-disguised by the dark pince-nez, and smiled with an expression appropriate to the skull-shaped candies of the Day of the Dead.

"Yes, it worked out very well, n'est-ce pas? Now you're identified forever with Licenciado Diego Velázquez, Chief of the Bureau of Cost Analysis. And such good will must be rewarded, mmh? A very special invitation for day after tomorrow awaits you at your hotel. Please be there."

"I'm not going to a hotel. I'm going to see my wife. At last, I can do that."

"Of course, Licenciado. First, I shall take you to your home."

"No, you don't understand. I'm going to stay there. I live there, with my wife."

The Director General issued a new order, then immediately turned to Felix. "Your invitation awaits you at the Hilton."

"You're not making any sense. My things are at the Suites de Génova."

"They've been moved to the Hilton."

"With what right?"

"The right of the person whose influence saved you from a charge of trafficking in drugs, mmh?"

"I don't want to hear another word about influence."

"But it's the supreme law in Mexico, n'est-ce pas? You will return to the Hilton. The same room. It's a perfect front."

"You don't seem to understand what I'm saying," said Felix, with the irritation of exhaustion. "The matter's finished. I did what I had to do. *I* did it, without anyone's help."

"I just came from the market, mmh? You have too much faith in the fatal powers of refrigeration. Señor Benjamin is growing cold. But forever this time. He's resting comfortably with a bullet in his skull."

Felix felt sick; he doubled over, nauseated. He didn't want to choke to death on his own vomit. The nausea subsided as the Director General spoke again with the velvety voice of a snake charmer. "I don't know what motives you attribute to the dear-departed Benjamin. You're a very passionate man, I've always said that. How I laughed at the mischief you played on poor Simon, and Señora Rossetti in the swimming pool, and Professor Bernstein! That takes much *culot*, n'est-ce pas? Come, Licenciado, the time for violence between us is past. Let go my lapels. Let us be calm, mmh?"

"Are you telling me that Abie didn't kill Sara because he thought she was Mary? Jealousy wasn't the motive for the murder?"

For once, the Director General's laughter ran its course. He laughed so hard he had to remove the pince-nez and wipe his eyes with his handkerchief.

"Sara Klein was murdered because she was Sara Klein, my dear friend. No one confused her with anyone else. What is it Nietzsche says about women? That man fears a woman in love because she is capable of any sacrifice, because anything not related to her passion is despicable? That is why a woman is the most dangerous creature in the world. Sara Klein was one of those truly dangerous ones. The name of her love was justice. And this woman enamored of justice was prepared to suffer everything for justice's sake. But also to reveal everything. Yes, the most dangerous creature in the world."

"Her love was named Jamil; you killed him."

The Director General shrugged off the commentary with belligerent indifference, as if to say, anything goes. He spoke with no attempt at self-justification. "When I visited Sara at ten o'clock that evening in the Suites de Génova, I warned her to be on her guard. I told her that Bernstein had killed the man called Jamil as Jamil attempted to kill Bernstein. In itself, this was credible; there was more than sufficient reason for Jamil to murder Bernstein, and vice versa. But I nailed down my version by asking Sara to call the professor. She did so. Bernstein admitted he'd been shot that evening, following the ceremony in the Palace. Someone had attempted to kill him but had succeeded only in wounding him in the shoulder. Sara cursed Bernstein and hung up the telephone, shaken with sobs. She believed what I had told her."

"But Jamil was already dead and as good as buried in a military cell in my name. Who shot Bernstein?"

"But of course, he was superficially wounded by Ayub,

who was following my instructions. It was to exacerbate Sara, to force her to break the last threads of her shattered fidelity to Israel, and to get her to talk. *Quel coup, mon ami!* A militant Israeli like Sara Klein passing over to our side and making sensational revelations about torture and concentration camps and the military ambitions of Israel. Just imagine, mmh?"

"She was planning to return to Israel. She had the tickets. She told me on the recording."

"Ah, a true biblical heroine, that Sara, a modern Judith, no? She told me, too. She would denounce Israel, but from within Israel. Such was the morality of this unfortunate but dangerous woman. I gave her some *cachets* of sleeping drugs and told her to rest. I would come by for her the following morning to take her to the airport. I arranged a guard in front of the Suites de Génova. My agents took note of everything, the serenade, the nun. But no one suspicious entered. The Israelis deceived us. Their agents were already inside the hotel. Their names were Mary and Abie Benjamin."

"But Abie admitted that my version was correct . . ."

"Of course, it suited him for you to think that passion was the motive for the crime. Not so, the motive was political. Sara Klein had to be silenced forever. They succeeded. But do not torture yourself, Licenciado. Abie Benjamin is dead inside a freezer, and you have your revenge, n'est-ce pas?"

Although he couldn't see out, Felix knew that they were driving through Mexico City. The two men did not speak for a long while. Felix's depression annulled an anger that lay beyond his fatigue, like the city beyond the curtains of the car.

"You robbed me of my only act, my one free act," Felix said finally. "Why?"

Deliberately, the Director General lighted a cigarette before responding. "The Hydra of passion has many heads. Ask yourself whether Sara Klein deserved to die as you imagined it, because of mistaken passion. You should have realized, that crime hid other mysteries, like those Russian dolls that grow in number as they diminish in size. No. Believe instead that in the end Sara Klein died the death she deserved. Othello's passion would not have suited Sara. Macbeth's passion, yes. All the waters of the great god Neptune will not erase the blood from our hands, Licenciado. I know that. Sara died with clean hands . . . But I believe we are almost there."

The Citroën stopped. Felix opened the door. They were in front of his apartment house in Polanco.

"I shall wait for you here," said the Director General after Felix got out.

Felix crouched down beside the door to peer toward the ghostly outlines of the man in the cushioned darkness of the French automobile. "Why? I'm home. I'll be staying here."

"Nevertheless, remember that I shall be waiting."

Felix closed the door and looked up toward the ninth floor of the building. He could see lights, but only from the dimmest lamps in the apartment.

47 IN THE ELEVATOR, he thought about the last time he'd seen Ruth. It seemed a century ago, not three weeks. He remembered his wife's expression: she'd never looked at him just that way, her eyes filled with tears and tenderness, slowly shaking her head, her brows knit, as if for that one time she knew the truth but didn't want to offend him by speaking it.

"Please don't go, Felix. Stay here with me. I'm not playing games now. I'm asking you sincerely. Please stay. Don't jeopardize yourself."

Tender, sweet Ruth, neither as intelligent as Sara nor as beautiful as Mary, but capable of sudden rages sparked by jealousy and cooled by affection. A freckled Jewish girl, she disguised her freckles with makeup, drops of sweat gathered on the tip of her nose, Señora Maldonado was a pretty Jewish girl, charming, active, his faithful Penelope, and now he was returning defeated from the wars against an invisible Troy. She was the woman he needed to solve all his practical problems, the woman who always had his breakfast ready, his suits pressed, his suitcases packed. She did everything for him, even putting in his cuff links. And all she asked was patience and compassion.

He took out his key ring. The keys to his home. Patience and compassion. He hoped Ruth would be patient and compassionate. They needed both more than ever before if they were to rebuild their relationship. She thought he was dead; how would she receive him? She knew him well, she remembered him with sadness, but she wasn't looking for him. Would she recognize his altered face, very little changed really, but enough to create doubts. Was it he or was it another? Would Bernstein be proved right?

He looked at himself in the hall, honestly believing the reproduction of the Velázquez self-portrait was a mirror. How would Señora Maldonado react to the fact that from now on she would be called Señora Velázquez? How would she handle the practical details, the documents, the family, the relatives? Neither the Director General nor I had explained that. Then Felix must have shivered: in the same way we had changed him, we were transforming his wife. Only a little, but enough to induce error, to provoke doubt. He felt like Boris Karloff about to touch the electrified fingers of Elsa Lanchester.

He heard a voice that was not Ruth's. It was coming from the living room. The double doors between the hall and the living room were ajar. He felt ridiculously melodramatic; how long is it before a young widow receives callers? When does the first suitor call upon Penelope? What is his name?

He paused with his hand on the doorknob. The living room was in deep shadow, only the dimmest table lamps lighted. No. It was a woman's voice. Ruth's visitor was a woman. It was late, almost eleven, but there was a normal explanation; Ruth was lonely, she needed company.

He listened to the voice of Ruth's visitor. "I had left you to follow him. But I had followed him to fulfill a duty he himself had pointed out to me. It was no easy job for Bernstein to take your place, to offer himself in your place, to dilute my sense of duty by adding to it a love different from that I'd sacrificed, your love, Felix . . ."

His hands were burning as he entered the living room, seeking the origin of the voice, blind to everything except the reality of that voice, Sara Klein's voice.

The tape whirred peacefully in the cassette. Felix pressed a key, the tape shrieked and spun forward. "That night, we went to bed together. With Jamil, all the frontiers of my life disappeared. I ceased to be a persecuted little German-Jewish girl . . ."

He pressed the *stop* key. Only then did he hear the rhythmical sound of a rocking chair.

He turned and saw her sitting there, rocking, unspeaking, dressed in a nun's habit, scattered rosary beads in her lap, tense hands gripping the arms of the chair, long black skirts hiding her feet, a white wimple framing an overly made-up face, enough to disguise the freckles but not enough to dissipate the drops of sweat gathered on the tip of her nose, rocking, rocking, in the shadows.

"You were never really converted, were you?" asked Ruth, rocking, rocking, with a torturously neutral voice.

Felix closed his eyes. He wished he could close them forever. He left the room, his eyes closed, he knew by heart the arrangement of his own home. He reached the front door and, as he opened it, opened his eyes. He had kept them closed for fear of seeing himself in the self-portrait

Ruth and Felix Maldonado had laughingly bought one day in Madrid. He ran down the stairway, skipping steps, crashing against the handrail, pressing the sweat from his hands against the cement walls of the stairwell. Asphyxia—he needed air, air from the street.

He was on the sidewalk, panting.

The door of the Citroën opened.

A pale hand beckoned.

48

AGAIN IN HIS ROOM in the Hilton, he slept twelve hours. The Director General had accompanied him to the room and given him sleeping pills and a glass of water; he stayed with him as he fell asleep. Felix Maldonado could barely stammer his last question; his tongue was thick and his teeth felt as soft as hominy. "I give up, I give up," he said with a calm delirium that the skull-faced man observed with curiosity. "Who is it who has this power, this power to change lives, twist lives at his whim and make us someone else? I give up."

The Director General was incapable of feeling compassion; when he felt a twinge, it was instantly converted into scorn. But he had said it once before, he preferred cruelty to scorn. "There is one question you haven't asked, even though it's the one that should most disturb you." In spite of himself, his intended cruelty took on overtones of pity. "Why did Sara Klein return to Mexico? Why did she travel from Tel Aviv to be here only four days?"

He didn't know whether Felix heard him; Felix was quietly delirious. True madness, thought the man with the pince-nez as violet as Mary Benjamin's eyes, is always serene madness, madness that doesn't interfere with what one calls normal life, madness that rises, bathes, eats breakfast, goes to work, eats, returns home, brushes its teeth, sleeps, and again rises at the sound of the alarm clock. The madness of someone named Felix Maldonado.

"She came here to see you, can you hear me? That's the only reason she came, to see you one last time. That should matter to you, but you never asked yourself that question, you never tried to find out. She loved you more than you loved her; her love for you was real, not nostalgia, or an equally impossible promise. Do you hear me?"

But Felix was sinking into sleep, repeating the question, I give up, who is it who rules the world? What can I do? I can't fight them, who are they? Who do all of you obey? I give up.

He would never remember clearly the words of the Director General. I would repeat them should he come again to my house in Coyoacán, if he ever decided that, after all, I was the lesser evil, the friend from his college days and the Museum of Modern Art film series and the Ontario Shakespeare Festival, the Castor who with Pollux shared the sofa-bed in the Century Apartments overlooking the Hudson. I would repeat exactly what the Director General had said that night as Felix Maldonado, a serene madman, sank rapidly into sleep, the sleep/dream that with all its powers, when it is dream and not merely sleep, *rêve* and not merely *sommeil,* can transform man:

"You are but one head of the Hydra. Cut off one and a thousand will replace it. You are governed by your passions, they defeat you. The eagle knows that. The two-headed eagle. One head is called the CIA and the other, the KGB. Two heads, but only one body. Almost the Holy Trinity of our age. Whether we know it, whether or not we want it, we cannot help but serve the ends of one of the two heads of that cold monster. But as it has only one body, in serving one head we serve the other, and vice versa. There's no escape. The Hydra of our passions is trapped in the talons of the bicephalous eagle. The bloody eagle that is the origin of all the world's violence, the eagle that murders a Trotsky and a Diem, that attempts more than once to assassinate Castro and then weeps crocodile tears because the world has become so violent and the Palestinians violently demand a homeland. At times, it is the beak of the Washington eagle that cuts off our head and eats it; at times, it is the beak of Moscow. But the intestines of the winged beast are the same, and the excretory passages are the same. We are the excrement of that monster. When the Russians supported the creation of the state of Israel in the forties, Bernstein served the KGB. He served the CIA as long as the North Americans gave unconditional support to the Jews. Now he is playing one against the other and hopes to use both as both use the Israelis: Soviet tanks so that Israel can suppress the Palestinians in the south of Lebanon; North American oil so that Israel can combat the Arab armies with North American tanks and planes. The Director General served the KGB during the period of Arab–Moscow cordiality, and the CIA when El Rais Nasser died and Sadat sought Yankee support and the Saudis and Kissinger reached an accord to create the oil crisis. Any day, the alliances can change radically. The two-headed eagle laughs and devours, devours and laughs, digests and shits, shits and laughs at our Hydra passions . . .''

The face of the Director General was disappearing behind the veils of sleep, until only two eyes of black glass glittered deep in a white skull.

At one o'clock in the afternoon, a waiter entered without knocking and wakened him. He was pushing a wheeled table with covered breakfast dishes, a newspaper, and an envelope. He left without speaking.

Diego Velázquez got up, dazed, coughing and sneezing. He pulled the table to the bedside. He drank the orange juice and lifted the cover from the steaming plate of eggs with hot sauce. The eggs nauseated him and quickly he re-covered them. He poured himself a cup of coffee and read the inscription on the envelope, Señor Licenciado Diego Velázquez, Chief of the Bureau of Cost Analysis of the Ministry of Economic Development, Hilton Hotel, City. He removed the card. The Mexican Academy of Economics is pleased to invite you to a colloquium to be held on September 31 at ten o'clock in the morning in the Salón del Perdón in the National Palace of Mexico. The President of the Republic will honor us with his presence. You are requested to arrive promptly.

The newspaper was open and folded to an inside page. In a black box beneath the Star of David was the announcement of the regrettable death of Abraham Benjamin Rosenberg. The burial will take place at 5 p.m. in the Jewish Cemetery. His wife, his children, and other relatives share with you their profound grief. Hebrew rites will be observed. The family requests no flowers.

At five o'clock, Diego Velázquez joined the hundred or so persons gathered in the chapel at the cemetery. They stood in line to file past the body of Abie Benjamin, incessantly chanting *Shema Yisrael Adonai Elohenu Adonai Echod.* That morning, Abie's body had been washed, his fingernails had been cut, and they had combed his hair over the hole burned in his head. He looked serene in his shroud, the yarmulke on his head, the tallith he'd worn the day of his wedding covering his shoulders and face, the cotton stockings hiding his icy feet. Diego smiled at the thought that this man was being buried in a pocketless white shroud so as not to carry with him any of the wealth of this world.

The person standing behind Diego Velázquez nudged him gently as he lingered before the body. Diego left the line and sat down to wait for the procession to the grave. He saw Mary's veiled, bowed head in the first row of mourners. There were no flowers or wreaths in the chapel.

He waited until everyone had left to follow the black sheet-draped coffin borne by ten men. Then he followed. A black-bearded man dressed in black and wearing a black hat was sweeping the ground behind the coffin. Perhaps he'd bought the broom in one of Abie's chain of supermarkets.

They reached the empty grave. The rabbi, a heavily veiled Mary, and the couple's children recited the Kaddish. Then Mary removed the black sheet and the coffin was lowered into the grave. It thudded dryly, then settled into the mud of the summer's intense rains. Mary took a handful of earth and threw it onto the coffin. Then the gravediggers took over, spading vigorously.

When earth completely filled the grave, the rabbi cleared his throat and began his eulogy of Abie Benjamin. Only then did Mary lift her dark veils, and her eyes with the golden sparks shone more brightly than the silvery sun of the hazy but rainless afternoon. At the last moment, God had been merciful to Abie. The heavens did not weep. The God of Israel is compassionate only when He is severe.

Mary sought the eyes of Diego Velázquez.

They stared at one another for a long moment, deaf to the rabbi's eulogy.

Mary smiled at Diego; she ran a moist tongue over her palely painted lips and half closed her violet eyes. She didn't move, but her body was that of a black panther, lustful and now pursued, beautiful because she was pursued and because she knew it. In spite of the black dress buttoned to her neck, Diego could imagine the deep décolletage of her brassiere, and the oil between her breasts to make the cleavage more noticeable.

He turned his back on Mary and walked slowly from the cemetery.

49 AT NINE O'CLOCK, he crossed the lobby of the Hilton and walked to the parklike grass-and-cement strip in front of the University Club to wait for a taxi. It was the worst hour. Taxi after taxi passed without stopping, ignoring the uplifted finger that signaled he was waiting for a one peso cab.

He had waited ten minutes when a yellow taxi broke away from the orderly line of one-peso cabs and worked its way to the curb, honking. Diego stopped it and got into the rear seat. He was the only passenger. The driver tried to catch Diego's eye in the rear-view mirror; he smiled, but Diego had no desire to converse with a taxi driver.

When they reached the Hotel Reforma, a girl dressed in white, a nurse, stopped the cab. She carried cellophane-wrapped syringes, vials, and ampules. Diego slid to the far side of the seat to make room for her. He felt as if he were coming down with something, and wished he could ask the nurse for a shot of penicillin.

Just before the traffic circle at El Caballito in front of the Ambassadeurs Restaurant, two nuns calmly entered the taxi. Diego knew they were nuns by the hair tightly drawn back into a bun, the absence of makeup, their black dresses, the rosaries and scapulars. They chose to get in the front with the driver. He treated them like old friends, as if he saw them every day. *"Hel-*lo, Sisters, how's it going today?"

The taxi was held up by a long red light. A nondescript man had run to the cab and attempted to get in after the nuns, but the driver shook his finger "no," and drove off against the red light.

He managed to slow for an instant beside the newspaper stand at the corner of Reforma and Bucareli to avoid a violation. The warning light flashed on, but at the moment the taxi started to move, a student ran toward them with his arms crossed across his chest, running lightly in his tennis shoes in spite of the load of books he was carrying; a girl emerged from behind the newsstand and followed him.

They got in the back, and the nurse had to squeeze close to Diego, but she didn't look at him or speak to him. Diego ignored her.

The driver left the mandatory taxi lane and drove with more than usual speed in the direction of San Juan de Letrán. Once again, with difficulty, as he had in front of the University Club, the driver worked his way back into the line of one-peso cabs. On the corner of Juárez and San Juan de Letrán, in front of Nieto Regalos, stood a fat woman in a cotton dress; she had a basket over one arm. She signaled the taxi; the driver stopped as the light changed from yellow to red.

The woman thrust her nose into the taxi and asked them to let her in, all the taxis were full, she'd be late to market, her chicks were about to roast in the heat, be good to her. "No, señora," replied the driver. "Can't you see I'm full?" As he crossed the intersection, Juárez narrowed to become Madero. The woman with the basket was left behind, shaking her fist, her voice drowned out by the mounting roar of traffic.

"Why didn't you let her get in?" asked Diego, immersed in the silence of his fellow passengers.

"I'm sorry, señor," the driver replied, unperturbed, "but I'm running full, and if I picked her up, the cops would put the bite on me. They're just waiting for the chance."

Diego exchanged glances with the nurse, the student, the student's curly-haired girl, and the two nuns, who had turned around to look at him. Incomprehension and coldness alternated in their distant, hostile eyes.

"Stop! Stop, I tell you!" shouted Diego, without conviction. They were all staring at him as if they'd never seen him before; they were all counting on the absence of memory, as if there were some time warp between Diego and the rest of humanity, like bad sync between an image and a voice on a movie screen.

Now the driver caught Diego's eye in the rear-view mirror and winked. An indecent, offensive wink that implied a complicity that had never been sought or agreed upon.

"All right," said Diego, exhausted. "Stop. Let me out here."

"Five pesos, please."

Diego handed the wrinkled bills to the driver and got out in front of the Hotel Majestic, almost on the corner of the Plaza de la Constitución.

He walked faster. He crossed the Plaza and presented his card to the Palace guard, beside the elevator. He was told to go to the Salón del Perdón, where the meeting was to be held.

Many people were milling around the great brocade-and-walnut Salón dominated by the historic painting consecrating the nobility of soul of the rebel Nicolás Bravo. At a distance, Diego saw a myopic Leopoldo Bernstein using his handkerchief to wipe the sauce splattered on his glasses from his breakfast eggs. He replaced the glasses, saw Diego, and smiled amiably. In one corner of the Salón, he saw the Director General in violet eyeglasses, visibly suffering in the bright daylight, the flashes of the press photographers and television lights; beside him, Mauricio Rossetti, staring straight at Diego and whispering into the Director General's ear. There was a moment of heightened whispering, followed by an impressive silence.

The President of the Republic entered the Salón. He advanced among the guests, greeting them affably, probably making jokes, pressing certain arms, avoiding others, effusively offering his hand to some, coldly to others, recognizing one man, ignoring the next, illuminated in the steady, biting light of the reflectors, intermittently divested of shadows by the flashes. Recognizing. Ignoring.

He was approaching.

Diego prepared his smile, his hand, adjusted the knot of his necktie. He sneezed. He removed his handkerchief and discreetly blew his nose.

Bernstein observed him from across the room, smiling ironically.

Rossetti was making his way through the crowd toward Diego.

The Director General waved his hand in the direction of the door.

The President was within a few steps of Diego Velázquez.

EPILOGUE

The official maps outline a large rectangle extending from the drilling platforms of Chac 1 and Kukulkán 1 in the Gulf of Mexico to the beds of Sitio Grande in the spurs of the Chiapas Sierras, and from the port of Coatzacoalcos to the mouth of the Usumacinta River.

The maps of memory describe the arch of a coast of luxuriant loneliness, the first seen by the Spanish Conquistadors. Tabasco, Veracruz, Campeche. A lime-colored sea, so green that at times it resembled a great plain, redolent of its riches of porgy, corbina, and shrimp, tangled with seaweed linking the calm waves that sink into the sands of beaches of moribund palm trees: a red, vegetal cemetery; and then a slow ascent through lands red as a tennis court and green as a billiard table, along lazy rivers thickened with floating hyacinths, toward the mists of the native sierra, the seat of the secret world of the Tzotziles: Chiapas, a lance of fire in a crown of smoke.

It is the land of the Malinche. Hernán Cortés received her from the hands of the caciques of Tabasco, along with four diadems and a lizard of gold. She was a gift, but a gift that spoke. Her Indian name was Malintzin. The stars baptized her, because she was born under an evil sign, Ce Malianalli, oracle of misfortune, rebellion, dissension, spilled blood, and impatience.

The parents of the doomed child, princes of their land, were fearful, and secretly they delivered her to the tribe of Xicalango. By coincidence, that same night another baby died, the daughter of slaves of Malintzin's parents. The princes told that this dead baby was their daughter and they buried her with the honors befitting her noble rank. The doomed child, as if her masters divined the

291

dark augury of her birth, was passed from people to people as part of tributes, until she was offered to the Teúl, the white-skinned, blond-bearded god the Indians confused with the benevolent God Quetzalcóatl, the Plumed Serpent, who had one day fled from the horror of Mexico, promising to return another day by sea, from the east, with happiness on his wings and vengeance on his scales.

Then the voice of the buried slave spoke with the tongue of the doomed princess and led the Conquistadors to the eternal, high, central seat of authority, of the power of Mexico: the mesa of Anáhuac and the city of Tenochtitlán, the capital of Moctezuma, the Lord of the Great Voice.

Cortés converted Malintzin twice: first, to love; second, to Christianity. She was baptized Marina. The people call her Malinche, name of betrayal, voice that revealed to the Spaniards the hidden weaknesses of the Aztec empire and permitted fifteen hundred gold-hungry adventurers to conquer a nation five times larger than Spain. The small voice of the woman defeated the great voice of the Emperor.

But beneath the land of the Malinche lie riches greater than all of Moctezuma's gold. Sealed in geological pits more ancient than the most ancient empires, the treasure of Chiapas, Veracruz, and Tabasco is a promise in a sealed bottle: to seek it is to pursue an invisible cat through subterranean labyrinths. The patient drillers penetrate two, three, four thousand meters deep into the sea, into the jungles, into the sierra. The discovery of one fertile well compensates for the failure of a thousand sterile ones.

Like the Hydra, the oil is reborn, multiplied, from a single severed head. Dark semen in a land of hopes and betrayals, oil fecundates the realms of the Malinche beneath the mute voices of the stars and their nocturnal portents.